SNOWY SEDUCTION

"I want you," he said, intrigued by the snow that caught on her hair, her thickly curled lashes, her full ripe lips.

She swallowed, and the pulse in her neck warbled. "You can't. You're engaged."

"That doesn't stop the wanting."

He leaned close to steal a kiss, pausing long enough for her to pull away from him. But she didn't move. She just stared at him with those big eyes full of wonder and passion.

His head dipped to hers, and he kissed the snow from her eyes, her nose, before settling over her mouth. Hers trembled slightly, and he felt that hesitation clear to his soul.

A gentleman would have ended it now. He should've apologized for his boldness. For taking advantage of the situation.

But Reid was no gentleman.

He was a bastard, and he intended to take all that Ellie Jo Cade was willing to give him. Still, he kept his hands trapped between her thighs amid all that fabric that deprived him of exploring her as he longed to do.

There was something wickedly alluring about just kissing her. It seemed more intimate, like a stolen moment that was as fresh as the new-fallen snow.

She tasted of frosty winters and just a hint of spice. She was the dessert he'd hungered for. He damn sure wasn't going to content himself with a sampling.

BOOK YOUR PLACE ON OUR WEBSITE AND MAKE THE READING CONNECTION!

We've created a customized website just for our very special readers, where you can get the inside scoop on everything that's going on with Zebra, Pinnacle and Kensington books.

When you come online, you'll have the exciting opportunity to:

- View covers of upcoming books
- Read sample chapters
- Learn about our future publishing schedule (listed by publication month *and author*)
- Find out when your favorite authors will be visiting a city near you
- Search for and order backlist books from our online catalog
- Check out author bios and background information
- Send e-mail to your favorite authors
- Meet the Kensington staff online
- Join us in weekly chats with authors, readers and other guests
- Get writing guidelines
- AND MUCH MORE!

**Visit our website at
http://www.kensingtonbooks.com**

A COWBOY CHRISTMAS

Janette Kenny

ZEBRA BOOKS
Kensington Publishing Corp.
http://www.kensingtonbooks.com

ZEBRA BOOKS are published by

Kensington Publishing Corp.
119 West 40th Street
New York, NY 10018

All Kensington titles, imprints, and distributed lines are available at special quantity discounts for bulk purchases for sales
promotion, premiums, fund-raising, educational, or institutional use.

Special book excerpts or customized printings can also be created to fit specific needs. For details, write or phone the office
of the Kensington Special Sales Manager: Attn. Special Sales
Department. Kensington Publishing Corp., 119 West 40th
Street, New York, NY 10018. Phone: 1-800-221-2647.

Zebra and the Z logo Reg. U.S. Pat. & TM Off.

ISBN-13: 978-1-4201-0658-9
ISBN-10: 1-4201-0658-9

First Printing: October 2009

10 9 8 7 6 5 4 3 2 1

Printed in the United States of America

Chapter 1

Maverick, Wyoming 1894

Blinding light rode into the room on an icy gust of wind and rudely reminded Reid Barclay that he couldn't get rip-roaring drunk today. He shot a scowl at the newcomer who didn't seem to have the sense to know they were letting out what little heat the potbelly stove could belch out.

Damn, was he going snow blind? He blinked a couple of times just to make sure she wasn't a mirage. Nope, nothing wrong with his eyesight.

A lady stood silhouetted in the doorway, as if debating whether to come in or skedaddle. The answer was as clear as the big blue sky that stretched to the horizon.

A lady had no business stepping foot in this hole.

He ignored the inclination to stand up straight in her presence, preferring to hunker over his whiskey while she stood in the open doorway like an ice princess, gilded in white light and prim bearing—the exact opposite of what this place represented.

Any second Reid figured she'd realize she was in a

bawdy establishment that made its money satisfying men's baser needs. Or in his case, trying to.

"Is this Mallory's Roost?" That sultry note in her voice was at odds with her prim appearance, putting lurid thoughts in his head that he had no call thinking about a lady.

"Yep," he said, in no mood to offer anything more.

She gave a shudder, but instead of hightailing it like any lady with a lick of sense would do, she stepped inside and shoved the door closed. Besides the wind that howled a protest at being shut out, the only sound in the Roost was the crackle of the stove and Reid's uneven breathing.

This lady oozed quality in a hovel that wouldn't know sophistication if it bit saloon keep Ian Mallory on his Irish ass. The tips of dainty black boots peeked from under her heavy tweed skirt. Fine-looking black gloves covered small hands that rested demurely at her sides. Her wrap hugged her narrow shoulders and didn't appear near warm enough for these environs.

He had just enough liquor under his belt to want to heat this lady up under a nice thick blanket. Dangerous thoughts for a man in his position.

He let his gaze drift up to her face, and her inquisitive eyes and lush lips hushed his heart a measure. He couldn't recall when that had happened to him last. To have a woman intrigue him so now—Hell, it was time for him to vamoose.

He'd heard the train chug in five minutes ago, and knowing he had a passenger waiting had chased off thoughts of getting drunk. Not that drink would solve his problems. But sometimes a man just needed to drown himself and his troubles in a bottle.

That would have to wait. It was time for him to collect Mrs. Leach's friend and head back to the ranch.

He would've too if that slight desperation he sensed in this woman hadn't stayed him. He couldn't pull himself away just yet, not until he found out why a young woman of quality would enter a grubby saloon.

He finished off his rotgut, then almost choked on it as the sweet scent of lilacs drifted over him, tempting him to forget the promise he'd made. He didn't have to look up to know the lady stood at his elbow, but he did anyway.

Dammit to hell but the uncertainty he glimpsed in those big brown eyes of hers had him wanting to reach out to her and tell her whatever was wrong would be all right. He knew better now than to make such promises.

He shot the lady a look that should've sent her running, but she hiked that pert little chin up as if telling him she wasn't one to bluff. If that chin hadn't trembled the slightest bit—Aw, hell, didn't she know it was dangerous for a woman to come close to a lone man swilling whiskey— a man who was wallowing in old regret and new longing?

"Was there a gentleman in here earlier?" she asked.

"Not that I recall."

She frowned and bit her lower lip. "Perhaps he left before you arrived—"

"I been here since yesterday, ma'am," Reid said and scratched his knuckles over the stubble he'd not bothered scraping off this morning. "Plenty of cowpokes and the like have come and gone, but nary a gentleman has passed through those doors."

"I see," she said, her mouth pinched in clear disapproval of his admission, and his appearance, if he guessed right. "Is the owner of this establishment here?"

Reid nodded in Mallory's direction, his curiosity

hiking up another notch. "That's him propping up the far end of the bar."

"Thank you."

Yep, no doubt about it. She was the embodiment of the vision that had tormented Reid's dreams for as long as he could recall. True elegance with a throaty voice that hinted of naughty. So what the hell was she doing here?

She set off at a good clip toward the end of the bar where Ian Mallory snored like a sawmill. Her boot heels clicked a jig, and her bustle swayed to the lusty beat pulsing in Reid's veins. Damn, but he'd sure like to see if her inviting backside was mostly padding or firm, natural rounding.

"Excuse me," she said to Mallory as she stopped a respectable distance from him.

Mallory answered her with a snore.

The lady tapped a foot impatiently on the floor and Reid bit back a smile, wondering what she'd do now. From what he'd seen so far, she wasn't the type to tuck tail and run.

She cleared her throat. "Sir, if I may have a moment of your time." She leaned close to Mallory, her voice louder and more commanding this time.

Like a schoolmarm. Or a general.

It took grit for a woman to walk into this place. A damn sight more gumption to stay. Just the type of woman who appealed to Reid.

Seeing his dream woman in the flesh brought all the old longing rushing back. A good dose of regret, too, though he rarely acknowledged it anymore. But what shocked the hell out of him was the beginning twitch of an honest-to-God arousal.

The past two years lust had been a stranger to Reid. God knew he'd tried to get back in the amorous saddle again as recent as last night, but nothing any woman did worked. Now, just being in the same room with this lady had nudged his cock awake.

About damn time. Now if only he were free—

She turned to Reid then, and indecision flitted over her inquisitive features. "Is he always like this?"

"He has his lucid moments, but they're rare."

Her mouth cinched up tighter than a banker's purse strings, but the gloved finger she slid between her neck and high ruffled collar was more telling than her tongue slipping out to dampen her full lower lip. That long-missed heaviness paid a teasing visit across Reid's groin again.

Yep, that part of him wasn't dead after all.

Reid gripped the empty shot glass in his hands, debating about filling it again. Drinking beat wishing to hell that he was holding soft womanly flesh, but he couldn't leave the old gal waiting at the depot much longer either.

She shook the sot. "Mr. Mallory. Please wake up."

"Uh, wha—" The old drunk roused from his stupor and stared at the lady, blinking like an owl.

Reid could well imagine what went through the shanty Irishman's head. Had he died and gone to heaven after all?

"And just how can I help you, miss?" Mallory asked as he straightened to his full five-foot-six height.

"I'm looking for Mr. Reid Barclay," she said. "The conductor at the depot said I could find him here."

Reid froze, his hand inches from grabbing the bottle of whiskey. Had he heard her right?

"Now what would a fine lady such as yourself be wanting with the likes of Reid Barclay?" Mallory asked, voicing the same question that swirled in Reid's head.

She slid Reid a dubious glance, before turning back to Mallory. "That's personal."

The whiskey Reid had swilled crashed like angry waves in his gut. He stared at her long and hard, but nothing about her stirred his memory. Why the hell was she looking for him?

"If that don't beat all." Mallory thumped a hand on the bar and let out a wheezing laugh.

"Well? Can you tell me where I can find Mr. Barclay?" she asked.

Mallory bobbed his shaggy head and pointed a gnarled finger at Reid. "That's your fine gentleman right there."

Reid pressed both palms on the sticky bar, more discomfited than offended by the Irish sot's mocking tone.

"Oh." She pressed a gloved hand to her throat and stared at Reid in clear disbelief.

Reid's mind churned with reasons, beyond the obvious one, why this lady had sought him out. Damn it all, but that one plausible cause wasn't reassuring in light of his physical reaction to her.

"Cat got your tongue?" Reid asked.

Again, that telling flush stole over her creamy cheeks. "Please forgive me. I was expecting someone more— I mean, someone far older and, and, and—" She waved a hand as if trying to catch words that had escaped her.

"Respectable looking?" he asked.

Her cheeks turned a fiery red this time. "Please don't take offense, but you don't look like the gentleman I'd imagined."

"None taken, ma'am."

She crossed to Reid, those sharp bootheels tapping out a lively ditty that had his blood pumping for a fare-thee-well. "I'm pleased to meet you, Mr. Barclay."

Reid inclined his chin a mite, his neck crawling with suspicion. "Barclay or Reid will do."

"Highly improper, but if that's what you wish." Her

cheeks darkened a smidgen, and for the first time she looked as uneasy as he felt.

"Why are you looking for me?"

"I'm Eleanor Jo Cade," she said.

She couldn't be the woman he'd been expecting from Denver—the one his housekeeper had recommended for the job in her absence. "Mrs. Leach's friend?"

"Yes," she said.

"Why? What?" Reid scrubbed a hand over his face, annoyed as hell that she had him stammering for words. He sucked in a deep breath and wished he hadn't as he drew in her sweet lilac scent.

"Why didn't you wait for me at the depot?" he asked, acting annoyed she'd come looking for him in this weather when he was really perturbed that she was a young, pretty and damned desirable woman.

Of course, the fact she was here in the saloon told him she was the type who took matters into her own hands. And dammit all for thinking that because his body jolted again at the thought of her taking him in hand. *Shit!*

"It seemed silly to wait when I could just as easily find you and we could be on our way."

There was more to it than that. The spark of panic in her eyes hinted she had another reason that she wasn't ready to divulge.

That alone was enough reason for him to send her on her way here and now and save himself a passel of grief. God knew he'd surely suffer misery in Miss Cade's company, for his thoughts were anything but gentlemanly around her. But he'd have a hellish time finding a suitable woman to replace Mrs. Leach at this late date and in this ungodly weather.

He blew out a disgusted breath at being caught

between a rock and a hard place. "Then by all means let us collect your baggage and be on our way."

Her sigh was a fitting reaction, but the wide eyes glittering with relief, coupled with those soft lips trembling into a smile, went too far. Yep, this little woman roused feelings in him best left dead.

Reid shrugged into his jacket and motioned to the door. "Stay here while I fetch the sleigh from the livery."

"I don't mind walking with you. It'll save time." She click-clicked across the wood floor like a spirited filly and out the door into the bitter cold.

Reid tossed five bucks on the bar and started after her. He would have preferred to lose ten minutes and regain his equilibrium, but it was obvious Miss Cade would rather tramp through the snow than spend another second in the Roost.

"You've got your hands full with that one," Mallory said.

"She doesn't appear to be the troublesome sort to me."

"Unlike yourself, Mr. Reid Barclay. For all that cultured talk you spout on a whim, I know you've got the heart and soul of an Irish rebel."

"What if I do?" Reid paused at the door and stared at the man who'd watched him go from rebellious boy to respectable rancher.

"Her type won't give you a roll in the hay and then go her way with a smile on her face. Remember that."

Reid inclined his head. "I'll bear that in mind."

"Will you? You always were a cocky bastard. But then you have the blood of nobles flowing in your veins."

Mallory, the wily old goat, knew the truth Reid held close to the vest. He was an English nobleman's by-blow, disowned by his father long before Reid's mother died giving him life.

"I'm still a bastard, Mallory." If Kirby Morris hadn't cut a deal when he had, he'd be a dead one by now.

"Aye, you did 'em wrong, boyo. They ain't coming back."

His mouth stretched into a grim line. He'd given his brothers just cause to hate him, and damned if he knew how to right the terrible wrong he'd caused so long ago.

Guilt was a bitch to live with.

"Perhaps I'll have the luck of the Irish after all."

"More likely you'll have the devil's time of it," Mallory said as he splashed whiskey into a shot glass, "when your past charges into your life with guns blazing."

A possibility Reid hoped to avoid. He stepped out and let the wind blow the rest of Mallory's dire predictions back inside.

No matter how much he groused about his fate, he'd made the right choice. Never mind it'd been the only one at the time. If his skin felt a mite tight for him at times, so be it.

He was ready to live up to his end of the bargain now. Or had been until he'd hired a fetching house cook that had him thinking of dishes best served warm in bed.

Reid squinted against a punishing sun, searching for Miss Cade. He spotted her easily down the street, thanks to a royal blue cloak snapping in the wind like a bull-fighter's cape. He hadn't known her hair was the color of whiskey until now.

The back of it was caught up in an intricate weave of sorts and that touch of red glowed in the sun.

Reid headed toward Miss Cade, his blood running thick and hot with need. He had a fondness for fair-haired women.

She tugged the full hood up and ended his rumina-tions of taking the pins from her hair and running his hands through it. By damn, but the lady was a sparkling gem amid a blanket of white. She'd be living in his house, a constant temptation for him to take what he wanted and damn the consequences.

He paused to let a buckboard churn by, the bed laden with goods and squealing children huddled down in a bed of straw. He knew the whole family worked their behinds off on their ranch due north of his, yet he'd never seen a happier brood.

Simple pleasures.

He'd never known what it was like to have the love of family until he'd lost it. Now there was no getting it back.

Reid caught a glimpse of Adam Tavish plowing through the muck in the street. He, too, seemed arrested by the sight of Miss Cade.

Though the U.S. Marshal swore he was on the trail of the Kincaid gang, Mallory told him that Tavish had been asking an awful lot of questions about Reid. It wasn't the first time a lawman had inquired about his past.

The fact remained that Reid had left word everywhere, all but begging his brothers to come back to Wyoming. He'd also baited a trap for the man accused of killing Lisa True, letting it be known that Slim was at the Crown Seven as well. But so far the only one sniffing around was the lawman.

As for Ezra Kincaid? He'd likely be watching.

If the old outlaw was out there, he was holed up planning his move. That worried Reid the most.

Truth be, he was relieved Tavish was dead set on stopping the old rustler who surely must be drooling over Reid's thoroughbreds. But that didn't mean he wanted to be on close speaking terms with Tavish.

Considering his past, Reid was careful to keep his distance from the local sheriff and the marshal. But with

Tavish reaching Miss Cade first and guiding her into the livery, he couldn't very well do that today.

Ice crunched underfoot as he made his way to the livery. He wrenched open the door, finding Miss Cade and Tavish squared off inside.

He knew the feeling.

Reid gave the livery boy a nod to ready his sleigh.

"I see you've met the marshal." Reid stopped beside Miss Cade, sparing Tavish a dismissing glance but feeling the man's curious gaze skewer him all the same. Was that annoyance he saw in her eyes?

"Yes, he was just assuring me that this is a quiet, lawful community," she said.

Tavish favored Miss Cade with his good-ol'-boy smile that didn't fool Reid one bit. "You never did tell me what brought you to Maverick, Miss Cade."

She flinched this time, a slight tremor Reid attributed to a case of nerves. Until he got a closer look.

The lady was clearly angry and her ire was directed at the U.S. Marshal. Damn, what had Tavish said to her earlier?

"I'm taking over Mrs. Leach's role of cook at the Crown Seven Ranch while she's away," she said.

Tavish thumbed back his hat, revealing a pair of observant green eyes that no doubt had saved the lawman's ass on more than one occasion. "Pardon me for saying, ma'am. But most cooks I've met tended to sample their fare a bit more than necessary."

It was the truth, but Reid took umbrage with the way Tavish looked at the lady, like she was a tasty morsel and he was starving. Never mind Reid had done the same earlier. She was his employee, and judging by her tight-lipped expression, she didn't wish to tarry in Tavish's company.

"So, where have you worked before, Miss Cade?" Tavish asked, his conversational tone at odds with his shrewd perusal.

A dull flush blossomed on the lady's cheeks, and the rigid set to her shoulders seemed an odd reaction, in Reid's estimation. "The Denver Academy for Young Ladies."

"Do tell?" Tavish's eyes took on a calculating glint.

"I fear I'd bore you with stories of teaching young ladies to acquire discriminating tastes," she said over the tinkling of harness bells. "Besides I am sure Mr. Barclay is anxious to be on his way."

"Another time then. Afternoon, ma'am." Tavish slid two fingers over his hat brim but stayed rooted to the spot. "Barclay."

Reid dipped his chin in farewell, then guided Miss Cade to the red sleigh. "You leave your baggage at the depot?"

"Yes. I have a small trunk and a carpetbag."

A rarity for sure. He'd warrant Cheryl would drag all manner of trunks and valises with her from England.

"After we retrieve your things, we'll stop at the mercantile. I suggest you select anything you need for yourself or the ranch now."

"I have everything I require with me."

"Fair warning, Miss Cade. We won't be coming into town for a week or more."

"I'm sure everything I'll need is at the ranch."

Reid expected she'd say that. So why did he have the sudden feeling he'd be going hungry this night—and in more ways than one?

Chapter 2

Ellie settled into the sleigh beside Reid Barclay, more than happy to put distance between herself and the nosy marshal. Heavenly days, the last person she'd expected to get trapped in a conversation with was the man who'd sworn to hunt down her pa and bring him in—dead or alive.

If her mind hadn't been focused on the mysterious glint in Reid Barclay's eyes and the jolt of sensual awareness his mere touch evoked in her, she would've paid attention to her surroundings. As it was, she'd rushed to the end of the boardwalk for a breath of bracing air and nearly bowled the marshal over.

Goodness, was Marshal Tavish always lurking in the shadows?

He certainly had been in Denver when her fiancé learned she was an outlaw's daughter and ended their engagement. He knew her secret. But had he guessed her true reason for coming to the Crown Seven?

Ellie bit her lower lip as worry nipped along her nerves. She couldn't botch this up, not when her pa's life was at stake.

Her pa. She'd grown from being a little girl who adored her daddy to a young woman ashamed of what he was. But because she'd loved him with a daughter's devotion, him staying away from her had hurt that much more.

He'd done it to protect her reputation.

But the truth came out anyway.

It stripped her of her dream of a family and cost her the coveted position in Denver she'd worked hard to achieve.

It forced her to seek a position across the country where nobody knew her. And it brought her here where she'd stepped into the role of another lie.

She could honestly say she didn't regret it overmuch. It seemed unbelievable that she'd see her pa again after so many years of just hearing of his exploits. She'd be able to talk to him. She'd be able to spend a holiday with him.

As Reid Barclay guided the sleigh toward the depot, she inhaled the crisp, cold air and embraced this rare opportunity that had been offered her. Or she tried to, at least.

Mrs. Leach had assured her that Mr. Barclay was an equitable boss. But she hadn't mentioned that he was a virile gentleman as well.

His nearness in the saloon had unsettled her to the point of distraction. But the occasional brush of his shoulder against hers sent warmth coursing through her body.

She was beset by a powerful urge to inch closer to him. That was highly improper conduct!

Why, she'd never been smitten with a man.

She'd been as intimate with her former fiancé as a woman could be with a man, yet he hadn't roused such raw yearnings in her with just a look or casual touch.

This illicit reaction to a stranger had her cheeks burning with embarrassment and her mind cluttered with confusion. In fact she wasn't able to draw a decent breath until he stopped at the depot and left her while he fetched her baggage.

Too soon he returned to torment her with his virility.

Heavenly days, she knew the perils of succumbing to one's torrid desires. She'd not fall victim to that again.

As Reid settled her bags in the sleigh, she focused on what brought her to the Crown Seven. Despite what was printed on the wanted posters, her pa was a horse thief—not a cold-blooded killer. She had to stop him from making a deadly mistake and she didn't have the luxury of time to make him see reason.

Even if she succeeded, this could very well be their last chance to be together as a family. She had to do this right.

She certainly knew how a household should be run, how to entertain frugally or lavishly. She knew what constituted proper meals.

The only problem was she didn't know how to cook.

Mrs. Leach had assured her there was nothing to it. She wasn't convinced of that then, and she wasn't so sure now.

As she tried and failed to recall the first thing about preparing something as simple as stew, she gave in to a shiver. What if she couldn't cook one edible meal?

"You chilled, Miss Cade?" Reid asked as he slid back into the sleigh beside her and his broad muscular shoulder settled against hers.

Heat blazed at his touch, sending flickers of warmth to dance within her. "Nothing more than a passing tremor. I'm sure the heavy blanket will stave off the cold."

"I hope you're right." He flicked the lines and the sleigh smoothly glided forward. "One more stop to make and we'll be on our way."

"Good. It's been a tiring journey and I long to—" Ellie bit her tongue, close to admitting she wanted to do nothing but rest. "I long to get settled and busy myself in the kitchen."

"Reckon you do. Your quarters aren't large, but you'll find them above adequate."

"I'm sure I'll be comfortable."

And even if she weren't, she wouldn't be at his ranch that long to suffer from a bit of discomfort.

As she'd told Mrs. Leach, headmistress Halsey expected her at the Falsmonte Academy in San Francisco the first of the new year. Ellie must not be late or she'd lose the once-in-a-lifetime chance to teach at the prestigious school for discerning young ladies. She'd lose the only job that'd come her way since the scandal.

"Mrs. Leach ordered holiday gee-gaws and reminded me several times that I was to pick them up while I was in town," he said as he stopped the sleigh before the mercantile. "I trust you know how to dress the house up with them."

"I've been told I have an artistic eye for such," she said, relieved to be in her element again. "Do you usually decorate the entire house?"

"Nope," he said. "Never celebrated the occasion before."

"Surely you're exaggerating."

He shook his head. "I was reared in an orphanage, Miss Cade. There was scarce enough funds for food and clothing."

How sad! Christmas had always been her favorite holiday, for it was the one time throughout her life that her pa made an effort to visit her, if only briefly.

He'd always bring her some small gift and regale her with wild stories of the West. He'd tell her he'd missed her and loved her and that he'd stay in touch.

But he never had.

She hadn't seen him for three whole years. She'd feared

he'd died. Then Mrs. Leach's letter arrived out of the blue and gave her hope.

"Last chance for shopping, Miss Cade," Reid said as he extended a gloved hand to assist her.

She rested her hand in his and secretly thrilled at the power encased in those supple leather gloves. This man might be a wealthy gentleman but he certainly was no dandy.

"If I may be so bold to ask, what has spurred you to celebrate the season now?" she asked as he escorted her to the door of the mercantile.

His handsome features took on a hard, distant expression. "We'll be hosting a wedding at the ranch," he said without a lick of excitement in his voice. "Seems fitting that the house look festive."

A wedding. Another detail Mrs. Leach had neglected to mention.

"Who's getting married?" she asked.

"Me. My fiancée will arrive in a week."

That was the last thing she expected to hear. But it was just the shake of reality she needed to put a stop to these inappropriate thoughts of Reid Barclay.

"When will the wedding take place?" she asked.

"Christmas Day."

One week from now! A bone-deep worry settled into Ellie.

Mrs. Leach hadn't mentioned she'd have to decorate the house and prepare a wedding feast. What else had the woman kept from her?

"After you," he said, holding the door open for her.

Ellie bustled into the warmth of the general store that overflowed with all manner of goods, as well as a goodly clutch of customers milling about. All paused to stare at the new arrivals, though the women barely paid her a passing glance.

He tipped his hat to a grinning trio of ladies huddled near the confectionary counter. Their soft, telling giggles had Ellie wondering if he'd captured the heart of the entire female population of Maverick.

He'd surely caught their interest, but then how could he not with those incredibly broad shoulders and long legs dressed entirely in black? And those eyes—

She'd never seen such an arresting blue that reflected her emotions back at her instead of revealing his own.

A robust woman bore down on them, her kindly face wreathed in a smile. "Good afternoon, Mr. Barclay. What can we do for you today?"

"Mrs. Leach said there was a parcel waiting here for me." He nodded to Ellie. "Anything Miss Cade wants, just add it to my bill."

"With pleasure," the woman said, giving Ellie a critical eye this time before flouncing off into a back room.

Without another word, Reid took himself off to the section sporting all manner of leathergoods. Ellie appreciated his broad back and firm backside before moving over to a table laden with fine hand-knit items.

"Can you tell us about the latest fashions in England?" one of the trio asked as she sidled over to Ellie.

She considered that a moment. "It's the cutting edge of hauteur, but as to specifics, I'm woefully unaware of what is in vogue there."

One of the trio frowned. "But you just came from there."

It was Ellie's turn to don a mantle of confusion. "No, I just came from Denver where I've lived most of my life."

The trio exchanged confused looks. "But aren't you Mr. Barclay's fiancée?"

"Heavens no," Ellie said, stunned they'd assume so.

"I'm a friend of Mrs. Leach's and I agreed to assume her duties on the Crown Seven Ranch while she's away helping her sister."

Instead of understanding, the trio took a collective step backward in perfect synchronization that would make a chorus line proud. The censure in their eyes was as unsettling as the sudden hush that fell over the store.

"Have you and Mrs. Leach been friends long?" one of the women finally asked.

Ellie hesitated for a suitable reply, for speaking the truth would surely rouse Reid Barclay's suspicions. She decided to expand minimally on a passing remark she recalled in one of Mrs. Leach's letters.

"You could say that," Ellie Jo said and affected a secret smile as if she were fondly recalling the past. "Mrs. Leach lived in Denver for a good many years."

Two of the young women raked her with a condemning look before walking away. The woman that tarried pulled her lips in a thin line of disapproval.

"There's no need to say more," she said, and turned up her nose and joined the small klatch that had formed near the rear of the store.

How rude! Ellie was a heartbeat from launching into a lecture on the merits of gainful employment for women when the storekeeper stepped in front of her.

"Pay them no mind," she said in a hushed tone. "They have nothing better to do than spread gossip, and would delight in causing trouble if you argue with them."

Ellie couldn't afford trouble, not now when so much was at stake. She turned her attention to the handmade woolens and gave the thick muff a longing look before crossing to the window.

Sunlight streamed through the panes and kissed the glass ornaments hanging on a small fir tree. She adored everything about Christmas. The carols sung with fervor. The gaily-decorated trees and sinfully delicious sweets.

The gilded and silvered Dresdens her aunt had imported from Germany were the rage among the upper class in Denver, but the homemade strings of cranberries and popcorn, and clusters of pinecones and berries dangling from ribbons brought back fonder memories of her youth.

She could just barely remember watching her mother sing as she decked the tree, but the mental picture was growing fainter as the years passed. She dreaded losing those precious memories, so the past few years she'd attempted to recreate them by stringing popcorn and cranberries—even if she hadn't had a tree to drape the garlands around.

She'd had Mama's cornhusk angel and her memories.

This year would be different. This would be a Christmas to remember for she'd have her pa to share Christmas with.

That was all the incentive Ellie needed to go forward with this deception. Even though she wasn't what she claimed to be, she'd do her best for Mr. Barclay.

Ellie sought out the shopkeeper again. "Pardon me, but I'd like to buy popping corn and fresh cranberries."

"There's a bag of cranberries in with Mrs. Leach's order. I'll add a pound of popping corn to it," she said.

Ellie rummaged in her purse. "I'll pay separate for it."

"No need," Reid said.

She whirled to face him. How could such a big man, made to look bigger in that heavy sheepskin coat, come up on her without her hearing him? And why did she have to be so aware of him as a virile man?

"I don't expect you to purchase my personal items," she said and laid her coins on the counter.

One black eyebrow hiked up. "You aim to eat all that popcorn yourself?"

"Well, no. But I'll use a good deal of it to decorate."

"Toss another pound of popcorn in our order," he said as he scooped up her money and handed it back to her. "I'm partial to popcorn, Miss Cade."

She knew she'd been bested, so she held out her palm. "Then popcorn you'll have, Mr. Barclay."

He smiled a wolf's smile that made her insides quiver with awareness, but when he dropped the coins in her hand and covered her palm with his in a time-honored gesture of affection, a jolt of sensual heat passed from him into her. She couldn't stop her tremor anymore than she could ignore her body's awareness of Reid Barclay.

In just the short time she'd been in his company, he'd made her feel more alive and desirable as a woman than she'd ever felt before. Surely he could hear her heart thundering.

He stepped back almost immediately, but the devilish twinkle in his eyes let her know he was aware of the effect he'd had on her. A new worry settled over Ellie, for the last thing she should do was court Mr. Barclay's favor that way.

Yes, technically she had nothing to lose but her pride. But that had taken a serious beating lately. Surely a respectable rancher such as Reid Barclay would boot her off his ranch if he knew of her shady past.

Never mind she was deceiving him as well. No, she'd go to her grave with this secret, for the ramifications involved not just her, but Mrs. Leach and her pa as well.

"Fill a bag with licorice whips and peppermint candies," he said to the shopkeeper.

"You're spoiling that boy," the shopkeeper said.

Reid snorted. "Not likely."

Ellie glanced around the store, but she didn't see hide nor hair of a child. Until she glanced outside.

A boy of ten, if he was a day, stood on the boardwalk looking in, his sack coat hanging on his thin frame and his bare hands fisted up in the sleeves. His cheeks were red from the cold, but his light eyes were fixed on the tall cowboy inside the store.

"Word got out that you've been helping him and his ma," the shopkeeper said. "There's been more talk."

"Let their tongues wag. They need help, and I can give it. Simple as that," Reid said.

"God will surely shine on you, Reid Barclay," the shop-keeper said.

"He'll likely send me straight to hell." He hefted the large box of provisions and caught Ellie's rapt gaze, but he simply nodded to the door. "Time we got on our way."

"Of course." She opened the door for him, then preceded him through when he chose now to stand on manners.

But she stepped aside in time to see him pass a small sack to the street urchin. "Make that last you, boy."

"I will! Thank you, sir," the boy said.

"There's provisions in the store for your family," Reid said. "You see your ma eats her fill."

"She will, Mr. Barclay," the boy said. "Ma is cooking up a storm on that new range."

"That's good." He tousled the boy's sandy hair. "Get on inside with you and collect that parcel."

"Yes, sir." The boy barged inside without a backward glance.

"That was a wonderful thing you did," she said.

He slid her an impatient nod toward the sleigh. She sensed he didn't want accolades for doing a good turn.

As he stowed their provisions in the sleigh, she was tempted to get in on her own. But he surprised her again.

Strong hands bracketed her waist, the thumbs pointing up to graze the underside of her breasts. Fire licked through her and she gasped as if truly burned by his touch.

He picked her up as if she weighed nothing, taking his own sweet time. Or at least time seemed to stand still for her before she felt the footboard beneath her.

Ellie was rendered speechless with the strength in Reid's hands. Hands that could bring pleasure to a woman. Hands that weren't immune to fighting. Hands that had known work.

The sleigh dipped as Reid climbed up and sat beside her. He surprised her by spreading a heavy buffalo robe over his lap and hers.

Those knowing midnight-blue eyes held a mixture of censure and amusement. But Ellie wasn't fooled.

Pa was from the old school. Why if he knew the liberties Irwin had taken with her, he'd likely track down the man she'd planned to marry and give him jesse. If he saw the way she was comporting herself with Reid Barclay . . .

His long, strong thigh stretched alongside hers like a fire-warmed log, and his hotter-than-an-ember hip pressed to hers. A delicious heat spread through Ellie.

She had absolutely no trouble imagining how well they'd fit together as man and woman. But what shocked her was how much she wanted to feel Reid's body pressed to hers with nothing between them.

Those were dangerous thoughts that could destroy her plans to start a new life in California. She'd never considered her wayward wants would be the obstacle to overcome.

She caught herself from leaning into the heat of him. Adhering to propriety would be a challenge around this man, especially since her thoughts seemed to stray into the dangerous and forbidden and he was a deliciously warm temptation she longed to cuddle up to.

Ellie listened to the steady ring of sleigh bells and focused on the reasons she'd agreed to take over Mrs. Leach's position. Nothing like reality to chill these inappropriate thoughts of her boss.

"How long will it take to reach the ranch?" she asked as they left the town of Maverick behind them.

"Better part of an hour."

Sixty minutes of sharing a buffalo blanket with Reid would test her endurance. There was nobody but her and Reid and miles upon miles of unbroken snow. Nobody would know if they held to propriety. Nobody but her conscience.

She'd failed to listen to it before. She vowed not to make that mistake again.

Though sitting close to him warmed her, she shifted to keep a respectable distance between them.

"You all right?" he asked.

She was chilled and nervous and so very lonely. "Just fine, Mr. Barclay," she said, and willed her teeth not to clatter.

"You can call me Reid," he said in that low, sultry tone that made her insides tingle.

A twinge of unease passed through her. He likely thought she'd offer him the same freedom to address her informally. But dropping those strictures could lead to loosening of other principles.

She'd made that mistake once. She wouldn't do it again.

Still, she had to trot forth a suitable reply that wouldn't offend. "Perhaps once we become better acquainted."

Which wouldn't happen because she'd be leaving after the holidays.

"Fair enough."

They lapsed into an easy silence after that. Ellie fairly bubbled with excitement over seeing her pa again. But she carried a good case of nerves as well. She only hoped that the recipe book she'd purchased would guide her should Mrs. Leach's receipts fail her.

She fixed her gaze on the snow-packed plains stretching out toward the bruised ridge of the mountains in the distance. It seemed she'd been staring at the same vista for ages.

"How do you keep from getting lost out here?" she asked.

The ghost of a smile teased his ruggedly handsome face. "As long as it's not snowing, there are landmarks to guide me."

She glanced at the sky that threatened more snow and prayed it would hold off. "What if it starts snowing again?"

He caught her gaze with his solemn one. "Then we hope my instincts are right."

Not a terribly reassuring answer, especially when the first fat flakes began falling. When the wind gusted and blew the snow right at them, she squirmed with the beginning twinges of panic.

She huddled into her hooded cloak and stuck her gloved hands up her sleeves. Still the chill seeped into her bones, for the brick at her feet had grown cold and the miniscule space between her and Reid seemed larger.

Out of necessity, she scooted close until the solid length of his body bumped hers. She saw nothing ahead but a wall of white. Even the sleigh bells sounded dull.

Just when she feared they were lost and would freeze to death, the snow stopped. The sun broke through the clouds as the sleigh popped over a rise and the ranch spread into view. She wasn't sure what she'd expected, but it certainly wasn't the patchwork of corrals and buildings of various sizes and descriptions.

The two-story stone house was far grander than she'd expected to find in Wyoming, let alone a ranch. The design was distinctly Italianate, reminiscent of the mansions in Denver.

Bathed in the afternoon sun, it looked like a square-cut topaz set amid a stark white cloud. A true jewel of the high prairie, fitting for a prosperous rancher.

Ellie straightened from her huddled pose as Reid angled the sleigh around to the back porch. This must be the servants' entrance, though the open terrace was larger than the front porch hanging on her uncle's home and looked twice as inviting. Wouldn't that man have a conniption fit if he knew what she was doing here?

She wouldn't be here long enough for her uncle to ever know. Which was just as well.

Her uncle would like nothing better than to see Ellie's pa hang, for he believed his sister deserved better than marrying a Missouri farmer. When her pa turned outlaw, her uncle's dislike turned to abhorrence. If she lived to be an old woman, she'd never understand such hatred.

Ellie welcomed Reid's help down and hoped her numb feet and legs would carry her inside. She took the satchel he handed her with fingers that were stiff with the cold.

Reid grabbed her trunk and carried it up the steps. "Hubert will see that you're settled in, but if you need anything, just ask."

"I will."

She followed, leery of accepting anyone's help so soon

after arriving. Until she spoke with her pa, she didn't know who she could trust.

The half-glass back door swung open, and a small wiry man of advanced years glanced from her to Reid. "Who, may I ask, is this woman?"

"E.J. Cade. Mrs. Leach's friend." Reid inclined his head the old man's way. "This is Hubert, butler and all-around nosy parker."

The butler's face remained impassive as he treated her to a quick inspection. So much for being friendly.

"This way, Mrs. Cade," Hubert said.

"It's miss," she said.

"Of course. Do forgive me for addressing you as one does the elevated female staff in England." An odd smile flickered over Hubert's face as he turned and walked into the house.

Ellie expected she would be given the room off the kitchen, but Hubert strode down the hall to a narrow rear staircase into the kitchen. She caught a glimpse of Reid pounding up the stairs with her trunk on his back as if it weighed nothing.

She wanted to follow now, for Reid would surely deposit her trunk and be gone about his own business. She wasn't ready to part company with him so quickly, though she should. But Hubert moved at his own pace which was slower than slow.

To dart around him would be horribly rude. So she schooled her eagerness and waited in the hall that was at least warm.

"This way," Hubert said at last, his features curiously benign as he stood at the bottom of the stairs.

"After you," she said when she heard heavy boots pound down steps on the other side of the wall—likely Reid going about his business.

Hubert hesitated a moment, then mounted the stairs in that same metered cadence that chafed her nerves. He opened the first door they came to and stepped aside to wave her in.

"Your chamber, Miss Cade."

"Thank you."

Ellie stepped into a compact room complete with a bed, dresser and armoire. Reid did an injustice by calling it adequate.

Why, it was far larger than the room she'd grown up in at her uncle's house. It was far more welcoming than her cramped garret room at the boarding house. And all this light!

Windows on two walls gave her a good view of the ranch outbuildings and lent the room a spacious feel.

She set her satchel down beside her trunk and crossed to the windows, thinking this vista surely rivaled any Christmas postcard she'd seen. "It's a beautiful sight."

"It has a certain rustic charm," Hubert said. "You'll find the kitchen in relatively good order. When Mrs. Leach was away, I availed myself of the facilities, though I am not adept in the kitchen."

That made two of them.

"I'm sure I'll manage." Though she knew she'd need a good deal of luck when she prepared her first meal tonight.

"If you require meat or game," Hubert said, "inform me and I'll send word to Moss."

"Moss?"

"The mess-hall cook," he said.

Ellie heaved a sigh of relief as she pulled the pin from her hat and set it on the dressing table. At least she wouldn't be expected to cook for a crew of hungry cowboys.

"Are you from England, Hubert?"

"Indeed. I was born in the Cotswolds."

"What brought you to Wyoming?" she asked.

"My former employer, Kirby Morris," Hubert said, and turned somber. "Would you care to inspect the kitchen?"

"I'd love to." She tucked up a few stray hairs that had escaped her bun, then followed the little man down the stairs.

The abrupt change in subject confirmed he didn't wish to say more about Mr. Morris. Ellie understood, for she'd never been one to talk about her past either. She'd divulged her secret once to her fiancé, and that brought about the end of her engagement and got her promptly dismissed from the Denver Academy for Young Ladies.

Still, her curiosity was peaked about Kirby Morris and how his very British butler ended up being in Reid's employ.

She paused once at the bottom and tried to place the low hum of masculine voices deeper in the house. She couldn't make out the words, but she recognized Reid's voice. Who was the other man?

"Your domain, miss," Hubert said, and she was obliged to join him into the kitchen.

"It's lovely." An understatement.

Though Ellie was a virtual stranger in a kitchen, she certainly appreciated the light pouring in the bank of windows. The cooking range was monstrous, larger than the impressive one her uncle had bought for his home. How she'd love to be able to cook appetizing meals on this stove.

Hubert opened a door along the back wall. "The pantry was recently stocked with essentials, though you may find it lacking certain items of import."

Ellie stepped inside and gazed up at the tins and

boxes of dry goods. A large flour bin took up the width along one wall. She ran a hand over the smooth tin surface, marveling it was as shiny as a mirror.

A door banged deep in the house, and a man's string of curses carried clear into the pantry. "If I get my hands on that sonofabitch, I'll string him up. Hubert!"

"Coming, sir." The old man sighed. "Excuse me."

The butler left, and she stood there gawking at the door as curses continued to fill the house. Reid sounded livid. What in the world had happened?

Ellie hurried across the kitchen and paused at the door that opened onto the main hall. She looked down it, but didn't see anyone. The torrent of foul oaths appeared to come from a room near the front of the house. Common sense told her that was likely where Reid's ranch office was located.

She certainly didn't want to get caught touring the house, and strolling down the main hall would likely do just that. A door to her right stood open, so she stepped inside.

Of course. The servants' entrance to the dining room. A long, dark table and more chairs than she cared to count dominated the spacious area. Her stomach pitched at the thought of satisfying so many palates.

She walked the length of the room, Reid's curses becoming clearer. His office must be next to this room, and he must've expended his anger because the house suddenly fell silent.

Ellie peeked out the other door into the main hall. Across from her, pocket doors were open to reveal a very formal parlor dressed in the richest looking brocades she'd ever seen.

She cocked her head. All she heard was the pounding of her heart and the metered ticking of a clock. She inched into the hall, her fingers sliding along the smooth paneled walls to the half-shut door. A peek through the crack confirmed this was an office, and a well-appointed library as well. But was it empty?

"I can't believe this has happened," Reid said, answering her unspoken question and sounding terribly close.

Ellie crept back toward the dining room door, careful to be quiet. She certainly didn't want to get caught eavesdropping.

"Did anyone see who took the stallion?" Hubert's question froze her in place.

"Booth claims Ezra Kincaid was seen riding him hell-bent for thunder," Reid said. "That old outlaw has got more guts than sense to pull a stunt like this."

Ellie's jaw nearly dropped to the floor. She ducked into the dining room and flattened her spine against the door. Her mind reeled with what she'd just overheard.

This made no sense to her. According to Mrs. Leach, her pa was here to exact revenge on the cowboy who framed him for murder years ago. Why in the world would he draw attention to himself by doing something as stupid as stealing Reid's horse?

Chapter 3

Reid stilled, catching a faint whiff of lilacs. Just like in the saloon, the swift warming of his blood left him a mite lightheaded.

So did the woman. Ellie must be close for her scent to reach out to him and glide over his skin, stroking, teasing and tempting. Feminine, yet unmistakably bold.

Yep, she was a daring one to march into Mallory's Roost because he was late to fetch her from the depot, and just as audacious to come near Reid's office when he was throwing a shit fit. Her boldness intrigued him, but it was her hint of wide-eyed innocence that gave him pause.

Sure as shooting she was the type woman who was trouble for a man like him. Hadn't Mrs. Leach told her that she was to mind her own business while she was here?

He whipped around to ask her that, but Miss Cade was nowhere to be seen. That didn't ease his mind none. She may not be near, but she'd gotten an earful.

He met Hubert's calculating eyes. The old man was like a hawk, always keeping an eye on him.

Though he couldn't prove it, he suspected Hubert kept Burl Erston apprised of what he was doing here at the ranch. If Reid didn't tow the line, Kirby's cousin would make good his threat and bring a heap of trouble crashing down on the two men Reid considered brothers.

"You get Miss Cade settled?" he asked Hubert.

"Indeed. I was introducing her to her domicile when you commenced bellowing."

"Reckon my voice carried."

"Like a bugle on the wind, sir."

Reid winced. He hadn't intended to vent his anger where his new cook could overhear. But she had, and if his suspicions were right, she'd eavesdropped on the rest of what had been said.

"Forgive me, sir, but are you certain this Ezra Kincaid stole Cormac?"

Being reminded that his prize stallion had been rustled from under his nose had Reid close to stomping mad again. "Middling so. Booth claims Frank Arlen saw the old outlaw riding off on the sorrel."

"How convenient Mr. Arlen happened by to witness the thievery."

The same thought had crossed his mind as well. "Booth said Arlen came around looking for work again. He was let go at the spread north of here that he'd been working."

"I'm not surprised."

Neither was Reid. Arlen had two streaks of lazy running down his spine.

"Did Mr. Howard mount a search for the stallion?" Hubert asked.

Reid shook his head. "By the time Arlen got around to telling him about the rustler, the tracks would've drifted over."

"The thief chose a perfect time."

That he had. Reid never expected Kincaid would steal

his prize stallion right off his ranch. Now if that wasn't rubbing his face (and pride) in a cow pie, he didn't know what was.

"Should I inform the cook of your dinner preference?" Hubert asked.

"Whatever she wants to dish up is fine by me." He'd been content with Moss's whistle berries, sowbelly and soda sinkers.

"Very well, sir. Will there be anything you require? Perhaps a brandy."

"I'll take you up on that later," Reid said. "Right now I aim to have a long talk with the hands. Since Kincaid found it so easy to walk off with one horse, he'll likely return for another."

Hubert's owlish eyes remained as emotionless as ever. "I hope that the thief has the sense to keep the horse stabled in this weather."

Reid hoped the same as he shrugged into his sheepskin coat. He headed for the back door, his bootheels hammering the floor, mirroring his anger. He had to make peace with the two men he'd wronged so badly, and so far he hadn't had a lick of luck locating them.

In the six months he'd been back here, he'd watched his herd of prize thoroughbreds thunder over the high plains, kicking up a cloud of dust.

And sometimes, when that dun grit settled, he saw a young woman lying in the middle of a dusty street, her calico skirts fanned around her as a red stain spread across her chest. He'd never seen her lifeless eyes, but he'd damned sure remembered the condemning ones of the sheriff.

He hung his head. Remorse mingled with the old anger that had never truly left him.

He'd struck a devil's bargain to save his hide, and ensure

the two men he called brothers weren't dragged into his nightmare. But he'd been lied to from the start. He hadn't realized how deeply he'd been deceived by Burl Erston until he'd returned to America six months ago.

Kirby was dead. Dade and Trey had vanished, accused of rustling cattle off the ranch, which had to be a damned lie. And Burl Erston held the controlling shares of the Crown Seven in his tight fist.

He'd known then that righting that wrong wouldn't be easy. It may prove impossible with a marshal out to make his mark and an old outlaw determined to even a score.

As he passed the kitchen door, he caught a glimpse of Miss Cade staring forlornly at the stove. He had the distinct feeling she was miles out of her element. She wore much the same look that he'd seen staring back at him in a mirror since the shooting.

Don't go looking for trouble.

Miss Cade could just as easily be piqued about the quality of the cooking contraption or the scarcity of needed goods in their larder. Whatever was amiss, Hubert could see to it.

Reid pushed out the back door and turned up his collar. A gust of bitter wind stole his breath and forced him to struggle with each step.

The coat of fresh powder blew sideways in a blinding curtain. No doubt about it, he'd gotten back here in the nick of time.

He grabbed the rope line at the end of the terrace and followed it toward the hazy shape of the outbuildings. Bits of ice pelted his face and stung his eyes, but his ire failed to cool. By the time he reached the long, low bunkhouse he was spitting mad.

He'd warned his crew time and again to guard those thoroughbreds. Somebody had let him down, and that somebody had better have a damned good reason for being derelict in his duty.

He pushed into the mess hall that smelled of rich meat juices, spice and working men. Eight pairs of eyes focused on him with myriad degrees of annoyance at having their supper interrupted.

He put his weight against the door to close it and stamped the snow from his boots.

"'Pears you brought in an avalanche," Moss said in that scratchy voice that held a hint of pain.

"It's coming down again," Reid said.

"Park it on a bench while I fetch you a plate of stew."

"Coffee will be enough for now." Reid ambled to the table and lifted a hand to stop his foreman, Howard Booth, from vacating his seat at the head of the long table. "I want to know everyone's whereabouts when Kincaid stole my stallion."

"We were on the trail of a wolf pack," Neal said, and indicated two other punchers who nodded agreement.

"I was busting ice so the cattle could drink," another hand said.

Shane flicked him a worried look that raised his suspicions. "One of the support posts on that lean-to snapped and brought down the roof."

"We lose any cattle?"

"Nope, but they scattered to hell and gone." Shane took a long sip of his coffee. "Took the rest of the day rounding them up again."

"Was the post rotted?" Reid asked.

"Nope." Shane ran his thumb around the rim of his coffee cup, as if drawing the moment out. "It's possible the cattle leaned into it and it snapped. Possible that somebody threw a line around it with the intentions of dragging it down."

Understanding dawned. "But the wood gave first."

Shane shrugged. "It made a damned fine diversion."

"Kincaid's handiwork," Reid said, and the men grunted and bobbed their heads in agreement.

"I had the hands run the herd into the paddock while I stabled Etain, Tara and Grania," Howard said, muddling the mares' Gaelic names as always.

Thoroughbreds straight from Ireland, dams to Reid's racing dynasty that he'd bought after selling Cormac's brother for a trifling fifteen thousand dollars. Unlike those American-born stallions, his mares' dams and sires were listed in *The English General Stud Book.*

Two were with foal. Tara was due for a season, and he'd told the men to keep Cormac away from her. All to keep the pedigree pure.

Now the stallion he'd hoped to sell in America was stolen, and he damned sure didn't have the money to replace him. The loss of that income dashed another dream of his to hell.

Reid ground his knuckles against the homemade table and ignored the stab of pain veining across his hands. He stared out at the ranch he'd thought was well-guarded. To think that old rustler had walked off with one blooded horse.

No, not a mere rustler.

Kincaid was a man bent on revenge.

Reid had thrown out bait, and the old rustler had rowed in on the river of bad blood that flowed between them.

He wasn't surprised. Kincaid wanted retribution for being blamed for a murder he swore he hadn't committed.

But the fact that he'd taken Reid's horse was a clear sign that he knew he was Slim, the drunken cowpoke who accidentally shot a woman in Laramie two years ago. Maybe

Burl had lied about paying to keep his real name secret. Maybe Reid hadn't changed as much as he'd thought, though he surely felt like an entirely different man.

For damn sure Ezra Kincaid aimed to get his pound of flesh out of Slim's hide. Well, Reid sure wasn't about to make it any easier for him than he already had.

Reid had done his time for a crime he didn't remember by going to England and agreeing to Burl Erston's demands. But he hadn't counted on Erston holding a rustling charge against his brothers over his head if he failed to do his bidding.

"I need to check on the horses," he said to Booth.

His foreman downed the last of his coffee and pushed to his feet. "I was just heading that way. Wouldn't be surprised if Grania didn't foal tonight."

He wasn't surprised. The change in the weather and herd change would make a temperamental dam even more skittish.

Shane caught his attention. "I put that post in the barn. See what you make of the marks on it."

"I'll head over there first," Reid said and moved to the door.

"You fetch Mrs. Leach's friend from town?" Moss asked as Reid reached for the latch.

He got a grip on the cold iron and remembered that forlorn look on Ellie's face when he'd left the house. "Yep. When I left, she was in the kitchen."

"It'll take a spell to get a decent meal on." Moss hefted a porcelain dinner pail. "Got enough stew in here to fill your gut tonight. All she'll have to do is whip up a batch of biscuits. If you want my help, that is."

It sounded good to him on this cold, bleak afternoon. "Much obliged. I'll take it up after I see to the horses."

Moss stepped back with his offering. "I can do it. Hell,

I intended to head up there anyway with a haunch of venison. One of the boys went hunting today."

"Fine by me." Reid tugged his Stetson down and turned his collar up. "Tell Miss Cade I'll be up for supper in about an hour."

"I'll sure enough let her know," Moss said.

Reid stepped out into the biting wind and pelting snow and damned his bad luck. Booth followed and they soundlessly trudged to the barn.

Their boots crunched the hard pack and the wind howled at their backs. It sickened Reid to think of the outlaw running the thoroughbred stallion in this treacherous weather. One slip on the ice could end the horse's life.

He'd kept them guarded the past six months, but now it seemed impossible. Though the horses signified the break he needed to start over, he couldn't ask any man to suffer this weather to keep an eye on them.

He could only hope if it was too bitter for his men to be out, it'd be too severe for Kincaid to strike again too.

He shouldered his way into the barn. Though cold, it was a welcome respite from the biting wind.

Booth strode to a post propped against a pen. "Take a good look at this about a foot up from the bottom."

Reid crouched and inspected the fir pole. He saw what Booth and Shane had noticed right off. Bits of sisal were caught in the rough wood.

"He used a rope, all right." He glanced at Booth. "After creating a distraction, why just steal one horse? Why not drive the whole herd away?"

"I wondered the same," Booth said. "Maybe something or someone scared him off."

He nodded, but he doubted that was the reason. Nope, this looked more like a taunt to him. Kincaid wanted him to know they were vulnerable. He'd want him jumping at shadows.

"I can't imagine him striking at night," Booth went on. "But I aim to keep an eye peeled on the stable and corral all the same."

"Don't expect you to stay up all hours in this weather."

Booth laughed. "Part of the job, boss. I need to be on hand if that mare foals tonight."

Reid was grateful his foreman watched his prize thoroughbreds. Still, he wasn't about to head indoors to the warmth and enticing woman until he checked out his horses.

"Let's go take at look at that mare."

After easing a molasses pie into a hot oven—the one dessert she felt confident enough to make—Ellie paced to the back door and stared out the frost-etched window at the expanse of white. She'd lived in Denver for a decade, so she wasn't a stranger to snow. But in the city, the winter landscape was broken up with scores of buildings, street lamps, lights glowing from homes and businesses, and people traveling on foot or in all manner of conveyances.

There was always noise of some sort.

Here, she'd never experienced such dense quiet. The only thing that broke the monotony of an endless white vista were the outbuildings standing dark and forlorn.

A frustrated sigh rumbled from her. She'd jumped at the opportunity Mrs. Leach offered her for two reasons. She'd get to spend Christmas with her pa. And hopefully, she'd be able to talk him out of taking the law into his own hands, as Mrs. Leach feared he was about to do.

Though her pa had known she was coming here, he'd

stolen Mr. Barclay's prize stallion and rode out of her life again.

The old pain of abandonment needled her heart again. How silly of her to think her pa would be glad to see her. That he'd at least hold off rustling for a few days while they shared a brief reunion.

She ran nervous fingers around her high, stiff collar. Would she ever see her pa again?

She rubbed her brow, annoyed with herself for getting her hopes up. And she was mighty annoyed with her pa, for now she was stuck here among strangers and cast in the role of housekeeper and cook until Mrs. Leach returned.

That time couldn't come soon enough.

She took a deep breath and schooled herself to proceed as she'd promised to do. When her task was over, she'd take the train to California and the job awaiting her there.

Until then, Mr. Barclay deserved no less than her best.

Mrs. Leach had left her a sketchy map of the housekeeper's domain, which helped immensely. A springhouse sat behind the house and a meat locker crouched nearby.

But what eased her mind was finding a note from Mrs. Leach. The good woman had addressed it to her and hidden it inside the pie safe.

In short, she told Ellie how she and the chuck cook worked in tandem regarding cuts of meat. All fresh game had to be requested, and then it depended on the luck of the hunter.

When Mrs. Leach had left, there'd been a pork shoulder in the stone meat locker adjacent to the springhouse. Several inviting meals came to mind.

If that meat was still there, she'd attempt to carve a

few steaks. With the dried mushrooms she'd found in a tin, she could make a savory gravy to dress the panfried pork steaks.

A few vegetables seasoned with spices and dressed with butter would make a passable first meal.

But first she had to ascertain if they had pork. To do that, she had to brave the elements.

"It is good to have such appetizing smells in the kitchen," Hubert said from the doorway of the pantry, startling her. "Is there anything I can do to assist you?"

She nearly made the mistake of asking him to go to the meat locker for her. No, if Mrs. Leach gathered her own ingredients for meals, she'd do so as well.

"Everything is in order," she said.

He gave her that odd look again, as if he knew she was a fraud and stumbling through meal preparation. "Very well. I was a bit concerned when I noted you'd not begun dinner preparations."

She bristled up at that, hoping she appeared indignant instead of defensive. "I decided to bake a pie while I apprised myself of what was on hand. Now that I have, I'll have supper on in short order."

"Excellent." Hubert's thin lips twitched with a hint of amusement. "Mr. Barclay will expect to dine promptly at five."

Thanks to being a clock-watcher, Ellie knew that gave her a bit less than forty minutes to have a meal on the table. While chicken-fried pork steaks and a medley of vegetables cooked on the stovetop, she'd put a whip on her just-baked pie and set the meringue.

Yes, her first meal was very doable—if she didn't have to fetch the meat from the locker. And if the pork was gone?

Her stomach quivered at the thought of failing her

first meal here. A simple vegetable soup seasoned with salt pork was sounding more appealing.

She marched to the cloak she'd hung on the hall peg with the intentions of shrugging into it and striding out the door. She managed to swirl the fabric around her shoulders in a show of impatience when the back door burst open.

A gust of icy wind swept down the hall and ripped her cloak from her hands. She yelped and grappled with the yards of fabric still cold from her long drive to the Crown Seven.

Ellie's head jerked up and her eyes surely went wide as saucers. For standing in the kitchen was an elf of a man from her dreams—short, rotund and swathed in a heavy red-and-black buffalo plaid coat.

Snow clung to his white beard and mustache, and his round cheeks were rouged from the cold. His green eyes stared at her with disapproval that made her shiver.

Ellie swallowed, unable to form words as she stared at the man. No, he couldn't be. He couldn't be that bold to steal a horse and return to the ranch.

"Reckoned since ya'll got in late I'd share my Irish stew," he said in a rusty voice she didn't recognize. "Though the only Irish in it is a touch of whiskey."

Her pa had changed drastically, packing so much weight on his wiry frame that he looked like a barrel. His black hair was now snow white, and a full beard hid his grizzled features.

Her heart set off on an icy race. No, he looked nothing like the father she'd known, nor did he resemble the man on the wanted posters nailed in jails across the west.

If not for his sour expression, he'd pass for the jolly old elf Santa Claus.

Somehow she managed to move forward to take the

offered pail from him. "Thank you for sharing your bounty." And for finding a reason to come to the house, though his darkening frown wasn't at all heartening.

"I'll set it on the stove," he said and took off in that direction before she could object.

She should have followed him into the kitchen, but she couldn't force her legs to work. Of all the reunions she'd imagined, this one had never occurred to her.

Surely he recognized her. Perhaps he was simply being cautious with Hubert in the house. Perhaps he truly wasn't pleased to see her again after all these lonely years.

He returned to where she stood in the hall. She noted his halting gait and wondered what had happened to him. The years had turned him into someone she barely recognized. Even his voice was scratchy, as if speaking took great effort.

She longed to step into his embrace and lose her breath from his bear hug. Even if his demeanor welcomed it, she didn't dare make such a bold overture with Hubert bearing down on them.

"I thought I heard voices," Hubert said, insinuating himself into this awkward moment. "Allow me to introduce Mrs. Leach's friend, Miss Cade."

"How do, miss," her pa said, his green eyes warming a bit.

Hubert made no sign of noticing as he continued with his formal introductions. "Miss Cade, this is Gabby Moss, the chuck cook."

At least she knew what to call him now. "How good to make your acquaintance, Mr. Moss."

If he felt as awkward as she, it didn't show. "The men went hunting today and bagged a couple of prairie chickens and a deer. I've dressed both and hung them in the meat locker."

"Thank you," she managed to get out in a voice that didn't quaver.

"Were they able to find Kincaid's trail?" Hubert asked.

Her pa shook his head, not meeting her eyes or the Englishman's. "Nary a sign of it. Boss had the men pen up the rest of them thoroughbreds."

"That should deter this thief," Hubert said.

This time she caught a hint of mischief flickering in her pa's blue eyes. Good heavens, surely he didn't intend to steal another horse? Surely he realized he was playing a dangerous game by passing himself off as a chuck cook while he was rustling horses.

"Reckon the weather will slow him—" Her pa broke off, scowling and sniffing the air. "What in tarnation's on fire?"

She drew in the smell of burnt sugar and scorched crust at the same time Hubert muttered a curse and hobbled toward the kitchen.

"My pie!" she said as black smoke billowed into the hall.

Chapter 4

Reid smelled the smoke before he saw the black cloud stringing across the dusky snow sky. He drew in a deep breath. Not wood smoke. No, this smelled sweet, like burned sugar.

What the hell?

A thousand improbable things went through his mind as he trudged toward the house. He caught sight of Ellie standing in the open door, fanning a towel and looking ready to cry. Smoke escaped the back door in puffs.

"What the hell happened?" Reid asked as he stomped to her, giving her a head-to-toe perusal that had her flushing red. "You start a grease fire?"

"No, I didn't do any such thing," she said and coughed.

He peered past her into the hall and noted the worst of the smoke had dissipated. All she was doing now was letting frigid air inside, but she seemed to be unaware.

He moved her back into the house and yanked the door shut. His eyes immediately watered from the lingering smoke.

"What was burning?" he asked.

Her narrow shoulders slumped. "My pie, I fear."

That didn't say much about her culinary talents. Just what had Mrs. Leach been thinking to recommend Ellie Jo Cade for the job of housekeeper and cook?

"Where's Hubert?" he asked, his patience shot to hell now.

Ellie pointed a shaky finger into the kitchen. "He's in there with my—with Mr. Moss."

He headed straight there, hoping he'd get answers out of one of them. "Well?" he asked the two older men standing before the stove.

"It appears that the damper was closed, which prevented the smoke from escaping." Hubert glanced down at the soot on his waistcoat and grimaced. "If I'm not needed, sir—"

Reid excused the fussy butler with a nod and turned to Moss, well aware Miss Cade had ventured into the kitchen at last. "You got anything to add?"

Moss stroked his cottony beard and snorted. "Your new cook smoked the place up but nothing's burnt 'cept what was in the oven. Appears to have been a pie of sorts."

"It was a molasses pie," she said. "My grandmother taught me how to make it."

"Did she teach you to open the damper on the cook stove before you fired it up?" Moss asked in a belligerent tone that nudged Reid to jump to Miss Cade's defense.

But before he could utter a word, she jutted her chin out and said, "Of course she did."

Moss slid her a steely-eyed look that brought fresh color to her face. "If what you claim is true, then why the hell was the damper closed?"

"It was open," she said, squaring off against the old chuck cook as if she'd done so many times before. "If the damper had been closed, the kitchen would have filled with smoke in a matter of minutes."

"Maybe you shut it right before I hauled supper in for you," Moss said.

Ellie reeled back, a look of abject hurt clouding her big eyes and slamming Reid back to the here and now. Somebody had closed that damper. Hubert would've needed a chair or ladder to reach it. But then so would Moss. And, hell, the ranch cook was just doing a good turn by bringing a pail of stew up for supper.

That left Ellie Jo Cade. She was the stranger, and the most likely one to have caused this stir.

"Why are you doing this?" she asked Moss, her voice suddenly small and trembling.

Moss's bushy white eyebrows slammed together. "Reckon you'd best look in a mirror and ask that question." He turned to Reid. "If you was smart, you'd haul this gal back to Maverick before she burns the house down."

"How dare you suggest such a thing," Ellie said.

Moss didn't even acknowledge her with a look. "I can throw a meal on the table any time, boss. You holler if you need me."

"I'll bear that in mind," Reid said.

That earned him a curt nod from the old ranch cook before he turned and tramped down the hall. Cold gusted in, then the door slammed shut and silence roared in the kitchen.

Reid rubbed his forehead where a headache pounded. First Kincaid steals his stallion, and now Miss Cade sets fire to the kitchen. Or did she?

He crossed his arms over his chest and faced Miss Ellie Jo Cade. "You got anything more to say?"

"I didn't close the damper." She looked Reid square in

the eyes and he saw the truth there as plain as day. "Please, give me another chance."

He fully intended to, because there was no way in hell he was hauling Mrs. Leach's friend back to Maverick in this weather. Never mind the chances of him finding a decent cook in town on short notice.

She looked disheveled, yet oddly alluring. But it was those eyes sparking with anger that made him pause.

"Who do you think closed it then? Moss or Hubert?"

The wiry butler sputtered to attention. "Not I, sir."

"I think Mr. Moss closed it when he left the pail of stew on the stove," she said, and seemed close to stricken by the very idea of him committing the deed.

"Why would he do that, Miss Cade?"

Her chin came up. "It's clear he doesn't want me on the ranch."

He had a feeling she was right, but there was more to it than jealousy. When they were arguing, he'd noted a familiarity between them. He sensed their quarrel went way back.

It was no secret that Mrs. Leach and Moss had been bed-partners at one time. Reid suspected that romance began while she was still in the business of pleasuring men for a living. But how did Miss Cade tie in with those two old-timers?

"What's to say you didn't close the damper to make Moss look bad?" he asked.

"I daresay that's because it was open then." Hubert wiped most of the soot off his waistcoat and grimaced.

"How long have you known Gabby Moss?" he asked Ellie.

"I don't know that man at all."

She wouldn't meet his eyes, and that told him she was

lying. Yep, there was something between the old cook and Miss Cade. But what?

"Yep, Moss made no secret that he wants you gone from here," Reid said.

She pinched her eyes shut for a heartbeat. "None at all."

"But you don't know why," he said.

She shook her head, looking defeated, when he suspected she wasn't one to give in without a fight. "Perhaps Mr. Moss is angry that I was chosen to replace Mrs. Leach."

He wasn't convinced yet that she could boil water, but he saw no sense in arguing the point. What was done was done. If Moss was trying to railroad Miss Cade, then keeping him out of the kitchen would forestall any more episodes like this.

"You might be right." Reid nodded at the porcelain pail sitting on the range. "That stew hot yet?"

Miss Cade turned to the stove and lifted the lid. "Nearly so. Would you like biscuits with supper?"

"I surely would."

He fished his pocket watch from his vest pocket and ran his thumb over the stag and forest design before he thumbed open the lid. Time always stood still for a breath or two, for he clearly remembered the Christmas that Kirby Morris gave him this watch.

It marked his right of passage as a man. The head honcho for this ranch.

And he'd failed miserably.

He snapped it shut and slid it back in his vest. "How long before it's ready?"

Her smile took his breath away. "I'll have supper on the table in twenty minutes."

"Fine. I got ranch business to tend to."

That was a damned lie, for he had nothing better to

do than stand here and watch her. But doing what he wanted would leave him hungering for something he couldn't have.

Ellie concentrated on following the recipe to the letter for two reasons. Her biscuits had to be edible. And keeping her mind on the job at hand kept her from dwelling on what her pa had done to her.

Though his betrayal hurt her feelings, she wasn't going to give up on him yet. He must have had good reason to do what he'd done. The way she figured it, she had two weeks to get her pa alone and talk to him at length.

In the meantime, she'd do her best to prepare meals that met with Reid Barclay's approval. She surely couldn't or wouldn't continue accepting her pa's handouts, for it was clear he wasn't happy to see her here.

She filled the tureen with stew and carried it into the dining room. Reid sat at the head of the long table looking incredibly handsome and unbelievably lonely.

"Would there be anything else you want?" she asked.

An intense heat flared in his eyes before they tempered to a molten blue, but the message was clear and bold and should have offended her. Instead, her body flushed as if she'd been stroked with fire.

"I'll take coffee after my meal," he said at last.

It was her cue to leave the room, but she couldn't seem to break the spell of his gaze until he looked away. Even then she trembled and had trouble catching her breath.

"Then I'll leave you to your supper," she said, and left the dining room with as much aplomb as she could muster.

Ellie fanned her hot face and tried to tell herself it

was the heat bottled in the kitchen that had her flushed and squirming. But it was a lie. How could one man evoke such intense longing in her with one look?

She didn't know, but she had to put a stop to this attraction. She'd made that mistake before. She surely wouldn't do it again, and with an affianced man at that.

Why, if Reid Barclay was a gentleman, he wouldn't make such an intimate overture to her. But he had, and that confirmed what she'd glimpsed in Mallory's Roost.

Reid Barclay wasn't a gentleman.

After putting on a pot of coffee for the cad who employed her, she slipped into the pantry. The pitiful remains of her pie sat cooling on the sill, looking more like charred wood than dessert.

She bit her lower lip to still its telltale quivering. She wasn't one to bawl at the least provocation, but, dammit all, it hurt something fierce knowing her pa wanted her to fail—wanted Reid Barclay to dismiss her. It broke her heart that her own father didn't want to grasp this opportunity to spend Christmas with her.

Did he fear she'd say something and expose him for who and what he was? Or was he more interested in rustling than in spending time with his only daughter?

She shouldn't be surprised if both worried him. Though he'd visited her at the holidays when she was little, she hadn't seen him or heard from him in the past five years. She'd feared he was dead, and with his death went any chance he'd redeem himself.

On her last birthday she'd shared her secret with Irwin, for she believed the man she was to marry should know about the past she'd kept hidden. She'd never dreamed her confession would show her Irwin's true colors in all their garish glory.

Oh, yes, she understood betrayal well.

She dropped onto the short bench with her warm pie cradled in her lap. Clearly this bench was more of a stool, and the only comfortable way to sit on it was to extend her legs out and let her stockings show. Not that she cared one whit what image she presented in this little corner of her temporary world.

With Irwin she was relieved to know what kind of man he really was before the vows were spoken. My, but she'd gotten an eyeful of a very vindictive sort.

Despite what he'd done—and that man had done plenty to ruin her reputation in his effort to shore up his own—she'd found the gumption to rally on. Yet now she felt as if time was conspiring against her.

Mr. Barclay expected her to cook a fine feast for his wedding. Her pa wanted her long gone. And all she wanted was the chance to spend what could be her last holiday with her ornery pa.

Men! She broke off a piece of burned crust and stuck a finger into the warm filling, scooping up a bit to taste. She would not think of Reid Barclay beyond the role of her employer. In fact she didn't want to think at all right now.

She scooped a bit of filling in her mouth like a lad who'd just filched a pie off a windowsill. As soon as the pungent taste exploded in her mouth she moaned her pleasure.

Past the telltale charring, it was a cross between mincemeat and raisin. Far better than she'd hoped to achieve. Why, if she'd been able to add a meringue to it—and if it hadn't scorched—this pie would rival one of Grandma Kincaid's molasses pies.

"You all right?" Reid asked, startling a gasp from her.

How could this man sneak up on her unawares? Not

that it mattered. Now that she knew he was an arm's length away her entire body began that unwanted tingling again.

There was no dignified way she could get to her feet, so she remained seated. "Other than smoking out your kitchen and burning dessert, I'm just dandy."

She poked two fingers into the pie again and stuffed the sticky filling into her mouth. Hopefully her uncouth manners would prompt Reid Barclay to leave her in peace. Or in this case, leave her to wallow in her personal misery.

"You're doing that all wrong," he said. "Let me show you how to make short work of that pie."

Reid plopped down beside her on the small bench, his bootheels scraping the floor as he extended his long, jean-clad legs the same direction as hers. She'd expected his black boots to have fancy stitching, but they were plain and the leather looked supple, thanks to the shine, evidence of frequent polishing.

Like an exuberant kid, he poked his long fingers into the sticky filling and scooped a large finger-full to his mouth.

Though she was typically quick to instruct others on proper etiquette, she couldn't seem to get her mind and mouth to work together. Reid Barclay was to blame, for each time he stole another bite his broad shoulder brushed hers and sent energy jolting through her.

Energy of the most titillating kind.

Heavenly days, the fact he was her boss and affianced didn't penetrate her mind. Neither did the fact that her pa had recently rustled Reid's prize stallion and was holed up right under Reid's nose, or that Reid would sooner see the old man hang.

Right now as he sat beside her helping himself to another taste of her charred molasses pie, he looked for all the world like a cowpoke. A very tempting cowboy.

Oh, this was dangerous sitting here in the pantry with this man. She started to get up just as he reached over to scoop up more filling, pressing the warm pan on her lap.

"Perhaps you should hold the pie plate," she said and made to pass it to him.

She accidentally bumped his elbow just hard enough to jar loose the wad of filling poised on his fingers. The gooey mass slipped off and dropped onto his jeans.

"Now look what you did," he said.

He didn't have to tell her to look. She couldn't drag her gaze away from the sticky brown mass resting close to his crotch. And were her eyes deceiving her or was that part of him shifting and lengthening?

Nope, she wasn't imagining things. Her heart pounded and the place between her legs began pulsing.

She tore her gaze away from his obvious erection and stared at the pie safe, forcing to mind one of Headmistress Halsey's dictums. *A lady never glances at a gentleman's private parts.*

Yet here she was, staring at Reid Barclay's crotch as if he were a randy cowpoke fresh off the range and she was a cow-town Cyprian leaning over a brothel balcony, ready to welcome him to her bed. Even knowing she had behaved brazenly, she was tempted to take another peek.

And what did that say about her? It certainly wasn't the image she'd honed all these years, nor was it the one expected of her at the Falsmonte Ladies Academy in California.

She had been certain she could handle such a delicate situation because she knew the pitfalls that awaited an unsuspecting miss. If learning by example were a prerequisite, her experience with Irwin certainly made her the perfect teacher for the young ladies of quality—a position she was to start in less than a month. What would Headmistress Halsey think if she saw her now?

That depended on how Ellie handled this situation. A lady with her experience should be able to extract herself from such a touchy predicament without undo embarrassment to herself or the gentleman. As for doing so gracefully—

She gave up all hopes of that. Without a doubt, her cheeks must be as red as the handles on the sad irons stored on the shelf beside the ironing board.

"I was doing fine as long as you were holding it," he said, the warm pie pan pressing into her thighs and rubbing shockingly low on her belly as he filched another piece. "This is a mighty fine pie, Miss Cade."

With effort, she found her voice. "The crust has the consistency of charcoal."

His warm breath fanned her ear and she shivered. "No fault of yours."

She cleared her throat and swallowed hard, thinking he was so close she could almost taste the hint of molasses on his breath. "I am relieved you believe that."

"I didn't at first," he said.

Ellie spared him a quick glance only to find his gaze was fixed on her mouth. She tried for a smile and damned the way her lips trembled.

"What changed your mind?" she asked.

"Seeing you sitting in here looking forlorn," he said. "If you'd burned this pie on purpose, you wouldn't do that."

Which meant either Hubert or her pa was guilty. She hoped Reid would tell her his thoughts, and what he intended to do about it. But he scooped up the last of the filling, which told her he was more interested in eating than talking.

She expelled the breath she'd been holding. Thank God, he'd about consumed all of the pie and this torment of sitting close to him would soon be over.

"Have the last bite," he said as he lifted his hand to her mouth.

He couldn't mean for her to eat the filling off his fingers, yet they remained poised before her. She licked her lips more from nerves than hunger.

"Thank you, but go on and enjoy it yourself," she said, proud she'd kept her voice from quavering.

But she was helpless to keep her heart from thundering like a stampeded herd. His eyes glowed with a sultry light that set her insides blazing hotter than the overheated stove.

The inviting curve of his lips as they quirked into a knowing smile had hers parting of their own accord. And mercy, but her thighs ached to do the same.

"I insist you enjoy the last of it." Something dark and deliciously wicked flared in his eyes.

"It isn't proper," she said, and this time her voice did tremble to betray her outward calm.

His dark eyebrows wiggled. "Few pleasurable things are."

How well she knew. She gave a half-hearted effort to pull away, denying the longing that danced a hoedown within her. It was a struggle to keep her quivering thighs pressed together, but she managed to retain that much dignity.

"Go on," he said, and this time she was sure his intentions were far from honorable as he pressed the morsel to her mouth, brushing the syrup over her lips. "You know you want to."

Oh, she wanted that and more. She knew it was wrong, but sitting this close to his powerful body and staring into his eyes that glowed with wicked promises pushed all thoughts of propriety from her mind.

She took a cautious bite and shivered as her tongue grazed his fingertips. The arousing scent emanating off Reid Barclay overpowered the sweet molasses custard melting on her tongue.

She couldn't have formed a coherent thought if her life depended on it.

He poked what remained into his own mouth and licked his fingers clean, his tongue curling around the exact same spot where her tongue had touched. His eyes closed in exaggerated ecstasy and his moan was a song that serenaded her longing.

This had to be the most wickedly wonderful thing she'd ever done with a man, for though she'd shared an intimacy with Irwin, it was over and done with so quickly she scarce knew what had happened.

With Reid Barclay she felt things she didn't know it was possible to feel. Being with him, touching him, brought her body fully alive, as if she'd been sleeping all this time, waiting for him to come along.

Reid clearly exuded an animal prowess that beguiled her on a purely primitive level. She knew if she made love with him, she'd remember every second for as long as she lived.

At that moment, she realized she was stuck on an uncharted island. For all her knowledge of the goings on between a man and woman, she knew pitifully little about seduction.

But there was no doubt in her mind that Reid Barclay was trying his best to seduce her.

She focused on their disjointed conversation thus far, desperate to gain control of the situation. What had they been talking about? The pie. Dear God, yes.

"If you're really that partial to molasses pie, I'll bake you another one," she said. "The next time the crust will be nicely browned and I'll add a fluff topping to it."

"Will you feed it to me, Miss Cade?"

She opened her mouth, but all that came out was a squeak. That had to be the most indecent thing he'd said yet.

Before she could rally her wits to tell him just that, his lips settled over hers. She was no stranger to kisses. Irwin had started out with frantic demanding ones, then dwindled to perfunctory pecks.

She'd never realized there was something else to savor. And she certainly savored this lazy stroking of tongues and glide of lips she was experiencing with Reid Barclay.

He tasted of rich sugar and brandy and delicious temptation, reminding her again of how very little she knew about men. Why, she'd thought he'd be demanding, taking what he desired without thought to her wants.

But he seemed in no hurry to do more than kiss and hold her. It was as if he knew what she'd hungered for all her life.

The gentle glide of his hands up her arms and down her sides, as if she was something rare and precious he was honoring. This unhurried melding of lips left her ravenous for more.

Their heated breaths mingled and chased off the chill of uncertainty.

Her spine, which had gone stiff with shock when their

lips first touched, instinctively arched to put her closer to the heat radiating off him. He drew her closer, and she hadn't realized he'd lifted her onto his lap until she felt the corded muscles in his legs bunch beneath her.

Against her hip, his erection reminded her of other delights they could share, successfully annihilating any resemblance of this necking to what she'd shared with Irwin.

For once in her life, she blocked out all thoughts of decorum and propriety and let herself enjoy this moment. Just once.

His mouth left hers to wander down her neck. She tipped her head back, giving him ample access, then realized that path led to danger.

"Please, we must stop this," she said, and was torn between relief and disappointment when he heaved a sigh.

"Your moral fiber is stronger than mine, Miss Cade," he said and rested his forehead against hers, his breath sawing hard and fast.

"Then I'm sorry for your fiancée." She pulled away from him to break the contact that kept her mind muddled.

"So am I."

Well, she couldn't fault him for his honesty. She did wish he wouldn't look at her so intently, for she was sure he was judging her unfairly by her actions thus far.

"I'm not one to take up with a man," she said in her own defense. "Especially a stranger."

"Didn't reckon you was," he said.

"Even if you weren't affianced, I believe a man and woman need to get to know one another before making any type of a commitment. That of course takes time," she said, and knew she was on the verge of rambling, but she couldn't seem to stop it either. "You know nothing about me, and all I know of you is you raise horses, you're from England, and you have a fondness for pie."

"I stole one off a windowsill once when I was a boy," he said.

That statement hung between them for the longest time.

"On a dare?" she asked, certain he'd done such a thing just to prove he could, for surely the privileged boy was given anything he whimpered for.

He gave a depreciating laugh. "Nope, my backbone was rubbing a hole in my belly."

She stared into his eyes that were near black with some emotion she couldn't name. Something dark and heart wrenching. Something that left scars of longing.

"Were you running away from home?"

He shook his head and gave another humorless laugh. "Hardly."

He got to his feet, a muscle drumming in his cheek as he extended a hand to help her up. She took it, feeling his withdrawal even as the warmth of his big hand stole up her arm for that brief moment.

"You'll hear soon enough," he said. "I was born and raised in America, not England."

"I didn't realize that."

But it explained so much. The lapses from cultured speech to rough cowboy lingo. So many questions filtered through her thoughts.

Ellie picked up the pie plate and scraped the burnt crust into the pail reserved for scraps, glad to have a few more seconds to gather her thoughts. She sensed there was far more to his story than he'd let on, but she was determined to start off on the right foot with him this time.

"Where do you hail from, Mr. Barclay?" she asked.

Silence answered her. She turned to find him gone.

Perhaps that was for the best.

No matter how attracted she was to Reid Barclay, the simple fact remained he was her employer, and an affianced gentleman. Though he'd certainly not let that deter him from making overtures with her just now.

As Miss Halsey advised in her manual, it was often left up to the lady to establish and maintain proper decorum. That was certainly the case here.

From here on out she'd do her job to the best of her ability, and when she had spare time, she intended to have a nice long chat with her pa.

She'd not do anything as reckless as falling into Reid Barclay's arms again and proving she was a true wanton at heart. No matter how much she longed to do just that.

Chapter 5

With her first day behind her, and a wedding scheduled to take place a mere week from now, Ellie certainly had her work cut out for her. Thankfully Reid had been content with a breakfast of eggs, bacon and fried potatoes the next morning. The simple fare allowed her to become better acquainted with the banquet range and feed him a meal that wasn't scorched or undercooked.

The second he left the house, she set her kitchen to rights and then fetched the popcorn popper from the pantry. She dumped a cup of shelled corn in the hopper, slid the wire lid closed, and set it over the hottest part of the stovetop.

As she slid the pan back and forth, Ellie tried to decide on how best to decorate the house. But all she could think about was the way Reid's mouth had fused to hers. Kissing him in the pantry had been positively stupid. And what had possessed her to eat from his fingers?

Ellie groaned and shook the corn popper a bit faster. She had enough experience to know where a kiss would lead. Yet she'd curled against him and moaned at each heated stroke and bone-melting kiss. Good heavens, she'd acted as wanton as the ancient Roman courtesans she'd read about. She'd been the loose woman she'd instructed young ladies not to be.

He was her employer and she the employee. Never the twain shall join in a compromising situation. Yet she'd done just that.

Well, no more! She was here to spend the holiday with her pa, though that prospect was looking rather dismal at the moment. And she'd given her word that she'd take over Mrs. Leach's duties in her absence.

She took a critical look at the kitchen. This house wasn't new by any stretch. The pine floor was weathered in the hall, and there were old scrapes and dings on the wallpaper.

Whoever had built it took care, for it was grander than any house she'd seen in the West. But it clearly lacked a woman's touch. And not just recently.

She couldn't see any indication of a woman's presence anywhere but in the kitchen. And then it was only evident in the floral linens hanging just so, and the single potted plant sitting on the far windowsill.

No, there hadn't been a woman living here in years—if ever, she thought as the shelled corn began popping in the hopper.

Ellie shifted her thoughts to decorating the house for the holiday wedding. She'd have to ask Reid to cut a tree for her. She'd also need a goodly amount of evergreen boughs. Some pine cones would be nice as well.

When no more corn exploded in the hopper, she carefully slid open the lid and dumped the fluffy, white popped corn into a large bowl. She'd string it and the cranberries later.

For now she needed to find out what all Mrs. Leach had ordered for the occasion. She was pleased by the array of artificial flowers and chenille pom-poms she'd found stored in the pantry.

The scuff of a shoe in the hall snared her attention. She looked up into Hubert's benign face.

"Is that popping corn I smell?" he asked.

"It is. I just popped some to make string garlands."

"Ah, pity." He turned to leave.

"If you want some," she said on her way into the pantry to fetch the box of decorations, "please, help yourself."

Surely one older man wouldn't eat it all. And even if he did, she had a goodly bag left to use for decorations.

Besides, if she was honest with herself, she welcomed the company. She returned with the box just as Hubert took a dish from the cupboard and eased onto the bench nearest the popcorn bowl.

She dug into the items Mrs. Leach had ordered. If she was lucky, there was enough so Ellie could fashion several nice sprays and festoons for the holiday wedding.

"Do you know how long Mr. Barclay has lived here?" she asked Hubert as she plucked another white chenille dove from the box and placed it with the others on the table.

"For nearly fourteen years," he said. "Mr. Morris had the house built then to his specifications shortly after he purchased the land. He and the lads moved in before winter."

She continued sorting the decorations in the box as if she wasn't dying to know how Reid Barclay came to live with a man named Morris. Was he a relative? A friend?

One thing was clear. Hubert had been here too.

"Am I correct to guess you worked for Mr. Morris for quite some time?" she asked.

"Indeed so. I was in his employ for nearly thirty years." Hubert lifted his chin as if proud he'd worked for one man for so long.

Reid Barclay was either that age or close to it, she suspected. No doubt Hubert could pinpoint Reid's age.

Ellie bit her lip as curiosity goaded her to ask the older gent to tell her more about his time under Morris's employ. But she was treading a fine line between congenial conversation between employees and out-and-out snooping on her part.

Annoyance skipped up her limbs. She'd instructed her students many times to exercise patience in all things, but she was having a deuced time applying what she'd preached. In fact, she couldn't remember when she'd been so bitten by curiosity to the point of shunning good behavior.

So she opted to voice the truth. "I'm afraid I'm totally confused, for I've no idea who Mr. Morris or the lads are, or how any of them are related to Mr. Barclay."

Hubert lifted his droll gaze to her. "It is a bit of a jumble to grasp." Instead of explaining, he crossed to the range and put on the teakettle. "Would you care for a spot of tea?"

"That would be nice," she replied, when she really wanted him to tell her more about her enigmatic employer.

"I will admit there were times during my employ when our roles blurred and Mr. Morris was more friend than employer."

"That's to be expected when you live with a person for that long," she said, and wondered what excuse she could drum up that would explain why she was in the pantry with Reid yesterday eating molasses pie off his fingers.

Hubert actually smiled. "Indeed so. I was not at all pleased when he told me he was coming to America for an adventure, but I tagged along just the same."

"Do you regret it?"

"There have been moments when I questioned my decision, as well as those living on this ranch," he said, his brow creasing as he carefully poured a cup of tea.

She wanted to press him to explain, but the impatient stride of footfalls in the hall warned her to hold her silence. She reached into the box of decorations just as Reid stepped into the kitchen.

He glanced from the table strewn with an array of faux flower sprays and fruit clusters to her face. "I smelled popcorn."

So much for using it to start a garland. "Help yourself."

Reid wasted no time dropping onto the bench beside Hubert and scooping up a handful of popped corn. He ate with relish, and for a moment she almost caught a glimpse of a hungry little boy ravenously devouring a treat.

She shook her head and went back to sorting the decorations. "I am glad you popped in because I need to ask you about the larger decorations."

One dark eyebrow veed over a piercing blue eye. "Go on."

"It's about the tree," she said.

"What tree?" he asked.

She rolled her eyes. "The Christmas tree. I think it should be a tall one, say six foot at least. I'll also need a selection of boughs for swags and decorations."

He shrugged and fished out another handful of popped corn. "I thought folks put the tree up on Christmas Eve?"

"Well, yes, traditionally," she said. "But since you are getting married on Christmas Eve, it should be done before then."

"Fine. We'll set it up the day before."

She flattened her palms on the table and leaned a bit

toward him to draw his attention away from the popcorn. "That's still waiting too long."

"Just when did you want to put it up?" he asked, rocking back and locking his arms over his chest as if displeased by her input.

"Today," she said, earning her a dismissive snort from Reid and a cough from Hubert.

The old butler recovered his manners first. "That would be seven days before the holiday, Miss Cade."

"I can count," she said. "Setting it up now would put us all in the holiday spirit that much sooner."

Reid's dark gaze skewered her with such icy dismissal that she shivered. "It's going to take a helluva lot more than a tree dressed up in ribbons, fruit and tin ornaments to put me in the holiday spirit."

She pursed her lips and counted to ten, then added another ten before she felt marginally in control. "It's your wedding, Mr. Barclay. I'm sure your bride would appreciate it if you showed a bit of enthusiasm for the celebration."

He shoved to his feet, jaw anvil-hard and shoulders racked tight. "I didn't pick the woman or the day, so don't expect me to get heated up over it all."

With that, he stormed out of the kitchen and down the hall, his bootheels striking the hardwood floor like gunshots. He marched into his office and slammed the door so hard the windowpanes rattled.

She blew out an exasperated breath. "Is he always this intractable?"

"He's often far worse," Hubert said and without another word of explanation, took himself off as well.

Ellie dropped onto the bench and cradled her aching head. She couldn't imagine anyone forcing Reid

Barclay to do anything he didn't want to do. Certainly not marriage.

Memories of their interlude in the pantry taunted her. Of course. He must have taken liberties with a lady and her family was forcing him to do the honorable thing.

If that was the case, how very sad for both of them.

However, that was even more reason to make the house as festive and cheery as possible. Despite the fact that Reid was playing the part of a curmudgeon, she felt it her duty as housekeeper to create a pleasant atmosphere for the bride.

With renewed purpose, Ellie set about making a list of what she'd need to turn this drab house into a sparkling jewel for the holiday wedding. Christmas was the most wondrous time of the year.

She loved this season. She loved her pa and was not going to let his cold reception darken her spirits or deter her. And she certainly wasn't going to allow herself to get moon-eyed over the groom ever again.

Reid sat at his desk drumming impatient fingers on the smooth surface. He should be drafting a letter to the potential buyer for his yearling thoroughbreds to confirm if the man was still interested. Instead, he was stewing over that confrontation with Miss Ellie Jo Cade.

She was a pushy one.

What the hell made her think that cluttering his house up with decorations would brighten his mood? Nothing was going to do that. Not whiskey. Not a willing woman. Not even the probability of him gaining his freedom by chucking it all here and now.

He was damned. Simple as that. When he looked in the mirror, he saw the man who'd betrayed the only friends he had by trusting Burl Erston to save his hide from hanging, and the ranch from bankruptcy. He saw a young woman lying in the street, dead. He saw the trust in his benefactor's eyes long after Reid had broken his promise to him by landing them all in this fix.

Burl Erston believed he had Reid over a barrel, that he was forcing his hand now. But the man couldn't be more wrong.

Reid's conscience was driving him to marry Cheryl. It had goaded him into letting it be known that he was back on the Crown Seven and was ready to face Dade and Trey, and anyone else he'd wronged.

He'd be a married man in seven days. God help him.

He scrubbed a hand over his nape and swore. Cheryl would be here any day now. Though it pained him to admit it, Miss Cade was right about one thing.

The house ought to look festive and welcoming for Cheryl. He owed that much to her, and to her father.

He pushed to his feet and headed across the room. Hell, with his luck, Miss Cade was one of them that went caroling.

He found her in the parlor, staring at the room and tapping a finger on her tooth. In fact she was so deep in thought he was sure she hadn't heard him come in.

He should've known better.

"If you've come to apologize for that tyrannical act earlier," she said, still not looking at him, "then I accept."

His fingers fisted, but he slammed a lid on his irritation and proceeded with why he'd sought her out. "You want to go with me when I cut down your pine tree?"

That brought her gaze to his. "You're willing to take me along to pick it out?"

That wasn't what he'd said or meant, but what the hell. A tree was a tree to him.

"Might as well get what you want," he said. "I figured if we left now we'd be back in time for dinner."

Her narrow shoulders drooped. "If I go, who will prepare your dinner?"

"I can grab a bite with the men," he said, nearly losing his train of thought as he caught the excitement in her eyes. "Hubert can fend for himself once."

"Excellent!" She hurried into the hall. "I'll just be a moment grabbing my cloak."

He smiled at her enthusiasm and headed toward the back door. "I'll hitch up the sleigh and meet you around back."

Reid shrugged into his sheepskin coat and pushed outside. He wasn't going to question the wisdom in going off alone with Miss Cade. Nope, he knew why he wanted to get her alone, and it didn't have a thing to do with collecting greenery or a tree.

By the time he readied the sleigh and headed toward the house, Miss Cade was waiting for him on the terrace. He started to get out to help her in, but she waved away his help.

"I can manage," she said, and matched action to words.

He settled the heavy buffalo robe over her lap, then gave the lines a snap. Bells jingled as the sleigh took off with a slight jerk.

"Will we have to go far to find a good tree?" she asked.

He motioned to the mountains in the near distance. "A good fifteen-minute drive there and back. Should be able to find a decent tree in no time."

Forty minutes later Reid was chewing on those words and not liking the taste one damned bit. Miss Cade wasn't just wanting a nice six-foot tree. She was determined to find the perfect pine tree among the hundreds here.

He stamped his cold feet and glared at her. "What's wrong with this one?"

She gave it a critical eye. "It's a bit sparse."

So was his patience. "Won't that give you more space for decorations and such?"

"I suppose it could." She turned away from him and walked off. "This one has possibilities."

Reid swallowed a curse and stomped over to her, hoping to hell she'd finally found the right tree. "You want this one?"

"I'm thinking."

"That's what I get for hauling you along," he muttered under his breath.

She shot him a damning glare, then turned her attention back to the tree. "Look! It's got pinecones on it."

"That good or bad?" he asked, because if she wanted them off there, he'd be more than happy to oblige her.

Anything to get her to pick a damned tree so he could cut it down and get back to the ranch before they both froze to death.

"I like them," she said at last, and then favored him with such a bright smile that he damned near forgot to breathe. "This is the one."

Reid tore his gaze from her and stared at the tree that looked no different than the other pines dotting this slope. Hell, there was just no figuring how a woman's mind worked.

He dropped on his knees and scraped the snow away from the tree so he could get to the trunk. Even then he had to lie on his gut so he could cut it down close to the ground like she wanted.

He gritted his teeth against the cold and wet seeping into his bones, but the work kept his mind off the enticing woman standing far too close to him. But not for long.

In no time, he'd chopped down the tree and had it loaded on the sleigh. It was just him and her and wild thoughts about getting warm under a buffalo robe.

"Let's get back to the ranch."

"Wait! I need evergreen boughs for my festoons," she said.

Damn! Thoughts of her haggling over which boughs to cut made his head pound.

"How many?" he heard himself ask and wondered if the cold had frozen his brain.

She frowned, and he knew before she spoke that he wasn't going to like her answer one little bit. "At least two dozen."

"Let's make this easy and chop down another tree."

"I suppose that's the wisest thing," she said, but he was already in the process of cutting another pine half as big as the first one.

That ought to give her enough evergreen to cover every shelf in his house.

His fingers were stiff and numb by the time he hefted the second tree onto the back of the sleigh. "Now can we go home?"

"We certainly can," she said, and her wistful smile wasn't lost on him.

Once she was settled in the sleigh, he climbed in beside her and clapped his hands in an attempt to thaw them some. Bits of ice flew everywhere.

"Good heavens, why didn't you tell me your hands were near freezing?" she asked.

He frowned. "They aren't that bad."

She gave an unladylike snort and grabbed his hands, sending pinpricks dancing over his palms. "They're like ice, but at least they aren't wet through."

"More reason to head home now." Because sitting in

a sleigh with her holding his hands was heating him up below the belt.

"We will once we take the chill off your hands," she said, and before he could voice an objection, she tugged his gloved hands between her thighs and clamped them tight like a vise to heaven.

At least a heaven he longed to see and feel and taste.

His heart stuttered to a stop while his mind raced with what she'd boldly done. She couldn't be that naïve, but the concern in her expressive eyes and the firming of her kissable mouth proved she was dead serious about warming his hands.

They still felt like chunks of ice, but the rest of him was heating up damned fast. Didn't matter that even if he had feeling in his fingers besides pins and needles, there was yards of petticoats and stiff skirt that barred him from stroking her skin.

That's what he longed to do. It'd been a long time since he'd felt this pull toward a woman. It was so strong he didn't think about anything but satisfying his baser needs. It was so powerful he damn near forgot his vow to marry Cheryl.

He should have pulled his hands from her then and there, for fat flakes of snow had begun falling again. Instead, he curled his fingers around her thighs.

She stiffened, and that jolt of awareness shot from her into him. Her eyes were huge and turning smoky and clearly surprised that something she'd started with innocent intentions was fast turning intimate.

"I want you," he said, intrigued by the snow that caught on her hair, her thickly curled lashes, her full ripe lips.

She swallowed, and the pulse in her neck warbled. "You can't. You're engaged."

"That doesn't stop the wanting."

He leaned close to steal a kiss, pausing long enough for her to pull away from him. But she didn't move. She just stared at him with those big eyes full of wonder and passion.

His head dipped to hers, and he kissed the snow from her eyes, her nose, before settling over her mouth. Hers trembled slightly, and he felt that hesitation clear to his soul.

A gentleman would have ended it now. He should've apologized for his boldness. For taking advantage of the situation.

But Reid was no gentleman.

He was a bastard, and he intended to take all that Ellie Jo Cade was willing to give him. Still, he kept his hands trapped between her thighs amid all that fabric that deprived him of exploring her as he longed to do.

There was something wickedly alluring about just kissing her. It seemed more intimate, like a stolen moment that was as fresh as the new-fallen snow.

She tasted of frosty winters and just a hint of spice. She was the dessert he'd hungered for. He damn sure wasn't going to content himself with a sampling.

He deepened the kiss, and she leaned into him and moaned as if welcoming him home. He took his time, his tongue coaxing hers to duel, their breaths mingling as one.

But what jolted through him like lightning and set his blood on fire was when her hands stole onto his thigh. She didn't squeeze or stroke or rub him. Just let her small, gloved hand rest on his leg. But that connection was the most erotic thing he'd felt in ages.

Sweat gathered on his brow and his crotch got a bit tighter than comfort allowed. This was do-or-die time. He'd have to take her here in the sleigh, or stop kissing her.

She pulled away from him, her eyes drowsy and her lips red and plumped from his kisses. "Please. We have to go home."

He wanted to read more into it, but she wasn't making any assignation for later. They'd had their stolen moment, and he suspected she'd agonize over what they'd done.

Not him.

He wanted her, and if the opportunity arose, he'd take her next time.

Chapter 6

She'd behaved shamelessly.

That realization played over and over in Ellie Jo's head during the short, tense drive back to the ranch. She failed to appreciate the beauty around her, made more magical by the fact that soft snow danced in the air like an enchanting snow globe she'd once seen on display in Denver. She couldn't even take pleasure in imaging how she'd decorate the house with all the evergreen she needed, or the joy she'd experience decking the wondrous tree Reid had cut down.

All she could think of was his mouth moving on hers. The firm, seductive strength that had surrounded her, though only their lips touched, was unlike anything she'd experienced in her life. The slightly tart taste of his kiss and the heat of a powerful man that had her sweating beneath her corset.

Her own boldness in heeding the vixen in her and laying her hand on his leg.

She'd never felt such strength—such blatant masculinity so well defined. His strong muscles had clenched beneath her palm and had her scrunching her own thighs in an instinct she'd recognized, but had never dreamed would happen to her.

The groan that had escaped him evoked an answering moan of surrender in her. He was as aroused as she.

She had only to move her hand up his thigh to touch his erection. She'd surely wanted to, so badly she shook with the need. And why shouldn't she?

She'd lost her virtue, so she had nothing to lose. She'd never had such a wickedly tempting thought in her life than to boldly invite Reid Barclay to take them where they both wanted to go, and realizing that popped the erotic bubble she'd been floating in.

No matter how wondrous this fiery attraction felt, it was all wrong.

Reid Barclay was affianced to another woman. Oh, he'd cut down the tree and boughs for Ellie, but he'd done it so his house would be festive for his holiday wedding. *His wedding!*

She stole a glance at the man beside her and felt her face flame with embarrassment. My God, she'd been ready to toss her skirts up for a stranger.

Despite what Mrs. Leach had told her about Reid Barclay, she knew nothing about him. Who was he really? Cowboy or gentleman?

The answer was obvious. Neither!

He'd kissed her senseless again without much provocation. She was certain he'd have gone further if she'd encouraged him.

This cowboy needed no encouragement. Reid Barclay was nothing more than a philandering rogue. She'd known that the moment she'd first met him in the saloon.

That was another thing that should have alerted her

to his character. The man had spent the night in Mallory's Roost.

Why, he was the worst sort for an impressionable woman.

She knew that, yet she'd fallen victim to his charisma. Her body was still humming with desire, even knowing the type of man he was.

Yes, that admission said it all.

Ellie had taken great pains to explain the pitfalls of such nefarious men to her charges in the Denver Academy for Young Ladies. She herself had fallen victim before and she'd vowed she'd do all she could to ensure other innocents didn't fall victim to such men.

She could not turn a blind eye now.

His betrothed was coming here with stars in her eyes and love swelling her heart. The poor girl must think she was marrying an honest man. A man who'd honor her all his days. A man who'd give her a home and family. A man who'd stand by her side if and when the storms of adversity blew their way.

Ellie curled her fingers into fists inside her muff as the sleigh topped the rise and the ranch spread into view. Yes, she knew the schemes such men employed.

She'd believed Irwin had been that honest man for her, for he'd said and done all the right things. He'd asked her to be his wife. So she'd not protested when their amorous forays went beyond propriety.

They were, after all, going to marry within the month. She believed she'd spend *that* night, and all those following until she or he left this earth, with Irwin.

She'd believed she could trust him with her darkest secret, for she'd thought a man of such integrity would understand her dilemma regarding those rare surreptitious meetings with her father, who just happened to be a notorious outlaw. How horribly wrong she'd been!

Well, she'd vowed then that she'd not let another woman suffer such indignity if she could help it. Never mind that she hadn't realized until after the fact that she hadn't truly loved Irwin as a wife should.

No man should trifle with a woman's affections, or cite her parentage as a reason to toss her aside. No man should make a woman make a terrible choice between marriage or disowning her father, and then persecute her for the only decision she could make.

Ellie well knew this type of man. She had vowed to instruct young ladies on how to avoid these rogues, and she would do no less now.

She took a bolstering breath as he guided the sleigh toward the house. "That was wrong of you to kiss me."

"Then why did you kiss me back?" he asked.

Of course he'd point that shortcoming out to her. "Why doesn't matter. I am your employee, not your mistress."

"You could be."

Those three words pulsed between them, leaving her shaking with anger at herself and him. Wealthy men were more inclined to take a lover. And hadn't Irwin suggested she do just that now that she was a ruined lady?

"I am going to pretend you didn't say that," she said as he secured the lines with strong, deft hands.

Though the idea of being Reid's lover appealed to her far more than it should, she'd not toss aside her career to be a rich man's paramour. She'd not be the scarlet woman.

If she couldn't find a good man to marry—she was growing less certain that breed of man existed—she'd spend the rest of her days instilling in young ladies the rewards of living a fulfilling moral life.

He climbed from the sleigh without a comment and

came round to give her a hand. A secret thrill went through her as she laid her hand in his.

Those long, strong fingers closed over hers, and her heart skipped a beat. Maybe two. For though his touch was perfectly proper, the blatant desire in his eyes spoke volumes.

He led her to the terrace and released her hand, giving the image of the perfect gentleman. She knew it was an illusion and yet she mourned his withdrawal.

This man was dangerous to be around, for his illicit need kindled the same craving in her. How in the world would she get through the next week in his company and retain her dignity?

She stared at the trees he'd cut and forced her thoughts on decorating the house. That was easier said than done with him standing close enough to touch. And mercy me, she wanted him to touch her.

"Please cut off all the boughs on this smaller tree," she said. "But leave the top foot or so intact."

"I'll take care of it for you."

She shouldn't feel anything but gratitude that he'd volunteered to do the task himself. After all, he had taken her with him to pick out what she'd wanted and cut the trees.

And then he'd kissed her.

"I don't suppose you have an iron tree stand." Surely he'd think she'd just shivered from the cold.

"Nope. Never seen one before either."

"Oh, dear."

She'd not given it a thought when they were in Maverick. But then her greatest need at the time was finding Reid Barclay and putting distance between herself and Marshal Tavish.

"Perhaps Mr. Moss will be able to advise you," she said.

Her pa had always found a way to stabilize the various trees he'd brought home to their cabin. She smiled, reminded of those simple pleasures again—until her gaze locked with Reid's and she read the promise of a far different pleasure smoldering in his eyes.

"I'll see what I can do." With a dip of his strong, square chin and the ghost of a devilish smile, he returned to the sleigh and climbed in.

"I trust you still intend to take your dinner with the men?" she asked, hoping she sounded more composed than she felt.

"Yes'm, but expect me at the house for supper," he said, then took off toward the outbuildings without waiting for her reply.

Not that she'd have anything noteworthy to add. Cooking and keeping his house in order was her job— not jaunting off in a sleigh with him and stealing a kiss.

Ellie pushed thoughts of Reid Barclay's seductive kisses from her mind and hurried to the meat locker to take stock of what was available. She had no idea if the dressed game birds she selected were grouse, sage hen or prairie chicken, nor did it matter for the recipe she had in mind.

She set off toward the house, relieved she had more than enough time this afternoon to prepare supper and make room in the parlor for the tree Reid would bring in later. She'd deck the house in Christmas gaiety and hope that revived her own lagging spirits. And not once would she go woolgathering and imagine that she was trimming the house in preparation for the Christmas wedding she'd longed to have one day.

In fact, if the bride-to-be realized what a cad Reid Barclay was, there'd likely be no wedding in this house. It would surely serve him right to be jilted.

He need not look Ellie's way for sympathy or passion. No, she knew his type and he deserved a comeuppance.

She'd been beguiled by him twice. She wouldn't play the part of a love-struck fool again.

"Ain't surprised a rich boy like yourself wouldn't know how to set up a tree," Gabby Moss groused inside the shelter of the barn as he nailed cross boards on the base of the tree trunk.

Reid bit back a laugh. He'd been born dirt poor and couldn't recall ever celebrating a Christmas.

This one would be no exception.

His marriage was a business arrangement as well as a promise made to the man who'd saved his life. He was doing this as much for them as for himself. Hell, any of his brothers would have done the same to keep Kirby's daughter from falling into harm's way.

He just wished his brothers were here too, because then he'd have something to celebrate. They'd have their ragtag family united again, and they'd hold title to his ranch.

He eyed the wooden braces the old man nailed on the cross boards. "You sure those will keep it from tipping over?"

"I've been doing this for many a year and ain't lost a tree yet. Speaking of which," Moss said, squinting up at him, "it sure took you a long time to cut down two trees."

Reid shrugged and continued chopping the boughs off the other tree. He sure as hell wasn't going to tell the old man he'd been out spooning.

"Miss Cade was particular about which one would suit." Moss nodded. "She picked a good one."

They each went about their task with only the nick

of an ax on wood or hammer cracking nail to break the silence. As always, Reid's thoughts strayed back to Miss Cade. How did a smart young lady become good friends with Mrs. Leach, a former madam and crusty old gal to boot?

"Mrs. Leach tell you much about Miss Cade?" he asked Moss.

The old man's mouth pinched tight. "She didn't tell me a damned thing about her. Why you asking?"

"She's living in my house." Passing herself off as a cook when it was clear she didn't know much about cooking. "You suppose she's kin to Mrs. Leach?"

Moss shrugged, seeming nervous all of a sudden. "She never said she was."

That told him nothing. He whacked off another bough, mindful that Moss had never been the talkative sort either. But he was holding his cards a bit closer to the vest right now. What did he know about Miss Cade that he wasn't willing to divulge?

"I just got a feeling she's never done this sort of work before," he said, pressing the point again.

"Well, she did forget to open that damper." Moss flicked him a quick glance. "You'd be within your rights to send her packing."

He shook his head. "I gave Mrs. Leach my word that I'd keep her on until she returned. Hopefully that'll be sooner instead of later."

"Your outfit," Moss said, and Reid was convinced then that the old man had closed the damper on her that day.

Yep, Moss knew more about Miss Cade than he was willing to tell. So much that he was willing to sabotage her first day here on the off chance Reid would fire her. Why would he want her gone?

"But if you know something about her that would bring trouble to the outfit, speak up," he said.

The old man squinted at him. "If there's trouble coming this way, it'll be because there's talk that Slim, that cowpoke that got away with killing that woman in Laramie two years back, is working here."

He took the old man's measure again and saw the same concern in his eyes that he saw in the mirror every morning. What he didn't know was how much Moss knew about his past.

He was guessing no more than gossip, and that ranged from him being a wealthy English lord to a cold-blooded killer. He damned sure wasn't the former, and he couldn't remember the details on the latter.

It was the not knowing those details had robbed him of many a night's sleep. Had it cost him the only family he'd known as well? It sure looked that way.

Moss gave the big tree a shake and made a satisfied grunt when it held tight. "You want me to tote this up to the house for you while you're checking them thoroughbreds?"

"Much obliged," he said. "That mare must be close to foaling."

"Reckon so." Moss pointed at the boughs stacked in a pile. "Whatcha going to do with them?"

"They go to the house too. Miss Cade wanted boughs to decorate with."

Moss gathered an armful. "I'll fetch them up there then."

"I'd appreciate it if you'd help keep an eye on the women," Reid said.

"I'll do what I can."

"Fair enough."

He didn't want either of them hurt. Though he was

going to do just that. He had to marry Cheryl and gain what he'd foolishly lost. And he was honor bound to repay her pa's kindness to him, Dade and Trey.

Kirby Morris had taken in three homeless boys with nothing but mischief on their minds. He'd taught them right from wrong and made men out of them. He'd made them a family while leaving his only daughter in his cousin's care. He'd given the boys this ranch so they'd never want for a home again.

But Reid had made a fatal error and lost it and his family. Now that Cheryl was at her guardian's mercy, he had no choice but to step in and see that she was spared a life of torment. Even if he weren't being blackmailed, he had to make sure that she inherited what should be hers alone—the Crown Seven.

But he didn't love her. He didn't even lust after her. Nope, he had it bad for Ellie Jo Cade, the one woman he wanted but couldn't have.

With the parlor ready to receive the tree, and a cake just put in the oven to bake, Ellie poured a cup of tea and dropped onto a kitchen chair to rest. It was no wonder women tended to show their age too soon, considering what they did daily to keep their houses in order.

She'd certainly made notes of the "little things" she'd taken for granted and would instruct the young ladies in her classes how to better manage their time.

"Would you mind company?" Hubert asked from the doorway.

"Not at all," she said. "Would you like a spot of tea?"

He gave her a toothy smile and took a seat across from her. "I'd rather enjoy that."

Ellie poured his tea, then resumed her chair and allowed herself to relax again.

The man was a pleasure to talk with, and she suspected he was aware of everything and everyone on this ranch. Just the man she hoped to form a camaraderie with.

"I would imagine in the time you've been here," she said, "you've gotten to know all of the cowboys."

"I have made their acquaintance. They are a breed of man unto themselves, rather withdrawn and possessed of a querulous mood at times."

An apt description from what she could see. "How long has Gabby Moss worked here?"

Hubert took a sip of tea and stared across the room, as if mulling over his reply. "Why do you ask?"

"I'm just curious," she said, more than a bit annoyed that he'd avoided answering.

"Curiosity is a perilous element. It can alleviate one's worries or push one into a tangle."

"Is that the voice of experience talking?"

Hubert inclined his head. "Quite so."

She studied Hubert in silence. If Mrs. Leach was aware of her pa's true identity, could Hubert be aware of it too?

Before she decided on a way to ask him without giving away her pa's identity, the back door opened and icy air gusted into the kitchen. The door slammed, something scraped the walls, and the heavy, uneven footfalls held a distant familiarity.

"Where ya want this here tree?" her pa asked in that oddly gruff voice that sounded nothing like him.

She stared at his cheeks reddened by the cold and his eyes glittering with mischief and felt her heart swell with love. No matter what he'd done, he was her pa and she loved him as only a daughter could.

"Well?" he asked when she didn't answer right off.

"In the parlor, of course." She got to her feet and was glad Hubert couldn't see her knees knocking beneath her skirts. "I see you built a stand for it."

"Just like I always have done." This time there was no mistaking the affection in his gaze.

Hubert got to his feet and gave the big tree a droll glance. "If I'm not needed, I will go abovestairs and attend to my duties there."

"I have things under control here," she said, and added a prayer of thanks that she and her pa would have a bit of time alone at last.

Honestly, she wanted to give him a piece of her mind for the shenanigan he pulled on her. And she wanted to fall into his arms and get the bear hug she had missed for so long. How could she love him and want to throttle him at the same time?

"Mr. Moss," Hubert said with a dip of his chin.

"Hubert," her pa replied.

She slid past her pa and trotted down the hall, anxious to get the tree settled so they could talk. "I have just the place for it at the front windows."

His uneven gait followed her at a slower pace and tempered her anger like nothing else could. What had happened to him since she'd seen him last? Why was he favoring a leg? Why did his voice sound scratchy and strained?

"Well, I'll be," he said. "You got it all set up."

She faced him then, and was sure she beamed from ear to ear. "I remembered that my pa used to place the tree in a tub and keep water in it so the tree wouldn't dry out." She took a step toward him. "I've missed you so."

He set the tree down with a thud and looked around, eyes alert and shoulders tensed. "No more than I have you, but that sure as hell don't mean I'm glad to see you here."

Her smile fell as reality came crashing down around her and with it a hurt so sharp and cold she had to wait a moment before she trusted her voice. "That's why you closed the damper. So Reid Barclay would think I was totally inept and fire me."

He bobbed his head. "Yep, but I should've known it wouldn't work," he said in a low, raspy tone. "You're too pretty for a man like him to let go."

Her face heated, she didn't comment on the compliment or on their employer for fear she'd let slip how far she'd fallen. Though her pa was an outlaw, she didn't wish to flaunt her moral slip to him.

Instead she focused on what was wrong between them when they should be thanking God to have this rare chance to spend a holiday together.

"Why did you do it, Pa? What's going on here that you don't want me around?"

"Rustlers," he said, and she nearly laughed at the seriousness of his tone until she realized he wasn't joshing her.

"You didn't steal Reid Barclay's stallion?"

"Hell, no," he said. "At the time, I was up to my elbows in blood and guts, butchering an elk."

"Then how could someone have sworn they saw you ride off on that horse?"

"That's what I aim to find out. If some polecat is passing himself off as me and stealing horses, I reckon he ought to be the one who hangs for it."

"As well he should," she said. "Were you aware Mrs. Leach contacted me because she feared you were about to place your neck in the noose?"

He shook his head, looking like a forlorn elf with his white hair that tended to curl and the long white beard that hid his features and the telling scar on his cheek so perfectly. "Nope."

It was just above a scratch of sound. "What is wrong with your voice?"

"I was hanged." He lifted his kerchief and his beard. A reddish welt encircled his neck.

Her stomach heaved as her mind raced with questions. "When did this happen?"

"Nigh on three years ago. I'd have died that time if the boss here hadn't come upon me when he did."

"Reid saved you?"

He shook his head and adjusted his kerchief again. "Kirby Morris. He owned this spread back then. Was dying himself, but he saved my hide. Never forgot that I owed him."

"Was this hanging the end result of the woman who was murdered in Laramie?" she asked, well remembering those headlines that appeared in the *Denver Post*, and her unwillingness to believe her pa could do such a thing.

"Nope, that happened six months later." His mouth puckered up in a belligerent knot. "I didn't kill her. Hell, I didn't even pull my sidearm that day until I was riding hell for leather out of Laramie with a posse riding my tail."

"Who shot her then?"

"A cowpoke named Slim," he said. "I got a glimpse of him, but I didn't stick around to argue the point."

She sat down very carefully. "You're saying you were framed for that woman's murder?"

"Yep. That's why I'm here," he said. "Nigh on a year ago I heard at Mallory's Roost that Slim was working on the Crown Seven. Thought I'd mosey up this way, hire on as chuck cook, and settle an old score between me and him."

She realized that Mrs. Leach hadn't been exaggerating. "Why haven't you?"

"Ain't found hide or hair of him yet."

With luck he wouldn't either. "Good. If you kill him, you'll be wanted for another murder."

He shrugged. "They ain't going to let Ezra Kincaid off the hook, Ellie Jo. If the law catches me, I'll hang. Sending Slim to the devil won't change a thing."

"Then remain Gabby Moss," she said, desperate for him to see reason, for him to live out his days in peace.

He shook his head, stubborn as a Missouri mule. "Slim must know who I am and why I'm here. I reckon he stole that horse of Barclay's using my name. Only one way this can end now. One of us has to die."

She recoiled from the finality of his decision. If there was just some way to prove her pa was innocent of the murder. But that still wouldn't absolve him of the years of rustling.

"Marshal Tavish is in Maverick," she said, taking his large, work-roughened hand in hers. "He knows I'm your daughter."

He curled his fingers and held on tight to her. "He question you about me?"

"Once." Shortly after Irwin publicly broke off their engagement, but she wasn't ready to divulge that ugly part of her past with her pa now. Maybe never. "I told him the truth, that I hadn't seen or heard from you in years. And I wouldn't have known if Mrs. Leach hadn't written to me."

"Figured she was the one who wrote you," he said. "Trouble is sure to come here, Ellie Jo. I want you to pack up and head back to Denver now."

"I'm moving on to California after Mrs. Leach returns," she said. "Were you able to repay Mr. Morris's kindness?"

Her pa smiled, looking more like his old self. "Reckon in a way I'm doing that now."

"How? By cooking on the Crown Seven while you're looking for a killer?"

He frowned and shuffled his feet. "Ain't got the time to explain it all right now."

Knowing him, he'd never find the time to tell her just what was going on around here. "Promise me that we'll have one last Christmas together."

He glanced from the tree to her and sighed. "All right."

"Thank you," she said, and prayed that nothing would happen to ruin this Christmas for them.

Chapter 7

Ellie had spent the last thirty minutes knocking snow off the boughs her pa had brought in and grousing over the unfairness of him being accused of a crime he hadn't committed. There had to be a way to help him, but she couldn't imagine what it could be at this point.

So she turned her attention to something she loved doing—decking the halls. Or in this case, the parlor.

She found a box of carpet tacks and a tack hammer in the pantry, dragged a ladder-back chair from the kitchen to the parlor, and set to work hanging swags and festoons of greenery.

The room was far warmer near the ceiling, and coupled with the exertion, a fine sheen of sweat gathered on her brow and dampened her nape. But she soldiered on and sang carols as she added the ribbons, chenille doves and assorted trims Mrs. Leach had ordered to each spray of evergreen.

It was beginning to look like Christmas now. The added scent of pine mingled well with the allspice and sticks of cinnamon she'd arranged in clusters.

Ellie stretched as far as she could to pound the last tack into the spray. Wham, wham, wham.

"What the hell is going on in here?" Reid asked from the doorway.

"That should be obvious."

She was in no mood to argue with him, not when supper needed her attention. She pushed away from the wall with all the intentions of stepping carefully off the chair. But she'd not quite given herself the right boost to lever her from the odd bent position she'd been in.

Her upper body leaned toward the wall again. Fast. It wouldn't have been a problem if she hadn't also been in the process of stepping down.

Ellie teetered for a heartbeat on the chair, unable to grasp the back, which was behind her. In fact there was nothing she could grab onto but air, and her wind-milling arms did her no good at all.

She tensed, knowing she was going to fall and fall hard.

A ripe curse split the air followed by the pounding of boots. Strong arms swept around her and crushed her to his chest, but her momentum took them both down just the same.

His back slammed onto the floor and with a pained grunt, he loosened his hold on her for a scant moment. Though his big body cushioned her fall, she still had that forward momentum pushing her up his frame.

So she threw her hands out to keep her from ramming her head into the wall. She hissed as the carpet burned her palms right before his hands tightened on her hips and stopped her with a jolt.

She lay there a moment to catch her breath, dreading to look down into his eyes. But she took the chance anyway, and oh, my, she wished she hadn't.

He looked mad enough to spit nails.

"Thank you," she said, and made to move off him.

His hands tightened, keeping her in the undignified sprawl she'd fallen into. Why, she hadn't realized until now that she was straddling him.

Her face flamed as her mind raced to recall what rule Mrs. Halsey cited for embarrassing incidents such as this. Nothing came to mind but how good it felt to be this close to him.

And wasn't that the point she'd argued with herself earlier? How could she maintain a proper anger for this rogue when his mere touch muddled her mind?

"Let go of me, please," she said with a bit more heat than was proper.

His hold didn't ease in the least. "Why'd you turn my parlor into a forest?"

She gritted her teeth. "I was decking the halls to lend a festive touch."

"How about undecking some of it?"

"Absolutely not." She pushed against the floor but couldn't budge an inch. "I did this for your fiancée. You do remember her and the wedding that is to take place here in six days?"

"Vaguely." He had the audacity to smile at her.

"Oh! You are wretched. A rogue of the worst sort!"

He laughed.

"Stop that," she said, and when he wouldn't let her go or shut up, she made to rap him upside the head.

She realized her mistake the second he captured her hand in midair. Before she could regain her leverage, his mouth was on hers.

Not a sweet, seductive buss of lips like before.

No, this was a full, amorous attack on her senses.

Her head spun. Her heart skipped several beats before

it began racing. Her trapped hands had the almost aching need to hold him close.

Just like the intimacy they'd shared in the pantry, his tongue made a sweeping foray into her mouth, setting off little explosions of need she hadn't known were possible. She should fight him off. Scream perhaps. Kick and of course stop kissing him and holding on to him as if he was her anchor.

But heavenly days, she'd never dreamed she'd lose all sense of time and troubles in a kiss. It was simply mind-boggling and confusing, because she shouldn't feel this way at all.

As if sensing that she was capitulating, he softened the kiss as well as his hold. That made this joining of lips and tongue and heated breath all the more wonderful.

For now, he was caressing her, and she was too lost in the sensations to resist. Why, she even heard bells.

This was meant to be. It couldn't mean anything else.

The rough clearing of a throat intruded on the moment, but she resented it when Reid ended the kiss abruptly. It took a moment for her vision to clear and for her senses to realize they were no longer alone.

A glance to the doorway confirmed the butler stood there, stoic as a statue.

"A sleigh and a wagon from town have arrived, sir," Hubert said.

"Who'd call on you at this hour?" she asked as she got off him the best she could without totally abandoning her dignity.

And she didn't dare look at the rogue for fear he'd be grinning.

"I reckon it's Cheryl and her guardian."

Her jaw dropped, and she did look at him then. "Your fiancée is here already?"

"It appears so." He rolled to his feet with fluid grace and extended a hand to help her up, not seeming the least bit alarmed that he'd nearly gotten caught dallying with her.

How could he be so cavalier?

Ellie took his hand without comment and gave her skirts a shake to set them right again. But there was no help for her hair. Half the pins were scattered on the carpet, which allowed the heavy mass to slide down her back in a riot of curls.

She certainly must look like she'd had a tumble with a man. His fiancée would take one look at her and know what a rogue Reid really was.

But no matter how she felt duty bound to let the woman see Reid's true worth, she refused to humiliate her. Enlightening her was something she must do in private, for she knew well the pain of a public unveiling of truths.

There was time for her to take Reid's intended aside and gently tell her the truth. The choice would be up to the woman whether to go through with the marriage or break the engagement.

Then Ellie could rest assured she'd done the right thing.

Leaving him to think what he might, she slipped from the parlor and ran to the kitchen to check her cake. She pulled the pan from the oven and set it on the range.

Her shoulders slumped. The top was very firm and browned a bit much around the edges, but she hoped it would be passable.

As for herself, she hastened to her room to repair her appearance. But even after she'd tidied her hair, her lips still tingled from his moving on hers, and the hum of sensual excitement coursed like a raging river.

* * *

Reid stalked to the front window, shoving the pleasure he'd found in Ellie's arms to the back of his mind. It wasn't easy. It sure as hell didn't put him in a good mood.

Any chance he'd had of having Ellie was over now that his intended had arrived. All she could be for him was a temptation.

She surely did tempt him to forget he'd agreed to marry Kirby's daughter, and that he wouldn't—couldn't—go back on his word. Didn't matter that Ellie had blotted out the ugly past he'd never be able to escape, if only for a few hours.

And wasn't that just the hell of it all? When he was with Ellie, he didn't think of the young woman who'd caught a stray bullet fired from his gun two years ago, or the blackmail threat hanging over his head ever since that day.

He'd had his neck saved but lost his freedom in the bargain. Now if he reneged on the deal he'd made with Kirby's cousin, Burl Erston would make good his threats.

He watched the righteous son-of-a-bitch climb from the sleigh and give the ranch a long perusal. Not once did he say a word to Cheryl or offer to help her from the sleigh.

She just sat there, like she was exhausted from the journey from England and waiting for somebody to take pity on her and bring her in out of the cold. What the hell made Kirby think that his cousin could raise his daughter better than he could've?

Erston was busy supervising the removal of luggage from the second wagon. The arrogant sonofabitch was oblivious to Cheryl.

Reid's anger shot up another notch. He pushed from the window and stormed to the door, of a mind to tear into Burl Erston.

But he couldn't. Not yet.

Erston wasn't one to offer idle threats. If Reid didn't tow the line, he'd marry Kirby's daughter off to an old lord who'd pay dearly to wed a young woman who'd give him an heir. He'd have Reid's brothers charged with rustling Crown Seven cattle, even though Dade and Trey were likely just taking what was theirs after they'd been run off their home.

Reid couldn't imagine the hell they went through after Kirby died and Erston took over. He couldn't imagine how betrayed they'd felt when Erston told Dade and Trey that Reid had sold them out.

Erston had lied to them, just as he'd done to Reid.

If Reid balked, there'd be no way that he could stop Erston from selling the Crown Seven out from under him. There'd be no way Reid could make amends to Dade and Trey.

Reid would lose the only home he'd ever known, and welch on a promise he'd made to Kirby long ago.

Nope, he wouldn't let Kirby down again, for losing the ranch would rob Cheryl of her birthright. Besides, he owed the Englishman for taking him in when he had nowhere or no one to turn to.

Kirby gave him a home and a family. Reid would damn sure see that Cheryl got her share, even if marrying him was part of the bargain.

In time, Ellie Jo Cade would be a fond memory of who he could've pursued if he hadn't screwed up his life before he'd met her.

He yanked the door open to find a liveryman from Maverick was helping Cheryl maneuver the narrow path in the snow. He saw the rapid staccato of her breath and guessed she was damned near frozen.

She stood on the porch looking like a lost waif,

probably wondering what new hell she'd been dragged to this time.

"I trust your journey wasn't too arduous," Reid said by way of greeting.

She gave a depreciating laugh and stepped inside the house. "It was taxing, but I endured without complaint."

Reid's fingers curled into fists, remembering well how she'd spent her days working at the Montvale School for Foundlings in England. She never complained that he could see, but then he guessed she'd never known anything different.

"Reckon you'd like to retire to your room and rest a spell," he said and closed the door.

"Yes, I would."

There was tension evident in the press of her lips, and worry lines fanned from her eyes. She'd never had trouble meeting his gaze straight-on before. Likely she and Erston had done nothing but argue the entire trip. Yet he couldn't help but think there was something else troubling his intended.

Cheryl glanced in the parlor that Ellie had painstakingly decked out but didn't comment on the effort or the festive effect. "I understand the Pearce farm is nearby."

"The sheepherder?"

"Yes, that's him," she said. "He moved to this area nearly three months past."

That he did, and gained the animosity of every cattleman in the county by bringing a herd of woolies with him.

"His spread is four miles northwest of here. You know him?"

"Mr. Pearce is my dearest friend's brother," she said. "I promised I'd visit him as soon as I arrived and deliver a package to him."

"Erston can drive you—"

"No!" There was no hiding the fact she was nervous to the point of shaking. "Please, Reid, he can't know I've asked about Kenton Pearce."

"I won't mention the sheepherder's name then."

"Thank you," she said.

She kept her gaze lowered, no different than she had in the whole year he'd spent in England. He'd never been able to figure if she was just shy, or if that docility had been pounded into her.

He sure wouldn't put it past Erston. Kirby had left her with his cousin shortly after her mother died. He claimed he couldn't think to go on and properly raise a child, especially a little girl.

So before coming to America, he'd handed her over into the care of Burl Erston and his wife. But Reid doubted it was a loving home.

One thing was for sure, Cheryl's life and view on the world would have been a lot different had Kirby brought her to Wyoming where he bought the ranch ten years ago. Maybe he feared it would be a mistake to bring a young woman into a house where he'd taken in three orphan boys. Would they have grown up as siblings, or would Reid have tendered an affection to her in time and ended up marrying her anyway?

He'd never know. Fact was he felt nothing but empathy for her now, and that was unfair to his bride-to-be.

She glanced out the door, then turned and finally looked Reid in the eyes. "Would you take me to the Pearce farm?"

"Reckon we can do it tomorrow."

The short ride over would give him time to talk to her in private. He wanted her aware of his plans to buy out Erston. He had to have her cooperation.

"I fear Mr. Pearce has been on tenterhooks awaiting

my arrival," she said. "Do you think it would be possible to visit him today? Just us."

Rousing memories of his earlier ride and scorching kiss with Ellie Jo flashed in his mind's eye to needle his guilt. Without a doubt, getting away from the house and the object of his desire was damn smart.

"Don't see why not," he said as Hubert joined them. "We'll plan on leaving as soon as you're settled in."

"Thank you." She fidgeted a moment, then stepped forward, stood on tiptoe and placed a fleeting kiss on is cheek.

He caught Hubert's censoring glance, and wished the brush of her lips on his face stirred something in him besides guilt. "I'll get the sleigh readied."

"May I show you to your room, Miss Morris?" Hubert said.

"Please," she said.

They were just starting up the stairs when the front door swung open and Burl Erston stomped in. "Bloody inhospitable weather. I can't fathom why Kirby wished to live in this god-awful environs."

"It's cattle country," Reid said.

"Yes, yes." Erston shrugged out of his frock coat and shook the snow from it, sending frozen pellets skittering over the floor Ellie had just swept. "I suppose it was a fitting home for the three street urchins he took under his wing."

Reid shrugged off the insult, for it was true. He, Dade and Trey had been boys, living hand-to-mouth by their wits and grit.

If they hadn't come upon Kirby when they did in St. Louis and saved his life, he doubted their paths would ever have crossed. He sure as hell wouldn't have grown to be a man in this fine home.

He dreaded to think how much different his and his

foster brothers' lives would have been if Kirby Morris hadn't taken them in and made men out of them.

And what did he do to repay the man's largess?

He got drunk on his ass and accidentally killed a woman instead of winging the old rustler who'd been hell bent on stealing his horse. Kirby had begged a loan from Erston in order to bribe the sheriff and keep Reid from swinging from the gallows.

Maybe it'd been better in the long run if he'd paid for his reckless stupidity then and there.

"Name your price for your shares," Reid said, knowing the only way to deal with Erston was to get right to the point.

"Thinking of buying me out, eh?" Erston laughed, an ugly chuckle that grated on Reid's nerves.

"Yep. You don't like it here, so why hang on to it?"

Cheryl's guardian shrugged, a gesture generations of Erstons had no doubt honed to snobbish perfection. "I don't intend to. But I invested a good deal in you and this ranch at my cousin's request."

Money-grubbing bastard. "Like I said, name your price."

Erston's expression turned cagey. "Where would you come by that much money?"

"I'm not without resources," Reid said.

"Interesting. I hadn't thought you'd rally in just one year." Erston stared at him as if waiting for him to explain, but hell would freeze over before Reid divulged how he'd come by a herd of thoroughbreds, or his plans to sell them so he could force Erston off the ranch once and for all.

"Good luck to you then," Erston said. "But bear in mind that should your partners fail to claim their shares by the end of Christmas Day, buying me out will cost you substantially more."

"A fact I'm aware of."

One that worried him endlessly too, for it wasn't just a matter of them abandoning their share of the ranch. It was the fact that something had happened to one or both of them.

"Pray tell, who is that delectable creature?" Erston asked.

Reid followed the direction of the Englishman's gaze, and his gut clenched. Ellie slipped from the powder room at the end of the hall and hurried into the kitchen, bustle gyrating and energy bouncing in each step. His groin tightened in response.

"That's Miss Cade, my housekeeper," he said.

"Help, eh?" Erston licked his thin dark lips. "Always a plus to employ women who are easy on the eye."

The insinuation was a gut-punch Reid hadn't expected. Damn strange considering he'd thought the same.

"Stay away from her."

Erston stared at him, one brow lifted in question. "You did say *miss.* Is she spoken for?"

"Not that I know of." Hell, he didn't know much about the lady other than she'd awakened his sleeping lust and she didn't know her way around the kitchen.

"Then what's to stop me from spending time with her?"

Nothing but the fact that Reid didn't want Erston to lay one smarmy finger on Miss Ellie Jo Cade. "Leave her be. If you've got a hankering for female companionship, take yourself off to Maverick. Ian Mallory has upstairs ladies at the Roost that'll satisfy your needs."

"Ah, so that's the way of it." Erston smirked. "Is Cheryl aware you've taken a mistress?"

Reid grabbed fistfuls of Erston's frock coat and shoved him up against the wall so hard the windows rattled. "Miss Cade is my housekeeper, nothing more, nothing less."

"Is she? Do you know I've never seen a cook with an enticing figure such as hers."

Neither had Reid. "She's not the type to trifle with."

And he knew it was true, yet she'd let him kiss her twice. Where would it have stopped?

"Tried and failed, eh?" Erston asked.

"Miss Cade is here to cook and clean in Mrs. Leach's stead. That's all there is to it," he said. "So keep your cock in your britches around her."

"For one who professes all is on the up-and-up, you are terribly defensive of her."

"She is a lady who works for me."

Erston's beady eyes took on an unholy gleam. "As I hold Kirby's shares of the Crown Seven, she's an employee of mine as well."

Reid tightened his hold and was rewarded with a choking sound from Erston. "Stay away from her."

"Very well," he said, clawing at Reid's steely grip. "I'll not expect more from her for now. But should Miss Cade express a willingness to become better acquainted with me, I shan't turn her away."

He shoved free of Reid and sauntered toward the stairs where Hubert had just made an appearance. "About time you presented yourself."

"I was occupied seeing Miss Morris to her room, sir," Hubert said with all the pomp one would expect from royalty.

"By all means do the same for me, and then see that my baggage is brought up posthaste."

"Yes, sir," Hubert said.

Erston had to be the most arrogant man Reid had had the displeasure of meeting. He loathed that the man had him over a barrel. But he surely understood why Cheryl wanted to get away from her guardian, for Reid was possessed of the same inclination at that moment.

Reid shrugged into his coat, settled his hat on, then headed down toward the corral to ready the sleigh. Maybe a jaunt over to the sheepherder's spread would help him steel himself for the inevitable. For what he dreaded most was becoming Cheryl's husband.

Ellie's thoughts were still churning with what she'd learned today about Reid and this ranch, long after she'd prepared a simple cake for dessert and slid it in the oven. It was all so confusing.

Kirby Morris had owned this ranch three years ago and had saved her pa's life. Now Reid was marrying Miss Morris. Could she be a relative?

And why was Burl Erston accompanying Miss Morris to the ranch? There was no mistaking the hostility between Reid and Erston, and the two surely hadn't tried to hush their terse conversation.

No, he seemed more interested in buying out Burl Erston.

Mercy, who did own the Crown Seven? Clearly it wasn't totally in Reid's control as she'd assumed.

It wasn't her business to know. Why, she'd already gotten so absorbed in listening to Reid warn the odious Erston to stay away from her that she'd nearly forgotten her cake.

She took it from the oven and set it on the rack to cool. It looked firm, but she did as the recipe advised and inserted a clean broom straw in the cake's thickest portion.

She held her breath and withdrew it, hoping it wouldn't deflate or be uncooked. The straw came out clean, and the top stayed mounded.

Still, she hoped her creation tasted better than it looked. One side was a tad thin and crusty, while the other was as fat as a goiter.

"Whatever you have prepared smelled so absolutely luscious I had to come see for myself," a woman said, her tone soft yet cultured.

Ellie faced Miss Morris, hiding her surprise at the woman's lack of elegance. Wholesome best described her.

"Thank you," she said.

Miss Morris smiled, and she saw the true beauty in the woman at that moment. "What I could not determine was if it was chocolate or spice."

"Actually, it's both."

"Excellent. Reid is partial to chocolate and it is wise to keep the head of the house satisfied in one area, at least." Miss Morris flushed and stared at the floor, leaving Ellie Jo to wonder just what she was implying.

"Is there anything in particular you'd prefer for your wedding dinner?" she asked.

Miss Morris's shoulders drooped. "Whatever you want to prepare is fine by me."

"You've no preferences?" Ellie asked, stunned.

"None that would make a difference for a wedding feast," she said. "Perhaps a favorite of Reid's would be wise."

After delivering that telling statement, she promptly took herself off. Good heavens, was she that unconcerned? Or had it been pounded into her to put her man's feelings above her own?

Ellie silently fumed over the woman feeling subjugated by Reid. She wasn't a rabid advocate of the suffrage movement, but she believed women should exercise their God-given rights. At the least, nobody should be dominated by another.

She slipped into the pantry for the tin of cocoa and box of powdered sugar to dust her cake, annoyed that she'd happened on another favorite of Reid's. Just thinking how enamored he'd been of that ruined pie—

Heat flooded her face as that intimate moment she'd shared with Reid waltzed across her memory, pausing to two-step with the most recent one in the parlor. Even knowing he was a philanderer didn't stop this powerful longing dancing in her.

Was that why Miss Morris was so acquiescent? Was the woman caught in Reid's sensual aura as well? Had he made an earlier overture to her and gotten caught?

It was hard for her to imagine Reid forced into a shotgun wedding, but stranger things had happened. Whether that was the case or not, she felt duty bound to get Miss Morris aside and explain the type of man she was about to marry. That should be easy for her to accomplish.

She knew the perils that awaited the gullible woman. Likely Miss Morris had already fallen victim to such a fate.

Though a woman couldn't recover lost virtue, she shouldn't be forced to endure a feckless marriage. She could go on to lead a full life, and perhaps even find a good man who'd understand that one slip didn't deserve a scarlet letter.

Trust should be earned, not blindly expected.

That was why she intended to confess her own fall from grace to Miss Morris. Holding herself up as an example should show that even a woman of her former station wasn't beyond letting her emotions rule her in such instances.

She wasn't a woman of loose morals, but she hadn't stopped Irwin from having his way with her because she'd wanted to feel deep love for him. He was, after all, her fiancé with the wedding scheduled for a month away.

She wasn't the type to lust after another woman's man either. Except Reid had made the first overture in the pantry, and again in the parlor.

That was really enough for Miss Morris to know.

To Ellie's shame, she still desired Reid with an intensity that incinerated sound reasoning. Try as she might, she feared those carnal yearnings weren't likely to fade into obscurity any time soon.

Chapter 8

"I've always been jealous of you and your partners," Cheryl said over the chink-chink of sleigh bells, breaking the silence that had fallen over them shortly after they'd left the Crown Seven.

"What the hell for?" Reid said as he guided the sleigh over the hardpack road.

She huddled under the buffalo robe. "You got to live with my father while I was fobbed off on Erston and his wife."

The heat in her voice was enough to melt the snow-pack. "Kirby thought he was doing the right thing by leaving you with his kin."

"A father and daughter is family," she said. "He didn't want me. That's quite clear."

Reid heaved a sigh. He'd heard this before and still didn't know how to debunk her claim. Likely Erston had planted the seeds of abandonment long ago, and they'd grown into a thicket of antipathy.

He could understand her feelings in this, for he was the unwanted bastard of an English lord. But he'd never attempted to contact the man even that year he'd spent in England.

If he found out today that his kin had left him anything, he wasn't sure how he'd react.

But Cheryl's situation was far different. Her pa left her with family. He hadn't left her in an overcrowded orphanage.

Still, he suspected Kirby regretted the estrangement between him and Cheryl. So much so that he gave her an equal share of Crown Seven as part apology and part inheritance.

"Kirby left one sixth of this spread to you," he said to remind her that her pa had legally included her in his chosen family, either by guilt or duty or whatever drove him.

"Burl retains one-third, correct?" she asked, showing no interest over owning part of the Crown Seven.

"He does, but once we're married, we'll own a third of it."

She frowned at that, and his gut clenched with renewed unease at the thought of making her his wife. "Do your partners own the other third?"

"They do, at least until the last day of this year," he said, determined to forge on and make the best of a bad situation. "If Dade and Trey don't claim their shares before then, they revert to Erston."

She made a face that pretty much summed up his own displeasure over that outcome. "You'll be under Burl's thumb forever then."

"Maybe not. Once my partners join with *us*," he said, putting emphasis on that word that prompted a puckering of her brow, "we'll have enough shares to hold sway in how the ranch is run."

"Then I hope your partners arrive soon."

So did he, for if they didn't, his only chance to break free of Kirby's cousin would be if he could get a good price out of his thoroughbreds and buy him out.

All he had to do was find a buyer for his horses before that damned old outlaw rustled another thoroughbred.

In the silence broken only by the tinkle of bells and muffled clump of hooves on the hardpack, he slid Cheryl a sideways glance to judge her mood. Appreciation for this rugged land shone in her eyes. If they had this in common, maybe they could kindle an interest in each other as well. Maybe he just needed to try a bit harder with her to get his blood pounding below the belt again.

Reid hauled back on the reins. Before the sleigh fully stopped, or he thought through the idea forming in his head, he rounded on Cheryl.

"I haven't done you right," he said. "For that I'm sorry, because you deserve a man that'll give you all of himself instead of a portion."

"What in the world are you talking about?"

"Us. If you'll let me, I'll begin making amends right now." He blew hard, as if running from the truth had winded him. "We've been affianced for a year now, and I've yet to kiss you like I should've done."

Her eyes went wide, then quickly narrowed. "That's understandable, as you left for America as soon as the arrangements were finalized."

Ran like hell was a more apt description. "Damned rude of me to do. Stupid to boot. A man fixing to part with his intended for nigh on a year should leave her with something to remember him by."

"Such as?"

"I should've kissed you till your drawers started smoldering, then pressed you for more until you either gave in or slapped me."

Her cheeks blazed an unbecoming shade of pink. "But you didn't. You comported yourself in a gentlemanly manner, for which I'm grateful."

"Are you?"

"Absolutely. Ours isn't a love match and there is no reason to pretend it could be such."

Her admission was as good as a wallop upside the head. No wonder she hadn't asked him once how he'd been or if he'd missed her. She was doing what was expected of her without complaint.

"You deserve better than me," he said.

She fidgeted on the seat, but he suspected it wasn't from cold. "Don't say that."

"It's the truth." He snapped the lines and set the sleigh in motion again. "You know I'm in a fix, that I let your pa and my partners down. Hell, if not for me, Erston wouldn't have any tie to the Crown Seven."

"Yes, he would have," she said. "Burl told me that my father wired him before you were arrested, asking for a loan."

He bit off a curse, for that proved Kirby hadn't believed that he, Dade and Trey could round up a herd of mustangs in short order. But they could've done it. Green breaking those wild horses for the army would've saved their asses, and all it would've cost them was a bit of time and a lot of sweat.

But what did it matter now? He screwed up before they'd had the chance to give it a try.

"So Erston was on his way to Maverick anyway?" he asked.

"Yes. I suspect that he saw this ranch as a means to

fatten his own purse one day," she said. "Your brush with the law just made it easier for him to achieve that end."

"I'm sorry as hell you got dragged into this," he said, and meant it.

"It will work out all right in the end," she said.

He hoped to hell so. "No regrets then that you'll be marrying a Wyoming rancher before long?"

She stared at her lap and smiled, looking as coy as a young girl. "None whatsoever. In fact, that day can't come soon enough."

This was more like the Cheryl he knew. She was a straight shooter like Kirby had been. But right now she was having the devil's time looking him in the eye.

He sensed there was something else she wanted to say, but she was holding back for some reason.

At least she wasn't dreading their marriage. But he couldn't shake the feeling that there was something different about her.

"You said Pearce is a friend of a friend?" Reid asked when the silence grew too loud for him to bear.

"Yes, he's the brother of a school chum from Shrewsbury. Their family owned a sheep farm there for generations, producing the most exquisite fleece." This time, she stared at the horse's gray ass instead of the one sitting beside her, for Reid surely felt like a fool.

"What the hell is going on, Cheryl?"

Her rigid shoulders seemed to lose their starch. "Mr. Pearce was a tenant farmer on land that Burl recently acquired from a baronet who'd squandered his fortune. You know how Burl covets property."

"That I do." But no matter how much money or land Erston amassed, he was still a money-grubbing businessman.

"Unfortunately, the baronet failed to tell Burl that the sheep on his land belonged to Mr. Pearce."

"Erston didn't believe him," Reid said.

"Not a word. When Mr. Pearce moved his sheep to another parcel of land, Burl accused him of stealing them and went straightway to the authorities."

Reid whistled long and low. "Mr. Pearce is wanted in England for rustling sheep?"

"I'm afraid so."

A crime punishable by death on both sides of the pond. He took another gander at the fat woolies penned near a ramshackle lean-to that served as a shelter.

"How did Pearce get himself and those sheep out of England?"

"I overheard Burl say he was shipping cattle to the Crown Seven, so I altered the docket a bit and told Pearce to have the sheep delivered to the ship." She smiled. "As he was obliged to travel under a different name, and all the papers were in order, nobody questioned him."

If that didn't beat all. He never would've figured Cheryl would do anything underhanded, but she'd surely pulled the wool over her pompous guardian's eyes.

"Why'd you do it, Cheryl?"

She gave him a look that said he was daft to ask such a thing. "If I hadn't stepped in, Mr. Pearce would have hanged for a crime he was innocent of."

Reid was still trying to digest the scheme she'd devised when the unmistakable bleating that annoyed the hell out of cattlemen drifted his way. He turned his attention back to the sheep farm.

A stocky man paused in shoveling a wide path to the front door of a cabin that looked like a brown box slapped down amid a field of blinding snow. His rough farmer's clothes and windswept hair lent him an unkempt look, but his smile was quick and affable.

Reid reckoned the sheep farmer hadn't had many visitors of the friendly sort to his spread. Even the man's dog wagged his tail in greeting. Dangerous things in a land where sheep and their herders were reviled.

"Mr. Pearce, I presume?" Reid asked her as he drew close to the cabin.

"Yes." Was her voice a tad breathy?

Reid tossed her a glance, and her wistful smile raked rowels down his spine. He'd barely gotten a hello from her, whereas her friend's brother gained a tender greeting and a sigh. *Hell!*

He secured the sleigh and jumped down, intending to come around and assist Cheryl. The quick-footed Mr. Pearce beat him to it with his dog yapping at his heels.

"I trust your journey was a pleasant one," he said, holding Cheryl's hand a bit longer than necessary as she fussed to right her skirts.

Cheryl cleared her throat and extracted her hand from Pearce's, though Reid would swear she did so reluctantly. "Quite, though I tell you truly it seemed to take forever to get here."

"What of your guardian?" Pearce asked, flicking a glance from Reid to her.

"As odious as ever." She pulled a small packet from her muff and handed it to him. "From your sister."

The sheepherder's eyes went wide. "How thoughtful of you."

The two stood there in the cold smiling at each other. Reid got the burn in his gut that told him there was more going on here than met the eye.

"I wasn't aware my near neighbor was a friend of my

intended." Reid stopped beside her, his shadow falling over the shorter man.

The sheepherder found his wits first. "Nor was I, but I've had good reason not to court a friendship with the area ranchers."

"It's a fact woolies aren't welcome here," Reid said, and hoped any trouble that visited this ranch didn't spill over onto the Crown Seven.

"Forgive me for neglecting a proper introduction." Cheryl made the overtures.

Reid brushed two fingers over his hat brim in greeting. But the introduction was interrupted when a small boy burst out the door and straight into Pearce.

"Papa." The towheaded boy extended his hands to Pearce.

A woman of advanced age hurried out next, wringing her hands in a stark white apron as she took in the visitors. "The scamp got away from me."

"That's all right, Mrs. Hatch." Pearce caught the boy up in his arms and straightened, almost in challenge. "Good to make your acquaintance, Mr. Barclay."

"Barclay will do in these parts," he said, taking the man's measure and judging him to be the forthright sort.

At least the boy had a father that cared for him. What Reid would've given for a moment of his father's time.

"As you wish." Pearce motioned to his open door. "Do come in."

Before Reid could say that they had to be getting back, Cheryl had followed the older woman into the cabin. He had damn little choice but to follow her.

"I've heard quite a bit about you," Pearce said.

Reid imagined that came from Cheryl, bemoaning the fact she was being forced to marry him. "I trust my fiancée didn't bore you."

"Actually, Miss Morris didn't talk of you at all. The barkeep at Mallory's Roost was far more accommodating." Pearce strode inside, leaving Reid to bring up the rear or stay outside and freeze his ass off.

He dreaded to think what drivel Ian Mallory had spouted about him, more so since the old sot knew about Reid's former life. "Cheryl told me about the fix you landed in with Burl Erston."

The defiant glint in Pearce's eyes told Reid it wasn't by choice. "An untenable situation, for which my only recourse was to disappear."

"Best make yourself scarce while Erston is in Wyoming," he said.

The truth of it was there were cattlemen out there just waiting for an excuse to go after a sheepherder. If it got out that he'd rustled stock in England, he'd be as good as hanged.

Pearce inclined his head in understanding. "I intend to stay right here and devote my time to ways to produce a superior fleece that is more resilient to the elements."

Reid thought to tell him he'd be wise to create a breed in Wyoming that could pack its own guns, but figured his humor would be lost on Cheryl and Pearce. Not that Pearce was paying him much mind again. While the sheepman took his son in another part of the cabin, the older woman scuttled off to prepare tea.

Tea. Reid despised it.

His gaze narrowed on his intended, fussing with her skirts again. She looked right at home on that fancy sofa that looked out of place in this crude cabin.

Pearce hustled from the kitchen with a tray bearing a pot, a trio of cups, and a tin of shortbread. He made a show of pouring tea, asking Cheryl's preference for sugar and seeing she sated her hunger, falling over himself with platitudes and never sparing Reid a glance.

In fact, the room shrunk to just the two of them, with Reid relegated to the part of field mouse in the corner, observing the two chatting about England and the weather and sheep.

But behind all the proper etiquette and niceties, Reid sensed a stronger undercurrent. A sense of closeness that went beyond friends.

Reid tapped his fists on his thighs, watching them through slitted eyes. By damn, had Cheryl taken a lover?

After thumbing through Eliza Leslie's cookbook, Ellie set to work preparing a beef bouilli for tonight's supper. Hopefully the fact it was elk instead of beef wouldn't matter.

The pot roast was simple, yet elegant. It would be a welcome change from the poor fair the guests likely endured en route to Wyoming.

She couldn't imagine embarking on such an arduous journey this time of year. Though Christmas weddings were in vogue in some circles, it was typically the bride's family who made the arrangements.

But then as far as she could see this upcoming wedding was far from normal or joyous for the bride or the groom. Neither had any immediate family present, nor had she heard that any friends would be arriving.

The groom didn't wish to marry the bride.

The bride exhibited no interest in her wedding or the groom.

In fact, they treated each other more like distant relatives than an affianced couple. How had he put it? *I didn't pick the woman or the day, so don't expect me to get heated up over it all.*

Even she and Irwin showed more devotion to one another than that, which had made her humiliation all the more painful to bear at the time.

So why was Reid being forced to marry Miss Morris? What was Erston holding over his head to get him to comply?

Those questions nagged at Ellie far too much. The fact he rebelled about his fate spoke volumes. She wondered now if he hoped to get caught trifling with her so he could get out of a forced marriage.

Well, she'd not be part of his game, no matter what it was. She was here to spend the holidays with her pa, and talk him out of making a deadly error by hunting down this Slim. And when the opportunity arose, she'd have a nice long talk with Miss Morris.

Thirty minutes later, Ellie's stomach fluttered nervously as she took the lid off her kettle and peered into the pot. Chunks of carrot, onion and potato bubbled around a hunk of meat immersed in a rich broth.

She sighed with relief, confident her first supper for the guests at the Crown Seven would be a success. True, she'd had to substitute elk for beef and potatoes for turnips, but her simmering beef bouilli was filling the kitchen with an appetizing aroma.

In another hour or so, it'd be perfectly cooked and ready to serve exactly at the precise time for the evening meal. And for once, triumph in the kitchen would be hers.

Ellie poured a cup of tea and settled onto a kitchen chair to relax. She'd wanted to prove she could manage a household with the same alacrity as she taught her students. But this sense of satisfaction was a surprise.

This thrill of accomplishment that left her nearly giddy must be what a housewife felt when she cooked a proper meal for her family. Her family. Would she ever experience that now? Would she find a good man who would accept a wife with a tarnished past?

The questions were ones she didn't care to examine too closely. She was not one to dwell on what couldn't be changed. If she couldn't be a wife and mother, she'd teach young ladies to be that paragon of womanhood.

There were worse fates that could befall a woman.

Her dessert was finished. Her entrée was simmering away nicely. And if the cloth ballooning over her crock was any indication, the dough for her light bread was ready for the next step.

She frowned. What was the next step? She fetched a pan from the pantry and read the recipe again.

"'Knead the dough well,'" she read silently. "'Divide into sixteen equal parts. Arrange the balls on a greased pan. Let rise once and bake until golden.'"

That sounded simple enough.

"I say, that is a most appetizing bouquet," Hubert said from the kitchen.

"Thank you."

She beamed at the compliment. That was a new experience she intended to savor.

Her smile wavered when she returned to the kitchen to find Hubert peering into her bouilli pot. Her blood ran cold. If he tampered with her meal, she'd be tempted to kill him.

"I didn't know you were so interested in cooking," she said, holding her pan before her like a shield.

Hubert replaced the lid on her kettle and straightened. "I was trying to deduce the herbs."

"I added bay leaf to the parsley and rosemary garni."

She set her pan on the table, relieved to have found bay leaf stored in the pantry.

"Ah, yes. As that particular strain of laurel doesn't grow in America, I had to import it for Mrs. Leach." He helped himself to tea. "The other herbs I grew myself."

Ellie paused in turning her dough out. "You did?"

"Indeed. Gardening is a hobby of mine, though the environs here make it somewhat a challenge."

She glanced at the Englishman and knew that very little had gotten past him in the years he'd worked here. "Tell me about Kirby Morris."

He frowned, and for a moment she feared he'd wiggle out of answering. "I'm not quite sure where to begin."

"What brought him here?" She began kneading the dough into a manageable form and hoped Hubert would continue talking while she worked.

"Cattle. He wanted to own a genuine ranch and poured much of himself into this place."

"It's a lovely home," she said and meant it. "Was there a Mrs. Morris?"

Hubert gave a slow nod. "She died in childbirth."

"And the child?"

"Miss Morris lived, and will marry Mr. Barclay in a few days." He took a sip of his tea. "I suggest if you have any further inquiries, you ask the lady or Mr. Barclay."

That must be his way of telling her that he'd not divulge more on that topic. Which of course made her think there was more to it. And made her want to know the details of this arranged marriage.

So she pressed him on another matter while she worked out her frustrations shaping the dough into balls. "You never did tell me if a cowboy named Slim worked here."

"Americans choose rather descriptive nicknames, don't you think?"

She nodded, having certainly heard some doozies. And it was clear he was avoiding answering her again, so she'd try another tactic to continue the conversation. If she was lucky, he'd tell her what she wished to know.

"From what I've read, there are English ones that are just as vivid," she said, taking a cue from him and alerting the topic.

"Such as?"

"Artful Dodger. Or how about Pip?"

Hubert's eyes widened. "Why, Miss Cade, I am surprised and delighted to learn that you've read Charles Dickens."

"He's a favorite of mine." She placed the last dough ball in the pan and wiped the dust and bits of dough from her hands. "I have read every book Miss Perry had of his."

"Miss Perry?"

"The headmistress of the Denver Academy for Young Ladies." She knew the moment the words left her mouth that she'd revealed a detail of her past that wasn't in keeping with her role as housekeeper.

"Is that where you learned to cook as well?" he asked.

"No. I learned how to present a proper table there as well as other social graces," she said, deciding that bit of truth wouldn't hang her.

But if he pressed her about where she'd learned her culinary skills . . . Well, she'd have to trot out a lie.

"If you'd like, you may avail yourself of Mr. Barclay's library. It isn't well stocked, but there are a few works there that I believe you'll find enjoyable."

"I'll bear that in mind." Ellie covered her pan of rolls with a towel and met Hubert's curious stare, holding her excitement in check over the offer of the library. "I'm not one to eavesdrop or bear tales, but I couldn't ignore

Mr. Erston's standoff with Mr. Barclay. Who does own the Crown Seven?"

Hubert winced. "That remains to be seen. Mr. Erston acquired Mr. Kirby's shares in the ranch upon his death, but four others hold claim to the land as well. Now if you'll excuse me, I must decant the wine for the evening meal."

"Thank you for enlightening me," she said, and was rewarded with a rare smile from the odd little butler.

Ellie popped her rolls in the oven. She would've loved nothing more than to rest, but she needed to set the dining room in order well before the guests arrived.

It took her longer than necessary to locate the proper plates and utensils. Longer still to position the tablecloth just so, like Miss Perry had taught her what seemed a lifetime ago.

Ellie had just set the table with the exquisite English Rose china and trimmed the wicks on the candles in the lone candelabra when she heard the scuff of a shoe. She turned, but instead of greeting Hubert, she stared into Mr. Erston's pale, assessing eyes.

"May I help you?" she asked, her face hurting from the forced smile of civility.

"I certainly hope so." He treated her to a long, exacting perusal that left her tensing from the obvious.

She would not tolerate this odious man much longer. "What would you like, sir?"

"Female companionship."

"I fail to see why you thought it necessary to tell me that—"

"Impertinent chit! I have a stake in this ranch, and all employees fall under my orders." He pushed away from the doorway and ambled toward her, his gaze wavering between lascivious and nasty.

Ellie didn't care if he was a president or king. She

squared her shoulders and fixed him with a cool look that had never failed to dissuade men from making an unwanted advance.

"I am the cook and housekeeper, Mr. Erston. Nothing more."

"That's what Barclay insisted, but I've learned that everyone has a price." He gave her a slow, appraising inspection that made her feel dirty. "I'll pay you handsomely if you'll entertain me into your bed each night while I'm marooned here."

She fisted her hands in the folds of her apron and resisted the urge to slap the arrogant Englishman. "Your lewd proposition is an insult to my character."

"A high-brow servant. How novel. Tell me, how much money would it take for you to shun your morals?"

"That degrading query does not dignify a response."

Head high, Ellie spun on a heel and marched back to the door opening into the kitchen. She'd just reached it when a steely hand clamped over her upper arm and jerked her back.

She slammed into Erston's chest and fought for balance. "Let me go!"

He held her tight, his eyes blazing with retribution. "I will not abide intractable servants."

"I won't tolerate a libertine."

"Haughty bitch." Erston caught her chin in his grip and squeezed, his cold smile telling her that he enjoyed hurting her.

The pain nearly stole her breath away. She feared that if he continued squeezing her face, he'd crack her jaw.

She tried to twist free, but his hold was unbreakable. His eyes blazed with nothing short of evil intent.

"Is something amiss?" Hubert asked, his tone curt and loud and the most wondrous sound she'd ever heard.

"A small misunderstanding with the help." Erston shoved her away and then gave an abrupt tug on his brocade waistcoat. "Think about what I said."

"I suggest you do the same, sir."

It was likely the wrong thing to say, for the curl of his upper lip promised more retribution.

Without a word, Erston stormed past an indignant Hubert and pounded up the stairs. A moment later an upper door slammed shut.

Good riddance, Ellie thought as she slumped against the wall and gingerly pressed her fingertips to her face. She winced and was sure there would be bruising.

Hubert rushed toward her, his actions reminding her of a blue jay whose nest had just been attacked. "I shouldn't have left you alone with him."

"Is he prone to forcing his attentions on the servants?"

"It would appear so."

She worked her jaw and winced at the stiffness setting in. It was clear Hubert was just as stunned and infuriated over Erston's behavior as she.

"At least now I know to be on guard while he's in residence," she said, then frowned as an unpleasant odor wafted her way. It took her a moment to place the source. "My dinner rolls!"

She raced to the kitchen range and opened the oven door. Her shoulders drooped along with her hopes as a charred odor rolled from the cavern and engulfed her.

Her earlier pride of accomplishment vanished as she pulled out the pan. Blackened hulks greeted her instead of golden-domed rolls.

"Oh, no!" She longed to lob the pan at Burl Erston's arrogant head.

Hubert muttered what sounded like a curse. "It wasn't your fault."

"The rolls are ruined just the same."

Ellie dropped the pan on the table, then lifted the lid on her beef bouilli. She held her breath for fear of what she'd find. It had cooked down considerably, looking more like a poor man's stew than the French entrée she'd envisioned.

The potatoes had split and were about to fall further apart. The onions had turned transparent and had completely lost their shape. And there remained scarce broth to spoon over the beef.

But it would have to do.

"It'll hold until I get biscuits baked," she said, more to herself than to Hubert.

"I gather time is of the essence here?" Hubert asked.

"Yes, supper can wait another thirty minutes at the most."

"Ah, and if Mr. Barclay fails to arrive by then?"

Her gaze slid to Hubert's. "Then they will be served an interesting version of stew."

To her surprise, Hubert smiled.

Chapter 9

Reid straddled a rackety chair and crossed his arms on its back, giving the illusion of relaxing when he was anything but. He'd watched Cheryl and Kenton Pearce for nigh on an hour now, trying to spot something that would prove they'd been up to some hanky-panky. But neither of them had done more than exchange brief cow-eye glances after Cheryl had swooned.

Of course, Pearce had been there to catch her. The sheepherder had acted with the utmost propriety, which was more than Reid would've done if it'd been Miss Cade.

A woman fainting was expected, considering how they cinched themselves up. It was the reason why Cheryl had a fit of the vapors that had spurred Reid's suspicion.

After listening to Pearce excitedly regale her with sheep breeds and fleece output in terms that bordered on lusty, Reid called an end to the visit.

That's when Cheryl demurred, rose and promptly fainted dead away into the Pearce's arms.

Now if that wasn't high drama worthy of the stage, Reid would eat his new felt hat with its Montana peak.

Ever since then, Cheryl had put on a fine show of

rallying from exhaustion. But though she said all the right things and looked woebegone, she overplayed her part with Pearce's help.

Yep, there was something between the two that went beyond friends. Reid just wished he could tell if they'd taken their friendship past the talking stage, because while he would tolerate a bit of flirting, he wouldn't stand for anything more.

"You're looking better now," Reid told Cheryl, which earned him a chastising frown from Pearce and a weak smile from her.

"I am endeavoring to soldier on," she said.

That she was, but for what reason? "You're doing a right fine job."

A flush stole over her face as she peered up at Reid. "I dislike inconveniencing you."

"You're not, but we're surely putting Mr. Pearce out."

"Not in the least," Pearce rushed to say.

"Still, it's time we headed back to the Crown Seven," Reid said.

"Do you think that's wise?" Before Reid could answer, Pearce was speaking to Cheryl. "I wouldn't wish for you to have a setback."

"I don't think there's any fear of that." Reid smiled at Cheryl and extended his arm to her. "Let's be on our way."

It'd be dark in another hour. Besides, Erston was at the ranch with Ellie and he didn't trust that Englishman any farther than he could toss him.

Cheryl got to her feet with surprising ease and rested her gloved hand on his. "Oh, dear. I feel dreadful causing such a ruckus my first day here."

"Don't be." He just hoped Ellie hadn't set fire to anything while he'd been gone.

"Thank you for your kindness, Mr. Pearce." Cheryl paused at the door, her expression as bland as milk.

"It was my pleasure," he said. "When you feel up to it and the weather is cooperative, I'd like to show you the Rambouillet rams I acquired."

"I'd enjoy that."

And that's all it took for them to launch into a discussion about woolies again.

Reid shook his head. To hear and see Cheryl and Pearce together, it was obvious that both of them had sheep on the brain.

'Course, there were some that said the same of him and his horses. But his plans had met with a serious backset. Just thinking of Kincaid stealing Cormac got him riled all over again.

Reid assisted Cheryl into the sleigh with Pearce hovering behind him like a nervous host. In moments, they set off back toward the Crown Seven. His intended was much more relaxed since her visit with Pearce. But was she happy because of the reunion with friends who shared a mutual love of sheep, or because she and Kenton Pearce were lovers? He wished he knew for sure.

Just because he'd spent nigh on a year looking for a woman who'd nudge his pecker into pumping again didn't mean Cheryl had been searching England for a man to scratch her itch.

"You seem troubled," Cheryl said.

He thought to deny it, then realized he should attempt to find some common ground with his future wife. "My stallion was stolen yesterday."

"Oh, dear. Have the authorities endeavored to find this rustler?"

Reid laughed, thinking Cheryl had a lot to learn about life in the West. "Take a look around you. There's miles upon miles of land for two lawmen and a posse to search. In weather like this, they'd rather stay by the fire."

"I've never seen so much open space before. It takes one's breath away."

"That it does. But don't let the beauty fool you. This weather is brutal. You've got to ask yourself if you could live here the rest of your life in the wild. Could you stand long winters of staying inside for weeks on end with nobody to talk to but your husband and the men that freeze their butts off tending your stock? Could you bundle up and work with them when the situation demanded it?"

"What if I said yes?"

"I'd say you were showing as much grit as your pa."

She frowned at that. "Tell me about him."

"He was a good man."

"That's better than knowing nothing." She huddled beside him, head bowed again. "Did he ever mention me?"

Reid heard the longing in her voice and debated about lying to spare her feelings. But it hadn't been that long back when he'd discovered that much of his past was a lie. He wasn't about to do the same to Cheryl.

"A time or two," he said.

The last time being before he agreed to leave America with Erston. He'd thought it odd at the time that Kirby wrangled a promise out of him to make sure his daughter got her shares of the Crown Seven. But he hadn't believed Kirby was that close to dying.

It explained why Kirby hadn't balked about selling his shares to Erston in exchange for securing Reid's freedom.

"I used to dream that he'd come for me and bring me here, but he never did," she said, her voice tinged with longing.

Reid could understand that, as he'd had the same hankering growing up. Reality could be cruel.

"Is everything all right, Cheryl?"

"Splendid. I'm so happy to be here."

This time, she flashed him a wide smile, but it was the truth in her eyes that convinced him. Made him feel guilty too, because he surely would've preferred it if she'd have stayed in England.

Rifle shots echoed across the high plain, repeating too damned fast for his liking. He guessed the source was less than a mile from the Crown Seven.

"Are those gunshots?" Cheryl asked.

"Yep. Hang on."

Reid flicked the reins over the horse's back, damning the fact he was in a sleigh instead of on horseback, worried sick that he was racing toward unknown trouble with his intended. But he didn't dare slow or backtrack to Pearce's farm, for there was the fear that cattlemen were out "thinning woolies" and Pearce's spread could be next.

He damned sure didn't want Cheryl anywhere near that kind of hate.

"What's wrong, Reid?"

"Damn if I know," he said. "But if I tell you to drop down and cover your head, do it. You hear?"

"Clearly. But if we're riding into danger, wouldn't it be wiser to return to Mr. Pearce's farm?"

"Told you before cattlemen and sheepmen don't always mix," he said. "Best thing we can do is get home."

She huddled under the buffalo robe. "Oh, God."

His gut was so tied up in knots he could scarce breath as he topped the last rise and his ranch came into view. He gave the whole a quick scan, noting the men gathered by the thoroughbreds' stable, staring north.

Reid's gaze followed that path. Booth Howard and a cowboy rode around the far hill and out of his view. Sunlight had glinted off their rifles pointing skyward, proof they were ready to use again.

Rustlers. Reid knew that was the cause of the commotion long before he raced the sleigh into the yard and hauled back on the reins. He spied Shane in the corral, saddling a horse.

Neal came running and steadied the sleigh. "Booth saw a man poking around the thoroughbreds, boss. When he hollered, the man forked a saddle and high-tailed it."

"Ready Kaw," Reid shouted to Shane, then he jumped from the sleigh and lifted Cheryl down. "Get in the house and stay there."

"What are you going to do?"

"Go after him."

She held tight to his coat sleeve. "You can't be serious."

"Yes'm, I am. I've lost a stallion to a rustler. I don't intend to lose more," he said. "Now get in the house."

Before she could offer further protest, Reid wheeled around and followed the path toward Shane and the restive gelding.

"Was the rustler riding Cormac?" he asked as the cowpoke cinched the saddle on his paint.

Shane shook his head. "He was on a dapple gray. You're thinking it was Kincaid?"

"Seems the logical choice."

Kincaid had probably sold his stallion by now and was back to nab another horse. It was damn clear the old man wasn't going to give up. Well, neither was he.

He gathered the reins in one hand and vaulted onto the gelding's back. The big animal pranced in place and quivered beneath him, but only for a heartbeat. Soon as he heeled the paint's flanks, the gelding set off in a burst of energy down the trail already pounded down by the others.

If his men cornered Ezra Kincaid, he wanted to be there before things got out of hand. For this might be the last chance he'd get to make amends for the wrong done to the old man.

A case of nerves beset Ellie the second she heard shots fired. She'd craned her neck at the window as two men road off over the snowy plains, but she had no idea what had happened.

Her mind wasn't eased one bit when Reid Barclay raced across the snow-packed plains a few moments later, kicking up a spray of white powder and looking more like an outlaw than a gentleman. What in the world had happened now?

She had been so busy baking that she hadn't even known he'd returned from his jaunt out with his fiancée. And just reminding herself that he was off limits to her soured her mood. Blast it all! Would the man continually break through her defenses?

"Your gingerbread smells delightful," Hubert said as he shuffled into the kitchen.

She smiled at the compliment and returned to the pan of icing she'd been whipping together before the shooting began. "Have you heard what happened?"

He took his time preparing tea before answering. "According to Miss Morris, she and Mr. Barclay heard shots as they were driving back from Pearce's sheep farm. Mr. Barclay fears that Ezra Kincaid has struck again."

She longed to disabuse Hubert and everyone else of the notion that her pa was rustling, but she couldn't for fear he'd be lynched or arrested, which in the end would amount to the same. If the law caught him, he'd surely hang.

"If nothing else, Kincaid is the convenient scapegoat," she said.

"Interesting observation," he said as he added sugar and milk to his tea and left her wondering if she'd said too much. "I suppose we won't know for sure who is doing what until he's apprehended."

She just hoped her pa wasn't the man eventually caught. Or if he was apprehended, that he'd spend his days in jail instead of being hanged. The memory of that ugly red welt on his neck sickened her, for he'd almost died then.

Ellie fixed her attention on the gingerbread men she'd set to cool and said a quick prayer of thanks to Kirby Morris for saving her pa's life. As for her cookies, they were a curious army of men with no two exactly alike, thanks to the fact she'd had the devil's time removing the cut cookies from the board to the baking pan.

Some were short and stout. Others where long and thin—like the elusive Slim that her pa had come here to find.

Though she longed to question Hubert about him again, she knew she dare not bring up Slim's name again. That would only rouse suspicion.

She turned down the top of a cheesecloth bag and filled it with white icing. A frown pulled at her brows, for the consistency was a bit thinner than it should be.

In fact, she had to fold up the open end to keep the icing from running out of her bag. Frustration danced along her limbs, for decorating cookies and cakes was one thing she knew how to do with aplomb. Yet this had all the promise of being a royal mess.

She had to pinch and release the end of the bag in minute amounts to keep the icing from pooling and creating too large eyes and buttons on her gingerbread men. Thankfully she didn't have to draw a straight line with it. But even so, the decorating looked heavy-handed to her.

"Are you all right, Miss Cade?"

"Just a bit frazzled from all the hullabaloo." She bit her bottom lip as she iced another lopsided smile on a cookie.

Hubert harrumphed. "Uproar is an apt description. One would think a man who'd eluded the law thus far would not take a foolish risk."

"One would think," she repeated.

She glanced at Hubert, wondering just how much he knew about Ezra Kincaid. Was he aware that Mr. Morris had saved his life once? Did he have a clue that Mrs. Leach knew Gabby Moss's true identity?

She suspected little ever got past Hubert, but she didn't dare come right out and ask. Still, the curiosity that she warned her students to shun got the better of her.

"I couldn't help but overhear Mr. Barclay yesterday," she said, setting one tray of iced gingerbread men aside and starting to decorate the second one. "I take it that Mr. Kincaid and he have had troubled dealings in the past?"

Hubert seemed absorbed in stirring his tea. "The rustler attempted to steal Mr. Barclay's horse several years ago."

"Here at the ranch?"

Hubert shook his head, either disagreeing with her or intentionally changing the subject, when Miss Morris burst into the kitchen. Worry lined her brow and a high flush rode the lady's cheeks, but Ellie suspected the latter was due to the cold instead of her sleigh ride with Reid.

Merciful sakes! Just thinking of her own outing with the ruggedly handsome rancher had her blushing.

Hubert got to his feet with effort, and she was reminded that the butler was of advanced age. "Do you require my assistance?"

"Not at all, though what Reid and I encountered upon our return to the Crown Seven has left me quite concerned," Miss Morris said.

"I'm sure Mr. Barclay will take all due precautions and return as soon as possible," Hubert said.

"As do I." Miss Morris blinked like a curious owl and gave a nervous glance behind her before continuing. "What concerns me is that when we heard gunfire, he refused to return to Mr. Pearce's farm, which was much closer, citing a hostility between the cattlemen and sheepherders."

"He was likely most anxious to return you here where you'd be safe," Hubert said.

"No doubt you are correct," Miss Morris said. "But that doesn't alleviate my concern for Mr. Pearce."

Ellie had the feeling the lady cared more about their neighbor than her fiancé. She had insisted Reid take her to the sheepherder's farm shortly after she arrived. But then Reid hadn't behaved like a man besotted with his bride-to-be either. He'd certainly played free around Ellie every chance he got.

"I feel quite certain that the recent troubles were confined here on the Crown Seven," Hubert said.

"I do hope you're right, and that Reid and his men roust this rustler soon," Miss Morris said, going very still when Burl Erston strode to the kitchen doorway and stopped.

"I've been looking for you, Cheryl," he said. "When

you are finished speaking with the staff, I need a word with you in the ranch office."

Terror streaked across the young woman's face so swiftly that Ellie would have missed it if she hadn't been looking at Cheryl.

"Very well," she said, her voice resigned and incredibly small.

Ellie watched as Cheryl preceded Erston down the hall, her head bowed and her shoulders set in a tense line. The closing of the office door seemed to roar in the house. Something was very wrong here.

The thought stayed with her as she finished decorating her cookies. It was hard to decide which threatened to dampen the holiday spirit more—Burl Erston's odious presence, or the rustler who was masquerading as Ezra Kincaid.

The back door opened, admitting a blast of frigid air and Reid Barclay. A tingling awareness streaked through her as she listened to him stamp his boots.

His steps lacked patience, but he paused at the hallway and glanced from her to Hubert. "Lost his trail this side of Medicine Bow."

"A pity, sir," Hubert said. "I'd hoped you would capture the miscreant this time."

"Same here." He squinted at the table, then ambled close. "Those gingerbread?"

She bobbed her head. "Yes. It wouldn't be Christmas without them."

His mouth pulled in that half smile that made her heart flutter. "If you say so, Miss Cade."

He filched a cookie and bit into it, releasing a pleased moan that was the best compliment she'd ever received from him. She suspected he'd devoured the cookie by the time he strode down the hall.

Hubert slid her a bland look. "I am sure Mr. Barclay will desire his supper soon."

Her pleased smiled vanished. Her bouilli! She'd totally forgotten to check on it while she was icing the cookies.

"I'll see to it immediately," she said, half dreading what she'd find.

She lifted the lid on her kettle and released the breath she'd been holding. The mouth-watering aroma perked up her flagging appetite.

Surprisingly, there appeared to be more broth than before. No doubt that was because the rest had cooked down so.

She spooned up a bit of broth to test. The rich savory taste was perfect—not too spicy, but not bland either. Ellie sighed and fetched the platter she'd set out on the side table. She hesitated for a moment, wondering if she should have asked if Reid preferred to be served rather than set a family-style service.

But owing to the way Burl Erston had treated her, she decided to take the easy approach that would get her in and out of the dining room in the shortest amount of time.

After slicing the meat thin and arranging it just so, she set it on the rear stove lid in exchange for a lovely serving bowl she'd set there to warm. She filled it with vegetables, annoyed there was nothing she could do about their well-cooked state.

Hubert appeared at her side, startling her. The butler certainly moved on cat feet.

"Should I ring that dinner will be served?" he asked.

Ellie smiled, pleased with her meal even though it was a far cry from the French entrée she'd imagined. "As soon as I fill the water glasses, you may announce that dinner is served. Oh, I need to light the candelabra."

"I'll attend to that task, then announce the meal."

Hubert made a smart turn and left the kitchen. Ellie placed her biscuits in a towel-draped basket, and then joined Hubert in the dining room.

As she filled the glasses from the tilting water pitcher she'd prepared earlier, Hubert went about lighting the candelabra. A warm glow filled the room.

Hubert inclined his head, then left the dining room. Ellie did the same, only she slipped into the kitchen.

His dulcet voice drifted from the parlor to announce dinner was served. Ellie filled a gravy boat with beef broth and gave everything one last look. She'd finally gotten a decent meal together, and she could hardly wait to see Reid Barclay's reaction to her offering.

Though she couldn't imagine that a man who'd eat pie with his fingers would fuss about filling his own plate. My word, just remembering the kisses they'd shared had her flushing from head to toe.

But that blush of excitement soon vanished under a hot wave of guilt. It'd been wrong of her to dally so wickedly with another woman's man. Wrong of her to feel no shame at the time. Wrong of her to long for his kiss again.

Ellie wouldn't allow it, of course. She wouldn't come between Reid and Cheryl, and she wouldn't forget Reid and her pa were at crossed swords, so to speak.

Determined to get through this meal service with a minimum of interaction with the diners, Ellie plastered a serene smile on her face and made to carry the platter into the dining room. She froze midway.

Burl Erston stood in the doorway, a half-eaten cookie clenched in his hand. "I've tasted worse."

With that scathing review, he entered the dining room. She allowed a calming breath and followed. When in the world had he slipped into the kitchen for that?

Reid was in the process of seating Cheryl at one end of the table when she entered. Erston had positioned himself midway between the two.

Ellie waited until Reid had taken his seat, then moved to Miss Morris's left. Though technically a guest, she was also the future lady of the house.

A wave of intense longing to be in this lady's shoes caught Ellie unaware. She recoiled from the feelings, hating that she'd coveted another woman's man for even a moment.

In her own defense, she'd never been so attracted to a man before. She'd surely never thought to act upon those urges. But the memory of doing just that brought heat rushing to her face.

"This smells positively luscious," Miss Morris said.

"Thank you."

Ellie hoped everyone thought the compliment had brought on her blush. She moved to Erston's left and stiffly held the platter while he forked hearty portions of the beef bouilli onto his plate.

"I'm quite famished," he said, the lust in his eyes conveying he hungered for a woman.

Why, the lout even took the liberty of rubbing his elbow against her stomach, no doubt his attempt to persuade her to visit him later. And if that failed, he'd likely take pleasure in watching her fumble.

She resisted the urge to dump the platter of meat in his lap and walked to the head of the table, head high and shoulders squared in a servile manner. But beneath her reserved façade, her heart pounded a little harder as she held the platter to Reid's right, and her mind replayed the scene with him in the parlor when he'd caught her decorating.

Ellie set the platter on the sideboard, surprised Hubert

was standing there with the bowl of vegetables in hand. The sideboard, she noted, held the basket of biscuits and the gravy boat of savory broth.

"Thank you," she mouthed to Hubert as she took the bowl from him, gaining a pleased smile in answer.

She offered the trio of diners the vegetables and broth in turn, anxious to be done with service so she could re-treat into the kitchen. Erston declined the vegetables but ladled copious amounts of broth over his heaping plate of beef.

Glutton, she thought as she returned to Miss Morris's left with the basket of biscuits. The lady had just taken one when Erston coughed and spewed his food.

"Good heavens, Burl. What's amiss?" Miss Morris asked.

Erston grabbed his goblet and downed the water. He set the goblet down with a clunk and stared at his plate, chest heaving.

"You all right?" Reid asked.

Erston turned hostile eyes on Ellie. "The meat is unfit for consumption."

"How dare you?" Ellie said, forgetting her station in the face of his insult.

Reid's deep cough brought her gaze flying to his. If his frown hadn't clearly displayed his displeasure, the napkin he used to catch the meat he spit out certainly did.

"A bit heavy-handed on salt, Miss Cade," he said.

"It can't be."

Ellie marched to the sideboard and took a sample of the beef. The second it landed on her tongue, she clamped a hand over her mouth and coughed. *Salt!*

She hadn't used it in this dish. But someone certainly saw fit to freely add it.

"I won't keep a cook of her ineptness," Erston said, as

if to remind her he had the power to dismiss her if he chose to.

No one in their right mind would, Ellie thought as she turned to face Reid.

He stared at Ellie without revealing an iota of emotion on his ruggedly handsome face. "What do you have to say for yourself?"

She wiped her hands on her apron, fighting back tears of shame and anger. "I didn't put salt in the beef bouilli."

One black eyebrow arched in dubious question. "You're saying that someone tampered with the meal."

Ellie nodded, praying Reid would believe her. "Yes."

"A likely story," Erston said, his mouthed quirked in morbid amusement now. "A serious matter is at hand here. What if she decided to poison us?"

"Then we'd all be dead or so sick that we wished we were," Reid said, his gaze questioning Ellie's again.

"I'd never do such a thing," she said with righteous heat, though at that moment she was tempted to do Erston grave bodily harm.

"In my manor, the cook is held accountable for everything that transpires in the kitchen," Erston said, staring at her with cold triumph in his eyes and confirming her suspicion that he was the saboteur. "I warrant she seasoned the dish overmuch and is attempting to fob the blame off on one of us."

Reid pushed to his feet. "I'd like a word with you in the kitchen, Miss Cade."

Too hurt and angry to argue in front of Erston and Miss Morris, she simply nodded and walked into the kitchen with her head high and her back straight. But the second she reached the pantry, she whirled to face Reid.

"You should know that when I returned from setting the table earlier, Mr. Erston was leaving the kitchen," she said, frowning at the memory. "At the time, I thought he'd come in to steal a cookie, but I believe he set out to ruin dinner and humiliate me."

"He proposition you?" he asked as he helped himself to one of the cookies heaped on the plate.

She grimaced at the memory. "He did, and I disabused him of that notion immediately."

He chewed slowly as if relishing the treat, as if taking this mishap in stride, but the hard glint in his eyes belied his calm. "If he tries anything again, you come to me."

"I will." She looked at the range and sighed, thinking her biggest challenge was ahead of her. "Now about supper. I'll see what I can whip up in short order."

"Don't bother." He headed for the door. "Moss had a big pot of beans on. There will be enough for us all tonight."

"Thank you," she said.

He took his coat off the peg and shrugged into it. "Keep an eye on him, Miss Cade. I don't want a repeat of what happened tonight."

Neither did she. But as he pushed out the door into the blistering cold, she wondered how in the world she could deter Burl Erston from more mischief.

Chapter 10

Supper ended up being the remnants of Moss's beans, rice and pork, though there was damn little meat to be found in the pot Reid toted back to the house. Still, with the biscuits Ellie served up, it filled Reid's belly.

Cowboy fare surely didn't suit his guests.

"It's filling," Cheryl said, though she'd only managed to eat a hummingbird's portion.

"This is beyond suitable," Erston said, yet for all his bitching and griping, he managed to finish off a bowl full. "I can't understand why you didn't insist on your cook preparing a decent meal."

"She did that already and somebody thought to ruin it." He held Erston's gaze with his own and damned near grabbed the man by the throat when he smirked.

Yep, Ellie was right. Burl Erston had ruined a meal just to make her look bad for turning him down.

His opinion of the man continued to sink.

"Where is the cook?" Erston asked when Hubert served them dessert. "Did you send her off already?"

"Nope. Told her to put this unpleasantness behind her and start fresh in the morning."

"I hold majority shares, so I'll be the one to say if she stays or goes." Erston bolted to his feet.

"Sit down," Reid said. "Cheryl is siding with me on this, so nobody has majority shares yet."

"Ah, but I will soon." Erston snatched up his wine goblet and finished it off, then tramped from the room.

Cheryl wilted on her chair and massaged her temples. "This is all so wrong."

"Yep, but it doesn't change what we have to do anyway."

The color drained from her face. Not the reaction he wanted from his wife-to-be.

"I'm quite exhausted," she said. "If you have no objections, I'd prefer seeking my room now."

"By all means rest up." For the rest of the week was going to try their patience.

Reid sat in the empty dining room long after his guests had left. He thought about seeking Miss Cade's company for a cup of coffee and another gingerbread cookie, but dismissed the notion and took himself off to his office.

Thank God Burl Erston wasn't in here guzzling his liquor and availing himself of the records. That wasn't any of his business as far as Reid was concerned.

The horses were his, passed into his hands before Kirby died. But though the thoroughbreds had thrived here while he was in England, the men hadn't a clue as to his breeding program.

The foals thrown were good stock, but he'd have to wait to breed the strong line he'd envisioned. That'd take time he simply didn't have.

Nope, the thoroughbreds would have to go. He'd never get out of this fix unless he came up with the money. The question remained—how much could he expect to get out of the horses?

A good hour passed as he reviewed the figures he'd haggled over for a month. Though times were hard, the land was worth a pretty penny.

That was a good thing if a rancher or farmer was selling. But it was bad if a man was hoping to increase his holdings.

Or in his case, buy out a disagreeable partner.

He tossed his pencil on the desk and rubbed his tired eyes. If only Dade and Trey would show up, he'd have a better chance of squeezing Erston out. But he hadn't heard hide nor hair from them in the year he'd been back, and God knew he'd spread the word that he needed to talk to them.

Guess their silence was his answer. They didn't want a damn thing to do with the man who'd betrayed them. They didn't want their shares of the ranch the three of them had called home.

He poured three fingers of Kentucky bourbon in a glass and leaned back in his chair. He wasn't one to dwell on the things he couldn't change.

His father had disowned him before he was born.

No family had ever stepped forward to take him in.

Not one soul who came into the Guardian Angel's Orphan Asylum in all the years he'd been there had wanted to adopt him.

Those were cruel blows for a boy to accept.

Even as a man he felt the sting of rejection every time he looked into Cheryl's eyes.

He tossed back his bourbon and poured another. That sleigh ride with his intended left him arguing with himself over whether they should go through with this.

Hell, Cheryl didn't want to marry him any more than he wanted to tie himself to her.

But he couldn't chuck it all. He had plenty of faults, but he wasn't one to break a promise. But he did wish they could postpone the wedding until after Christmas.

That'd give Dade and Trey time to get here to claim their shares. And then? Well, then things could get interesting, because they'd have majority shares over Erston and could force him out.

But that wouldn't happen if the boys didn't show.

Kirby had opened his home and his heart to him when he had nothing. He'd given him a share in the Crown Seven. All he'd asked was that Reid make sure that Cheryl got her shares.

That wouldn't happen if he took off like Dade and Trey had done. Even if he was a hard-hearted bastard, he couldn't up and move in the dead of winter with a herd of thoroughbreds and no place to hang his hat.

He tossed back his liquor and grimaced as it burned a trail down this throat. Hell, he might as well make the best of a bad situation. Besides, after he and Cheryl were married and they'd bought out Erston, they could quietly divorce. She could still be a damned good partner in the ranch.

He splashed more bourbon in his glass then went still as death as the clear strains of a Christmas carol drifted into his office. Ellie. He recognized her voice right off, even though she was singing real soft.

She didn't have an angelic voice. No, there was a throaty quality to it that called to something in him that he didn't understand, that left him quivering and wanting.

As for the song, he'd heard it a time or two over the years. The Guardian Angel's Orphan Asylum always saw fit to put on a Christmas show in the hopes the holiday spirit would move folks to welcome an orphan into their homes.

He left his office and crossed to the parlor.

She was in there, busy draping popcorn and berry garlands around the tree.

Singing. Swaying. Smiling.

He leaned a shoulder against the doorway and watched her, glass cradled in his hand and a sense of longing pounded in his chest. For the life of him, he couldn't imagine why she was so heated up over the coming holiday.

But then he'd never celebrated Christmas in his life.

She stepped back and gave the tree a critical look, hands perched on rounded hips and head tilted at an angle that had him longing to step in and kiss that sweet place behind her ear and trail his lips down her neck.

She stepped forward and moved a shiny glass bell from one bough to another. All the while she was humming, when earlier she'd been down in the mouth over Erston salting her dinner.

"What put you in such a good mood?" he asked.

She whirled to face him, eyes wide and cheeks kissed with color. "It's Christmas. Or nearly so."

He didn't need to be reminded, seeing as that would be his wedding day as well. But that shouldn't make any difference to her, unless she was counting the days until Mrs. Leach returned.

"What's so special about Christmas?"

"Nearly everything," she said, taking a gilded glass boot from the box and hanging it on a bough. "It's my favorite holiday of the year."

A glance at his parlor proved she surely liked decorating for it. Why, it was looking as gay as the front window in the mercantile.

He motioned to the boughs liberally placed around the parlor, to the tree that was fast becoming loaded with shiny glass balls, strings of popcorn and berries, and gilded cardboard Santas, cherubs, animals, and fruit. For the life of him he couldn't see the point in going to such fuss.

"You always do all this decorating at Christmas?"

"To varying degrees," she said. "My aunt put up modest decorations because my uncle was mindful of the cost. But the owner of the boardinghouse was as excited about Christmas as I was, so we went all out decking the halls."

"That makes you happy?"

She flashed him a dazzling smile that threatened to melt the cold resolve around his heart. "Everything about Christmas makes me happy."

"Everything?" he repeated, wondering what the hell else she aimed to do.

"Oh, yes! I love the caroling, and gathering with friends and family to share memories and give gifts. It's a time when magic dances on the frosty air, and glittering decorations brighten the gloomiest winter day."

He shook his head. Only time he sang was if he was night-watching a restless herd, or so drunk he thought to serenade a fetching calico queen. Only time he met up with friends was over a game of cards, or in a saloon. Those memories were best forgotten.

As to family, he had none.

"Never done none of that," he said.

His hand stole to the watch pocket of his vest and the solid, comforting feel of his timepiece. The beginnings of a smile pulled at his mouth, because he did understand the awe in receiving at least one gift in his life. But he hadn't thought to do the same.

"I can't believe you've never celebrated Christmas," she said.

"It's always been just another day to me, though I recall that Mrs. Leach fixed a special dinner that day and invited the hands up. But she never went all out decking the halls," he said, taking the term she'd used with such glee.

"Of course not everyone does go to such lengths to make a home festive," she said. "Didn't your parents celebrate the holiday at all?"

He shrugged and handed her what looked to be a glass horse's head with twisted wire halter and reins. One thing he never talked about was his past, though he was tempted to share a bit of his with Ellie. Was that what she meant by getting together and sharing memories?

"Wouldn't know if my folks did or didn't." Though he imagined his father followed the holiday tradition to the letter with his legitimate family in England. "See, I was raised in an orphanage and never knew my parents."

"You didn't have any relatives to go to?" she asked as she hung the ornament on the tree.

"None that would have me," he said, refusing to let the old pain of abandonment get a hold on him anymore. "Reckon the closest I've ever come to family was when Kirby Morris took me, Dade and Trey in off the streets."

She was silent for the longest time as she added another glass ball to the already crowded tree. "Dade and Trey. Are they the lads Hubert referred to?"

"That's them."

"Are they coming for your wedding?"

He rubbed his palm over his nape and heaved a weary sigh. "If they do, it'll surprise the hell out of me."

It'd ease his mind too, for once the three of them

banded together again, Burl Erston wouldn't have a leg to stand on.

"From what I've heard and deduced, it sounds as if Mr. Morris was a very good man," she said.

"That he was."

Reid still couldn't get over the fact that Kirby claimed he, Dade and Trey had given him a better reason to make a new life in the West. Damn shame it ended up being a short one.

She gingerly unwrapped something on the table, then stared up at the top of the tree. "I need your help with this."

"Just tell me what to do."

She handed him a doll made of what looked like corn-husks. It was far from the fancy decorations already on the tree, but the way she cradled it had him guessing it meant something special to her.

"Would you please put the angel atop the tree?"

"Sure thing." He took it from her, then eased his hold when the husks crackled. "She looks like she's been around awhile."

Ellie's sweet laugh danced around him like glittering bits of frost. "My mother made this when I was a child."

He stared at the plain cornhusk angel again and felt a stab of envy that she had something to treasure from a parent. With care, he slipped the angel over the top spear of the tree, and refused to let the sense of right-ness he felt with this woman gain a foothold.

"You done now decking the parlor?" he asked when she just stood there staring at the tree all misty-eyed.

"For tonight." She smiled at him, eyes twinkling with merriment again. "I have to finish hanging the stockings for you and Miss Morris by the fireplace."

He laughed at that. "Don't bother on my account."

"You, sir, are on your way to getting a lump of coal."

"No doubt you're right, for St. Nick never saw fit to drop a cookie or toy in my stocking."

She sighed, her smile wistful. "One is never too old to wish on stars or enjoy Christmas to the fullest, for it's a time of joy and hope for all."

"I'm not so sure about that."

"Believe me, Mr. Barclay," she said as she bustled past him on her way to the door. "There is always time for hope."

He watched her leave and felt the ache of loss settle in his gut. He took in the festive parlor one last time.

She was right about it brightening his spirits some. But he'd given up hope long ago when he'd cried for the family that never came. He vowed never to let himself feel that vulnerable again.

Ellie stood before the range she'd yet to make friends with and attempted to get the morning meal cooked. Bacon, she found, pretty much cooked itself. But instead of an accompaniment of eggs, Reid Barclay requested flapjacks, of all things.

Mixing the batter wasn't hard at all. Apportioning the correct amount of batter on the griddle took practice.

The first ones were far too large. Not only did they burn on the bottoms, but the first one she flipped sailed over the others and plopped onto the floor.

She managed to turn the second one over on the grill, but it landed atop another one. Sweat popped out on her brow as she tried and failed to separate the two.

So she started over and poured far smaller circles onto

the sizzling grill. And all the while she was haunted by what Reid had told her last night.

She'd never guessed the big cowboy had been an orphan, or that he'd never celebrated Christmas in his life. Why, she wouldn't be surprised if he'd never been honored at his birthday either.

So though he was a rogue and a scoundrel when it came to fidelity, she felt compelled to show him how wonderful Christmas could be—starting with a good breakfast.

The smaller flapjacks were far easier to turn without mishap, but she still burned three of them.

Hubert trudged into the kitchen, his face dour as always. He pointed to the platter of dark flapjacks— some whole, some torn in half during the flipping process. "Are those Mr. Barclay's breakfast?"

"No, those are mistakes."

He made a sound much like a suppressed laugh. "Mr. Barclay wishes to know if breakfast will be served soon."

She flicked the older man a harried glance and managed to turn over the last hotcake without incident. "A few minutes more at best."

That proved to be true, and she soon had a stack of flapjacks. A check of the coffee pot proved there was plenty on hand should Reid want more. Later, she'd steep tea for Miss Morris.

She rightly didn't give a fig what Burl Erston preferred. The wretched man could make due with the fare she'd set out. And if he didn't like it?

Ellie ground her teeth as she carried the just-warmed plates into the dining room, then went back to the kitchen. She had to bear in mind she had cast herself into the subservient role here, but it galled her to have to wait on the likes of Burl Erston.

After transferring the bacon to a plate and leaving a generous serving of meat and cakes for Hubert, she declined the butler's offer to help and carried breakfast in to Reid.

Her gaze flicked to the head of the table where he held court, cradling a cup of coffee in his big hands. Her insides fluttered just thinking of those same hands bracketing her waist and drawing her near.

"I apologize for the delay," she said, damning the flush that stole over her face as she set the plates before him.

"Smells good," he said, taking up his fork. "Looks good too."

She said a quick prayer that it tasted good as well.

"Would there be anything else you'd like?" she asked.

"I'd appreciate it if you'd pull up a chair and share the morning meal with me."

She'd like nothing better than to partake of a leisurely breakfast with him. But that would surely overstep her bounds.

"Your guests would be appalled to find the help sitting at the dining table."

He snorted and pushed to his feet. "My guests will be abed for another hour. Join me, Miss Cade."

She bit her lower lip, sorely tempted. It had been a trying morning getting this much done.

"Very well."

Ellie poured herself a cup of coffee and added sugar to the brew, content to stir it and watch Reid. Never mind that she'd been practically salivating over want of the beverage.

The man was an enigma she longed to solve. But the fact that he would soon be another woman's husband gave her no reason to pursue it. No reason but curiosity.

"I trust you purchased a Christmas gift for your fiancée?"
He frowned. "Nope."

"You should, you know," she said, sounding far too breathy to her own ears.

"You got any suggestions?"

"Something to commemorate the day, like a locket."

"You may have to help me with that." And then he winked at her and returned to his breakfast.

Oh, this was wickedly wrong. How could he play the part of a gentleman rancher one moment, and a seductive cowboy set on charming her out of her bloomers the next?

That question nagged at her as she took a seat next to Reid and satisfied her hunger with a few pancakes drizzled with syrup. They turned out far better than she'd expected.

Ellie forked the last of her pancake in her mouth, feeling like a fumble bunny when flecks of sticky breading stuck to her chin. She licked her mouth to catch them, but that one morsel eluded her reach.

In an instant, Reid's hand shot toward her to capture the crumb. The pad of his thumb streaked over her skin, gliding up to catch the crumb. But instead of brushing it aside, he brought his thumb to his mouth and flicked the crumb off with his tongue.

Ellie's mouth went dry and a pulsing heat expanded low in her belly. Desire. She knew it instantly, even though she'd never felt this intensity of the emotion before. Even though she'd never before behaved so wantonly.

She found herself equating this instant with the treasured ones that wives must surely share with husbands before the children rouse from sleep. This must be a reflection of what it is like before the day's tasks call them away. That halcyon moment when the world revolves around just the two of them.

All that was needed to make it perfect would be if he fit her in his arms and kissed her.

As if reading her mind, his head bent toward hers. Ellie's eyes lowered a bit in erotic surrender as Reid bent closer. Closer.

The clearing of a throat tolled like church bells.

Ellie scrambled to her feet and nearly upended a chair, damning the fact that Hubert had caught her and Reid in a compromising situation. Again.

"Marshal Tavish is here to see you, sir," Hubert said, looking at Reid and not once at her.

Not so for the marshal. He strode into the dining room and treated her to a swift accusatory look before facing Reid.

She went cold inside, for she knew in that instant that something had happened, and her pa had taken the blame again.

Reid regarded the lawman with the same annoyance he would anyone who'd interrupted him and Ellie. But what surprised him was the tension that crackled between the two. Damn, did Ellie share a past with Tavish?

"What brings you out this way?" he asked the marshal, drawing those cool appraising eyes back to him.

"Just got done following up a lead that took me in a circle." Tavish thumbed his hat back, and there was no hiding the fact that the lawman was pissed off to all get-out.

"How so?"

"Rustlers hit Rocky Point Ranch last night," Tavish said. "The hands didn't see a thing, but a cowpoke on his way back from Medicine Bow spotted a man riding for thunder north with a trio of horses."

Reid checked the impulse to ride to Josie's spread. She had a husband now, and any problems fell on him. Besides, she and Yancy were spending Christmas with his kin back east.

"How many head they lose?" Reid asked.

"Hiram said three good saddle horses were taken. The most notable being Yancy's roan gelding."

"Who'd you say spotted the rustler outside Medicine Bow?"

"I didn't," Tavish said, his poker face revealing nothing.

Just what the hell was going on here? Why wasn't the marshal being straight with him?

"This witness," Ellie said. "I gather he was able to recognize the outlaw.

"True enough, Miss Cade. He swears he saw Ezra Kincaid hightailing it north with that roan and two other mounts."

Reid chewed off a line of mumbled curses that would've had a reprobate blushing, then he wanted to kick himself when Ellie turned an alarming shade of red. Dammit all!

"You'd think that old man would have the good sense to retire," he said.

"Yup, but it 'pears that ain't the case." Tavish frowned at Ellie. "Something ailing you, Miss Cade?"

"No, I'm fine. It's just unsettling to know an outlaw is so near."

"I'll catch him," Tavish said.

Reid wasn't so sure. The old man had slipped through a host of knotholes over the years. He wouldn't be surprised if Ezra did it again.

"Oh, before I forget, Dan at the depot asked me to pass this letter on to you." Tavish dropped the note beside Reid. "Y'all have a good day."

Reid opened it with high hopes it was the letter he'd been expecting. The first lines dashed that hope.

It was from the preacher in Maverick. The man had gone to Sheridan to visit family, and was stuck down with the ague. He doubted he'd be up to returning to Maverick in time for a Christmas wedding, and asked if it could be postponed until the following week.

It could be put off indefinitely for all Reid cared. But a deal was a deal and he wasn't apt to get out of this one.

He slipped the note in his vest pocket. Still and all, this could be the lucky break he'd been hoping for, or the deal breaker that would rob him of everything he'd worked to achieve.

Chapter 11

Ellie couldn't recall ever being this nervous in her life. She'd thought the marshal would take his leave and ride off, but he and Reid had trudged straight to the bunkhouse and slipped inside. Was her pa in there? Would the marshal recognize him?

She hugged her aching stomach and pressed her face to the icy glass again. "Oh, just go," she said.

"Is something amiss?" Hubert asked.

She spun away from the window and faced the butler's curious stare. "No! I was just working up the fortitude to visit the meat locker."

It was impossible to tell if Hubert bought that whopper or not. "If you'd like, I'll make the journey there for you."

His offer touched her, but she couldn't let him do that. Her pa would venture there midmorning, and this would be her one chance to talk to him without anyone else around.

"Thank you for volunteering," she said, and smiled her gratitude as well, even though her nerves where twanging like out-of-tune banjo strings. "But this is a task I prefer doing myself as I need to know what meat is available."

"Then I'll take myself off and see if I can be of service to Mr. Erston," he said, and actually grimaced.

Her heart when out to the butler as he turned and shuffled off, for dealing with the Englishman was a trial neither of them needed. At least Erston seemed to respect Hubert, which was more than he did for her.

The whicker of a horse had her whipping back to the window. She scrubbed the frost off the glass with her sleeve and caught a glimpse of the marshal riding off. Thank God!

Still, she watched and waited a good fifteen minutes before the cook shack door opened and her pa ambled forth. She wasted no time shrugging into her wrapper and adjusting her heavy shawl over her head. Her pa reached the meat locker and disappeared inside.

She stepped outside, and the cold took her breath away. But she pushed thoughts of discomfort aside and walked carefully down the path to the meat locker, her sturdy boots barely making a sound on the hardpack snow.

She'd worked up a bit of warmth by the time she reached the squat building and ducked inside. Her pa straddled a stool inside, clearly waiting for her.

"You have to leave Wyoming," she said after she gave him a hug and received a crushing one in return. "Go to California—"

"I ain't going nowhere until I find the varmint who's using my name to rustle horses." His green eyes snapped with anger and dared her to argue.

"Don't be a fool," she said, rising to the challenge. "Let the law catch him."

Her pa snorted. "He's too damn smart for that, which is why he's slipped by the law for so long."

Her nervous stomach did an uneasy flip again. "Do you know who he is?"

"Maybe." He scrubbed his whiskers and stared at the wall, as if trying to place the rustler. "I caught a glimpse of him last night. Least I think it was him."

"Where?"

"On the ridge beyond the stable." His bushy white eyebrows met over his bulbous nose, giving him the look of a disgruntled elf. "I can't be sure, but he sure looked like the man who killed that young woman in Laramie two years back."

"Slim?" she asked, and he bobbed his head. "You should tell Reid."

"Hell, Ellie, I can't tell nobody but you," he said, and she knew it was true.

She'd trusted one man with the truth before, and he'd betrayed her confidence and abused her affection.

"So what do we do?" she asked.

She caught the longing in his gaze before he hardened his features. "You pack up and leave."

"Absolutely not!"

He got to his feet with effort and came toward her, grasping her shoulders and staring nearly eye to eye with her. "Listen to me, girl. He knows I'm here on the Crown Seven. That's why he let it be known he was working here so I'd take the bait."

Fear wrapped icy arms around her. "You're scaring me, Pa."

"I aim to," he said. "What worries me is that Slim just might have figured out who you are."

She felt the blood drain from her face.

Six months ago, she'd have pooh-poohed that notion. But Irwin freely prattled about how he'd nearly gotten trapped into marrying her—an outlaw's daughter.

That had cost her the coveted position she'd achieved at the Denver Academy for Young Ladies. But her reputation was smeared when her pious uncle upheld Irwin and admitted he'd taken in his wife's niece out of pity. That changing her name to Cade couldn't cleanse the bad blood that flowed in her veins.

She was fortunate that the headmistress at the Falsmonte Ladies Academy was unaware of her past. But was that secret on the verge of being released again?

"If Slim can't lure me into a trap," her pa said, "I fear he'll use you to draw me out."

Ellie cupped her pa's grizzled face in her palms and pressed her forehead against his. "I'm not leaving, not when I may be able to help you. Not when we have a chance to spend Christmas together."

"Ah, Ellie, it's too damned dangerous for you to stay."

"Three days, Pa. Christmas is just three days away." She pulled back and stared into his eyes that were clouded with worry. "I won't think of leaving before then."

He scrunched his mouth in a knot and fixed her with a flinty-eyed look that used to make her laugh so hard she'd cry when she was a child. She wasn't laughing now, not in the face of so much danger.

"You're as hard-headed as your ma," he said at last.

That made her smile. "You don't suppose I got a bit of that Missouri stubbornness from you?"

His mouth twitched. "Maybe a bit."

"Now that that's settled," she said, content to remain in the circle of her pa's arms a bit longer, "you need to tell me what this Slim looks like. In case he comes snooping around, that is."

Her pa nodded agreement. "Slim ain't nothing to brag on. He was as rangy as a half-starved coyote. His hair was brown and straight as a stick. But with it being winter and men bundling up like bears, I can't tell if he's as rope-thin as he was two years back."

That fact would make it less likely to spot him right off, and could allow the killer to get too close. "Did he have any distinguishing features?"

"Yep, a reddish mark aside his face," he said, letting go of Ellie at last and stepping back from her. "That's why I know it was him I saw snooping round here."

She shivered with cold and worry. "I'll be mindful of a distinguishing birthmark."

Her pa nodded and heaved a sigh. "You'd best get back to the house before you freeze."

"In a moment. I've read the account in the newspaper, but I want to hear how you ended up getting blamed for that shooting in Laramie," she said, and smiled when he tensed up.

"Well, it all started over a fine stallion that caught my eye the minute the cowboy rode into town on him," her pa said.

"Imagine that," she said, and gained a hushing scowl from her pa.

"Town wasn't crowded that day, and that fine horse was tied up right outside the stable in the open." Her pa scrubbed a hand down his beard, and she could almost see him as he'd been that day, near drooling to steal a horse and having to bide his time.

"Piano music and laughter was spilling from the saloon across the street, and the old men that'd been warming a bench in front of the mercantile finally left." Her pa's eyes twinkled with the devilment of a much younger and much bolder man. "I'd just untied that stallion when the saloon doors burst open and a couple of cowboys staggered onto the boardwalk. One of them shouted, 'Shoot that rustler,' at the same time a woman let loose a scream from inside the livery."

Ellie went still, for this was a diversion from the

account she'd read in the newspaper. Even owing to her pa expounding a bit, she realized the truth in his words.

"Lisa True?" she asked.

He bobbed his head, his expression puckered in anger. "She came tearing out of the livery and scared the living hell out of that stallion I'd hoped to use as a shield until I could gain the saddle. He reared and tore the line right from my hand. Left me standing there in the wide open. And that's when the shooting commenced. I tell you truly, I couldn't have been more exposed if I'd been standing there buck naked."

She shivered violently, but not from cold. No, she was reliving the fear she'd held close to her heart every time she imagined her pa taking a deadly risk and nearly dying for it.

"So you shot back at the cowboys and ran," she said.

He sucked his lips in and glared at her. "I ran all right, but I didn't fire a shot."

She frowned. "But the witness said you shot Lisa True."

"The witness lied to save his own hide," he said. "Half a dozen shots peppered the ground around me."

She closed her eyes on a groan, sickened to think of him caught in the crossfire.

"Two came from the livery, but the shooter was aiming at the woman instead of me."

"Lisa True?"

"Yep. Out of the corner of my eye, I saw her stumble and fall, but as I felt no pain, I kept running till I'd cleared the back of the livery." His gaze met hers, and her stomach clutched at the sadness darkening his eyes. "I got a good look at him in that split second I ran by."

"You saw a thin man with a scarred face," she said.

He nodded, and long moments passed in silence while her pa stared at the ground and shook his head.

Ellie guessed she knew what bothered him. He'd been the witness to a murder, but because he was a wanted man, he couldn't do a damn thing about it.

"How'd you ever get out of town alive?" she asked.

He smiled, though it leaned to the wry side. "I knew they'd have a posse on my tail faster than a hound could lick a pot, so I smacked my old horse on the rump and sent him thundering off, and then I ran into the livery and climbed into the loft."

She smiled in kind. "Hiding in plain sight, just like now."

"Pretty much. I just went real still while all the shouting and cussing went on outside," he said. "One man shouted out that she was dead. That Slim killed her, and I knew that had to be the feller I saw in the livery."

They were back to a close version of what was common knowledge. Slim Cullen had been arrested for Lisa True's murder, and her pa barely escaped capture for rustling.

"It weren't until later that I read where a witness came forward and swore I'd fired the shot that killed that girl," he said, his gruff voice resigned. "But I didn't do it, Ellie. I was too busy running to pull leather."

Reid lounged behind his desk and tried his damnedest to avoid looking at Burl Erston seated across from him. He'd never liked the man, but it was a miserable trial to be in the same room with him now. The only way he managed it was by reminding himself that before long, he'd have the means to buy Erston out. Or at least he was still holding out hope that the buyer from Kentucky was still interested in his thoroughbreds.

"I fail to see any bloody reason to wait for her to join us," Erston said.

"I do," Reid said. "She's my fiancée, and what I have to say concerns our wedding."

Erston's beady eyes sparked with malevolent intent. "Your wedding is an arrangement that she has no say in. Let's get on with the reason for this meeting."

Reid's gaze lifted to the doorway and his intended. Her face was paler than usual and her eyes were drawn, as if she'd been ill recently. He nodded to the chair beside him, and she hurried across the room like a mouse.

"So sorry to have kept you both waiting." She slid onto the chair near Reid and offered up a weak smile.

"As well you should be," Erston said. "Well, get on with it now that she's graced us with her presence."

Reid unfolded the letter and handed it to Cheryl, gaining pleasure when Erston puffed up like a toad. "I got a letter this morning from the preacher in Maverick. He's down with a fever and doubts he'll return before next week."

"So find another minister," Erston snapped.

Reid leaned back in his chair and regarded the tyrant who had made the last two years of his life sheer hell. He hated to guess how wretched he'd made Cheryl's life.

"Maverick has one preacher," Reid said. "You'd have to travel to Laramie to find another, and hope he didn't have plans for the holidays."

Erston glared at him across the table. "Which is precisely what you should be doing instead of wasting our time discussing it."

"I'm willing to wait." Reid turned to Cheryl who sat still as a stone. "What do you want to do?"

"I really don't care," she said, gaining a grunt of approval from Erston. "Though I can't see the harm in putting it off either."

Erston slammed his fists on the desk. "I can, as I have no wish to remain in this frozen tundra any longer than necessary. So saying, if you won't endeavor to find a replacement minister, than I shall."

Reid had expected as much. "By all means do what you feel you must."

Erston lurched to his feet, his complexion ruddy and his eyes glinting with hate. "I know what game you're up to and it won't work."

"I'm simply passing along news." He slid the telegram toward Erston, but the narrow-minded tyrant refused to look at it.

"Rubbish! You're hoping to put the wedding off in the vain hope that your friends will crawl out of whatever hole they're hiding in and claim their shares." Erston sneered. "They won't come, for they've no wish to be arrested for cattle rustling."

That brought Reid to his feet and got his anger flowing in a swift black river through his veins. "What the hell are you talking about?"

"Crown Seven cattle disappeared at the same time your *foster* brothers left the ranch," Erston said. "It wasn't a coincidence, as I have witnesses who attested to the fact that they drove the animals away."

"They were only taking their share and you know it."

Erston's thin lips pulled into a smile that was as twisted as his mind. "It's on the books as rustling. They'd do well to stay out of Wyoming."

"You low-life sonofabitch!"

"Curse me all you want," Erston said. "In the end I'll gain control of this ranch and there will be nothing either of you can do to stop me."

With her sage hens seasoned and roasting over a slow flame, Ellie set to work on her housekeeping duties. If nothing else, taking this job gave her a realistic view of what being a housewife entailed.

She'd certainly make adjustments in her lessons for discerning young ladies at the Falsmonte Ladies Academy. If a woman didn't manage her time well, as Ellie had failed to do, she'd find herself working sunup to sundown.

Add the extra duties of a holiday, a wedding and houseguests and she was quite frankly run ragged.

Still, the house wouldn't clean itself. And with Mr. Erston away inspecting the ranch and stock, and Miss Morris retired to her room likely seeing to her wedding preparations, this was the perfect opportunity to spiff up the parlor.

She removed the feather duster and carpet sweeper from the closet and hurried into the parlor. Not only would the house be spic-and-span in an hour or so, she'd work off her frustrations by Bisselling the carpets.

Unfortunately her thoughts kept drifting to a certain rugged cowboy with a devastatingly kissable mouth and oh-so-nimble hands. It was an absolute crime that he commanded her thoughts so. Why, she'd bet he had the same effect on every woman he met.

Perhaps when she finished her chores, she'd have that talk with Miss Morris. She'd certainly want to know that the man she was planning to marry had a roving eye.

Having decided on that course of action, she took stock of the parlor decorating. She could have used more ribbons and pinecones, but her meager supply was exhausted quickly.

All that remained were the chenille doves and white roses for the wedding itself. Another thing she must discuss with Miss Morris, and soon.

If the lady had a bouquet already, then she'd use the

items on hand to further brighten the parlor for the ceremony. If it actually took place.

Reid hadn't bothered to close his office door earlier when he'd explained to Mr. Erston and Miss Morris that the minister would be delayed. Though she hadn't heard, and wouldn't guess, how Miss Morris took the news, it was obvious that Mr. Erston was violently opposed to an extension.

If she had her druthers, she'd prefer the ceremony take place next week as well, for she'd be on her way to California then. She wouldn't have to watch Reid marry another woman.

Ellie grabbed her supplies and damned the jealousy that sank its green fangs in her. Her future rested in teaching privileged young ladies how to comport themselves in all situations. She'd do well to heed her own instructions.

She hurried upstairs, glad she wouldn't have to worry about being caught in a bedroom by Burl Erston. But while she reasoned she should attend the guest rooms first, she passed both of them and entered the large room at the end of the hall. Reid's bedroom.

A naughty thrill shot through her as the owner's bracing scent of mint and citrus eddied around her. The four-poster bed dominated the room. A rich burgundy quilt was tossed haphazardly over it.

No doubt the linens were a tangle beneath, and the thought of Reid's long limbs twisting this way and that on this bed sent a fresh rush of longing coursing through her. She'd do well to purge these carnal thoughts from her mind. But knowing it and doing it were two entirely different things.

She began humming a carol and set about stripping the bed, finding yesterday that if she was singing or humming, she wasn't plagued with thoughts of Reid Barclay. Doing something she was used to and excelled at restored her self-confidence.

In no time she had fresh linens stretched over the large feather mattress and rearranged the quilt just so. A final dusting of the dark chest of drawers and dresser and like woodwork spruced the chamber up.

She ran a hand over his pillow, lingering where his head would rest tonight. A curl of longing fluttered within her, so intense it nearly took her breath away.

If she was careful, she could steal into his room and satisfy this need to be in his arms. But that's all she'd ever have with Reid Barclay. Stolen moments.

It wasn't enough, and the memory of one night of passion would only taunt her for the rest of her days.

Ellie jerked her hand back and quit Reid's room. She'd do well to push all thoughts of him from her mind and focus on tidying the other rooms.

She made quick work of cleaning Burl Erston's room. With her supplies in hand, she stepped into the hallway just as Miss Morris's door burst open.

Their gazes touched briefly before the young woman took off at a run down the hall to the lavatory adjacent to the bathing chamber. A moment later the sound of retching drifted to her.

Good heavens, if she'd contracted some illness, then everyone in the household could be feeling the effects by evening. That would not only put a damper on the wedding, but on Christmas as well.

The young woman stepped into the hall, looking white as snow. "I'm dreadfully sorry."

Ellie's heart went out to her, for she'd never seen anyone look so forlorn. "That's all right. Let's get you back to bed. Do you have other symptoms?"

"Nothing but a queasy belly," she said, though she dutifully returned to her room and allowed Ellie to press the back of her hand to her brow.

"You aren't feverish," she said. "Do you have a nervous disposition?"

Miss Morris shook her head, and a tinge of pink colored her cheeks. "It could be the tart I ate this morning. Mr. Pearce's housekeeper had made lemon curd, and she gave me one to take home. I guess I should have eaten it right away."

Ellie was just glad the woman hadn't gotten sick off her cooking. "How do you feel now?"

She sighed. "Tired."

"Then rest," she said. "Would you like anything?"

Miss Morris shook her head and crawled onto her bed.

Ellie tarried a moment, then left and hurried toward the kitchen. She hadn't the heart to tell Miss Morris about Reid's weakness. And if the spicy scent filling the house was any indication, her sage hens were on their way to being overcooked.

Chapter 12

Burl Erston climbed the stairs with slow deliberation. He'd learned long ago that the swiftest way to achieve wealth and possessions was through the misfortune of others. Unlike his father and his cousin Kirby who'd adhered to the damnable Golden Rule, Erston had increased his holdings by acting swiftly when an opportunity, or misfortune, presented itself.

He'd held tight control over his business ventures and personal life at home and abroad. His wife, after all, had done as bidden without argument, with the exception of raising Cheryl.

He'd granted his wife what she wanted, simply because he never guessed the meek child of his cousin's would be so stupid as to become seduced by the first man who'd showed interest in her. To make matters worse, he was nothing more than a bloody sheep farmer!

If only he'd been a peer or at the least a tradesman.

As Cheryl was of age, he couldn't stop her from marrying Pearce. So he did the next best thing. He set out to ruin Pearce, which proved to be far easier than he'd thought.

Pearce had disappeared from England with the law hot on his heels, and Cheryl was back in his control. But to keep her in line, he dangled the very real threat of doing bodily harm to Pearce and his son should Cheryl think to follow the man.

She'd instantly demurred. Or so he'd thought. He'd never suspected that she had defied him and used her private funds to transport Kenton Pearce, his son, and a flock of sheep to Wyoming.

The law in America cared little about an imported British thief in the wilds of the West. But there were other means to bring Cheryl to task.

Whatever reunion she hoped to achieve here would never happen. His jaunt to town today resulted in him finding a man of dubious character who'd gladly eliminate that distraction for a price. That would bring her back in line.

He rapped on her door and girded his patience while he waited for her to answer.

"We need to talk," he said the moment she opened the door.

"Not now. I don't feel well."

She looked like hell too, but he refused to put this off. "I know about Pearce."

She staggered a bit and grabbed the jamb for support. "How?"

He allowed a terse smile. "I overheard you confiding in your future husband. Did you tell Barclay that Pearce was your lover?"

"Don't be ridiculous."

He clucked his tongue. "I never realized what a conniving bitch you were."

Her sharp indrawn breath was her only reply, hinting that his words could indeed inflict wounds. Or not.

It was difficult to tell with someone as deuced crafty as Cheryl. To think she'd gulled him the past year.

"Tell me, what did you plan to do after you set Pearce up on this remote Wyoming ranch?"

"What difference does it make now that you know the truth?" she asked.

Erston smiled, his mind working for a means to twist what he'd just discovered to his advantage—blackmail was a wonderful weapon. Cheryl's condition became evident on the journey over and made it easier for him to bend her to his will.

"You wouldn't have transported your lover here and abandoned him," Erston said, thinking out loud. "Of course, at the time you likely didn't know you carried his bastard."

Cheryl's hand moved to her midsection in a telling protective gesture. "Why can't you allow us to live as we wish?"

"Perhaps I will once this business with Barclay is concluded."

"You're mad."

"If so, you'd do well to remember what I'm capable of. Barclay was not exaggerating when he said that some ranchers resent sheep and will go to any length to destroy them."

"What have you done?"

"You should ask yourself that question," Erston said. "Remember that you brought your lover here. If those men who've been burning out sheep farms decide Pearce is the next to go, there's naught anyone can do."

She pressed a hand to her mouth, looking ready to toss her lunch again. "Damn you."

Erston laughed, having been damned more times than he could recall. "Now then, as time is of the essence, you must seduce your betrothed tonight."

"I can't."

"You can and you will. Bedding Barclay shouldn't be a hardship for you." He slid her a nasty look. "Come now, don't look so down in the mouth. If all goes as planned, you won't have to suffer his touch for long. He'll believe he planted his seed in you."

Cheryl bit her bottom lip. "I don't want him hurt. I don't want anyone hurt."

"You should have thought of the consequences before you became Pearce's paramour." Erston crossed the short hall to his own room, pausing at the open door and keeping his voice pitched low. "Do as I said, or everyone on that sheep farm will suffer. Do I make myself clear?"

"Nauseatingly so."

"Good. I want it done tonight."

Cheryl heaved an audible sigh. "Very well."

He closed his door and exchanged his damp, cold traveling clothes for a warm suit. The only saving grace in this debacle was that if he'd not discovered the depth of her deception before now, then it was likely Reid Barclay wouldn't figure it out either. By the time he pieced it together?

Erston smiled. It'd be too late, for Barclay would be dead. He was due his recompense for raising his cousin's child, and would gain all in the end—the apportionment his cousin had left Cheryl in England, and this desolate ranch that would be worth a pretty penny.

No, she was worth more to him dead. Same with Reid Barclay. It was just a matter of time before he rid himself of the leaches and gained title of this god-forsaken ranch in the middle of nowhere.

* * *

Ellie waited as long as she dared, but when Mr. Erston began complaining loudly, she had no choice but to serve dinner. Thankfully, Hubert took pity on her and stepped in to serve the meal.

Though Miss Morris ate very little, there was barely enough of the sage hens and rice left to cover the plate she'd set aside for Reid. She only hoped that whatever he was doing, he wasn't doing it on an empty stomach.

She set his plate on the warming tray just as Mr. Erston pushed open the dining room door. "I want meat for my supper," he said. "Cook it well, and do provide enough this time."

"I'll see what's available," she said.

He glared at her. "For your sake, you should hope there is beef."

He strode down the hall to Reid's office, slamming the door in his wake.

"I can see why he feared someone would poison him," she said.

"Indeed so," Hubert said. "Pity we're out of arsenic."

Reid crossed his hands over the pommel and squinted at the break in the fence. "Frank Arlen mention where he was headed when he saw Kincaid?"

"Said he was heading up to Medicine Bow." Shane grunted as he stretched the top line of barbed wire that had been cut. "Said a ranch up that way was hiring on."

"They'd do themselves a favor if they pass Arlen over."

The cowboy had been the epitome of lazy while he worked for Reid. But there was something else about the hand that troubled him.

A good part of it was that whenever trouble befell an

area ranch, Arlen seemed to always have just ridden past or overheard something.

Though cowpokes tended to blow with the wind, Reid couldn't believe that Arlen was lucky or unlucky enough to happen by after trouble hit a ranch. Didn't help Arlen's credibility none that Reid suspected he had the ability to look a man in the eye and lie through his teeth.

"Only one set of tracks here," Shane said.

"I can't see Ezra Kincaid riding back here to cut the fence and not take a horse for his trouble."

"Maybe somebody scared him off."

Like Arlen? No, he couldn't swallow that as being true.

Yet the tracks led Reid to believe somebody had made another try for the horses. But what if he hadn't? What if someone else was setting things up to make it look like Kincaid was fixing to rustle the horses?

Reid stared out over the high plains that stretched on for miles. There were countless arroyos, gorges and blind canyons where a whole herd could get lost. Wouldn't be any trouble for a lone man to hole up there, waiting to strike when the devil prodded him.

The sheriff had told Reid that's what he'd done before and after Burl Erston paid to have him turn a blind eye to the charges against Reid. Even as Reid had made ready to return to America last year, Erston had warned him that he'd be safe as long as nobody figured out what he'd done.

He'd believed Erston, yet a chance visit to the jail proved that wasn't the case at all.

There were no posters with Slim Cullen's name or likeness on the sheriff's walls. But there was a detailed one of Ezra Kincaid, blaming the outlaw for Lisa True's murder.

The wanted poster claimed it happened when the

notorious outlaw starting shooting when he'd been spotted. Though Kinkaid had denied stealing a horse, poor Miss True caught a bullet that snuffed out her life.

It could've happened that way. But did it?

Reid rubbed his gloved hand over his brow, but the memory of that day remained too murky to see through to the truth.

"I don't have a good feeling about what's going on around here," Reid said.

"You worried about the womenfolk?"

"Yep. Hard to say what manner of man we've got lurking round here."

Shane nodded, his expression growing solemn in a snap. "What do you want me to do?"

"Keep your eyes peeled for anything that smells of trouble."

"You can count on it, boss."

Reid was, and hoped he hadn't made a mistake trusting the cowboy.

The pounding of hooves drew near, and he glanced back, half expecting Booth Howard to join them.

He spit out a curse, having seen that big chestnut gelding too recently. Now what?

"Looks like the marshal's got him a posse," Reid said, gaining a muttered curse from Shane.

Tavish reined up a good ten feet back from Reid. "Afternoon, Barclay. You putting in a gate?"

"Nope. Wires were cut," he said. "All the stock is accounted for."

"Reckon that's Kincaid's work. Like I told you, he's been seen in the area." Tavish stared at Shane stringing the last piece of barbed wire to close the breech. "Kincaid's getting bolder to cut a fence in the open like that."

"Maybe he likes rubbing the law's nose in it that he can operate in the open and not get caught."

"He's doing a good job of it." Tavish's saddle creaked as he shifted his weight and his breath clouded before him. "How many men you got working for you?"

"I'm down to ten. Why?"

"There's talk that one of them is Slim Cullen."

"Don't recall nobody by that name signing on." Reid caught Shane's worried look. "You got any man by that name in the bunkhouse?"

"Nary a one," Shane said.

"Looks like you were mistaken, Marshal."

Tavish snorted. "I'm not surprised. If he's here, he's probably using a different name."

Reid nodded. He damned sure was. "What'd this Cullen do?"

"Got on the wrong side of Ezra Kincaid." Tavish shook his head. "Kincaid is out to prove he didn't commit the murder he was accused of doing two years back, so I'm not surprised he'd concoct some story to shift the blame from him."

"You any closer to finding him, Marshal?"

"Not a damned bit. Best be careful."

"I intend to be," Reid said.

Tavish gave the repaired fence one last glance, then he reined his horse and trotted off to join the two deputies riding with him.

"I don't like waiting for Kincaid to strike," Shane said.

"Neither do I." But if he moved too swiftly, he'd likely scare him off.

Hell, he may never know who really killed Miss True. Himself, or Ezra Kincaid.

* * *

Supper was another trial, and not just because Ellie had browned the cutlets a bit too much. The diners held about as much gaiety as if they'd gathered for a wake.

Miss Morris barely tasted the veal medallions and rice but nobody seemed to notice but Ellie. Of course she'd made a point to observe the lady following the aftermath of her stomach affliction this afternoon.

Though hours had passed, the woman retained a bleached pallor that snuffed out the spark in her brown eyes. Even her mouth looked pinched.

For the life of her, Ellie couldn't imagine why the lady had left her bed and come to supper. She'd surely excused herself to return to it after dessert was served.

A pity Burl Erston hadn't contracted the ailment. But she was thankful he took himself off to bed early as well, citing weariness from his travels.

Once she'd cleaned the dining room, Ellie set to tidying up the kitchen. She'd never minded being alone with her thoughts, but tonight she kept dwelling on a certain rugged cowboy. Or rather on his past, which sounded so lonely she wanted to cry.

Of course that sparked a host of feelings that were dangerous for her to feel toward him. Compassion, empathy, and the desire to comfort him.

Yes, the last could certainly get her into trouble.

She was in the process of storing the gingerbread cookies in a tin when Hubert shuffled into the room. "Now that the household is abed, I shall retire to my room with a spot of tea and one of your gingerbreads."

"By all means, help yourself," she said. "I suppose I'll seek my own bed as well, though I'm not the least bit sleepy."

He set his tea to steep and plucked two cookies from

the tin. "Neither am I, but an hour or so of reading more of Mr. Twain's rousing tale should exhaust me."

"That's an excellent idea and one I intend to follow." She set off toward the hall, then paused at the foot of the back stairs. "You're certain Mr. Barclay won't mind if I borrow a book?"

"Not at all. Good night to you." Hubert gathered his tea and cookies and headed for his room.

Ellie strode down the hall, the click of her heels loud on the wooden floors. Though the house was dark as well, the glow from the moon on the bank of snow lit the night well enough that she could see to navigate the house.

Unfortunately it wasn't enough light to read the titles of the array of books on the shelves in Reid's office. She lighted a lamp, adjusted the flame and began thumbing down the spines of books. Cooper. Emerson. Dickens. Poe. Twain. Verne.

My, he certainly had an impressive library. Or had this collection belonged to Mr. Morris?

Not that it mattered. The books were just begging to be read—heaven knew she'd read them all at one time or another. But one seemed more appropriate to enjoy this time of year than the others.

She eased the book from its niche, careful not to make a sound, mindful of the beat of her own heart. The creak of a chair across the room startled her so that she nearly dropped the book.

She whirled toward the sound. Her jaw dropped as her gaze clashed with Reid Barclay's darkly magnetic eyes.

"What did you choose?" he asked.

She clutched the book to her bosom. "*A Christmas Carol*. Hubert said I could borrow one to read."

He pointed at the bookcase, and that's when she noticed he held a heavy glass, half filled with amber fluid. "By all means, help yourself."

"Thank you," she said.

She wasn't surprised to find him drinking alone in the dark. After all, the first time she'd met him he'd been imbibing.

At the time she hadn't realized he'd been troubled. But she recognized it now, just as she recognized the powerful pull he had on all her senses.

She had her book, so she should go. Instead she took a step toward his desk.

"I've read that it often helps if you talk out your troubles," she said.

He let out a soft laugh that shivered over her skin like a silken ribbon. "I can't see that it will."

"How do you know if you've never tried?"

He lifted the glass to the sculpted curl of his lips and drank, his throat working in a slow roll that sent another shiver through her. "Join me?"

"I shouldn't," she said.

She wasn't a teetotaler by any means, but drinking with Reid in the velvet hush of night was dangerous on so many levels. But she wanted to. Oh, how she wanted to.

"Tell you what," he said. "You be my drinking buddy tonight, and I'll talk as long as you want."

Warnings flashed in her head that this was a bad idea, for liquor would surely lower her inhibitions. With Reid, they tended to fall into obscurity already.

But need, or a like desire to talk, had her slipping into the chair before his desk. "All right. But just one."

He flicked her a wicked smile that had her second-guessing her decision. Before her moral bent could prod her to her feet, he'd poured a generous amount of liquor in a glass and handed it to her.

Her fingers curled around the heavy glass and the heady aroma of fine brandy made her nose twitch. But it was those sparkling eyes of his, daring her to drink, that made her take that first sip.

Warmth filled her mouth and glided down her throat, expanding into a swirl of heat in her belly. "What has you sitting here brooding all alone?"

He rocked forward and braced his arms on the desk, the glass cradled between both hands. "You ever been where you had no control over the way your life was heading?"

"Yes," she admitted. "But most people have had that feeling at least once in their lives."

He took a drink and stared at her, but she couldn't read any emotion on his face. Not anger. Not resignation. Not even a trace of hope.

"Is this about your wedding, Mr. Barclay?" she asked.

"Reid." His gaze burned into hers this time.

"Reid," she repeated, certain she flushed over the intimacy of addressing him so. "Well, is it?"

He leaned back in the chair again, the leather creaking as he shifted. "That's part of it."

"Go on," she said, and took a drink to still her sudden chills which had nothing to do with the cold and everything to do with the sensual pull he had on her.

"In a nutshell, Kincaid has stolen one stallion and likely aims to rustle more," he said, the heat of anger sharpening his voice.

She bit her lip to keep from saying that wasn't true, that her pa had been here on the ranch the whole time. But she couldn't do it, for that would surely get him hanged and have her booted off the ranch.

"In this case the rustler does have control, for he's waiting for your guard to be let down," she said.

"That's it." He refilled his glass and offered her more, but she declined. "The buyer who showed interest in my horses has yet to reply to my letter."

"Well, it is Christmas. There are those who celebrate the season with family and friends." And as soon as she said that, she was reminded that Reid had none of the first and few of the second.

"There are those who will travel to any lengths to make a fuss over the day, and this one appears to be no exception," he said. "The preacher who was conducting the wedding sent me a telegram. He went north to visit kin and is down with a fever. He won't make it back here until next week."

"Your wedding has been postponed?" she asked.

He shrugged, but tension racked his broad shoulders and tightened the cords in his strong, bronzed neck. "Yep, unless Erston can round up a preacher before then."

No wonder Miss Morris seemed so sad. Ellie would be too if the Christmas wedding she'd dreamed of having had been delayed.

"What about your friends and family, Ellie? Why did you come here instead of spending Christmas with them?" he asked.

Oh, if only he knew the truth! "Because I chose to do a favor for a friend."

And hearing that lie spoken made her sound selfless when that wasn't the case at all. She didn't know Mrs. Leach, and wouldn't have come here if the woman hadn't sought her out and informed her what her pa planned to do.

Her misery grew when he seemed to mull over her reply an awful long time, as if trying to decide if he should take her at her word. She struggled to keep her expression sunny, even though her lie needled her with guilt.

Here she was, poised to face the holiday she loved most because of the generosity and love and good will it represented, and she was lying to the man who'd blindly agreed to give her a job. It suddenly didn't matter that he was less than gentlemanly.

She was a fraud who'd abused his benevolence.

She was the scarlet woman who dreamed of him in the dead of the night.

"If you could have anything you wanted for this Christmas, what would it be?" she asked, certain he'd want her pa swinging for rustling his stallion.

"You."

He didn't embellish on it. He didn't offer up any excuse. He just stared at her with a carnal hunger that left her quivering and ravenous for the same.

How in the world was she to reply?

She couldn't. Because instead of jumping to her feet and upbraiding him for his lascivious bent, she met his gaze without trying to hide the longing in her heart.

Ellie rose and weaved slightly. The brandy, the man and the suggestion were too powerful a combination to fight.

"Good night, Mr. Barclay," she said, addressing him formally in hopes that would break her seductive thoughts.

She tore her gaze from the heat of his and hurried to the door. But no matter how much distance she put between them, she couldn't escape her own desire for him.

Just as she pushed open the door and rushed into the hall, he said, "Sweet dreams, Ellie. Best lock your door."

She didn't pause to respond. If she dreamed, it would center around Reid Barclay. And there was nothing sweet about what she longed to do with that cowboy.

Chapter 13

Ellie slipped into her bedroom, closed the door and locked it. Her heart was still beating too fast and her thoughts jumbled from Reid's bold admission.

Knowing he wanted her, and hearing him say it were two different things. All pretenses were gone.

He'd made his wants clear.

It was up to her to walk away or succumb to the dark desires he stirred in her. Though she'd managed to walk away from him earlier, she wasn't sure if she was strong enough to resist him again tonight.

In the mood Reid was in, she half feared he'd visit her tonight. And in the mood she was in, she'd likely welcome him.

The locked door gave her time to think about what her body ached to do. It might be the deterrent that would send Reid down the hall to his own bedroom.

And if it wasn't?

She hugged the book to her chest. All thoughts of reading until she was too tired to keep her eyes open had vanished, replaced by the lure of satisfying this wicked longing with Reid.

She didn't dare attempt to lose herself in a book now, for if Reid saw the light on, he might take that as an invitation. If he knocked on her door, she'd have to make a choice. She wasn't sure she'd be able to turn him away.

Being that bold wasn't like her at all. True, she'd known one man in her life, but she'd never lusted after any man as she did Reid Barclay.

And it was all wrong.

He was affianced.

Cheryl was sleeping in the room down the hall.

And lest she forget it, she was here to share the holiday with her pa and keep him from making a foolish mistake. Letting the virile cowboy seduce her would only cause heartache.

Ellie donned her nightgown and climbed into bed. The springs twanged in the stillness.

Her face flushed just imagining how loud the springs would sing if Reid was lying beside her. Good heavens, everyone in the house would know.

She flopped on her side and drew the covers over her head, willing sleep to come. A dreamless sleep, thank you very much.

Ellie prayed her rest wouldn't be tormented with thoughts of the seductive cowboy down the hall, and dalliances that were oh, so tempting, but should never be.

But sleep didn't come, even after she'd heard Reid seek his room. Even when the hour grew late and silence hummed in the house like an angry old bee.

Everyone was abed and asleep. Everyone but her.

She was about to light the lamp and read until she fell over with exhaustion when an unmistakable click sounded in the night. She froze, listening.

That had to have been a door opening very slowly, as

if someone was being careful not to make undue noise. And was that the scuff of a shoe?

She was sure it must be. Someone had left their bedroom. Were they in need of the lavatory? Or had Reid decided to pay her a visit?

Ellie sat up and clutched the covers to her bosom, her head canted to pick up any telling sound in the hall. The seconds stretched out, each one seeming longer than the one before it.

The footsteps she'd expected to hear moving down the hall toward her room never came. In fact, she heard nothing but the hammering of her heart. Had she been mistaken?

Just when she'd convinced herself she'd imagined the sound, another click echoed in the night, this one even softer than before. And much farther from her room.

Ellie leapt from the bed and padded barefoot to her door. She pressed her ear to the panel, trying to pick up a telling sound in the hall.

Nothing. It was deadly quiet.

Someone had left their bedroom and entered another room. She was certain of it. Considering Reid's earlier horny mood in his office, it was fairly obvious what was going on.

Ellie's hands fisted against the cool wood door, and hated herself for that moment's jealousy. It was perfectly understandable that Reid and Cheryl would share a tête-à-tête in the wee hours of the morning. Intimacy between an affianced couple was expected.

After all, she'd allowed Irwin that liberty after they were engaged to be married. And look where that had ended!

Ellie crossed her arms over her bosom and prowled

the room, too restless to climb back into bed. This house was large, but not big enough to ensure privacy.

If she'd heard that door open and close, others would too—especially Burl Erston whose room was adjacent to Reid's. How cavalier of Reid to ravish Cheryl when her guardian was in the next room, privy to any sound they'd make.

A door banged open this time.

Ellie stopped in her tracks. Heavy footsteps sounded in the hall, but not for long and nowhere near her room.

Now what? Was Reid leaving Cheryl's room so quickly?

Ellie wrinkled her nose, wondering if that was the way of men. Her own foray into intimacy had been over before she knew what had happened.

But she'd expected Reid Barclay to have more finesse than Irwin possessed. She'd thought he'd take his time loving a woman. Damn, she'd thought about that far too often.

"Blast it all, Barclay! Have you no decency at all?" Erston asked.

Ellie knew she should mind her own business. But she couldn't.

She opened her door a crack, getting a narrow view of Reid's room at the end of the hall. Burl Erston stood in the doorway holding a lighted candle and looking like she envisioned Mr. Dickens's Ebenezer Scrooge.

God knew Mr. Erston was of the same temperament. However she didn't think he would be having an epiphany anytime soon.

"Did you think you could postpone the wedding and continue trifling with Cheryl?" Erston asked.

"What the hell are you talking about?" Reid's voice echoed out of the dark, sounding muzzy from sleep and a surfeit of alcohol. "What the hell are the both of you doing in my room?"

"Attempting to stop my ward from being abused again," Erston said. "But it's obvious I was too late. Return to your chamber, Cheryl."

"Please, Burl," she said.

"Now!" he said, his voice cracking like a whip.

Ellie jumped and clutched her fists under her chin, unable to believe the woman who'd barely paid Reid attention had sneaked into his room tonight. But Cheryl rushed from Reid's room wearing only a nightdress.

She'd gone to him.

Cheryl stopped beside Erston, her face pale as moonlight. But instead of saying more, she shook her head and fled to her room.

"There will be no more talk of a postponed wedding," Erston said after Cheryl closed her door.

Reid appeared in the doorway, hair mussed and wearing the same clothes he'd had on earlier. "Nothing happened here tonight, and even if it did, putting the wedding off till next week won't hurt a damned thing."

"I don't trust you," Erston said. "If you'd lie about seducing her, you would likely lie about your intention to marry her. I won't let it happen."

"I'm not reneging on our agreement."

"I should hope not," Erston said. "Kirby took you in and gave you a home, but he wouldn't have tolerated you ruining his daughter and then abandoning her. God knows you hurt him enough when your shenanigans nearly cost him this ranch."

"Don't talk about what I did wrong," Reid said. "You bailed me out of a jam and hustled me off to England because Kirby asked for your help, but it was you who demanded a big share of the Crown Seven for your trouble."

"What transpired then was between me and my cousin," Erston said.

"Like hell it was."

Tension crackled in the silence.

Reid stared at Erston, and even from this distance Ellie could sense the anger rolling off him. "We'll talk this out in the morning."

"At length." Erston stormed back to his room and slammed the door in his wake.

Ellie must have made a sound, for Reid looked down the hall to her room. His anger and confusion reached out to her in the darkness, coaxing her to come closer.

Her fingers tightened around the brass knob and her mouth went dry with a need so intense she could barely breathe. It took all her willpower to close and lock her door—not to keep him out but to forestall the temptation to go to him.

After a solitary breakfast the next morning, Reid sprawled in the chair behind his desk and stared at the nearly empty decanter of bourbon. His head still pounded with a hangover that anger made more miserable.

Last night, he'd set out to dull his desire for Ellie with bourbon. It hadn't worked.

So he'd staggered to his room in the wee hours of the morning and fell into bed, too liquored up to bother undressing. When Erston's bellowing had invaded his dreams and jerked him awake, his cock had been semi-hard.

It wouldn't have been like that if he'd screwed Cheryl. Yet she'd been huddled beside him in bed, clutching the bedclothes to her chin.

The last person he expected to find in his bed was Cheryl. She'd made it clear the day before that she didn't expect him to put on an amorous front. Hell, they'd never even kissed, so sleeping together was a monumental step.

Which was why he suspected a trap long before Erston accused him of seducing Cheryl.

It didn't make sense, since he aimed to marry her as agreed. Why go to the fuss of making it look like they'd been intimate? Did Erston think to blackmail him with that now?

Erston swaggered into the office like a conquering general and looked down his hooknose at Reid, certainly giving that impression. "I'm off to Maverick this morning to find a minister. After your tryst last night, it's imperative the wedding proceed as planned."

"A week isn't going to make any difference one way or the other," Reid said.

"It will to me." Erston's fingers tapped out an impatient beat on Reid's desk. "Though the damage has been done, I hope you can restrain yourself until you've exchanged your vows."

"Nothing happened last night."

Erston's sneer hinted he didn't believe that. "Deny it all you like. The wedding will proceed as planned."

He turned and marched from the room.

Reid bit off a ripe curse and combed his fingers through his hair. He wasn't agreeing to do anything until he and Cheryl had a good long talk about why she'd sneaked into his room last night.

Since she hadn't ventured from her bedroom yet, he'd check his mares first. Talk could wait until he finished that chore.

He pushed to his feet and strode to the door, catching sight of Ellie vigorously running the carpet sweeper over the fine rugs. No doubt she'd heard everything, just as she had last night.

For a moment, he had the urge to go to her and defend himself. He didn't want her thinking less of him, which was a switch from his usual attitude of not giving a shit what anyone thought.

But Cheryl's visit to his room had altered the course they'd agreed upon. He had to know why she'd done it. Then he'd figure out how to deal with Burl Erston and protect Cheryl from that bastard's machinations.

Ellie strode down the hall toward Miss Morris's room, worry dogging her steps. It was midmorning and the lady hadn't come down for breakfast yet.

Last night's misadventure had certainly cast a pall over the house this morning. It had been deathly quiet since Reid had left shortly after breakfast. Even Hubert had busied himself elsewhere in the house.

Ellie understood the lady's need for privacy, but she didn't want her suffering in silence either. How odd that days ago, she'd felt it was her duty to take Miss Morris aside and tell her what a scoundrel Reid was.

Now she hesitated doing so, simply because Reid hadn't gone into Miss Morris's room as she'd thought. The lady had taken the initiative and slipped into his room.

Or had she?

It was all so confusing. Should she believe her eyes? Or should she believe what was beating in her heart?

Maybe she just couldn't face the fact that he'd admitted he wanted her, and when she refused him he'd turned to his fiancée in the dead of night. Maybe she just didn't want to admit how vulnerable she was around Reid. Maybe she was deluding herself by refusing to allow how much this hurt her.

All that aside, it simply seemed too convenient for

Burl Erston to catch his guardian in Reid's bed last night. Like Reid, she couldn't see why the wedding couldn't wait until the minister could get here.

She stopped at Miss Morris's door and took several bracing breaths before rapping smartly on the panel. Not waiting for the lady to reply, she asked, "Would you like me to bring up tea or a light brunch?"

"No, nothing, thank you," Miss Morris said, sounding calm and not the least bit depressed.

"Should you change your mind, I'll be in the kitchen," Ellie said.

"I'll bear that in mind," Miss Morris said.

That pretty much slammed the door on further dialogue.

Ellie returned to the kitchen and the quandary of what to do about the noon meal. She imagined Mr. Erston would spend the bulk of the day in town in his search for a minister. She doubted Miss Morris would venture from her room. But Reid would surely expect a meal.

As time was short and her culinary experience already strained, she decided on a simple fare of noodles seasoned with braised chunks of antelope. Mixing the dough was simple enough, but rolling it thin and cutting the strips was a challenge.

The back door opened and closed. Ellie worked a bit faster, certain Reid had returned and would be hungry as a bear.

But instead of the tall cowboy who occupied her thoughts too often, Hubert shuffled into the kitchen. Mercy, she hadn't known he'd gone outside, too.

He stared at the dough covering the table before sliding her a curious look. "Dumplings?"

She frowned and dropped the strips that wanted to

stick together into the boiling water. "Noodles, though these will be a bit fluffier than usual."

That was an understatement. They were too thick, too wide, and would probably be as heavy as wood shingles. As soon as the dough hit the boiling water, the noodles expanded to twice their size.

He glanced in the pot, then went about fixing himself tea. "Ah."

That exclamation said it all.

She groused to herself and dumped the last of the noodles in the pot. If she couldn't master something as simple as noodles, how in the world was she going to prepare the Christmas feast? Or for that matter, the traditional plum cake for the wedding?

And just thinking of the wedding put her in a sour mood again. The questions she'd wrestled with last night while sleep eluded her were clearing in her mind now.

Reid had openly pursued her for a clandestine romance, proving he'd be an unfaithful lout to his fiancée. Yet Cheryl had showed more concern for Kenton Pearce, than Reid.

If not for that episode last night, she'd be convinced that Cheryl wanted nothing to do with Reid. And yet if Cheryl did care for Reid, then why in the world hadn't she shown any interest in her wedding?

The holiday promised to be an interesting one in more ways than one. If she could just think of a way where she could spend uninterrupted time with her pa.

"I suppose Mr. Barclay will invite the cowboys to the house for Christmas dinner," she said, an idea teasing her mind.

"Indeed, Mrs. Leach insisted we all dine together on that day," Hubert said. "Mr. Morris never argued."

How sad that had been the extent of their Christmas

celebration here. Hopefully this year would be far different.

She slid the cast-iron lid on the skillet just as a recognizable thud sounded in the house. But the gust of cold air that usually followed the opening and closing of a door didn't come.

"Did you hear the front door open?" she asked.

He sipped his tea and carefully returned the delicate cup to the saucer. "No, I didn't."

She glanced down the hall toward the front door, but didn't see anything amiss. How odd, she thought as she added the braised chunks of meat and drippings to the noodle pot. Perhaps Miss Morris was moving around in her room.

Hubert gave a loud sniff and frowned. "I say, have you something in the oven?"

Oh, no! "My pudding!"

She grabbed a heavy towel and lifted the peach tapioca from the blazing cavern. Regulating the temperature of the oven was a mystery to her.

Her dessert didn't smell burnt, but the edges were a tad brown and crusty. She'd have to avoid serving those parts in order to salvage the dessert.

The back door slammed shut, leaving no question that someone had entered. The heavy footfalls left no doubt to his identity.

Ellie didn't have to look up to know Reid had come in. Even if she hadn't recognized the assured, resolute cadence of his steps, she was beset by an innate sensual awareness that he was close.

He stopped at the doorway to the kitchen and looked in. "Smells mighty good in here."

"Thank you," she said, unable to stop beaming at the compliment.

A tense moment passed where he just stood there looking in, then with a negligent shrug, he ambled into the kitchen. "I'll take a cup of coffee if you've got it."

She hurried to oblige and hid her surprise that he pulled up a chair and straddled it, as if in no hurry to leave her company, as if mingling with the help was the most natural thing to do. "How is your mare?"

His mouth quirked to one side. "She foaled a fine dun colt about an hour ago. He ought to fetch a pretty penny."

"Excellent news, sir," Hubert said. "Have you heard from the prospective buyer yet?"

"Nary a word." Disappointment tolled in every word.

Hubert frowned, worry etched on his aged face as well. "That's unfortunate, sir."

"Will it be difficult to find another buyer?" she asked as she fetched the tureen from the cupboard.

"Hard to say." Reid hunkered forward and curved his hands around his coffee cup. "There are plenty who want them, but few who'll pay what they're worth."

"Do you have to sell now?" she asked.

He snorted. "I do if I want to buy out Erston."

So that was it. Reid needed the money off the thoroughbreds to purchase Erston's shares.

"Perhaps the lads will arrive after all," Hubert said.

A fleeting bleakness darkened Reid's eyes, the emotion so filled with angst that her heart ached for him. "I have to be ready in case they don't."

She turned back to the range and the task of pouring the noodle mixture into the tureen. No wonder he was guarding the horses. They represented his freedom from Burl Erston.

Before she finished, the back door banged open and harried footsteps came their way. She looked up just as a cowboy stormed into the kitchen. The wild look in his eyes made her blood run cold.

"Trouble, boss," the cowboy said. "One of the men spotted three armed riders headed toward Pearce's sheep ranch."

"Oh, dear," Hubert said, and wilted in his chair.

"How long ago?" Reid asked, slamming his empty cup down.

"Reckon ten minutes," the cowboy said.

"Not much I can do except get in the middle of trouble."

"You need to get over there just the same," he said. "Neal said Miss Morris set off toward Pearce's farm a good twenty minutes ago."

"She what?" Reid asked, the surprise in his voice mirroring Ellie's shock.

When in the world had the lady left the house? And then it dawned on her. When she'd put the lid on the skillet, she'd thought she'd heard the front door open.

Hubert had denied hearing a thing. But his hangdog expression made her suspect that wasn't the case at all.

"You knew she left," Ellie said to Hubert.

He nodded, clearly miserable over the truth. "Miss Morris begged me to have a sleigh readied for her. She expressed grave worry over Mr. Pearce and his family."

"So you helped her," Reid said.

Hubert said, "I didn't see the harm in her traveling over while her guardian was away."

Reid shoved to his feet and headed to his office. "All right, Shane. Who's with her?"

"Nobody," the cowboy said. "Neal readied the sleigh for her like Hubert asked. When he looked up, she'd gotten in it and took off."

"Saddle Kaw, round up a couple of hands and be ready to ride in five."

"Will do, boss," he said, and raced from the house.

Chapter 14

Reid stormed back in his office, unlocked his gun cabinet and strapped on the pair of six-shooters he'd hoped he'd never have to use again. He grabbed his Winchester, shoved cartridges in his pocket and stormed toward the door.

Ellie stood in the parlor doorway, worry etching lines around her expressive eyes. "What do you want me to do?"

Kiss him like there was no tomorrow. Give him something sweet to savor on his tongue as he rode into God-knew-what kind of trouble.

"Hope to hell I get there in time," he said.

She reached out and grabbed his arm, and the strength of her grip gave him the support he needed right now. Why in the hell couldn't she be the woman he was to marry?

The idea slammed into him and sent his senses reeling. He didn't have the luxury to pine for someone he couldn't have, for following where his desire led would hurt both women in the end.

"Be careful," she said, her voice breathy like he'd imagined it would be after she came in his arms.

Reid nodded and jammed his hat on, shoving thoughts of Ellie Jo Cade aside as he trudged out the door. Now more than ever he needed a clear head.

By the time he reached the corral, Shane was tightening the girth on Kaw's saddle. Four other hands sat their mounts, ready to ride.

Though Reid held no love for sheepherders, he couldn't let Cheryl ride into what would likely be a lynching or worse. He just hoped they'd get there in time to stop trouble from rearing its ugly head.

Shane unhooked the stirrup from the saddle horn at the same time Reid reached Kaw and released the paint's lead line with a snap. The big gelding tossed his head, nostrils flared.

Reid swung into the saddle. "Let's ride."

He leaned forward and let the powerful gelding find his balance and speed on the snow. Seconds ticked by like hours, each one more agonizing than the next, making the five-mile ride feel like twenty.

As Pearce's sheep ranch came into view, Reid hoped Cheryl's insistence on visiting the sheepherder wouldn't be the death of all of them.

Reid spotted the trio of gunmen ringing a sleigh that was surely his. Beside it stood a man he'd bet was Pearce. All of them looked up as Reid and his men rode up to them.

He stared at the cowpoke he'd shared more than a few drinks with at Mallory's Roost. "What brings you out this way, Jonah?"

The cowpoke shifted uneasily in the saddle. "Heard some fool set up a sheep farm here."

"Yep. This here fool is a long-time friend of the woman I aim to marry." Reid nodded to the wide-eyed woman in the sleigh and the man standing protectively at her side.

"Didn't know you was fixing to get harnessed to a woman," Jonah said, and gained snickers and grunts from the two men with him.

"Now you do." He smiled at Cheryl and was relieved when she smiled back, albeit a troubled one. "Cheryl is Kirby's daughter. You remember Kirby, don't you?"

"Kirby Morris?" one of the men asked.

Reid inclined his head. "One and the same."

"Shit." The two men with Jonah shared a look, then turned and rode off.

"Believe I'll follow them a spell," Shane said, and put action to words.

Jonah turned pale, and Reid reckoned he knew why. Truth was, there were few cowboys who didn't recall Kirby with respect, partly because he'd given most a hand on the Crown when they needed it, or tossed them a dollar or two at Mallory's Roost.

Generous to a fault pretty much defined Kirby Morris.

"Hell, yes, I remember him," Jonah said, and looked straight at Cheryl. "Your pa was a right fine man."

She blinked, no doubt having trouble believing that, since he'd given his only child to his cousin to raise and hadn't bothered to contact her once during her life. "I am beginning to realize there was more to him than I'd realized."

Jonah dipped his chin and faced Reid again. "I'll pass the word on."

"Much obliged," Reid said.

The cabin door opened and Pearce's little boy ran outside with the older woman on his heels, trying to catch him. "Papa!"

Pearce shielded his son behind him, looking torn

between leaving Cheryl's side and returning his son to the cabin.

Jonah stared at the group for a long moment before he dipped his chin again. "Merry Christmas to you all," he said, then reined his mount and started down the road.

Reid heeled Kaw and started after him. "Jonah!"

The cowpoke reined up in a spray of white powder. "Afraid you'd want to know more."

"Damned right I do." Reid crossed his wrists over the saddle horn and leaned forward. "Why'd you come here?"

"A man paid me to pay this sheep farm a visit, and not a friendly one."

"Who?"

"Don't know his name, but he paid well," Jonah said.

"Describe him."

Jonah did in exacting detail. Burl Erston.

"I ain't giving him his money back," Jonah said.

"Don't expect you to."

The cowpoke's brow creased with deep furrows. "You'd best bear in mind that if the job don't get done, he'll hire someone else to do it."

That was a given, but he saw no need to show his hand. "Just what did he tell you to do?"

"Kill anyone I found here." Jonah shifted in the saddle again, the creak of leather loud in the frigid tension that bounced between them. "I don't kill women and children."

He glanced back at the ranch and the young boy Pearce was now holding. Hell, Erston was lower than he'd thought.

"If I can hang on, I'll be needing hands in the spring," Reid said.

"I'll be back then." Jonah reined his horse around and rode off.

Reid sat there for long moments, all alone, determined to dam up the river of rage coursing through him before he returned to Cheryl and her sheepherder.

First she crawls into his bed in the middle of the night, and then she takes off alone to visit her damned sheep breeder. Why hadn't she told him?

Why would she?

If she and Pearce were as close as he suspected, she wouldn't want him anywhere near them. He headed toward the pair, reminded that shouting and such wouldn't solve a thing. Never mind that was the one thing he longed to do.

"I am indebted to you," Pearce said.

"Damned right you are. Those men were hired to barbeque your sheep on the hoof, and anyone else on this farm."

That brought Cheryl out of cowering in the sleigh. "Surely you're exaggerating."

"Nope. They were paid to turn this farm into a cemetery."

"Burl," she said, her teeth clattering from the cold— or cold reality.

Reid nodded, seeing no sense in lying to either of them. In fact, it was time they had a talk.

Pearce paled. "If what you say is true, then why did those men abort their plan when you arrived?"

Reid allowed a half smile. "They hold a lot more respect for Kirby Morris than they do for Burl Erston."

Pearce nodded, but deep concern clouded his eyes. "Will they return?"

Reid gave that a moment's thought as he swung from the saddle and landed on the packed snow. "They shouldn't, but you can't be sure in these parts. Watch yourself."

Pearce flicked a glance at the woman in the sleigh. "I shall be very careful with everything and everyone I hold dear."

Cheryl flushed, and not a pretty blush either. Nope, it bordered on the embarrassed kind tangled up with guilt. And hell, was that whisker burn on her face?

Reid's narrowed gaze honed in on Pearce again. The fair-haired sheepherder needed a shave.

"What's been going on here?" Reid asked.

Cheryl seemed to wilt in the sleigh. "Burl discovered that Kenton was living nearby."

Reid shook his head, knowing there was more to it than that. "He told you that?"

"Last night, he threatened to harm Kenton if I didn't do as he bid." She sent him a look that pleaded for discretion.

Mighty obvious she didn't want him telling Pearce what she'd done last night. Did Cheryl think he was too blind to see she had an interest in Pearce?

Hell, if she wanted to pussyfoot around the truth in front of Pearce, then by all means he'd let her do it. But once they were alone, he wanted to know the whole damned story.

"Mr. Barclay deserves the truth," Pearce said at last. "Please, let's all go in the house and talk."

"All right." Reid extended a hand to Cheryl, aware he was forcing her to choose between him and Pearce.

She fidgeted with her hands and turned that ungodly shade of red again as she looked from one to the other. Finally, she reached out and rested a hand on Reid's forearm with all the caution one would afford a pit viper.

He didn't need higher learning to realize his intended dreaded touching him. So why the hell had she crawled in the sack with him last night? If Erston hadn't barged in, how long would she have lain beside him like a log?

The answer was clear as the blue sky stretching as far as the eye could see. All night. Erston had blackmailed her to go to his room, but she couldn't force herself to take it any further.

The second her feet touched the ground, she extracted herself from Reid. He wasn't jealous. No, he'd have to feel more for Cheryl than brotherly concern before that emotion came to life in him.

But his pride was sorely tweaked for landing in this fix neither of them wanted. The problem was, he could see no way out for either of them.

While Pearce and his son escorted Cheryl toward the cabin with all the propriety a man could afford a lady, Reid secured Kaw's line to the back of the sleigh. He took a moment to admire the high plains he'd come to love.

Untamed. Endless. Rugged and unforgiving.

He could live out his days here. But did he want it bad enough to marry a woman who didn't give two hoops in hell about him?

He pushed away from the sleigh and trailed them, mulling over the rash idea forming in his head. A flash of light from the grove of cottonwoods snared his attention.

His gut clenched as he realized he was about to relive a nightmare. He'd seen a similar warning flash off a rifle some months back and hadn't reacted as fast as he should, earning him a bitching headache and a scar aside his temple for his trouble.

Panic shot up through Reid like a thermometer lying in the hot noonday sun. Had one of the gunnysackers riding with Jonah returned to take another try at Pearce or his woolies?

Reid sought out the sheepherder who was walking shoulder to shoulder with Cheryl. Out in the open. An easy target.

"Get down!"

Reid sprinted toward the pair as a rifle shot exploded from that hill. He shoved her so hard he knocked her off her feet.

The sheepherder swore and knelt to help her just as a bolt of fire sliced a trough aside Reid's head. He'd been shot.

"Sonofabitch!"

He sieved air through his teeth and fought against the hot wave of black rolling his way, staring at Cheryl and Pearce through a blizzard of white dots, knowing he'd soon lose his hold on consciousness.

"Oh, my God! *No!*" she shrieked.

The same thought crossed Reid's mind as the wave crashed over him and sent him tumbling into sweet oblivion.

Ellie dumped the dust from the Bissell just as the sleigh topped the rise. Ever since Reid had ridden out her stomach had been tied in knots.

So she'd done everything she could to keep busy. The lone shot that had echoed on and on frayed her nerves. That's when she'd given up sweeping the rugs before she wore a path in them.

She shielded her eyes to get a better look. Reid's paint gelding was tied to the back of the sleigh, trailing along at a good clip.

Two people sat inside. Their faces were shadowed, but Ellie knew Reid and Cheryl were in the sleigh. Reid was bringing her home—

No, Cheryl was driving the buggy.

Hope I get there in time, he'd said.

She tore her gaze from Reid to the two men riding

behind the sleigh, one holding a rifle as if expecting trouble. Or more of it?

A sick dread washed over Ellie as the sleigh slid past the house and headed for the outbuildings. Reid was slumped beside Cheryl with a bloody cloth tied around his head, looking more dead than alive.

The carpet sweeper fell from her cold hands. She clutched her coat close around her and trudged through the snow, her heart thundering like stampeding mustangs.

"Boss has been shot," Shane shouted as the sleigh rocked to a stop before the cook shack.

And Ellie's heart nearly stopped beating right then and there. She choked back tears and curses a lady should never let fall or never utter and ran harder.

By the time she came abreast of the sleigh, she was breathless and terrified what she'd find. Cheryl sat like a stone on the seat, eyes too wide and face too pale.

"What happened?" Ellie asked.

Cheryl blinked back tears. "Reid was shot protecting me and Mr. Pearce."

"Let's get him inside so Moss can stitch him up," a man said.

Her gaze flicked to Moss. The old man leaned against the door to his cook shack, wiping his hands on his dirty apron, eyes alert.

"How bad is it?" Moss asked.

"Barely a scratch," Reid said, his gruff voice the sweetest sound Ellie had heard this day.

"His head is bleeding horribly," Cheryl said, scrambling from the sleigh with Pearce's aid.

Moss nodded. "Head wounds do that."

"It isn't that bad," Reid said.

Ellie pushed forward, wanting to see for herself. Wanting to assure herself that he'd be all right.

"Bring him inside, boys," Moss said.

Shane and Booth shouldered Reid inside, proving to Ellie that it was worse than Reid claimed if it took two men to help him walk. Cheryl and Pearce moved to the doorway of the shack and stopped, succeeding in blocking the way.

"What happened?" Ellie asked Cheryl.

"It was all so dreadful. Those armed men came first, but Reid diverted them." Cheryl shook her head, looking close to tears. "Or so we thought."

Ellie gasped, thinking of the trouble Reid had alluded to before—the trouble that'd been pinned on her pa. "Rustlers?"

Cheryl shook her head, seeming at a loss to explain. "I don't know."

"Likely it was gunnysackers," one of the cowboys said, and several others grumbled agreement.

Of course. Ellie had heard of such deadly clashes between the cattlemen and sheepherders when she reached Maverick. But she sensed there was more to it than that.

Cheryl looked guilty.

"Exactly what happened?" Ellie asked.

Pearce looked away, the picture of guilt.

Cheryl sighed long and hard, then recounted what had happened before the shot rang out. "One moment we were talking and the next Reid was shoving me from harm's way. I'm quite sure he saved Mr. Pearce's life."

"How fortunate for Mr. Pearce."

"Exactly."

Cheryl stared at the sheepherder, her features momentarily registering relief, gratitude, and adoration before she stiffened, as if realizing she'd shown her true feelings. The woman wasn't putting on a show of dramatics.

No, Ellie knew that the emotions gripping Cheryl were

real and wrought from the heart. She was genuinely worried about Mr. Pearce.

That was perfectly understandable. It was obvious to Ellie that there was an intimacy between Cheryl and the sheepherder that went far beyond the bonds of friendship. Far beyond propriety.

How could she do that to Reid? Ellie turned her back on Cheryl as she tried and failed to douse her spurt of anger.

"You still out there, Miss Cade?" Moss asked.

Ellie turned to the cook shack and the old man standing in the doorway. "Yes, as plain as the nose on your face."

"If you got the stomach for it, I could use your help," Moss said. "My hand ain't as steady as it used to be."

If she had the stomach for it? He had to be kidding. She couldn't do more than fetch and carry for him. But with all eyes on her, including Reid's, she demurred and stepped inside the shack.

Reid slouched on a straight-back chair, eyes narrowed and sensual mouth pinched into a flat line of fury. Blood oozed freely from a gash near his temple.

"What do you want me to do?" she asked.

Her pa nodded to a tin box on the table. "You good at stitching?"

"As in sewing?" she asked, her voice squeaking at the end.

"As in closing up a wound," he said.

Merciful sakes . . . Ellie swallowed the sick sensation that bubbled up in her throat. He wanted her to stitch up Reid's wound.

"Well?" he asked.

"I-I'm a good seamstress, but this—" She sucked in air in a room that seemed to suddenly be short on it. "I don't know if I can."

My God, how many times had she watched her mother

tend wounds on her pa and the other outlaws? She'd sat there then and hadn't flinched at the blood and cussing that went on in an outlaw camp. But then again she'd only been eight years old.

"Get it done, Moss," Reid said.

"Best think twice about what you're asking." The old cook stuck out a hand that shook, not with fear but clearly with some sort of palsy. "Your head will look like a crazy quilt if I stitch you up."

"It doesn't matter—"

"Give me the needle and thread, Mr. Moss," she said, shrugging off her coat and rolling up the full sleeves of her blouse. "Silk floss if you have it."

"Got it right here."

"I'll need whiskey to sanitize it."

"Whiskey will do him more good inside than poured on his head," Moss said.

She glared at her pa, wondering why he was fighting her over this. Did he want Reid to be in pain?

"Then give him a glass, and a small one for me," she said.

Moss shrugged, but it was his frown that hinted he didn't think using whiskey to cleanse the wound was necessary. All the more reason for her to be the one to take care of Reid.

She threaded the needle, then plunged it in the scant half cup of liquor Moss provided.

"Booth, you and Shane ride over to Pearce's and see if you can find any tracks," Reid said, teeth clenched against the pain he must be enduring, or that he knew was coming.

"We'll get right on it, boss."

"You sure about this?" Reid asked Ellie after the two cowboys left.

"Of course." And if she told herself that enough, maybe it'd be true.

It shouldn't be that different to close a seam in cloth than it was to close a gash in a man's head. Even if the head was a hard one. Even if that head belonged to a man who heated her blood with one look.

Her mother had learned to do this shortly after she'd married her pa. By damn, she should have inherited some talent from her parents. God knew it wasn't cooking.

But did she have the grit for this? She was a teacher of young ladies. She'd been away from rough men and danger for most of her life.

She'd never had to help the man she loved, knowing she'd never be able to have more than stolen moments with him.

"Ellie?"

He said her name softly, like a caress.

It was what she needed to fling off her reservations and do what she must. She moved to stand between Reid's legs so she'd be close and have good light. His warm breath fanned her bosom and his spicy scent encircled her, drawing her closer.

She masked her shiver of desire under a feigned grimace of revulsion and dabbed whiskey on the angry slash on his head. Reid's rasp of indrawn breath echoed in the room and helped her regain her composure, if only a little.

She wet her fingers in the whiskey and squeezed the gash together. His skin was cool, but the blood oozing over her fingers was warm and sticky.

Her stomach stuttered again and she swallowed hard, startled that the room had grown suddenly warm. *Concentrate.* At least four pairs of masculine eyes were watching her, wondering if she could do it.

She wondered the same. *Concentrate.* Four small stitches should close it and leave a barely noticeable scar.

The first stitch was the hardest to make. She glanced down at Reid's face, dreading to see pain etched on his handsome features.

For a heartbeat, she spied vulnerability and longing in his midnight-blue eyes. Then he blinked and the emotions were gone, replaced by a wall of stoic masculinity.

Ellie took it for what it was—strength in the face of adversity. She turned her attention back to closing the wound. A second stitch. Then another.

Her brow beaded with perspiration in the close room. She heard each breath each of them took. She stopped herself from flinching at each creak of the floorboards when someone shifted their weight.

But it was the steady puffs of breath fanning her bosom that had heated her to an uncomfortable level. She didn't have to look down to know Reid was watching her—that his face was inches from her bosom, that she only had to lean a bit closer for him to kiss her as she longed to be kissed.

How selfish of her. He was wounded and likely devoid of intimate thoughts. He wouldn't dream of engaging in love play now.

Still, her nipples peaked and rasped against her chemise, sending tingles of need coursing through her. The heat off his widespread thighs seeped through her layers of petticoats and melted her resolve to remain unaffected by him.

Even while her mind said no, her body screamed yes. She wanted his hands stroking her from head to toe. Wanted his mouth to blaze an uncharted course over her body.

Ellie finished the last stitch and knotted it, proud each one was evenly spaced and smooth. "Do you have scissors?"

"You'll have to look for yourself," Reid said. "There's nobody here but us."

She glanced around the room and saw that her pa had left. "I was too busy to notice."

Too overcome with naughty sensations was more like it. She leaned over the table for the scissors and pressed her leg against his.

Heat fluttered through her like a thousand lightning bugs, setting off little fires everywhere they lit. It was wrong of her to feel such driving need for another woman's man, even if Cheryl Morris was more attentive to Kenton Pearce than the wounded man she was to marry.

Why, if Ellie were engaged to Reid, she never would've left his side. She certainly wouldn't be torturing herself now with the longing to sit on his lap. Straddle him perhaps?

The muscles in her thighs tightened and thrumming pangs of desire centered between her legs. She couldn't continue thinking this way, but she was helpless to stop the images from forming.

Yes, if Reid Barclay was her man, she'd ease down onto his powerful thighs. She'd run her hands over his broad chest. Her fingers would memorize every line in his face.

Her lips would press to his in a kiss that would know no end.

She'd love him with her heart and her body.

But he wasn't her man, and he'd never be. For even if he wasn't promised to another, she was still Ezra Kincaid's daughter.

She knew firsthand where the truth would lead her. Heartache.

Chapter 15

Ellie dabbed whiskey on the scissor blades and damned the fact she was torn between the two men she loved. And why did she continue to torment herself over something she could never change?

She'd not sully something as beautiful as making love with Reid with a lie. The truth could break her heart, and end her pa's life.

For one simple fact remained. Her pa was a wanted man. She had to keep his secret to keep him safe, and she wouldn't enter into an affair with Reid based on lies.

"You all right?" Reid asked.

"I am now that this is done." She snipped the floss and scooted away from him and the temptation she didn't dare satisfy. "What happened at the Pearce farm today?"

Raw fury flashed in his eyes. "Erston hired those men to kill Pearce and burn him out."

"Are you sure?"

"Yep. I talked to one of the gunnysackers, and he admitted that Erston paid him to kill Pearce," he said. "I was sure he'd given up doing it and rode off, but when I saw sunlight glinting off metal near the tree line, I knew some-body was out to pick Pearce off."

Chills tripped up her arms as she envisioned what had happened. "You got to Pearce first and took the bullet meant for him."

"In a manner of speaking. I shoved Cheryl out of the way first. Pearce knelt to help her." He heaved a sigh. "That's when I was shot."

"You could've been killed."

"So could Pearce." He frowned. "Or Cheryl."

He risked his life for them, and what was his thanks? Why, they hadn't even stayed around to ensure he was all right.

She crossed to the open door and looked out. Mr. Pearce's horse was tethered to the cast-iron ring in front of the house.

She fisted her hands in her skirt. How deuced bold of Miss Morris to invite her sheepherder into Reid's house. But then, last night proved Miss Morris went after who she fancied, for she'd strode into Reid's room to sate her desires.

Today, Miss Morris seemed more interested in Mr. Pearce. Oh, yes, Ellie knew what those knowing looks cast at him meant.

The Englishwoman was dallying with both men. "We need to get back to the house."

"What's got you so riled?" Reid asked.

"I'm not angry," she snapped, her peevish tone prov-ing she was indeed provoked. "I just don't care to spend the day here in the cook shack."

Which was a lie. She'd love nothing better than to spend quiet hours here with her pa.

Reid stepped so close his leg crushed her skirt against her thighs. "Looks like Pearce is still here."

There was absolutely no venom or annoyance in his voice. Was the man that dense?

Ellie said what was on her mind. "It isn't seemly that she's entertaining a man in the house."

"Hard to stand on decorum out here in the West."

She faced him, uncaring that her cheeks burned as hot as her temper. "That became evident after that episode last night. Really, I'd think your fiancée would be too worried about you to consider leaving your side."

One side of Reid's mouth kicked up in a grin. "I told you before this is an arranged marriage."

"That still doesn't give her the right to entertain a gentleman in your absence," she said. "Especially after last night."

"About that," Reid said. "I didn't invite Cheryl into my room."

"That hardly matters—"

"Yeah, it does." His big hands cupped her shoulders, and it was all she could do not to lean into him. "Nothing happened, Ellie."

"Really, your personal affairs are none of my business." She didn't want to hear how he'd been caught making love to Cheryl. She certainly didn't want to shake and stew with jealousy, especially now when he was so close she could grab him and kiss him like she longed to do.

"If I'd wanted to bed her, I'd have visited her room," he said, his warm breath fanning her flushed face. "But the only woman I thought of seeing was you."

A giddy rush of pleasure washed over Ellie at his words, which proved she was a lovesick fool. Had she learned nothing from her humiliating tryst with Irwin?

"Is that why you told me to lock my door?" she asked.

"Partly."

His hands settled on her waist and he eased her from

the door and prying eyes, branding her with his touch. Not one protest or admonition she knew a lady would employ to dissuade lotharios came to mind. Even the vow she'd made to stay away from him deserted her.

No, all that crossed her befuddled mind was that Reid was going to kiss her and she was going to enjoy it.

Oh, yes, she should protest. At the least she should slap the handsome face that was descending toward her instead of reaching up, grabbing his head and pulling him closer.

His mouth came down on hers with a need that stole her breath away, possessive and demanding that she give all. Not that she could deny him anything.

She opened to him, letting him have his way and doing a like amount of tongue dueling herself. Her palm slid over his chest to where his heart thundered. His big hand shifted to her breast, weighing, squeezing. The fact that she was standing here in her pa's cook shack just flitted out of her mind.

Any man who could kiss a woman till she ached to shuck her clothes and inhibitions had to be a master in pleasing her in bed. And Ellie longed to feel him inside her, to know the joy of being thoroughly loved by a man who knew what he was doing—if only for a little while.

Next week she'd be at the ladies academy in California, endeavoring to teach young ladies to guard their virtue. To never behave as wantonly as Ellie was at this moment.

Stopping this sensual attack was the sane thing to do. But she let out a surrendering moan instead and shifted closer to him.

Surely she'd know soon if he was as physically aroused as she, but the layers of clothes robbed her of that discovery. And then he pulled away and smiled down at her, the hand at her waist tethering her to him while he rubbed one hardened nipple into an aching bud.

"I leave my door unlocked." He kissed her forehead, the gesture so tender it brought tears to her eyes. "You're welcome anytime."

With that, Reid Barclay ducked out the door and strode to the house. He held his head high, and his tight behind beckoned her to follow and fondle to her heart's content.

The audacity of him to work her into a frenzy of need and walk away! Of inviting her into his room tonight.

Why, she should be spitting mad that he'd insulted her honor so. She should despise him for being an admitted cad who wanted to dally with Ellie right under his fiancée's nose.

But she was none of those things.

No, Ellie Jo Cade had decided then and there that despite the danger, she was going to take him up on his offer.

Hubert was waiting for Reid at the back door, his dour face revealing that he was none too pleased with the turn of events. If he only knew the conclusion Reid had come to, and what he'd been doing with Ellie.

"Mr. Pearce has taken his leave," Hubert said, the tone implying it wasn't a moment too soon.

"Where's my lovely fiancée?"

Hubert laughed without humor. "In her room, sir. We were fortunate that Mr. Erston is on his jaunt to Maverick, though I am sure we won't enjoy the reprieve from his company much longer."

"Wearing you down, is he?"

"Like a rasp on a worn sole." Hubert squinted at Reid's head. "I understand Miss Cade tended your wound."

"Yep. Did a fine job."

Took his thoughts completely off that niggling head-ache and onto his cock. Damn, but he'd feared that part of him was dead. It had been ever since he'd agreed to marry Cheryl.

But now, even the fact that he'd go through with the marriage didn't make his cock wilt like a field flower in the sun. Nope, Ellie had cured him. If he could just figure out a way that she could continue administering her healing touch to him when this unpleasant business was behind him.

Speaking of which, it was time to lay his cards on the table. "Ask Miss Morris to join me in my office."

"Yes, sir." But Hubert didn't budge. "Is there anything else you require?"

"Let me know the moment Erston returns."

Hubert nodded and trudged off.

Reid strode to his office, dropped into his chair and winced. He'd have to watch those quick moves for a day or so. Nothing strenuous. Though he might have to go at the vigorous exercise he had in mind for tonight a mite slower.

He leaned back in his chair, folded his hands behind his head and grinned at the plaster medallions on the ceiling. With Ellie, slow was a good thing. Yep, he fully intended to savor her for as long as he could. And then some.

Cheryl slipped into the room and paused, staring at him as if waiting for him to summon her closer. No doubt that's how Erston had treated her all her life.

"Come in and have a seat," he said.

She did, and for a change she met his gaze. "Shouldn't you be in your room resting?"

"No time for it," he said. "Erston will be back soon, and I want this settled between us before then."

She stared at her clasped hands and sighed. "Very well. Go on."

Reid sat forward and eyed his intended. There was a new tension in her face that hadn't been there before. Though Reid would like to think concern for him had caused it, he suspected her angst was over a certain sheepherder who nearly got himself shot dead today.

He shook his head. For once, he and Cheryl had something in common—they lusted after someone other than each other.

"What's going on between you and Pearce?"

Reid expected denial. Hedging at the least.

But this was Cheryl, and in the short time he'd known her, he appreciated the fact she was a straight shooter.

"I love him, and he loves me," she said.

He let her confession soak in for a minute or so. "Is that why you helped him escape England?"

"Yes. I couldn't let Burl ruin Kenton." She shivered. "Or worse."

"How'd he end up owning land nearly on top of us?"

She smiled. "Inheritance from his father," she said. "Kenton and his wife planned to move to Wyoming after Thomas was born, but she died in childbirth."

A commiserating pang of empathy burst within him, for his mother had died giving him life as well. God knows what would've happened to him if Kirby hadn't taken him in and given him a home.

Dammit, he'd screwed up in Laramie and cost Kirby and his foster brothers grief. He wasn't about to fail Dade and Trey again.

"This doesn't change anything," he told her. "Erston can make all our lives hell, and he isn't above bringing trouble down on Kenton Pearce again."

Her troubled eyes lifted to his, and her bosom

expanded with the ragged breath she took. "I know that, but I still can't marry you, Reid."

Whoa. He hadn't expected a flat-out refusal, especially after she'd sneaked into his room last night.

Reid leaned back in his chair and worried his lower lip with a thumb and forefinger. Something here just wasn't adding up right.

"You mean you don't want to marry me," he said.

"There's little difference."

"There you're wrong." Reid hadn't wanted to marry Cheryl either, but Erston had him over a barrel. "Listen, I'm not about to force you into my bed, but we have to make a show at it. Once the ranch is in our names, we can step back and change things."

"I don't care about the ranch," she said.

"Don't say that."

He drove his fingers through his hair and winced. Dammit, he couldn't lose the ranch, not when he was this close to reclaiming his home, not when he had a chance now to right the wrongs he'd done.

"It won't be that bad," he said.

She shook her head and got to her feet. "I'm so sorry, but I just can't go through with it," she said. "I never meant to cause you harm. Please believe me."

Reid stared at her, welcoming the anger building in him. He'd been promised this ranch if he married her. Now she was trying to back out of the deal.

Hell! Reid cradled his head, certain it was going to explode from pain instead of resentment.

"We agreed to marry, Cheryl," he said. "There's no backing out now."

"Things have changed, Reid. I can't marry you." She flicked him a pitying glance that he found mighty damned annoying considering she'd just cool-as-you-please jerked the rug out from under him.

Reid pressed the heels of his hands to his aching head and wondered if he should just chuck it all. But he couldn't.

There was more at stake here than owning a chunk of land.

Reid settled on a different tactic to get her to see reason. "Cheryl, I know you've got an eye for Kenton Pearce—"

"We're lovers," she said.

Holy hell! He hadn't expected her to own up to sleeping with Pearce. But at least he understood her reluctance now. Not that it changed one damn thing.

He realized she was staring at him with expectant eyes, clearly waiting for him to comment on her confession. "I'm not one to judge, Cheryl. But I do expect you to honor your vows while we're married."

"You're serious," she said, seeming shocked by that.

"Yep. The wedding takes place on Christmas Day at the ranch, or as soon after as the preacher can get here."

She clutched her hands to her bosom and backed away from him. "I won't do it, Reid. I won't agree to it."

"Calm down, Cheryl," he said. "Just hear me out. Once we marry—"

"No—"

"Look at it as a business deal," he went on. "Hell, we can divorce in one year."

Her eyes bugged. "Are you mad? I am not going to marry you for a minute, much less a year."

"If you're fretting over the scandal of a divorce—"

"I'm not, because I won't marry you, ergo I won't divorce you. What part of that don't you understand?"

"You're being bullheaded," Reid said, his patience shot to hell and his nerves fraying to fringe along with it. "Look, nobody but us will know if the marriage is consummated. We stay married long enough to force Erston out, then we part ways. You'll always have your share of the ranch, but you'll be free to go off with Pearce."

"That's it, isn't it? You're willing to do anything to gain the title to this ranch."

"It's my home, and I've never made a secret that I wanted it," he said.

But he held back admitting he was being blackmailed by Erston. That if he failed to marry Cheryl, he'd lose his share of the Crown Seven and the thoroughbreds.

A slow burn of anger kindled in him at the thought. Those horses were his. He'd worked his ass off to buy them from Kirby over the span of five long years. He'd been careful with his breeding program so he'd get top dollar off them. He damn sure wasn't going to hand them over to Burl Erston now.

Cheryl sent him a commiserating smile. "I do regret that my decision makes it more difficult for you to achieve what you want—"

"It makes it impossible." Desperation curdled in his gut. "Marry me as we'd agreed, Cheryl. That's not asking too much of you."

"Yes, it is," she said with more heat than he thought her capable of, and then in a hushed voice added, "I am with child."

Ah, hell, he couldn't have heard her right. "You're what?"

"I am carrying Kenton Pearce's child and I will not cheat him of his heir or have our child stigmatized so you can gain title to this ranch. Now do you understand?"

Reid clenched his jaw so hard his head hurt, understanding all too well. Not only would Pearce hate him for doing it, the child might come to resent him later on.

He swore long and hard as the only option he could live with loomed before him. Hell, he was going to fail his brothers again. He was going to lose his hold on his dream.

Cheryl worried her hands and stared off over the snow-crusted plains for the longest time.

"Does Erston know?"

"Unfortunately, yes," she said. "He's threatened physical harm to Kenton if I balk."

Yet she was prepared to risk all. Hell, he wouldn't be surprised to learn Erston had fired that shot that had hit Reid. He'd suspected all along it had been intended for the sheepherder. He'd simply assumed a cattleman was responsible.

"This will have to be handled carefully to outwit your guardian," he said at last.

She sighed. "We feared we'd have to elope. After the fact he can't do anything to stop us. But I'm worried about you as well. This decision hasn't come easily."

Few touchy ones did.

"I've got an idea," Reid said. "You'll have to trust me, Cheryl. Do exactly what I say without balking."

He felt her gaze burn into him for the longest time, assessing him maybe. Trying to gauge whether to put her faith in him or not.

"Can you do that?" he asked.

"I don't know."

Reid had promised Kirby he'd see that Cheryl got her share.

But to make that happen, he'd have to betray his brothers again. He'd begged them to come here and partner with him.

Now if they came, he'd be gone. And so would their claim to the Crown Seven.

Chapter 16

Reid was midway to the corral when he heard the jarring ring of bells. He looked up the drive and caught sight of a sleigh nearing the ranch, traveling too damned fast.

In moments, Burl Erston skidded past him and managed to bring the sleigh to a jarring stop, hauling back on the lines with brute force. The horse scrambled to regain his footing and tossed his head, seeming to favor a foreleg.

Reid ground his teeth and stomped toward the Englishman. Nothing pissed him off as much as a man mistreating a horse.

"If I catch you overdriving my horses again," Reid said, blocking Erston's exit from the sleigh, "you'll live to regret it."

Erston looked down his hooknose at him. "You're a bit touchy about a mere beast of burden."

"In the West, a man's life could depend on his horse."

"Ah, how I've missed your quaint adages this past year."

"Cut the bull, Erston." He stared at the frail man sitting beside Erston. "Who're you?"

"Thaddeus Arch, Baptist circuit rider."

"He missed the eastbound train, so I made it worth his

while to delay his journey," Erston said. "The wedding will take place tomorrow."

Damn the man for pushing the issue. "Why the rush?"

"There is no reason to delay things any longer." Erston's beady gaze challenged him to argue. "Besides that, the reverend would like to be on his way east before Christmas Day."

Instinct spurred Reid to argue the point, but he reined in the impulse. For once Erston was right. There was no earthly reason to put the wedding off for a few more days when they could get this over with sooner.

He damn sure wanted his tie to Erston severed soon.

"Then the wedding will take place tomorrow," he said. "But that has no bearing on my deadline to buy you out."

Erston smiled. "Indeed not. If you can get your hands on that much money in short order."

Reid walked off without bothering to reply. Time was too short to stand around jawing to a man he didn't have anything more to say to now.

Nope, he'd have it out with the Englishman tomorrow after the wedding.

A spirited whicker echoed from the paddock. His gaze fixed on the thoroughbreds milling around in the snow, their coats shimmering like velvet and clouds puffing from their nostrils.

He'd like nothing more than to continue the breeding program he'd started. Instinct told him that he had contenders in his herd.

But even though Erston gave him, Dade and Trey time to reclaim their shares, Reid would still have to part with the horses to buy the bastard out.

Reid fingered his watch from his vest pocket and thumbed open the lid. He'd have just enough time to visit Pearce's spread, then double back to Maverick.

He had to send off a wire again to Mr. Fitzmeyer—a horse breeder of high reputation outside Sedalia, Missouri.

When Reid met the man in England a year back, the horse breeder had expressed interest in Reid's stock. He'd promised that he'd pay top dollar whenever Reid was willing to sell.

He hoped to hell that offer still held.

In moments he'd saddled Kaw and swung into the saddle. A glint from the back of the house caught his eye.

Ellie Jo. She tossed something out in the snow, probably another meal gone wrong.

His mouth hitched up in a grin as he reined Kaw down the lane. He could get used to having her scorch his meals if she'd promise to heat up his bed every night.

Ellie watched Reid ride off until he was no more than a speck on the horizon and she was shivering from being out in the cold for so long. She hurried back into the house and headed toward the cooking range that defied her at nearly every turn.

She'd debated about attempting to fry a game hen for Sunday supper, but since the only thing she'd been able to prepare with a degree of success was soup, she set to work utilizing the stock from lunch to make a succotash of sorts.

It was thick and well seasoned, though the noodles had cooked to death. Just as well, she thought, since they weren't that appetizing.

Sinkers, her pa would've called them. They'd certainly done just that when she tossed them into the snow a bit ago, melting a path all the way to the bare ground.

She stood at the stove and rolled her shoulders, but

the tension was bone deep. What a strange course her life had suddenly taken.

Up until six months ago, she and Irwin had faithfully attended church services on Sunday morning, then he'd take her to his family's house for dinner. It was a very tense affair, with mother Framer being critical of everything Ellie said.

At times, her future mother-in-law's opinion even extended to the size of the mutton sleeves on her blouse, or the decreased padding in her bustle, or the loose bun she wore atop her head, which was coming in vogue.

As mother Framer endlessly explained to Ellie, a banker's wife must always present a reserved image. In short, Irwin's mother expected Ellie to be a replica of her.

Ellie had her own mind and knew how to use it, though she'd pushed her niggling worries aside. Her error.

She'd thought that by trying to heed to the Framers' wishes, Irwin and his mama alike, she'd become part of a normal family. That she'd find love.

Well, if the Framers were normal, Ellie wanted nothing to do with them. She'd been honest with Irwin, and look where that had gotten her.

Scorned. Tossed aside like yesterday's garbage.

Why, Irwin and his mother had succeeded in painting a figurative red letter on her back for all to see.

She counted herself lucky that the gossip was confined to Denver. Still, she was careful to keep her new position at the Falsmonte Ladies Academy in California secret for fear Irwin and his mother would deem it their duty to inform Mrs. Halsey she was the daughter of a notorious outlaw.

If she lost that job, she didn't know what she'd do.

Hubert trudged into the kitchen, his face more dour

than usual. "Mr. Erston has returned, accompanied by Reverend Arch."

She paused in paring a potato. "Then the preacher will be a guest through Christmas Day?"

"Actually, no," Hubert said. "The wedding date has changed."

"When is it to take place?" she asked, suspecting it would be far too soon.

Hubert gave a disapproving look. "Tomorrow."

She gaped, wondering how in the world she'd be able to prepare a wedding feast in such short order, wondering too how she'd be able to watch Reid marry Cheryl Morris.

"Is something amiss?" Hubert asked.

She shook her head, refusing to admit her heart was breaking. "I was just thinking of all I need to do tonight."

Which was a lie. Her thoughts centered entirely on Reid's bold invitation to come to his room tonight.

The audacity of the man to suggest such a thing on the eve of his wedding, with a houseful of guests.

Anger bubbled within her, but not all of it was directed at Reid. No, she was just as angry at herself for considering it, for this would surely be her last chance to lie in his arms.

All she had to do was sneak down the hall in the dead of night to satisfy her desire. She'd have a beautiful memory to hold the rest of her days of the one man she couldn't resist.

The afternoon westbound train had just pulled out when Reid rode into Maverick. He left Kaw at the livery and trudged down the boardwalk toward the depot.

Folks wreathed with smiles bustled along, their arms laden with packages. Children pressed their noses to the window of the mercantile, oohing and ahing over the toys on display.

Reid snorted and moved on. He hadn't known such things existed until he, Dade and Trey had run away from the Guardian Angel's Orphan Asylum when they were twelve.

That first winter they'd lived on the streets was an eye-opener for them, for though Dade had lived with his pa in the real world for five years, it'd been a poor existence.

The three of them had bonded in the orphanage though, forming a family of sorts that included Dade's little sister. But it wasn't long until she was adopted, and the boys faced the cruel fact that few folks wanted to take in half-grown boys.

Reid wasn't about to be apprenticed out to some trades-man. He wanted to be a cowboy, and his foster brothers felt the same.

Escaping the orphanage wasn't hard. Even hopping a train headed west proved easy enough, thanks to the help of an old hobo who showed them the ropes.

But living on the streets by their wits hardened them. Still, he could still recall that night before Christmas when they'd stood in the cold outside a fancy store in St. Louis, captivated by the toys in the window and proving they were still boys at heart.

He'd had his eye on the set of carved horses, each one so realistic he could almost imagine owning such a fine herd one day.

Now he did.

And now he had to sell them to realize another dream.

He stamped the snow off his boots and pushed inside the depot. Old Dan looked up and smiled at him through his window.

"What brings you into town?" Dan asked.

"Need to send another telegram to Missouri."

He took his time with the wire intended for Mr. Fitz-meyer and handed it to old Dan, along with the couple of dollars it cost to send it. "I'm spending the night at the Roost, so if Fitzmeyer replies, I'd appreciate you letting me know right away."

"I'll surely do that," Dan said, casting him an odd look before tapping out the message.

Reid headed out the door, suspecting word of his mar-riage tomorrow had spread through town. He had no desire to accept congratulations or condolences for get-ting leg shackled.

Folks would find out the truth soon enough.

He turned his collar up against the stiff wind and trudged through the muck and snow to the boardwalk. The harmonizing of a carol came from up ahead, but it failed to lighten his mood, for unless he trumped Burl's hand, he didn't have a damned thing to celebrate.

Yet here he was, fixing to hope for the best. The bell over the door tinkled as he stepped inside the mercantile.

The apple-cheeked owner's welcoming smile wavered just a fraction. "Afternoon, Mr. Barclay. I understand congratulations are in order."

"Wedding isn't till tomorrow."

He moved to the glass counter where an array of jew-elry was displayed. He'd put off buying a ring for Cheryl, and he regretted it. She deserved that much from him.

"What can I get for you?" the shopkeeper asked.

He pointed at a tray. "What have you got in wedding rings?"

"I have several fine rings, from simple gold bands to ones set with diamonds." She set the tray before him and pointed to the row of rings. "Diamonds signify true love."

He let that comment slide by him. "Let me see the etched one."

She obliged and he deemed the ring to be of good quality as well as attractive. But his gaze kept flicking back to the gold band set with diamonds. True love. Was such a thing possible?

"I'll take this one," he said, handing the etched band to her to package up.

"Will there be anything else?" she asked.

He picked up the one set with diamonds and turned it this way and that, noting that the light seemed to spark fire in the tiny stones. Dare he go after what he really wanted?

He handed it back to the shopkeeper. "I'll take this one too."

"Very well, sir," she said. "Would you like them placed in separate boxes?"

"Yes'm," he said as he fished out his money.

He tucked the boxes in his vest pocket and left, knowing word would spread through town that he'd bought two wedding rings. He just hoped to hell he made one woman happy.

A fine snow began falling as he made his way toward Mallory's Roost. He pushed inside the saloon, where a cloud of smoke hung from the ceiling and the stench of liquor drifted on the stale air.

Five cowboys sat at one table swapping lies, swilling rotgut and playing poker. Two of Mallory's gals hovered nearby, tempting the men to continue playing and buying booze.

Reid ignored the lot of them and headed to the bar. He braced a boot on the rail and braced his forearms on the bar top.

"Whiskey, and not the watered-down brew," Reid said.

Mallory muttered a curse but fetched a bottle from

under the bar and sat it in front of Reid. "Heard you'll be a married man tomorrow."

"Figured word had spread." Reid poured a glass and tossed it back. "What else is being said about me?"

Mallory snorted. "That the sheriff in Laramie took a bribe to set you free and pin the murder on Ezra Kincaid."

That explained the odd look old Dan at the depot gave him, and the reserved one from the shopkeeper. Hell, he was surprised the truth hadn't gotten out before now.

"Who can I thank for enlightening folks?" Reid asked.

"Frank Arlen," Mallory said. "He was in here the other night, three sheets to the wind and swapping tall tales with a couple of cowpokes."

"That sounds like Arlen. Full of lies and bullshit." But this time he told the truth.

Mallory nodded. "He was grousing about how he'd worked briefly for the Crown Seven, and that you'd fired him."

"Yep, and I don't regret it." Arlen was the laziest man on the spread, and caused nothing but trouble among the men.

"Aye, he seems to relish brewing trouble," Mallory said. "He thought it amusing that Kincaid had stolen your stallion, and went on to say it nearly happened two years ago as well."

"The local papers told all back then," he said, though he'd not seen one of them. "All except the part about Erston paying the sheriff to turn a blind eye. I supposedly escaped, and then a witness came forward and pointed a damning finger at Kincaid, and exonerated me."

Even so, some folks suspected Reid was guilty.

Mallory snorted. "Arlen claims to have witnessed it."

That brought him up short. "If that's true, then why didn't he say something to me when he hired on?"

"Maybe he thought to use what he knew later on," Mallory said. "Arlen bet he'd bring Kincaid in and collect the reward."

Damn! Arlen wouldn't care if Kincaid was dead or alive either.

The door opened, shooting an arrow of bright light and bitter cold into the saloon. Mallory muttered a curse and walked off.

Reid poured another drink and glanced at the newcomer, mindful of the last time he was here and Ellie Jo walked in.

A black hat pulled low over his brow shaded the man's face, but he recognized the man just the same. Marshal Tavish.

"I'm obliged you came to town," Tavish said. "Saves me the trouble of riding out to your spread."

Reid sipped his whiskey and held the burn in his mouth before sending it to his gut. "You got something to say, then say it."

Tavish braced his arms on the bar and caught Reid's gaze with his own. "You've got quite the reputation. What I can't decide is if you're innocent or guilty."

That was the same question Reid had wrestled with for two long years. When he had roused from his stupor the day after the shooting, he was plagued with the nightmare of a woman lying dead in the street, and the damning accusation that he'd killed her.

Didn't matter that he'd been aiming at the outlaw about to steal his horse. The bullet that took her life had come from his sidearm.

Or had it?

"Afraid I can't help you," Reid said.

Tavish shifted and the brass foot rail trembled a bit, as

if the marshal had jammed a boot on it too. "You're not going to defend yourself?"

"Nope. I was too drunk to remember what happened."

The marshal placed two bits on the bar and raised a finger. A moment later, a mug of frothy beer came sliding down the bar toward him.

"I read up on it, and it seemed mighty convenient that a witness came forth after you'd escaped from jail." The marshal took a drink and eyed him. "I heard a substantial amount of money was donated to the local sheriff at that time."

His nape grew uncomfortably warm from anger and embarrassment. Obviously Erston had convinced Kirby the safest bet was to pay off the local law. But had the bastard bought a witness too?

Reid wished to hell he knew.

He faced the marshal but kept his emotions carefully banked. "You thinking of hauling me to jail?"

"Nope. A witness swore Kincaid killed her."

He wasn't convinced. "Reckon the man who brings in Ezra Kincaid will make a name for himself."

"Reckon we'll see." The marshal finished off his beer and pushed away from the bar. "Did you know who she was?"

"Who?"

"Lisa True, the woman you may or may not have killed."

He shook his head. "Never saw her before, and never heard nothing about her either."

The marshal drew in a slow, chest-expanding breath and stared at Reid with eyes that had gone black with some emotion he couldn't read. "It's a sad fact that the attention of that crime centered on Ezra Kincaid and you. Her name isn't even mentioned on half the wanted posters I've come across."

There was no mistaking this time that Marshal Tavish had more than a passing interest in this murder. That fact put him in a mighty touchy situation.

"Hell, you knew her," Reid said.

That's why he was busting his ass to find Ezra Kincaid. That's why he was keeping an eye on Reid as well.

Tavish scowled at the wall, his expression as cold and hard as ice. "She was on her way to my sister's wedding in Pine Bluff when she got waylaid."

Ah, hell! "What happened?"

"Nobody knows. She missed her train, and the sheriff there assumed she'd gone to the livery to hire a buggy." Grief clouded Tavish's eyes, then vanished under that cool regard again. "The mortician said she'd been abused recently."

Reid set his back teeth, disgusted to think some man had raped her. "I sure as hell wouldn't do that."

"I have trouble believing the old rustler would do such a thing either," Tavish said.

"That means there was likely a third man, and he got away with having his way with her."

Tavish gave a curt nod. "Just what I thought."

A new worry sank its teeth in him and wouldn't let go. "What if the killer and the rapist are one and the same?"

"Then he'd best hope I don't find out he did it." Tavish made to leave.

"One more thing," Reid said, and the marshal stopped beside him. "According to Mallory, Frank Arlen swears he'll bring Kincaid in and collect the reward."

"You think he knows where he's hiding?"

He snorted. "Maybe. Arlen can look you in the eye and lie through his teeth. I'd guess him to be brave enough to shoot Kincaid in the back and haul his carcass in to the law."

"I'll bear that in mind."

The marshal turned and walked out the door without another word. Not that there was more to say.

Tavish had vowed to see justice served. But they both knew he had a snowball's chance in hell of finding the lowlife who'd raped Lisa, and he knew the unknown would hound him all his days.

Chapter 17

Reid hadn't even bothered to come home last night. That fact stuck in Ellie's craw as she hurried around the kitchen, frantically trying to put together a wedding feast.

Not that she expected a crowd.

Not that the bride had showed any excitement over her special day or all the trouble that she and Hubert were going through.

Well that wasn't entirely true. Miss Morris hurried down the rear stairs and into the kitchen. One look was all it took to see the woman was beset with a case of nerves.

"I have a huge favor to ask of you," Miss Morris said.

Ellie crossed her fingers and hoped the lady didn't request some extravagant dish for the wedding dinner. "What would that be?"

"I would like for you to be my bridesmaid."

Oh, this was just too cruel. How could she stand there so close to Reid while he pledged his troth to Miss Morris?

"I don't know how I can do that, and have the wedding dinner ready afterward."

"Bother the dinner," Miss Morris said. "Please, I desperately need a woman by my side."

For one brief moment she was tempted to tell Miss Morris that her husband-to-be was a philandering cad. But the hope she saw in the woman's eyes dashed that thought.

"Very well, but you'll have to take me as I am," she said, giving her gray skirt a shake. "Sans apron for the ceremony, of course."

"Of course." Miss Morris beamed. "Thank you so much."

After giving Ellie's hands an affectionate squeeze, the young woman turned and dashed up the stairs again.

Ellie released the groan she'd held back earlier. This was going to be the most trying day of her life, but she hadn't the heart to disappoint the bride.

She simply felt that Miss Morris had been cheated out of enough traditions. There'd be no piano music to accompany her down the makeshift aisle Hubert had created in the parlor and that she'd festooned with greenery and ribbons.

The bitter weather robbed Miss Morris of a fresh bouquet, and the silk and chenille one Ellie put together in the wee hours of the morning was a pitiful substitute.

And last but not least, the tension pulsing in the house made it feel more like a wake than a wedding.

She checked the tiny watch she had pinned to her bodice. Her eyes bugged.

Her plum cake should've been removed from that testy hotbox ten minutes ago.

She made a mad dash for the oven and removed the cake. Her shoulders slumped. The top was far too brown and the edges were crusty. She only hoped that a layer of white icing she whipped up would hold in what little moisture remained in the cake.

As for her entrée, she decided on veal cutlets—or rather a version thereof, since she was substituting venison for veal. The accompanying vegetables were scalloped onions and a potato puff casserole.

The latter had sounded easy to prepare, but her mixture was a sticky mass that would never pour into the deep dish as the recipe instructed. She was debating whether to add more milk or butter when someone pounded on the back door.

She looked up, expecting Hubert to answer it. But when the knocking continued and the older man failed to make an appearance, she wiped her hands and hurried to the door.

The last person she expected to see standing on the other side was Kenton Pearce. But there he was with a nervous smile pasted on his face. He held a small boy in his arms, and a stout older woman stood by his side.

"Good afternoon," he said. "I'm Kenton Pearce."

"I know who you are," she said.

He cleared his throat. "Of course. This is Mrs. Hatch and my son, Thomas. Mr. Barclay instructed us to use this door for obvious reasons."

Good heavens! Did Reid invite Pearce to his wedding?

Apparently so, for the sheepherder was clearly dressed in his Sunday best. Well it wasn't her place to voice her objections. Nor would she referee any shouting matches that were likely to ensue once Burl Erston saw the sheepherder had been invited to his ward's wedding.

She stepped back and waved them in. "You'll have to excuse me while I see to dinner."

"May I be of assistance?" Mrs. Hatch asked.

Ellie was sorely tempted to accept, but it was beyond polite to put a guest to work. "Thank you, but I can manage." She hoped.

She returned to her potato mixture and the dilemma

of reducing it to a thinner consistency. She grabbed the butter and caught the older woman's frown.

Flustered, she set the butter down and reached for the bottle of milk. The old woman nodded.

"I typically add crumbled bacon and a small fried onion to the mixture," Mrs. Hatch said.

She wasn't about to ignore sound cooking advice. "I have some bacon already crumbled." Left over from breakfast.

She easily filched an onion from the ones she'd set to boil and cut it up to add to the mixture. To her amazement, it poured like thick cream into the deep dish.

With that out of the way, she iced the plum cake in drifts of fluff while Mrs. Hatch prepared a gravy from the drippings. They finished at the same time, and shared a knowing smile.

"I'll never be able to thank you enough for your help," Ellie said.

"Pshaw! Think nothing of it."

The clearing of a masculine throat drew all their attention. "Mr. Barclay requests your presence at the wedding."

Ellie would rather go hide in her room, but she knew she couldn't. She removed her soiled apron and gave her simple gray day dress a close scrutiny. Thankfully it was devoid of grease, flour and batter.

They filed down the hall to the parlor. Mr. Pearce and Mrs. Hatch took chairs on the groom's side.

A look around showed that most of the Crown Seven cowboys were in attendance. All stayed on the groom's side, kept their hats on and their guns strapped to their sides.

Ellie stood at the back with her trembling hands clasped together, hesitant to take the walk down the aisle where the groom waited. My, but he was a devastatingly handsome man.

Reid wore black trousers, a black shirt, black hat, and a black gun belt strapped low on his lean hips. The hard angles of his face were devoid of expression, and his broad shoulders were racked tighter than a coat stand.

But when his gaze honed in on hers, she felt the burn of desire clear to her soul. Damn the man! How could he stand here at his wedding and flick her a look that promised untold pleasures could be found in his arms?

Hubert stood beside her. "It is time to take your place, Miss Cade."

"All right."

Except it wasn't all right to walk toward the preacher and Reid Barclay. It was sheer hell.

Her knees knocked and her heart threatened to pound out of her chest. She'd dreamed of this moment herself, but she'd been the bride. She'd been head over heels in love with the groom.

And her pa had been there to give her away.

Simple traditions.

But nothing about her life was simple anymore.

Oh, she had no doubt Reid could satisfy her wildest dreams. But their opportunity had come and gone.

Yes, she loved him. Yes, she wanted him. But she wouldn't be a married man's mistress.

Remembering that put a bit of starch into her spine. It also helped if she didn't make eye contact with the groom. Now if she just didn't feel his gaze on her—

Hubert looked into the hall, then stared at Reid and nodded. Now what was that about?

The bride stepped into the parlor, her hand resting lightly on her guardian's. All the cowboys stood, but none removed their hats.

Cheryl Morris sent a shaky smile at Reid. Ellie didn't dare glance his way to see if love shone in his eyes. She just wasn't that strong.

Mr. Erston escorted Miss Morris toward the preacher and Reid faster than was seemly. But he came to an abrupt stop the moment he laid eyes on Mr. Pearce.

"Bloody hell!" Erston said. "What's he doing here?"

"I invited him," Reid said.

Miss Morris flicked a longing look Mr. Pearce's way, and Ellie wondered again if Reid Barclay was blind. But then fidelity didn't mean anything to him.

If it did, he wouldn't have taken liberties with Ellie.

"Who gives the bride away?" the wiry preacher asked in a commanding voice.

"I do," Erston said.

He guided Miss Morris toward Reid and made a show of handing her into his care. With a smirk, he turned and took the lone chair stationed on the bride's side.

"Is there anyone present who objects to the joining of these two people?" the preacher asked.

"I do," Reid said.

Erston shot to his feet.

So did Kenton Pearce.

"What is the meaning of this?" Erston asked.

"Sit down, Erston," Reid said.

"Do not attempt to order me about," Erston said. "Now get on with this wedding."

"Gladly." Reid backed up. "Take your place, Kenton."

Before Ellie could blink, the sheepherder leapt forward to stand as the groom. This wasn't happenstance. This had been carefully planned by Reid, Cheryl and Pearce.

Why, she was so touched by his selflessness that tears stung her eyes. Lord knew she wasn't one prone to such.

"You can't do this," Erston thundered, on his feet again.

"The hell I can't." And to prove it, Reid pulled his gun and leveled it on Erston. "Now sit down and shut up."

Erston defied him for all of thirty seconds before the whisper of guns drawn from leather forced him to sit. A cold premonition passed over her heart as she watched the Englishman.

She'd never seen such blazing hatred before.

The preacher glanced from the bride to the groom, then launched into the ceremony. Ellie listened to the words and the obvious devotion of the bride and groom as they made their vows.

She lifted her gaze to Reid, but his attention remained fixed on Burl Erston. He'd cause them all grief. She was certain of it.

"Do you have a ring?" the preacher asked.

The sheepherder's face flushed red, and his eyes flashed an apology to the woman who'd soon be his wife. "No."

"Yes," Reid said, and pressed something into Pearce's hand.

The man turned to Reid who merely shrugged. "Get on with it."

"I have a ring," Pearce said, and Miss Morris sniffled as he slid the etched gold band on her third finger.

"It's beautiful," she said, clutching Kenton's hand while sending a smile to Reid.

He nodded and continued his vigil, watching Erston. That man was far too quiet.

"In the eyes of God and man, I pronounce you man and wife," the preacher intoned. "Go on and kiss her."

Pearce swept his bride into his arms and kissed her with all the passion young lovers can elicit.

Ellie finally took a decent breath. This was the first

wedding she'd ever been a part of, and she was sure she'd never forget a moment of it as long as she lived.

The newlyweds broke their kiss, but remained in each other's arms as they turned to Reid.

"Thank you," Pearce said.

Reid dipped his chin. "Treat her right or you'll answer to me."

"I'll adore her all my days," Kenton said, and Ellie knew he spoke from the heart.

The new Mrs. Pearce slipped from her husband's arms and crossed to Reid. "I never knew why my father favored you so until today." She reached on tiptoe and placed a kiss on his cheek. "I love you like a brother. Remember that."

His mouth pulled into a crooked smile that melted Ellie's heart all over again. How could she have misjudged this man so?

"You'd best be going on your honeymoon," Reid said.

Ellie sensed that the newlyweds wanted to say more, but Burl Erston's presence was a poison that tainted the special day.

As the couple filed out, Mrs. Hatch and young Thomas followed. Ellie did the same as they hurried into the kitchen, casting one more glance back at Reid just to assure herself that he was real. That she hadn't dreamed this up.

"I don't know where you're going, but please feel free to take any of the food," Ellie said to the Pearces.

Cheryl and Kenton shook their heads, but Mrs. Hatch jumped at the offer. "If we could have a meal for today, I wouldn't have to raid the kitchen of our new benefactor so soon."

Ellie produced a large porcelain dinner pail, sensing

they weren't traveling that far. Just what had Reid arranged for them?

Mrs. Hatch took a fair portion for their meal. "Thank you for your kindness," she said again.

Then they were all off in Pearce's sleigh. They would do fine. But if the shouting coming from the parlor was any indication, Reid Barclay was in for the fight of his life.

"You'll live to regret your defiance," Erston said.

Reid laughed. His only regret regarding this decision was not making it sooner. "Don't bet on it."

Erston walked to the tree Ellie had fussed over and stared at it a long, tense moment. "You stood a chance of retaining this ranch, but I doubt you'll be able to hold on to it now."

"I've got until the end of Christmas Day to claim my shares and buy you out."

"So do your former partners," Erston said. "Either of them could come forward and offer me a fetching sum for my shares in this desolate ranch."

It was a possibility Reid was aware of. "It's their right, same as mine."

"Ah, yes, the brotherhood of the urchins. I would think this past year has taught you that they don't want any dealings with you or this ranch."

"It's likely they never received my letter."

Erston snorted. "It's likely they don't give a damn. Or," he said, adding emphasis to that one word, "they are waiting for the moment to seize control of the ranch and boot you off as thanks for deserting them."

Had he planned it that way from the start? "I didn't leave out of choice."

"They don't know that."

Reid studied the man who'd controlled his life for the past two years and knew he hadn't been the only one under Erston's control. Win, lose, or draw, those days were over.

He wanted answers, and by damn he'd have them now.

"What did you force Kirby to do?" he asked.

"Besides hand over his shares to me to finance the payoff to the law?" Erston let out a chuckle that grated on his nerves. "Kirby was dying. He had no need for anything but atonement for deserting his daughter."

That wasn't the way Reid had heard it, but he wasn't in the mood to argue over that point. "How often did you remind Cheryl that her pa didn't want her?"

Erston hiked a shoulder. "It came up when the need arose."

"What was in it for you?" Reid asked, flat out.

The Englishman rocked back on his chair and stared at Reid for so long he was sure the man was refusing to answer. Just when he was about to ask another question, Erston spoke.

"Kirby owned a small parcel of land in Bath and I wanted it."

"To sell?"

Erston nodded. "I've no interest in being a financially strapped landowner."

Meaning he intended to do as Reid had suspected all along and sell his shares of the Crown Seven as soon as possible. So why send him back here for a year? Why insist that he marry Cheryl in America and combine their shares in the ranch?

The answer was as obvious as the new scar on his head. "You never intended for me to marry Cheryl. But if we did, she'd end up a young widow."

"How bloody astute. You, more than the others, looked

on this ranch as your home," he said. "I knew you wouldn't willingly part with your shares."

He was right, though he still couldn't believe his brothers hadn't cared enough to fight for the ranch Kirby had left them. But then they'd believed that Reid had double-crossed them and stole their shares.

"You could have had me killed in England," he said. "Why go through this elaborate ruse to return here?"

"The laws are far different there," he said. "Kirby told me that it wasn't unusual for a man to die from a well-placed bullet and his killer would never be found."

That day at Pearce's ranch made sense now. The cowboy he'd intercepted had fessed up that he'd been hired to wipe out everyone living at the sheep ranch. That was done to switch the blame from Erston to the gunnysackers out to rid the high plains of sheep and sheepherders.

All the while a lone gunman was lying in wait. "You ever stop to think what would have happened if one of Pearce's herders had caught that bullet?"

"Are you insinuating my aim is less than adequate?"

"I'm still alive," Reid said.

"Unfortunately."

Reid's disgust for Burl Erston shot higher than a just-tapped oil vein. "Hubert has taken the time to pack your bags, and Shane saw they were loaded onto a sleigh. I'll give you five seconds to clear out."

"You can't be serious," Erston said.

"Yeah, I can." He whispered his Colt from the holster and took a bead on Burl Erston. "One."

"Good God, Barclay," he said, shooting to his feet. "Have you lost your mind?"

He thumbed back the hammer. "Two."

"Damn you!" Erston stormed from the house, slamming the door in his wake.

Reid holstered his Peacemaker, well aware this war wasn't over yet. Nope, if the sale of those horses didn't go through, he could kiss this place good-bye.

Chapter 18

After partaking of the wedding feast she'd partially had a hand in, Reid thanked Ellie for her help and left the house. Another mare was due to foal, and since he'd sent two hands over to Pearce's farm to help keep watch, he had to pitch in and help with the horses.

Ellie suspected he enjoyed it, but she also knew he'd miss this ranch more than he would the stock. Though he was proud of his horses, he could replace them in time. He'd not replace the memories he'd created here with Kirby Morris, Dade and Trey.

Yes, she'd certainly seen a different side to Reid Barclay today. With Cheryl married to the man she loved, there was nothing standing in the way of Ellie following her desires. Nothing except fear over how he'd react when he learned she was Ezra Kincaid's daughter. Dare she trust her heart again?

She wasn't sure.

With the house put back in order and enough leftovers to do Reid, Hubert and her for supper, Ellie bundled up and left the house. Maybe it was her imagination, but it didn't feel as cold out.

This evening would be the perfect time for her to visit at length with her pa. Before long her time here would be over, and her new position in California would begin.

But the excitement and gratitude she'd felt at joining the Falsmonte Ladies Academy was absent. She didn't know when she'd ever see her pa again. And Reid? Well, he'd be just a memory she'd hold close to her heart.

She made it to the cook shack without any problem and rapped on the door. When nobody answered, she pounded on the panel a bit harder.

The door to the bunkhouse opened and a cowboy poked his head out. "If you're looking for Moss, he's gone hunting."

"Oh, thank you."

The cowboy ducked back inside the bunkhouse and closed the door. Now what?

A sound from the stables across the way caught her attention. Reid stood there, staring at her.

Should she return to the house? Or go to him?

"How is it going?" she asked him.

"Not far from birthing," he said, and started toward her again, his long legs eating up the distance in no time. "I need a couple of old blankets for when she foals."

"Does it take long?" she asked as she trailed him into the barn and to the room filled with all manner of saddles and tack.

"Hard to say. Every birth is a bit different." He draped two blankets over his shoulder. "This one shouldn't be foaling now, but the stallion broke free and got to her."

"Do you need any help?"

He stopped and looked down at her. "Nope. You ever see a horse born before?"

She shook her head. For all her education, the mystery of birth was still that. A mystery.

He glanced from the stables back to her and heaved a sigh. "If you want to watch, and think you have the stomach for it, then come ahead. But you can't do anything that'll stress the mare."

"I'll do exactly what you tell me to do," she said and fell into step beside him.

That earned a wicked wink and set her mind churning on things other than horses. Despite the bite of cold, she felt her face flushing as well, but if Reid noticed, he didn't comment.

He opened the stable door for her and she hurried inside, surprised it was light and relatively warm inside. Restive whickering came from a stall midway down the aisle.

The horse circled the pen, her sides quivering. "She's about ready," Shane said, his voice pitched soft.

Reid laid the blankets beside a stack of towels and slipped inside the stall. "Easy girl," he said, running a hand over the mare's bulging belly and beneath. "We're getting milk now."

The mare nickered softly and made one more circle of the pen before going down on her front legs, and then easing her body down on the bed of straw. Ellie's heart pounded as the mare kicked her leg before dropping her head down.

Reid talked softly to the mare, reassurances mainly, as he caught the tail in a soft cloth that held it out of the way.

She had an unobstructed view of the mare, and watching the changes come over the horse was both a shock and a thrill. Watching the gentle manner that Reid fussed over the mare filled her with renewed compassion.

He cared. There was no other explanation for it.

The mare whickered and kicked again, and Ellie's

mouth dropped open as the animal's sides bulged. The birthing itself happened in a span of minutes.

Reid wrapped a towel around the baby horse and rubbed it down while the mare delivered the afterbirth. Shane quickly saw to that while the mare gained her feet and gave a great shake.

"What a fine foal," Reid said.

"Is that a female or a male?" she asked.

"Female, with the same strong lines as her mama." He smiled at her, and the uninhibited joy on his face took her breath away. "You want to come in and take a closer look?"

Ellie tossed a nervous glance at the mare. "Will she mind?"

He shook his head. "Etain's a gentle one." He reached out to pat the mare's shoulder.

She took him at his word and slipped inside the stall. The foal stood on wobbly legs that looked far too long and fragile to support her.

"She's just beautiful," Ellie said, and reached out to pet the newborn.

The foal sniffed and nuzzled her hand. "She's trying to suckle my fingers."

"That's good. Let her suckle them while you lead her to the mare's udder."

Ellie did, moving at a snail's pace and nearly overcome with awe when the foal exchanged her fingers for the mare's teat. The mare whickered and nuzzled the foal.

"It's a miracle," she said.

He smiled. "It happens every day."

"Maybe, but I've never seen anything this wonderful before," she said, looking around the stall and thinking of another birth that happened ages ago and gave cause to celebrate Christmas.

Life.

That's what Christmas was about.

Life, love, and the promise of tomorrows.

Shane returned. "I can handle it from here on."

"Yep, this one doesn't look like it'll cause us trouble." Reid took Ellie's arm. "Let's head back."

She smiled, for she didn't trust her voice. She didn't argue either when they stepped outside into the still beauty of an early evening and he draped an arm around her and hauled her close.

As they walked toward the house, she realized she'd never felt this close to anyone. Just with Reid.

He dropped his arm from her when they reached the house. She ducked inside and moved toward the kitchen, thinking the house never seemed so quiet.

"Would you like coffee?" she asked.

"Nope. I've got to clean up, then tend to some book-work." He stopped at the bottom of the stairs and looked back, his eyes dark and sparking with passion. "I'll be done with it in an hour. If you want me then, I'll be in my room."

After giving her another wink that left her tingling, he turned and tramped up the stairs.

Ellie stood there for a long time.

This was it.

He'd invited her to his room, and she surely knew it wasn't to talk.

It was all up to her whether to run to her room and bolt the door, or take that walk down the hall.

Well past an hour later, Reid prowled his room like a restless cougar. His blood pulsed in thick hot waves and his cock stirred with that first twitch of an arousal.

He welcomed the sensation even though he cursed the predicament he was in. The light was on low. He was ready to pleasure a woman. Not just any woman.

Nope, he wanted Ellie Jo Cade under him. Wanted to get lost in her expressive eyes as he buried himself in her heat.

Thinking of how thoroughly he longed to love her kept him hard while his senses fired sheet lightning. Soon. It had to be soon or he'd lose his damned mind.

He groaned and combed his fingers through his hair. The heavy need settling in his groin had him walking with care. Had him fretting too. What if she didn't come?

The glow of a full moon drifted through his windows, ribboned across the floor and spread like a blanket over his bed. His empty bed.

The house had fallen quiet hours ago, like it had been tucked in for the night. Would she come to him?

He wasn't sure. He could go to her, but he wouldn't.

If they had sex, it had to be her choice. She had to come to him first. Dammit, he wanted her to come first.

He wanted her. He needed her so damned badly.

Reid stomped to the door and dropped his forehead on the cool, smooth wood. He pressed both palms on the panel and felt his blood surging like a swollen river of need.

His teeth hurt and his skin felt close to busting. He damned sure couldn't close his eyes without seeing her inviting smile. He couldn't stomp around the room like a maddened bull because the rub of his pants on the swollen tip of his head had him close to coming.

He couldn't draw in a decent breath without smelling lilacs, for crying out loud.

He'd hurt to be inside a woman before, but never this bad. He'd never felt this needy. This vulnerable. He'd never been this unsure of himself and so sure of the crazy ideas twirling in his head like a killer twister dancing over the ground.

But the notions wouldn't stop either. If he could hang on to the ranch, he'd be free to go after Ellie. If he lost the ranch and everything he owned, he could offer nothing but hard times and heartache.

Over the pounding of his heart he heard a creak. A door? It had to be.

Reid slid a hand to the door handle, his fingers curling around the knob like a shadow, laying siege to it like a thief in the night. But he couldn't bring himself to wrench it open.

But as time stretched out, a taut silence wove a knot of tension in the house. Had wishful thinking conjured up that sound? No doubt it had, for nothing stirred in the house except his longing for Ellie.

She wasn't coming.

It didn't matter why. She wasn't going to take him up on his challenge.

Fine.

He'd put her from his mind.

Except he couldn't.

Go to her, fool.

He pinched his eyes shut and drew in a labored breath, then another. His fingers tightened around the cool brass knob so hard he felt the raised design branding itself in his palm.

One more breath. Then another. He wasn't a chickenshit, but he sure as hell was acting like one now.

He respected women. But he'd never ached to love a woman like he did Ellie.

Damn his pride. He'd beg her if he had to, but he'd sate his lust this night.

Reid wrenched open the door. And forgot to breath.

For Ellie Jo Cade stood outside his door wrapped in lilac-scented shadows and seductive magnetism. She'd come to him, garbed in a simple wrapper that he ached to peel her out of.

Restless energy hummed between them. He heard her swallow. Saw her timid smile and telltale shiver.

"Well?" Her question whispered over his heated skin like a fingernail trailing down his spine.

"You talk too much."

Reid slinked an arm around her narrow waist and hauled her in his room. As he eased the door shut with a barely discernible click, his mouth claimed hers.

She tasted of mint and excitement, opening to him with a throaty groan that vibrated over his skin and arrowed to his crotch. Damn, he'd half expected his body's explosive reaction to her, but he hadn't considered she'd be a noisy lover.

Hell, he hadn't thought of much beyond his driving need to bury himself inside her. Now!

He fumbled to twist the key in the lock with a hand that was all thumbs, then wrapped both arms around her and pulled her flush against him. He swallowed his own noisy groan as those twin nipples shot fire straight through his body.

His cock jerked and his thinking blurred. Hanging on to rational thought was nigh as impossible as closing the barn door against a howling wind.

He was almost there when she did some sort of gyration that had fireworks going off behind his eyes. His cock bucked like a just-lassoed mustang.

"Oh, yes, yes, yes, yes," she said on a reedy moan.

Music to his ears. Seductive music.

He'd have to keep kissing her to muffle those little

sounds of pleasure that were bubbling up from her like champagne, popping in his blood and intoxicating him with her ardor. Had he ever been with a woman who was this passionate?

Not that he could recall.

He'd never let a woman get the better of him, but he was fast losing ground to this seductress.

Another abnormality, for he'd been pleasured by high-priced women who knew all the tricks. He knew them all, and prided himself on his ability to keep a cool head while he pleasured a woman.

He never lost control until he spewed his seed. Soon as he'd recovered from attaining his release, he took charge of the situation again. Always.

Except with Ellie.

With her everything was different. Everything was new. Everything was perfect.

He backed her toward the bed and worked a hand between their fused bodies, pausing once to let his mouth love hers. If he didn't get her naked and under him soon he'd go off for sure.

A long sultry moan burst from her and bounced off the walls.

"Shhh."

"Shhh," she repeated against his lips, and the buzz of that touch raced from his mouth to the throbbing end of his cock.

Shit, he was going to blow his head. Too soon. He dragged in a shaky breath that smelled of lilacs and hot need.

Whoa up, cowboy. Your ride's gonna be over before it starts if you don't slow down.

But slowing down seemed to be the farthest thing from Ellie's mind. It was up to him. What'd he been doing? Her buttons. Getting her naked. Keeping her quiet, or at least muffled so Hubert wasn't privy to everything they did.

"Where's the fire?" he asked when he knew damned good and well flames were licking through his blood.

"You talk too much." As if to prove her point in tossing his words back at him, she darted her tongue in his mouth and kissed him until he quaked.

Hot damn! He was going to die right here with the most god-awful aching hard-on he'd ever had in his life.

He popped the last button off her wrapper and shoved the garment off her, raining kisses from her mouth to the high frilly collar of her nightgown. He'd never seduced a woman who was so primly dressed and so hot to handle.

She was a perfect blend of cultured and naughty. Refined and wild. And she was his.

His mouth trailed to her ear and down her neck where a pulse frantically hammered away. He could hear it drumming, or was that his blood pounding in his veins?

He bunched her nightgown up her hips to her waist, grabbed her waist and hoisted her onto his big bed. But instead of shucking his clothes, he followed her down because she had two hands full of his shirt.

But that was okay. He had her where he wanted her. In his bed, on her back, naked. Well, near naked.

His big fingers fussed with the buttons on her gown, working one loose. Two. All the while those long legs of hers were wrapping around his hips and drawing him to the heat of her.

His cock felt too full and tight. His nerves twanged like guitar strings that'd been plucked too hard. Raw need vibrated through him like a war cry.

He forgot who was seducing who here. Hell, he didn't care.

That wasn't like him. He tried to regain the control he'd lost the moment he dragged her into his arms. To hell with it.

Sweat streaked his face and trekked down his back as he struggled to unbutton her damned nightgown. She had no such problems opening his shirt.

That first whiff of cool air on his heated skin cleared his head. Not that it lasted. Her palms flattened on his bare chest and skimmed circles on his skin, creating friction sparks that surely could be seen in the darkness.

He gritted his teeth and kept working the damned button, trying not to think how her hot mons rubbed his swollen cock each time she arched her back. He gave up getting her naked and tried to rip off his own clothes first.

Her palms skimmed up his chest and her thumbs raked his nipples. A guttural moan burst from him.

"Shhh," she said on a wicked laugh.

He couldn't take the torment one second longer. He reared back and tore his shirt up and over his head, flinging it aside. Or trying to.

One arm remained in a sleeve, but he could live with it. He freed the last tiny damned button on her gown and whisked it over her head.

For one moment, he drank his fill of her beauty in the waning moonlight, of the eyes that sparked with desire and challenge. Of the generous bosom crested with pink nipples, rising and falling in desperation and begging for his hands and mouth.

He bent to adore one globe just as her fingers skimmed the scar aside his head, her touch so light he almost didn't feel it. He pushed the memory of getting shot from his mind and turned his attention back on the woman in his bed.

Her hand drifted over his shoulder and hung on while the other closed over his cock. He bucked once, nearly coming in her hand.

"Easy."

"I don't want easy," she whispered, leading him as easily as a stallion ready to rut a mare.

That first touch of wet, hot woman jolted through him like lightning, swift and electric. Spasms rippled through him as she lifted her hips, seating him deeper.

He held himself up on arms that trembled, wanting to sink into her slowly, savoring every inch.

She had other ideas. Faster than he could blink, she wrapped those long legs around him and brought them together in a clap of thunder that made his ears pop.

The fit was tight and perfect, like they were made for each other. A romantic notion he'd have laughed at before, but it was there before him, and the sense of oneness was just getting stronger the longer he stared into her big eyes.

And then she smiled. A cat-licking-cream pleased smile. She had him by the balls and knew it.

He rocked his hips and pushed all the way inside her. Her eyes rounded in surprise, and he smiled down at her. *Now who's in control?*

Before he could savor that victory, her muscles tightened around his length and pulled at him. All the blood in his body rushed to his cock and a low groan rumbled from him.

Her eyes glazed with lust, her lips flushed and parted in surrender, her breath coming hard and fast as she moved and shifted and drove him mad with want. He knew instinctively that this was the calm before one helluva storm that was about to crash over them.

Some part of his brain that wasn't fogged by lust told him to kiss her and keep kissing her. Their mouths fused in hungry abandon as their bodies bucked and arched in a frenzied rhythm. To hell with finesse and control. She was giving as good as she got, and he was damned lucky just to hang on this long and enjoy the ride of a lifetime.

Knowing he couldn't last long enough to give her pleasure, he reached between them. Before his fingers grazed the damp hair where they joined, she stiffened and let out a keening wail that would've awakened everyone in the house and bunkhouse if he hadn't swallowed the sound.

Damned good thing too, because those spasms exploding in her pushed him over the edge. His own hoarse groan ripped from his mouth and into her. On and on . . .

With his desire and good sense spent, he had barely enough strength left to roll to his side. He smiled and gathered her close. Satisfied. Replete. Complete.

That last feeling scared the shit out of him. But now that he'd had her, he wasn't about to ever let her go.

Chapter 19

Hubert greeted Ellie with a smile and a cup of coffee the second she stepped into the kitchen. "Did you sleep well?"

Ellie damned her telling flush. She took the coffee, walked to the table and sat. Gingerly.

"I rested well last night." After she'd spent herself making love with Reid—not once, but three times.

She pressed both palms to her overly hot cheeks. Thank God she'd gone to his room, for her room was nearly directly above Hubert's. There'd be no denying what happened then.

"As tomorrow is Christmas, I took the liberty of fetching the turkey from the meat locker and placing it in the roasting pan in the pantry," he said.

"Thank you for remembering."

She'd totally forgotten she had to thaw the bird before she could stuff it. But cooking was the last thing on her mind.

After putting bacon on to fry, she grabbed her wrapper and hurried out to the meat locker.

All she thought about was the long night of making love

with Reid Barclay. She'd never imagined it could be that wonderful. Or addictive.

She couldn't stop smiling as she slipped into the dining room to ready the table for breakfast, only to find that Hubert had done that as well.

She turned to leave when Reid's voice echoed from the adjacent office. "You're sure he didn't board the train?"

"Positive, Mr. Barclay," a man said, his voice unfamiliar.

"Very well. Thanks for letting me know and for bringing this telegram right out."

"You're welcome, sir."

She waited until the man left before turning to hurry back to the kitchen. But Reid's curse stopped her before she'd taken two steps. What in the world had happened now?

"Alert the men to be on guard," Reid said. "God knows what Erston will get in his head to do."

"I'll step up watch on the horses, too," Shane said.

"Damn right," Reid said, a spate of silence keeping time with her too-rapid heartbeat before she heard him let out a relieved sigh. "Fitzmeyer is on his way out to look at the horses. If they meet the confirmation of his standards, he'll offer for them."

"That's damn good news, Slim."

No! Ellie froze, not believing her ears. She couldn't have heard right. Shane couldn't have called him Slim.

But all the denying in the world wouldn't change the truth.

"Arlen ever mention that he'd witnessed the shooting in Laramie?" Reid asked.

"Nope," Shane said. "Never acted like he equated you with Slim. 'Course, most the hands working here now don't know your nickname. After you left, Kirby insisted we call you Reid, but I'll admit I forget at times."

"So do I."

Shane laughed. "Well, you sure as hell don't look the same."

"Amazing how a haircut and a few extra pounds can change a man," Reid said.

Ellie could attest to that, for she hadn't recognized her pa right off. Her pa. Good heavens, what would he do when she told him about Reid?

She just stood in the dining room, rooted to the spot, filled with a sense of disgust and dread and heartache that made her want to vomit. She'd found Slim Cullen.

The man who killed poor Lisa True.

The man who walked off scot-free while her pa took the blame.

The man who she'd lost her heart to.

All her fanciful dreams withered before her eyes. She wanted nothing to do with the cowboy who'd murdered a woman. How could she have misjudged this man so? Surely if he was a killer, she'd see evidence of his cruelty. That possibility that she was mistaken gave her hope.

She couldn't equate the killer she'd read about with the kind, gentle man who'd helped guide a foal into this world. She couldn't believe the man who'd loved her tenderly throughout the night had gunned down a woman.

Yet Reid was Slim, the man her pa had come here to settle a score with.

If she held her secret, her pa would end up running for the rest of his life. He'd never find a moment's peace with such a high bounty on his head. He'd likely hang for a murder he didn't commit.

If she told her pa, he'd likely shoot Reid on the spot.

She hugged herself and stole back into the kitchen,

careful not to make a sound. What to do? What the hell was she going to do?

The opening of the backdoor interrupted her fretting, but only for an instant. A moment later her pa ambled into the kitchen, bundled up against the cold with a cloth sack slung over one shoulder.

She stared at the jolly old man in front of her until the fog in her head cleared. Not Santa Claus but her pa. An outlaw sure to hang if he was caught.

"Bagged a couple of fat rabbits late yesterday." He laid the sack on the table and helped himself to the coffee.

She looked from him to the bag, touched by his kindness, torn by indecision. This was her pa. The man she'd come here to talk out of making a grave error. The father she'd longed to spend one wonderful Christmas with before she moved to California and a new life.

But how could she do that now and keep the truth from him?

"What's ailing you, Ellie Jo?" her pa asked. "You look like you've just lost your best friend."

No, just the love of her life.

She didn't dare speak for fear she'd start bawling as much from anger as heartbreak. So she focused on the injustice of it all in hopes her torment would ease some.

While her pa had spent the past two years ducking the law, Reid was living in England, free from worry, because her pa took the blame for the murder he'd committed.

Now, Reid had returned to the West under his given name, no doubt confident that nobody would recognize him. And even if they did, he'd been dismissed of the charges.

Nobody was after him but her pa. He was looking for a rangy cowpoke, not the muscular rancher Reid Barclay had become. But he couldn't hide the scar that her pa had remembered seeing, albeit it was at his temple instead of his cheek. And his eyes were so dark a blue they were nearly black at times.

Those were easy enough mistakes to make from a distance. Why, she hadn't even noticed Reid's scar until last night when they were wrapped in each other's arms.

This time she couldn't stifle the tormented groan that tore from her.

"Ellie Jo? What's wrong?" her pa asked, his big hands closing over her trembling shoulders. "You're scaring me, girl."

She was scaring herself. Up until this morning, her plans had been so cut and dried. And now?

Now all she had to do was tell her pa that Reid was Slim Cullen. But she just couldn't do it. For no matter what she did, she'd likely make a decision she was going to regret.

Oh, God, she was going to be sick.

"I'm a bit under the weather," she said at last, and smiled into his worried eyes. "Nothing for you to concern yourself with."

Furrows marched across his wide brow. "You having one of those woman things?"

If it were only that simple. "Just a stomach complaint."

"I've got just the thing." He bustled into the pantry as if he knew his way around.

Ellie slumped on a chair, needled with more guilt for lying about her upset stomach. Oh, it was churning, but the cause was nerves.

They certainly weren't about to calm anytime soon, for if she did what was right by her pa, Reid would suffer. If she followed her heart and pretended she didn't know Reid was Slim Cullen, her pa would never gain the vengeance he sought.

The decision should be simple.

Slim Cullen shot down a young woman in the street.

Blood was thicker than water.

But for the life of her, she couldn't imagine Reid Barclay was a cold-blooded killer anymore than she believed it of her pa.

Her pa returned to pour hot water in a cup. He set it before her. "This here will set you straight."

She took a sniff but couldn't recognize the spice. "What is it?"

"Sweet flag tea," he said. "You've been drinking it since you was a little tyke."

She smiled, remembering how her mother would filch a few of the wild iris roots she'd dug so she could grind them for sachets. But she didn't recall the effects of the tea.

"Go on and drink it down while it's hot," he said.

"Is this a purgative?"

"Nope, it'll just calm your innards."

Ellie took a cautious sip. Warmth that had nothing to do with the temperature of the tea danced over her tongue.

She finished the brew with her pa watching and handed him the cup. "Thank you."

"No need to. If that doesn't help, you just holler and I'll fix you another cup."

She smiled. "I will."

"I still don't like the idea of you being here when trouble is sure to come," her pa said. "God knows what Slim will take into his head to do."

If he only knew. "I'm not leaving until after Christmas."

Her pa rubbed his knuckles along his jaw. "Anything you're wanting from town?"

"Nothing."

"You remember that Christmas you begged for that fancy doll you'd seen in the general store?" he asked.

She did, and she was surprised he recalled it. "You gave me a horse instead."

He chuckled, though it had a nervous edge to it. "I could steal a horse better than I could a doll."

"That's what I always thought," she said, and smiled without rancor.

"I'm sorry I wasn't a better pa," he said. "But I aim to make up for it in time. If Barclay will have me, I wouldn't mind staying on right here and live out my days as Gabby Moss."

And risk discovering that Reid was Slim?

Her head started pounding anew. "I've got a better idea. Come to California with me. I'm sure you can find a similar job on one of the ranches there."

He stroked his beard, looking everywhere but at her. "Reckon I can think on it."

"Please do," she said.

For she feared if she didn't separate the two men she loved, they'd surely end up killing each other.

Reid rocked back in his chair, propped both feet on the polished corner of his desk, and stared out the window. The Chinook winds had commenced at dawn, bringing much welcome warmth to the high plains.

In places, he could see the ground, proof the snow-eating winds were prevailing. It'd make it easier for them all to get around.

And it'd make it easier for Kincaid to rustle horses.

Nervous energy hummed through his veins. He hoped his brothers would arrive to claim their shares and bury the animosity they must surely feel for him. He hoped to hell Fitzmeyer got here soon and bought his herd, for that was the only way he'd be able to buy out Burl Erston. If he failed—

Hubert drifted into the room, as quiet as a shadow. "I told Miss Cade you wished to see her immediately."

"Thank you, Hubert."

"Do save your gratitude, sir. Miss Cade said she cannot spare the time to chat with you."

Reid frowned, the coffee cup he held frozen in midair. "It wasn't an invitation."

"I daresay it wouldn't have made any difference."

She was snubbing him? After the night they'd spent together? Well, damn!

"What chore has engaged Miss Cade's time?" he asked.

"She said she needed the bracing air to clear her head and is taking a walk."

He shoved to his feet. "Alone?"

"Yes, sir," Hubert said. "I advised her to stay close to the ranch proper."

Reid looked out the window, but didn't see her. It wasn't safe for her to wander around with Kincaid and now Erston likely watching the place. Either might take it in their head to cause her harm in order to make him suffer.

"May I remind you that she's not the type to be tri-fled with," Hubert said.

He glanced back at the old man and smiled at the censoring glint in Hubert's eyes. So she'd gotten to him as well.

"Rest your fears. The lady is in good hands with me."

Hubert cocked a brow, as if questioning that. "Sounds carry in this house, sir."

Ah, that explained it. "Discretion seems to be the order of the day."

"Indeed, even if it does come a day late."

"Right." Reid eased out the door, but he hadn't taken two steps when Hubert's next words stopped him.

"Honor is a good companion as well."

He smiled—the old butler was a staunch champion of Miss Cade. "You made your point, Hubert."

"Excellent, sir."

Reid grabbed his rifle and headed down the hall to the backdoor. The dainty wedding band set with diamonds was tucked in his pocket, but the decision to ask her to marry him rested heavy on his heart.

His whole future depended on Fitzmeyer buying the herd. If he lost the ranch, he'd have nothing to offer her. But after last night, he didn't want to let her go either.

He stormed outside, his nerves arcing like sheet lightning. The temperature had warmed a good thirty degrees, and with a bright sun bearing down on them, the snow was disappearing fast.

Where the hell could she have gone?

He scanned the ranch, paying particular attention near the outbuildings. He finally spied her near the paddock, talking to Shane. She was fine.

There was no need for him to go after her. No need other than the one tying his gut in knots that something wasn't quite right.

He took off that way, his sense attuned to danger. Shane pointed to him and she turned. He couldn't see her face at this distance, but he could tell that her body stiffened.

Yep, something was wrong.

He knew he'd satisfied her—no woman could've faked the pleasure she'd exhibited. Maybe in the light of day she had second thoughts about coming to him last night.

She stared at him a good long time before starting his way. They met on the track between the barn and the stable, and this close he could see even more clearly that something was bothering her. Hell, she couldn't even look him in the eyes.

Unease danced along his nerves, for though he knew Ellie Jo's body like his own, he didn't know a thing about the woman herself. But he intended to find out damned fast.

"What's wrong, Ellie?"

"Nothing. I just wanted to see how the foal was doing."

"And take in the bracing air to clear your head?" he asked, repeating the excuse she'd given Hubert.

Her cheeks flushed a telling red. "I am not in the habit of entertaining a man."

"I know that."

He nudged her chin up with his hand and stared into her eyes. No doubt about it. Something was troubling her.

"Regrets?" he asked.

She shook her head.

"Good." He grabbed her hand and tugged her behind a shed where they'd have privacy from the ranch hands.

"What are you doing?" she asked.

"Fixing to say a proper good morning."

He pulled her close and captured her lips with his. He felt her hesitation, but it lasted less than a heartbeat, and then she laid a hand on his chest and kissed him with abandon.

His blood chugged through his veins like a train under full steam, hot and running wild. He welcomed the rush of desire that engulfed him, still a bit stunned she could bring on such a potent arousal. But he needed her in his life for more than carnal satisfaction.

He'd never thought it possible to care this fiercely for a woman who wasn't his kin. Though he hesitated putting a name to what he felt, he readily admitted one thing: he wanted to spend the rest of his life in Ellie Jo's arms.

He angled closer and let his hand drift from her nipped-in waist to her bosom, drinking in those heady moans she made. He took satisfaction in sparking those telltale shivers in her too.

Even with all the damned layers of clothes women wore, he felt her breast plump in his hand. Even before his thumb grazed her nipple he knew it'd peeked into a hard bud.

He tugged on her lower lip, then slid his mouth over her chin and down her throat. She tipped her head back in surrender and he pressed his lips to the pulse in her neck, feeling her blood pound as fast and thick as his own.

Yep, there was no doubt in his mind that she wanted him as much as he did her.

He pulled back and stared at her eyes that were dark with passion, at her full, rosy lips that curled just so, as if begging him to return to them. If only he could offer her more right now.

"Stay with me, Ellie Jo."

He might as well have thrown ice water on her. She stiffened, her eyes wide and filled with a pain that speared him clean through.

She shook her head, pushing away from him. "No."

A gentleman took a lady at her word without question. But her refusal was a slap in the face that he hadn't expected. He damned sure wasn't ready to accept it, never mind that he couldn't come right out and ask for her hand right now.

"Why?" he asked, not caring that his voice cracked.

She shook her head again, seeming nigh frantic now. Hell, he knew nothing about her. She could be married for all he knew. Could be running away from an abusive sonofabitch.

Reid caught her chin and forced her to look at him. "You can't deny how you feel about me, Ellie. I've felt it too. Because of that, I deserve more than a one-word refusal."

Two fat tears slipped from her eyes and spilled over her cheek. His gut twisted, knowing he was the cause of her pain. But dammit all, he was hurting too.

"I-I won't because—" She sniffed and pinched her eyes shut. "Because you—" She broke off on a choked sob, drew in a shaky breath and looked him dead in the eyes. "If you must know, I've accepted a position at the Falsmonte Ladies Academy in California."

"Doing what?"

Her chin hiked up and her eyes narrowed. "Teaching young ladies comportment, and how to avoid situations like I've faced."

If she'd said she was going to be their cook, he wouldn't have believed her. But looking at her now, standing before him all prim and uptight, he knew she was telling the truth.

She wasn't a stranger to the bedroom, though she certainly seemed surprised by the depth of sensations he kindled in her last night. No, she wasn't talking about him and her.

Ellie must be referring to another man in her life. Jealousy coiled like a viper in him. The man must have hurt her real bad. Hell, she'd probably given her heart to him, and couldn't see taking that kind of risk again.

"You pining for him?" he asked.

She shook her head. "I've put that behind me."

"Bullshit." He grabbed her shoulders and dragged her against him, arrogantly pleased when she molded to him that instant before propriety kicked in and she went stiff in his arms again. "You're afraid that whatever went wrong with him and you will happen again with me."

She didn't deny it. She just stared at him, looking absolutely miserable again.

"What the hell did he do to you?" he asked, giving her a little shake this time in hopes it'd rile her to be honest with him.

She shoved his hands away and stepped from his grasp. "You want to know? Fine, I'll tell you. I was good enough to be the banker's mistress, but not his wife."

He looked away, because he hadn't offered her more either. "You know I'm caught in the cross-hairs here, waiting to hear from the horse breeder and hoping a message comes before Erston gains total control."

"Owning land is a good thing," she said. "But it should never define the man."

"Maybe not, but if I fail, I won't have a roof over my head."

She sent him a sad smile. "If you're half the man I think you are, you'd pick yourself up and start over fresh. You'd succeed because down deep you will never be happy until you have your own home."

That dredged a bark of laughter from him, because she was right. He feared ending up on the streets again. It grieved him to think he'd lose Hubert and the cowboys who'd worked their asses off for Kirby, and now for him.

"Tell me the truth this time," he said, and had the satisfaction of seeing her face redden again. "Why'd you agree to do Mrs. Leach's job when you didn't know a damn thing about cooking?"

"I had nowhere else to go," she said. "She was friends with the owner of the boardinghouse I was forced to leave, and offered the job. I didn't realize it would be so hard to do something that should come naturally for a woman."

He didn't doubt there was truth in this story, but he had a hunch she was still holding something back. She didn't trust him enough to be honest with him.

It hurt like hell, knowing that Ellie was prepared to walk out of his life. He didn't know how to change her mind about staying. He wasn't sure if he should even try.

"All right. You've made your wishes clear," he said. "But promise me one thing. In a year or two or ten, don't look back and say no man wanted you. Because that would be cheating us both."

She pinched her eyes shut and hung her head. For one moment he thought he'd gotten through to her. He hoped she'd see that leaving wasn't the answer.

"I've got to get dinner on," she said, and started off to the house at a good clip.

He let her go, confused by what had happened today. She still wanted him. The way she responded to his kiss convinced him of that much.

But something was standing between them, beyond what she'd claimed. He damn sure aimed to find out what that was.

Chapter 20

Reid leaned back in his chair and pinched the bridge of his nose, his eyes and mind tired from ciphering. It was the day before Christmas and nothing had changed. No matter how much he went over the figures, it still came down to him needing thousands of dollars to buy out Erston.

His thoroughbreds were prime, but he wasn't sure he could demand that kind of money for them. Folks were still struggling after last year's depression, himself included.

Of course, he'd expected to return to Maverick to find that Kirby and his brothers were holding on to the Crown Seven. Instead, he came home to find his benefactor had died, his brothers had vamoosed with the cattle, and the foreman was struggling to run the whole ranch, including the breeding program Reid had started with the thoroughbreds before his nightmare began.

One hard rap preceded his door swinging open. Booth Howard strode in, his hat pulled low and his sheepskin coat gaped open.

"Help yourself to bourbon and pull up a chair."

His foreman declined both, his nose wrinkling and his brow furrowed. "What in tarnation is that smell?"

He sighed. "Miss Cade forgot she put the giblets on to boil."

He didn't see the sense in mentioning that had happened because she was putting out a grease fire that just happened to be his beefsteak dinner.

"We're fixing to play a few rounds of poker in the bunkhouse," Howard said. "You're welcome to join us."

There was a time Reid would've jumped at the chance. Now, he didn't have the money to lose, or the inclination to enjoy the game.

His thoughts had jumped between this ranch and Miss Cade all day. Here it was going on evening, and he didn't have a solution in hand for either.

Howard leaned against the liquor cabinet, a wry smile tugging at his mouth. "Kincaid was seen north of the ranch today."

"When?"

"Don't know for sure. Reckon close to midday," he said. "I put an extra man on to help Shane at the stable."

"Good." He sure as hell couldn't afford to lose another thoroughbred. "When did you hear about it?"

"Right after he was spotted." Howard held up a hand when Reid made to protest. "The reason I didn't tell you was because I ain't so sure he was anywhere near the Crown Seven."

He leaned back in his chair and took a sip of bourbon. "Why are you doubting it?"

Howard snorted. "Because Frank Arlen was the one who spotted him. I passed him on the way back from checking the back section."

Arlen had certainly spent undue time in the vicinity of

the ranch of late. Peculiar for a man who was out of a job in the dead of winter.

"What the hell was Arlen doing on the Crown Seven?"

"Claimed he was on his way here to tell you he'd seen Kincaid," Howard said. "I don't trust him at his word."

Reid tapped his fingertips together, finding it peculiar that Arlen just happened to be passing by each time Ezra Kincaid made a teasing jaunt across Crown Seven land. "Anybody else spotted Kincaid in all this time?"

"Nope, just Arlen."

Mighty interesting. More so since the man had even been in Laramie the day Lisa True died at Kincaid's hands.

"What do you know of Frank Arlen?" he asked.

"He's a drifter. Far as I can tell he ain't held down any job longer than a season." Howard's expression hardened. "He's got a mean streak with horses and women."

Another strike against the lazy cowpoke. "Anything else?"

"He ain't above hiring his gun out," Howard said. "But he's the type that'll lie in wait and pick a man off, partly because he don't put much effort into anything, and partly because he's a piss-poor shot."

Reid twirled his empty glass on the table, thinking. "Would he rustle?"

Howard shrugged. "Probably, if he had a ready buyer. You thinking he might have made off with Caelte?"

"Could be. Nobody has claimed to see that stallion but Arlen." Nigh on twenty thousand dollars in prime horse-flesh, gone in a blink. "Whoever's behind all this had to be close. I want you to search all the line shacks near here. If we're lucky, you'll happen on the old outlaw."

Howard nodded. "Soon as we catch that rustler, we'll drag his sorry behind into Maverick. There's a reward on him."

"Bring Kincaid here," Reid said. "I want to talk to him before we hand him over to the law."

"I'll get on it tomorrow." Howard straightened. "If you change your mind about the game, come on down."

Reid pushed to his feet after Howard left and prowled his office. He hadn't felt this restless in ages.

At the window, he paused and looked out over the only home he'd ever known. Ellie was right. It scared the shit out of him to think he'd lose it.

It was home, yes. But Kirby had trusted him to hold it together in the lean times.

He'd done it. Hell, he'd been ready to head west to round up mustangs when Kirby took him aside and told him he was dying.

Reid swallowed hard, remembering that moment like it was yesterday. He'd rode up in the mountains past the tree line where nobody was around.

He'd cussed and ranted and raved, and then he sat on a rock and cried, the first time he remembered shedding a tear in his miserable life.

Then he did the stupidest thing of his life. He rode into Laramie and proceeded to get rip-roaring drunk. He was grieving for the man before he ever drew his last breath.

The rest Reid didn't remember.

He pushed to his feet and left his office. The house was quiet save the ticking of the grandfather clock.

A full moon shot beams through the front window to lend a glittering magic to the ornaments hanging on the tree. He jammed his hands in his pockets and stepped into the parlor scented with cinnamon and pine.

Ellie had gone to a lot of fuss. Had she taken time to enjoy it?

He didn't know. Nearly every time he saw her she was working or attempting to cook.

The soft strains of a guitar drifted on the night air, the melody one he'd heard a time or two from carolers strolling the streets of Maverick. He'd never understood what folks got out of it besides cold feet and a strained throat.

Same with the tree and all the fripperies. He didn't know where Ellie had found the time to string popcorn and cranberries, but she'd embraced that job with glee.

Finding the right tree was no different.

His mouth quirked in a smile as he recalled that day. She'd frustrated the hell out of him, and sparked a fierce desire in him too.

He moved to the sofa he never recalled using and sat in the dark, finding an odd peace as muted moonlight flickered over the bright ornaments on the tree.

He'd never been one to ruminate, but he caught himself wondering how different his life would've been if his ma would've lived. Would he have found that set of carved horses in his stocking? Would he have celebrated this holiday with a glad heart?

The glow from a lone candle arced into the parlor a heartbeat before Ellie walked in. She lit the globe lamp, then set the candle on a table near the tree, humming the melody Shane was picking out on the guitar.

She kept her back to him as she secured small tins on the boughs, taking her time. When she'd finished that, she went back to each one and stuck a small candle on the holders.

She lit each one and stepped back with a pleased sigh.

He tore his gaze from her and took in the tree twinkling with candlelight. "That's mighty pretty."

She whirled to face him. "I didn't know you were in here."

"You were intent on your chore." They stared at each other across the room, her eyes wide and misty. "Sit with me?"

To his surprise, she crossed to the sofa and sat beside him. He hesitated a second before draping an arm around her shoulders and tucking her against his side.

A sense of rightness hummed around him. "Do you always go to this much fuss?"

She laughed. "Sometimes I do more, especially in the school."

"We never had a tree in the orphanage," he said. "Kirby never bothered with one either."

"Perhaps it is more woman's work. My pa didn't put up a tree either the first year after my mother died."

He recalled her mentioning it shortly after she came to work here. "How old were you?"

"Twelve."

The same age he'd been when he'd struck out on his own with Dade and Trey. "Did you see your pa much after that?"

She fidgeted with her hands. "He came to visit when he could."

He suspected that wasn't much. "He still alive?"

"Yes."

She didn't offer more, but even if she was a mind to, Hubert chose that moment to join them. He set down a heavy tray and gazed at the tree.

"It is quite lovely, Miss Cade," he said.

"Thank you."

Hubert glanced at Reid cozied up on the sofa with Miss Cade. "I've prepared my yearly eggnog. Would you both care for a glass?"

"That would be nice," she said.

Reid nodded. As he recalled, Hubert's eggnog was mighty potent stuff.

The old servant handed them their glasses of eggnog, then returned to the tree and the book he'd set on the chair. He took his seat and put on a pair of wire spectacles.

"If neither of you object, I'll read a Christmas Eve poem an acquaintance of mine sent me." His gaze lit on Reid's in silent challenge, dragging a smile from him.

"Fine by me," Reid said.

As long as Ellie would sit here beside him, he'd go along with damn near anything.

"Please, go on," Ellie said.

Hubert opened the volume and began. "'Twas the night before Christmas . . .'"

Reid sipped what must be hundred-proof eggnog and listened to Hubert's animated voice recanting the light-hearted poem. When Hubert was finished, he closed the book, removed his spectacles and rose.

"Goodnight all," Hubert said. "Pleasant dreams."

Reid and Ellie remained on the sofa, but he sensed the tension returning to her. Hell, did she think he expected her to sleep with him again?

Though he'd like nothing better, he knew that wouldn't happen again unless she wanted it. That time might never come.

"I want you to have this." He fished in his pocket and pulled out the ring, then pressed it into her palm. "If things had gone different, I'd have asked you to be my wife."

She stared at the small gold band. "I can't accept this."

"Sure you can." He leaned forward and kissed her brow, drinking in her lilac scent. "Keep wishing on cornhusk angels, Ellie. One day they might come true for you."

With that he got to his feet and walked out of the parlor. But instead of seeking his room, he stepped outside just as Shane sang the last chorus of a carol.

A warm breeze swept over the plains, feeling more like spring than winter. But winter would return with brutal force.

And in the dead of night, he'd remember snuggling with Ellie on the sofa one warm evening while an old man recanted the magic of Christmas.

He wanted to marry her.

Ellie curled in bed long into the night with the gold band clutched tight in her fist. She couldn't recall her heart ever being this heavy, for while Irwin had broken off their engagement because she wasn't good enough, Reid withheld asking because he was afraid he'd have nothing to offer her.

Never mind that he was Slim Cullen, the man her pa was gunning for.

Never mind that her pa was an outlaw that Reid Barclay openly reviled.

He wanted to marry her, and if the situation was right, he'd have proposed.

She pinched her eyes shut and squeezed out a tear. What would she have said?

Maybe the better question was, what would he have done when he learned the woman he wanted to marry and her father had deceived him from the start?

Oh, she should have told Reid the truth right then.

Tomorrow, she thought as she slipped the ring on her third finger. She'd tell him all tomorrow.

* * *

Ellie woke in far brighter spirits at the crack of dawn. She admired the lovely ring Reid had given her before threading it on a ribbon and tying it around her neck.

The gold band nestled between her breasts, close to her heart. This was the only way she'd dare to wear it, but that didn't diminish its significance.

He'd marry her if he could.

That meant he cared.

And a man that cared that much, to buy a wedding ring for a woman he didn't think he could marry, would surely understand why she'd held her secret for so long.

It was high time Reid learned the truth. Not just about her. But about her pa as well.

Surely there were enough hands on the ranch who could attest to the fact that Gabby Moss was busy working when someone used his name to rustle Reid's prize stallion.

Surely Reid would see that as well.

She dressed and hurried to the kitchen, determined to outdo herself. Considering her past efforts, that shouldn't be difficult.

After wrestling the turkey roaster into the oven, she laid out a buffet line in the dining room and set to work on breakfast. She'd just returned from setting out the platter of bacon when the back door opened and three cowboys ventured in.

"Ma'am," Shane said. "Was we to take breakfast here as well as dinner?"

She removed the second batch of hotcakes to a platter without a mishap. "I don't see why not. Just head into the dining room and take a seat."

The trio didn't budge. "You sure about that?"

"Of course I am," she said as she got a firm hold on

the platter. "That table is large enough to accommodate a crowd. Just follow me."

She bustled into the dining room just as Reid entered from the other door. "Good morning! You're just in time. Dig in."

He glanced at the cowboys. "Well, you heard the lady."

After flashing Reid a smile, she ducked back into the kitchen. One meal down and the main one to go.

"Ellie!" Reid shouted.

Please, don't let the hotcakes be undercooked.

Dread settled over her shoulders as she returned to the dining room. "Do you need something?"

"Yes, you." He motioned to the chair next to Hubert. "This is Christmas. We'll all eat together."

"Oh, of course." She slid onto a chair, noting the cowboys seemed as nervous about her being here as she was. "Is this everyone?"

"No, ma'am," Shane said. "We're eating in shifts so the stock won't be left unguarded."

That reminder put a bit of a damper on her mood. She'd be glad when the rustler posing as her pa was caught.

"Neal and Moss ain't got back from town yet," one of the young cowboys said.

"But they will return for dinner?" she asked, more than a bit unnerved to hear her pa had left the ranch, today of all days.

She was under the impression that he'd been very careful about venturing around too many people. Just because he'd changed his appearance so drastically didn't mean that someone wouldn't recognize him.

The cowboy frowned, glancing from his peers to her. "Neal said he'd come home today, but Moss—" He shook his head and frowned. "He was supposed to be back last night."

The forkful of pancake she'd just chewed dropped into her stomach like a lead ball. "You don't suppose something has happened to him?"

The cowboy shrugged. The other two didn't bother to comment. In fact none of them looked concerned, including Reid, which only served to crank her anxiety up another notch.

"Moss likely decided to celebrate the holiday at Mallory's," Reid said, and sent her a meaningful look that she finally understood.

Her cheeks burned. Good heavens, she didn't care to imagine her pa seeking female companionship. Not that she didn't want him to be happy. It was just that imagining him off entertaining a lady clouded the picture she had of her parents in happier times.

"Mighty fine breakfast." Shane rose and added a nod to the compliment.

"Thank you," she said, inordinately pleased.

The two younger cowboys got to their feet as well, with one still chewing the last hotcake he'd just shoveled in.

"Much obliged, ma'am," said the one she'd been talking to, and the other nodded his thanks.

"I'm delighted you enjoyed it," she said. "Did you both get enough to eat?"

They tripped over themselves, nodding and thanking her again as they backed out of the dining room.

"I'd better cook some more," she said, and hastened into the kitchen.

As before, the bacon cooked itself with very little tending on her part.

But this batch of hotcakes took more pains, and not just in timing them right to flip. The batter had thickened, and they tended to be twice the size of the first ones. It didn't help that her thoughts kept turning to her pa.

After going through the first batch that were less than attractive and far browner than she liked, she managed to fill a second platter with hotcakes.

She delivered them to the table at the same time three more cowboys arrived for breakfast. Like the others, they made short work of the food and coffee, requiring her to fill the pot twice.

If only her Christmas dinner would be as much of a success, she thought as the last trio of cowboys dawdled over their coffee, discussing ranch details with Reid. She gathered the dirty dishes in a neat stack and started toward the kitchen.

The back door banged open and shut, and boots pounded on the floor. A cowboy burst into the dining room, breathing hard.

"You ain't going to believe this, boss," he said.

Ellie held her breath, hoping the rustler hadn't struck again.

"I'm listening, Neal," Reid said.

"The marshal threw Gabby Moss in jail," he said.

No! Ellie tightened her hold on the plates as her world tipped on its axis. It couldn't be, she thought, her head buzzing and growing far too warm.

"Except he ain't Moss at all but Ezra Kincaid himself," Neal finished.

"What?" Reid thundered.

That's when the buzzing in her head drowned out all other sound. She lost her hold on the plates, letting them drop with a clatter while her knees buckled and she crumpled in a heap.

Chapter 21

Ellie came awake with a start, mindful of exactly what had happened. Her pa was in jail. Dear heavens, the truth was out.

Things were still a bit muzzy, but she couldn't dawdle. She made to rise, desperate to get to him now.

"Whoa up there," Reid said, pressing her shoulders back down on the sofa. "You're not going anywhere until we figure out why you fainted dead away."

Uh-oh, this wasn't going to be pleasant or easy.

"Perhaps I ate too much."

"Try again."

She blinked to clear the remaining fog from her vision and wished she hadn't. Reid looked angry and tense, so unapproachable she wanted to scream.

"Shock," she said, which was the truth.

His gaze narrowed to slits. "Over?"

She swallowed. "Gabby Moss being arrested."

"Now why would that upset you so?" he asked, his voice deceptively soft and his gaze incredibly intense.

She pinched her eyes shut and said, "Because he's my father."

Ellie was certain she'd never heard such deafening silence in her life. She was afraid to move. Afraid to breathe. Afraid to look at him and see out-and-out hatred blaze in his eyes.

She chanced a peek at him, then another.

He stared at her without heat. Without censure. In fact, he stared at her as if she were a stranger, and one he wasn't too anxious to know.

"Ezra Kincaid is your pa," he said at last, and she bobbed her head in answer.

He looked away, and that's when she saw the muscle hammering away in his cheek. He wasn't angry. No, he was furious.

She'd expected that, but still it hurt. "I've got to go to him, Reid."

"Not yet. Not until I get some answers." But he did move aside and let her sit up.

She straightened her skirt and clasped her trembling hands together, feeling sick, and scared and angry as hell too. "What do you want to know?"

"What was your part in this?"

"There wasn't a conspiracy," she said, fidgeting with her fingers now.

"Don't lie to me, Ellie," he said. "Mrs. Leach convinced me to hire you while she was away. Why?"

She couldn't very well deny that fact. "In her own words, she hoped I could stop my pa from putting his neck in the noose."

He tossed his head back and gritted his teeth so hard she could hear bone grinding. "She knew he was Kincaid."

It wasn't a question, but she bobbed her head anyway. "She told me she recognized my pa shortly after he hired on."

One dark eyebrow winged upward. "I always suspected that Mrs. Leach knew him back in her sporting days."

"Yes, she admitted as much to me. Pa knew where I lived, but he'd decided to stay out of my life so I wouldn't be shamed or shunned." Ellie gave a short laugh, for despite his caution, she'd been shamed and shunned anyway. "Anyway, Mrs. Leach contacted me some weeks back. I hadn't even known where he was, or that he had assumed another name. She didn't even tell Pa she'd written to me."

"Why'd she do it?"

She'd asked herself that many times. "She was worried that Pa had become obsessed with finding Slim Cullen."

He groaned and scrubbed a hand over his mouth. "Do I have any secrets left?"

Plenty, she imagined. "I didn't tell Pa that I'd found out you were Slim."

He flinched. "Where's my stallion?"

"I wouldn't know, and neither would Pa," she said. "Someone is rustling and using his name."

He pushed to his feet and strode to the window, his spine one tense, unyielding line of masculinity. "All right. We'll head into Maverick and see what Moss has to say."

Ellie didn't bother to paste a polite smile on her face as she stormed into the jail. The long, tense drive into Maverick had frayed her nerves.

Marshal Tavish was seated at his desk. He straightened at her approach and offered a smile.

"I've been expecting you, Miss Cade."

She marched up to his desk and slapped both palms on his desk. "How did you know it was him?"

"That was just luck on my part," he said, as the door opened again and Reid walked in. Tavish paid him a passing glance before facing her again. "I was at the mercantile looking to buy a new knife when your pa came in to buy a gift for his daughter."

"Oh, no," she said, swaying under the immense guilt.

Tavish shook his head. "Moss neglected to buy a doll for his daughter years back when she asked for one, so he was set on making amends to Ellie Jo."

Ellie dropped onto the chair, heartsick that he'd gotten in this fix because of her. "You knew who I was."

"Yep. It was easy to see then why a teacher took on the cook's job at the Crown Seven." Tavish tipped his head to the side and eyed her. "I knew then that Gabby Moss was the notorious Ezra Kincaid."

"Did he put up a fight?" Reid asked.

"Nope, he was docile as a lamb and admitted who he was."

"What happens now?" Ellie asked, fearing she knew but needing to hear all the same.

Tavish shrugged. "He waits for the judge to come through. If he's lucky, he'll spend the rest of his life behind bars. If he pulls an unsympathetic jury, he'll hang."

She pressed a hand to her roiling stomach, fearing she'd retch. "I'd like to talk to him now."

"I need a word with him too," Reid said, and Ellie bit back a groan at the verbal sparring that was sure to come.

"Don't know about that," Tavish said.

"Please," she said. "It's Christmas Day."

Tavish removed his felt hat and combed his thick hair back, then took his time settling it back on. But his gaze flicked between her and Reid with cold appraisal.

"Please," she repeated.

The marshal scowled, but gave an abrupt nod.

"I'll give you two ten minutes with him. The door stays open. Agreed?"

"Yes, fine," she said.

Anything as long as she could talk to her pa and figure out a way to commute his sentence.

Ellie rushed up to the cell where Kincaid sat on a cot with his elbows on his knees and his chin in his hands. The old outlaw caught sight of her and struggled to his feet.

"Ah, hell," he said.

She grasped the iron bars. "Why did you come to town and take such a foolish risk?"

"I aimed to give you something you'd pined for instead of the grief and shame that was passed off on you all these years." Moss sent Ellie a smile that brimmed with affection and worry before flicking Reid an uneasy glance. "I ne'er meant no harm."

That excuse was spewed by outlaws all across the West. Reid curled his upper lip and struggled to keep a tight rein on his anger. But it was a losing battle.

"You sonofabitch," Reid said, and Ellie let out an affronted gasp. "Where's my stallion?"

"Wish I knew," Kincaid said. "It's the God's honest truth I didn't steal your horse."

Reid expected the denial. "You're a horse thief."

"The best that ever was for many a year." Kincaid bobbed his white head, showing no repentance at all. "Those days are behind me. Hell, they have been for nigh on two years."

"Bull. You likely hired on at the Crown until you figured out how to make off with those thoroughbreds."

A broad smile spread over Kincaid's craggy face and

set his eyes to twinkling. "Barclay, if I was still in the business you wouldn't have a blooded horse left to your name."

The same thought had crossed Reid's mind as well. Why had Kincaid only stolen one horse when he had ample opportunity to ride off with the herd?

"A man claims to have seen you riding off on Caelte," he said, not about to be gulled again by the old man or his fetching daughter.

"A man swears I killed a woman in Laramie too, but I didn't." Kincaid looked him dead on, letting him read the truth in his eyes—a truth that heaped guilt on him.

"Then why'd you come to the Crown?" Reid asked.

"I got a bone to pick with the no-account who gunned down that woman in Laramie," Kincaid said. "Word was that Slim Cullen was working at the Crown Seven."

"That he is," Reid said, and earned a groan from Ellie and a jaw-dropping look from the outlaw.

Kincaid folded his arms over his bulging middle. "Well, I ain't laid eyes on him yet."

Just what kind of bullshit was the old man trying to pull now? "You claiming Ellie didn't point Slim Cullen out to you?"

Kincaid jutted his chin forward and scowled at his daughter. "She sure as hell did not. Why didn't you come to me right away, Ellie Jo? That man's a woman killer."

She shook her head, looking flustered and plain bone-weary. "I just don't know what to believe, Pa."

Kincaid let out a sound of disgust, wrapped gnarled fingers around the iron bars and stared dead on at Reid. "Tell me who he is. I got a right to know."

"You blind, old man?"

"I must be 'cause I sure as hell ain't laid eyes on him the whole year I been working at the Crown," Kincaid said.

It was Reid's turn to wonder what the hell was going on. Not one bit of recognition was evident on Kincaid's face. Ellie's expression was just as puzzled.

He'd had more than his share of lies, broken vows and double-dealings the past two years. He wanted to shed light on the truth.

"Reid Cullen Barclay is my given name," he said. "But since I was tall and lanky most of my life, folks called me Slim."

Kincaid scowled. "You can't be him."

He laughed without humor. "Just what Kirby told me when they dragged me out of jail and convinced me I'd best spend a year in England with Kirby's cousin until the furor died down." Saved his butt, though that salvation came at a mighty hefty price.

"I'll be switched," Kincaid said.

"Your memory clearing, old man?" Reid asked.

"Like a full sun burning off a foggy morning." Kincaid looked him over from head to toe and nodded. "You was rail thin, all right, with hair curling down past your collar. And so damned drunk you could barely stand up."

"Yep, I'd spent way too many hours and all my money in the saloon that day when you came to town to steal my horse," he said. "I'd just found out Kirby Morris was dying of cancer, and I decided to drown my grief in rotgut."

Kincaid downed his head. "Didn't know Kirby was bad off then."

"You knew him?" he asked.

Kincaid nodded at Ellie. "She can tell you the particulars. Suffice to say if it weren't for Kirby Morris, I'd be dead."

He had no trouble believing Kirby would've lent a hand to the old rustler.

"Yep, I surely wouldn't have repaid his help by stealing your horse," Kincaid said. "Hell, I hadn't even known you were one of the boys Kirby spoke of until I hired on at the Crown."

"Sounds like you have a convenient memory," he said.

"My mind is sharp, boy."

"Then how come you couldn't recall the face of the man who murdered Lisa True?"

"Time's up," Tavish said.

Kincaid shook his head and stared at Reid with an intensity that rocked him to his soul. "I remember him. Make no mistake about it. I'm telling you right now that you ain't the cowboy I saw kill that woman."

That claim tumbled over and over in Reid's head. He wanted to believe it was true. God, how he wanted to believe he hadn't taken an innocent life.

But he'd be a fool to trust the old outlaw. A desperate fool.

"How can that be, Pa?" Ellie asked, voicing Reid's doubts. "You swore Slim Cullen murdered that woman, and Reid is that man."

Kincaid jutted his chin at a belligerent angle. "I don't give a damn what Barclay calls himself. He didn't shoot that young woman dead."

Ellie stared at her pa, seeming as confused as Reid felt. "Then who did?"

"The feller we're looking for, is who," Kincaid said.

"That's a mighty interesting story," Marshal Tavish said from the doorway. "Barclay. Miss Morris. Time for you to be heading out."

"But it's Christmas," Ellie said. "What harm can be done if I spend a little more time talking with my father?"

Tavish thumbed his hat back. "The sheriff has strict rules here, ma'am. Ten minutes with a prisoner."

"Look around you, Tavish," Reid said. "Most folks are home with their family, including the sheriff. Well, her kin is right here in this cell. No reason why she can't visit with him a bit longer."

"Please," Ellie said.

Tavish stared at them, looking about as obliging as a grizzly. "You got twenty minutes, then you skedaddle."

The marshal tramped away from the doorway, leaving it open as he had before. With luck, he'd hear something that would send him off hunting the man who'd stolen Reid's stallion.

And if Ezra Kincaid was duping him? God help him.

"If you're lying about what happened that day, old man—"

"I'm telling the God's-honest truth," Kincaid said. "You ain't the cowboy who killed that woman."

So who'd murdered her?

While Ellie and Kincaid reminisced about Christmases past, Reid forced his mind back to that dark day in Laramie, hoping more would come to light this time. He remembered riding into town, his heart heavy over the news that Kirby was dying.

He couldn't bear the thought of losing the man who was like a father to him. It shamed him to admit he'd failed Kirby.

They were in debt, and they had just a few ways left to recoup their losses or risk losing the Crown Seven. He'd stalked into a saloon and commenced drinking— inwardly crying in his liquor.

It hadn't taken long before the rest of that day was a blur, thanks to the fact he was a handkerchief away from being three sheets to the wind.

Reid stared at the old outlaw, letting his claim play over and over in Reid's mind until the truth settled into his soul. He hadn't shot Lisa True by accident. Another cowboy had murdered her.

Damned convenient. Believing he'd killed an innocent woman allowed Erston to strong-arm Reid into doing his bidding. It heaped guilt on him that he'd lived with for two long years.

He saw a killer every time he looked in a mirror. He called himself a coward for letting a rustler take the blame for that woman's death, even if Kincaid was an outlaw that would likely hang one day.

"What's troubling you, boy?" Kincaid asked.

"I need to know what you saw the day Lisa True was shot down in the street," Reid said.

Kincaid paced his cell. "Well, it all started with me figuring out a way I could steal a fine horse I had my eye on."

"My horse?" Reid asked.

"That's the one."

"I waited a good long time before trying to make off with that horse," Kincaid said. "I was a hairsbreadth from getting that line untied when that woman screamed and ran from the livery."

He frowned. "That should've drawn a crowd."

"Oh, it did," Kincaid said. "Thing is, most folks saw me by the horses and right off figured I was fixing to steal them. That's when I took off running."

He had a disjointed memory of staggering outside and seeing the old outlaw by his horse. "I shot at you."

"You shot wild, blowing a hole in the sign over the livery. But Slim Cullen, or the cowpoke I thought was him, had true aim." Kincaid shook his head, looking guilty. "It happened so damned fast. One minute that cowpoke was chasing her from the livery, and the next he pulled his gun and shot her down."

"Good thing he didn't see you," Reid said.

"He did," Kincaid said. "Stared me straight in the eyes. I was sure he'd drop me there on the sidewalk, but when folks started running toward the livery, he vamoosed. I damn sure did the same."

"How many horses did you make off with?" Reid asked.

"Not a damned one. I lit out of town and didn't look back," he said. "It was later when I heard they'd arrested Slim Cullen for her murder."

That they had. Reid rubbed the tense cords in his nape, his memory clear about when he woke in a jail cell to learn he'd killed a woman and would surely hang.

The old outlaw paced the cell like a caged bear. "All this time I thought that no-account was Slim Cullen. What I wouldn't give to run into him again."

"Would you know him if you saw him?" he asked.

"Damn right I would. I'll never forget those cold eyes of his," Kincaid said. "They glittered like blue ice. You see anybody that fits that bill?"

"Don't know for sure."

Reid paced back and forth, sorting it out in his head, trying to place where he'd seen eyes like that. When he did, his blood ran cold—not with fear, but with fury.

"Sonofabitch," Reid said, knowing if he was right, the killer was right here in Maverick.

"You know who he is," Ellie said, laying a hand on his arm, searching his eyes with hers.

"Maybe. Had a cowpoke working for me with eyes that color." Reid looked from Ellie's worried face to her pa's scowling one. "Describe this man who shot Lisa True."

Kincaid screwed up his face and stroked his beard. "He was rangy as a starved coyote. A mite taller than Ellie."

Five-eight then. So far it fit the man Reid had in mind. "Go on. What about his hair? Complexion?"

The old outlaw shook his head, as if trying to rattle those details out of hiding. "His hair hung over his collar and was mighty dark. From where I stood it appeared to be in need of a hard washing."

"You said he had a scar on his cheek," Ellie said.

"He sure did." Kincaid stopped pacing, his eyes widening as if something else had just occurred to him. "There were bloody tracks on his face, too."

"She scratched him," Ellie and Reid said at the same time.

Reid flicked a glance at the doorway and saw the marshal's shadow there. He could imagine what was going through his mind as he bent his ear to their conversation.

The real killer had either coaxed or dragged Miss True into the livery and had his way with her. She must have clawed him up in the process and got away.

Only to get gunned down when she was moments from freedom.

"Damn the man to hell," Reid said, snaring Kincaid's angry gaze with his own. "When he spied you fixing to rustle a horse, he saw it as the means to cover up what he'd done."

Kincaid nodded. "He knew I'd run."

"You listening, Tavish?" he asked.

"Yup." The marshal stepped into the door opening, his expression tight with anger.

Tension crackled in the jail, gathering momentum like an avalanche sweeping down the mountain.

"That witness in Laramie," he said, having a feeling in his gut that he wasn't mistaken this time. "He was Frank Arlen."

"Yup," Tavish said.

Ellie stepped close, her fingers tightening on his arm. "The man who saw Pa steal your stallion?"

"One and the same."

Arlen had stolen Caelte. He tried stealing Reid's blooded mares. He likely was the man who took that pot-shot at Reid the other day when he'd been kissing Ellie and dreaming of sinking into her and forgetting the world and his troubles.

"He's been watching the ranch all along," Kincaid said, frowning at his daughter who didn't seem to be aware how familiar she was with Reid.

Not that he minded, but this wasn't the place to tell a father that he had designs on the man's daughter.

"Ellie Jo, I want you to leave town tomorrow," Kincaid said. "Go to California like you planned now before—"

"No! I'm not leaving yet."

Kincaid dragged his gaze to Reid's, and there was no denying the fact that the old man was worried sick about his daughter. "Bet Arlen recognized me and knew if I tried defending myself, I'd end up right here."

That fear had played into Arlen's hands and kept the old man from venturing out. Hell, Reid could count the times on one hand that Kincaid had made a foray into town. The last time when he came to buy a gift for Ellie, he'd gotten caught.

Now how the hell was Arlen going to view that news?

"It's the God's honest truth that I'm leery of a convenient witness," Tavish said.

Reid felt the same, though there was nothing convenient or happenstance with what Frank Arlen had done. The man was careful to plan his moves so someone else took the blame. He just had to get the marshal to see that.

"I always thought a good poker player made the best criminal because he had the right amount of smarts and bravado." Reid glanced at Tavish, wanting the lawman to read the truth in his eyes. "Arlen overplayed his hand."

Tavish scrubbed a hand over his chin as if considering his opinion. "Interesting that Arlen happened to be in Laramie when Kincaid killed Lisa True. He claims he was riding near the ranch and saw Kincaid passing by. But maybe Arlen was driving off horses he'd just rustled at Rocky Point Ranch."

"As you said, he's a convenient witness."

Tavish scrubbed a hand over his mouth. "If you're right, then it'll be interesting to see what Arlen does next. If you're wrong, the rustling will stop now."

And if he was right? What the hell would Arlen do?

Chapter 22

"What are you going to do about Frank Arlen?" Ellie asked after Tavish put an end to her visit with her pa and hustled her and Reid out of the back room.

"Nothing much I can do," Marshal Tavish said.

She stared at him, unwilling to believe the law could be so blind. "But my father saw him shoot that woman."

The marshal laughed, which only made her madder. "You expect me to take the word of a horse thief?"

"I expect you to at least consider all the possibilities." But the marshal had closed his mind to Ezra Kincaid's version of that day in Laramie because he was an outlaw.

Marshal Tavish dropped onto his chair and rocked it back on two legs. "Find a witness to back up Kincaid's claim and I'll track down Arlen. But even if you do, remember Ezra Kincaid is a horse thief and he has to stand trial for that."

That took the argument out of her. She'd always known this day would come, for her pa had spent many a year rustling. But she'd also thought she'd be removed from the brutal reality.

At best, she expected to read of his arrest, trial and

either his imprisonment or death. She'd not dreamed she'd see him locked in a cell facing an uncertain fate. She'd not realized her heart would ache so.

Strong fingers closed over her arm. She looked up into Reid's fathomless blue eyes and smiled, glad she had someone to turn to if only for a short while.

"We'd best get back to the ranch," he said.

She nodded, hating the sting of threatening tears. This day had started with such promise. The first Christmas she'd spent with her pa in ages.

And now it would mark one of the darkest days of her life.

The last person he expected to see swaggering down the boardwalk toward him was Burl Erston. But then today marked the deadline to claim the shares of the Crown Seven, so it stood to reason Erston would come forward.

"I trust your two partners have not braved arrest for cattle rustling and come forth to claim their shares," Erston said, smiling because he knew damned good and well that Dade and Trey hadn't shown up.

Reid refused to give him the satisfaction. "The day's not over."

"Indeed not, but I'll be glad when it is so I can return to England," Erston said.

He snorted in agreement. "It'll be a damn fine day for me when I buy you out."

"Whether you do or don't is no concern of mine," Erston said. "If you can't afford to buy my shares, I have a gentleman in line who is most interested."

"Who?" he asked, dreading that Erston would sell out to one of the larger cattle outfits.

"I'm not at liberty to say." Erston made to move around him.

Reid stepped in his path. "I've got a right to know who is interested in the Crown Seven."

"You have a sixth interest and that's all." He pushed past Reid and headed down the walk.

"You're bluffing," Reid said.

Erston stopped and faced him again, his smile downright sinister. "Quite the contrary. Depending on the outcome of today, I'll either sell my third of the ranch tomorrow, or the two thirds I'll gain from your partners' default."

"Damn you!" Reid bunched his hands at his sides when he longed to drive a fist into Erston's pompous face. "You gave your word that you'd give me time to buy you out."

"Oh, you've had ample time, but now you have until midnight." Erston smiled and tipped his hat. "Merry Christmas."

Go to hell, he thought.

"What are you going to do?" Ellie asked as he escorted her toward the buggy.

"There's not a damn thing I can do but hope my partners get here today."

For it was possible that tomorrow he wouldn't have a place to hang his hat, or pen his herd.

The Chinooks continued to reduce the snow to slush and made the buggy ride back to the Crown Seven comfortable, but Reid didn't comment on the balmy weather or anything else. He was just too mired in worry over the ranch and doing the right thing by Ellie.

She was silent, too. He suspected her thoughts centered on her pa, for she clearly cared deeply about the old outlaw.

Kincaid was just as concerned about his daughter, and for good reason.

Frank Arlen was dangerous, and it was anyone's guess what he aimed to do next.

"Your pa is right. It'd be best if you headed to California," he said, breaking the silence at last.

He felt her gaze on him, but he stared straight ahead. "Are you anxious to get rid of me?"

"Not by a long shot."

He wanted her where he could watch her, hold her in his arms as she slept, and make love to her. But Arlen was out there skulking around. He had no idea who Erston had cut a deal with. And he was losing hope that Fitzmeyer would arrive in due time and buy the thoroughbreds.

He glanced her way. He'd never seen her look so forlorn. God knew she had good cause.

Hell, she shouldn't be alone in this world. She shouldn't be teaching girls how to live the life that she wanted to lead.

He knew she'd looked forward to spending this Christmas with her pa. She'd been cheated of that. She'd been cheated of so much.

"Did you know that Kirby Morris saved my pa's life once?" she asked.

He shook his head, not having a clue. "When did that happen?"

"Three years ago," she said. "A couple of cowboys caught him stealing a horse and strung him up."

He vaguely remembered hearing a couple of cowpokes brag over hanging a rustler.

"They must not have known who he was," she went on,

"or they'd have hauled Pa to the marshal to collect the reward."

The reward wouldn't have been worth near what it was after the shooting in Laramie. "Kincaid don't look nothing like his wanted posters."

She smiled. "I know. Actually, I didn't recognize him right off."

That told him she hadn't seen her pa in far too long, reminding him she'd been alone. "How'd Kirby figure into this?"

She caught his gaze this time, and the sadness in hers was a gut punch that caught him off guard. "He found Pa swinging from a rope and cut him down."

Reid laughed at his benefactor saving an outlaw's life. "Kirby was good at lending a hand to those in need."

"Pa spoke highly of him," she said. "You never did tell me how you came to know Kirby Morris."

That memory was clear as window glass. "Dade, Trey and I were living on the streets in St. Louis when we came on two thugs beating the hell out of a man who turned out to be Kirby Morris. I was the oldest at twelve and Trey had just turned ten."

"You were just boys," she said, concern ringing in her voice.

He smiled. "We didn't let that stop us from jumping in and fighting off the others. When Kirby found out we were street urchins, he offered to take us west with him."

They'd wanted to be cowboys, and going with Kirby put them closer to finding Dade's sister. Or so they thought. They hadn't any idea just how big and untamed the West really was.

"We took him up on his offer and became a family of sorts," he said.

They topped a rise and the ranch came into view. His breath caught like it always did when he saw it this way.

This was home, and he damned sure was willing to fight for it, and the legacy Kirby left them.

To Ellie's surprise, Hubert had taken the turkey from the oven when he deemed it was cooked. Shane had added his culinary contribution of salt pork and beans. Booth Howard had boiled enough potatoes for an army.

With the biscuits she'd made this morning, they had a passable Christmas dinner. As before, the cowboys ate in shifts so at least three were always on guard.

Sharing Christmas dinner with these hardworking men reminded her of her youth in the outlaw camp. There was no pretense there either. Just smiles and appreciation for the food before them and another day of freedom.

She could get used to this. But would she be denied the chance?

"I rode over to Rocky Point around noon," Shane said when the meal was over and he was sipping his coffee. "The Pearces are anxious to move back to their spread."

Though it wasn't a glamorous honeymoon, Ellie would be content to do the same with Reid. She'd be happy with him anywhere.

"How much longer will Cheryl and Kenton have to stay there?" she asked.

Reid helped himself to more coffee that was as strong and addictive as he was to her senses. "Until Erston gives up trying to ruin their lives and goes home."

"I wonder where Erston is staying?" she asked.

"Hard to say," Reid said. "So far nobody has owned up to taking him in."

The hard glint in his eyes told her that worried him most of all. Erston still held Reid's future in his hands.

"Arlen's the one to watch," Reid said. "He's got his eye on the horses, and he'd do anything to get them."

The men murmured agreement, but the nervous glances they shared with each other scared her. Arlen had abused a woman and killed her in cold blood. She dreaded to think how low the man could sink when it came to stealing a herd of thoroughbreds.

"He won't be able to pin the blame on Pa," she said.

"Maybe that's his angle," Shane said. "With Kincaid in jail, he figures we'll let our guard down."

Reid stroked a finger over his chin as if mulling something over. "That's not a bad idea."

"What're you getting at?" Shane asked.

"Simple. We let Arlen think we feel secure now that Kincaid is in jail." He pushed to his feet and the men did the same. "He'll make his move then."

Shane slid her a passing look before turning to Reid. "If we're all keeping watch over the horses, who's going to keep an eye on Miss Cade?"

"She's heading west on the train tomorrow," he said.

She stared into his emotionless eyes and wanted to scream. He wouldn't even take the time to drive her into Maverick, preferring one of his men haul her off his ranch, and out of his life.

"Is that what you want?" she'd asked him, her chest too tight with heartache to draw a decent breath.

"It's the best thing, Ellie."

No. He couldn't have been more wrong.

* * *

The walls of Ellie's room pulsed in the hushed quiet. It had to be close to midnight, and though this day had been exhausting, she wasn't the least bit sleepy.

She stood at her window and looked out over the Crown Seven Ranch bathed in moonlight. The probability that Frank Arlen was lurking in the shadows had her nerves throbbing.

Coming here had sounded so simple when Mrs. Leach had asked her to assume her position at the ranch. She thought she'd have ample opportunity to talk her pa out of satisfying his vengeance, and spend Christmas with him as well.

But everything had gone wrong.

She hadn't expected to get involved with Reid Barclay and fall hopelessly in love with him. She certainly hadn't suspected that Reid was Slim Cullen, the man her pa was gunning for.

Her head ached anew as she tried to sort it all out. Reid was Slim Cullen. He'd been arrested for Lisa True's murder.

But according to her pa, he was innocent.

Frank Arlen was the real killer.

Ellie fisted her hands against the cold window glass, letting the chill seep into her soul. She was frustrated and heartsick that her pa was in jail. He could hang for something he hadn't done and there wasn't a thing she could do to help him.

Yes, he'd chosen this life long ago. But he was her pa. The worst crime he'd committed was stealing horses. She didn't want to see him die.

Like Reid, he wanted her to take the train to California tomorrow. He wanted her away from here in case the worst came to pass and he was hanged.

California seemed a lifetime away from her now.

Yes, she was qualified to take young ladies under her wing, and she enjoyed helping others. As Irwin had commented, her job at the Denver Academy was the proper one to hold.

She grimaced at that. She'd lived so many years being proper.

Even her tryst with Irwin had been appropriate to a degree, for he was her fiancé. They'd been weeks away from the date he'd set for the nuptials—never mind that she advised the young ladies in her charge to abstain from such lurid activities in the event the wedding was cancelled, either by design or tragedy.

She'd been so hungry for love she'd ignored her own advice. To think of the pains Irwin went through to make sure the lights were out.

Why, the first time she made love she'd expected light-trails in the sky. But she never saw so much as a spark.

He'd fussed that they only bare what was necessary for their coupling. He'd gone about his duty with the same punctuality he employed in business, getting it over and done with in an economy of movement.

Irwin would never have fed her molasses pie with his fingers. He wouldn't have held her close to his heart in the dead of night. Skin to skin. Hearts beating in tandem in that slow, sultry rhythm that begged for the night to go on and on.

She dropped her forehead on her fists and closed her eyes, shivering as the structured walls of her future rose around her like a cold, damp fog. The two men she loved wanted her to take the train to California tomorrow morning.

Her pa wanted her safe and settled in her new position.

Reid simply wanted her off the ranch in case trouble descended. He hadn't even looked her in the eyes when he'd shuffled her out of his life, letting Shane drive her to town.

This would be the last night she'd spend in this house.

Ellie pushed away from the window, hugging herself when it was Reid's arms she longed to have enfold her. She wanted his lips tempting and worshipping hers in turn, his body pressing her down in the mattress and taking her to a place where there was only pleasure.

All she had to do was let her heart go and feel the love that surely must brighten the room on the darkest of nights. A shudder of remembered delight skidded through her, too quickly gone, too brief to sustain her.

Should she follow the safe, structured road, or her heart?

Her fingers closed around the gold band dangling from the ribbon around her neck. He couldn't or wouldn't ask her to marry him with his future up in the air.

All she could be was his lover, and even that couldn't last much longer. But she had tonight—

Her foolish heart begged her to toss respectability to the winds. Her heart knew it needed the love and attention Reid offered her to flourish. Her heart only knew he could fill the empty void she'd lived with all her life— if not forever, then at least for now.

Ah, but her mind was the enemy. It reminded her that even with commitment, the heart could be broken.

She'd gone on after Irwin ended their engagement without suffering a broken heart. In fact, she'd been furious with the self-righteous man, and with herself, for trying to fit into his world.

With Reid, she wouldn't be able to walk away unscathed. Though she'd harbored an affection for Irwin, it was nothing compared to the all-consuming love for Reid Barclay that warmed her blood.

He was the love of her life.

He had the power to destroy her.

Yet even knowing it, there was no way in hell she'd leave tomorrow morning. She couldn't walk away without talking to him one last time. Without kissing him. Touching him. Loving him with all her heart and soul.

Ellie shook her hands at her sides and expelled a heavy breath, having made the only decision she could. She'd have tonight with him.

She'd march to his room now, just like she did before. She'd offer herself to him, no promises, no regrets.

She tiptoed to the door, heart thudding madly as she relived that long walk down the hall to Reid's room. She turned the knob and eased the door opened. And bit back a shriek.

Reid stood outside her door, somehow managing to look relaxed and virile at the same time. A crooked smiled tugged at his mouth.

"Going somewhere?" he asked, his voice pitched to a seductive whisper.

"To you."

He held out a hand, palm up. She slipped hers in his and marveled at the power he exuded, the chafe of his calluses that sent shivers of awareness coursing through her.

He stared at her the longest time with only the barest ribbon of moonlight swirling around them. She feared he'd change his mind—that he'd be noble and send her away.

Before she could find the words to beg him to take her, he drew her down the hall and into his room, and closed the door. "I'm not giving you the chance to change your mind."

"Good, because my mind is set."

The only thing she wanted at that moment was to love him like there was no tomorrow, because for them there likely would only be this moment.

When Mrs. Leach returned, Ellie would make the trek to California and assume the life that had seemed so enticing months ago. And every night she'd dream of him, of this sizzling passion that arced like sheet lightning between them, and of what could have been.

Then he kissed her, and she melted into him and pushed all thoughts of responsibility and morality from her mind. Tonight she wanted nothing to encumber her. She refused to let anything or anyone mar this night.

Her hands tore at his shirt while he seemed in no hurry to remove her clothes. Even his kisses were leisurely samples of pleasures to come.

"I need you, Reid. Now."

"Slow down, sweetheart."

The endearment brought her up short. She could never be anything more than his lover.

She pulled away, barely able to make out his features in the semidarkness. "Why didn't you light a lamp?"

"Prying eyes," he said as he whisked her dressing gown up and off her, leaving her standing there in nothing but a flush of need. "As much as I long to admire you in the altogether, I won't risk drawing attention to my room tonight."

Because Arlen could be watching, she knew. It gave her yet another reason to resent the man, for he was robbing her of embedding this visual memory of their last night together on her mind.

"I'll open the curtains," he said, fitting action to words as he drew back the coverings on both windows.

A silvery glow spilled into the room and left her standing in a pool of moonlight. She covered herself, then thought the gesture foolish as he stalked toward her, a predator intent on its prey.

"Never hide yourself from me," he said, and she hoped that meant there would be more nights like this for them.

His palms skimmed up her sides and set off sparks a blind man could see. She dropped her head back on a moan. Is this what she'd have as his mistress? Would their passion flare in the dark only to die in the light of day?

His mouth closed over one breast and he suckled her dry, driving all sane thoughts from her head. For surely thinking that this was how she wanted to spend the rest of her life wasn't sane.

She was an educator. A woman who'd worked hard to achieve that distinction. Yet here she was, naked as the day she was born and frolicking in the arms of a man who couldn't offer her anything but this moment.

Surely love was a divine madness. Surely this was the best moment of her life, she thought as he picked her up and laid her on the bed. He followed her down, his mouth meandering down her body to linger at her belly.

She sucked in air and grabbed for him, waiting to pull him back up over her, knowing she had to touch him. To hold on. For what was to come would leave her undone.

Her body quivered and bowed upward to his seeking

mouth, her flesh hot and wet and taut with expectation. She breathed the heady musk of him into her lungs, absorbed the salty essence of him through her skin.

Had she been told she'd come to crave this, she'd have denied it with an insulted gasp. Now? Now she clutched at him to hurry him on, to give her the release she needed.

And then his mouth was on her, his breath a scalding brand. One flick of his tongue and she shuddered and came in a dizzying aura of lights. Too soon.

A laugh of satisfaction rumbled from him, distant as she floated among stars. But that incredible mouth of his brought her back to him.

His mouth slid up her chest and his tongue laved the pulse point in her throat.

With each kiss, each caress, rational thought escaped her a bit more. Not that she wanted to think any longer. She wanted to feel his hard body molding over hers, then the throbbing pulse as her inner core cried and stretched when he eased into her, inch by delicious inch.

She ripped his shirt off him and skimmed her palms up his heaving chest, lingering over the male nipples that peaked against her palms. So different from her, yet so alike.

He rolled onto his back, dragging her with him. She draped over his bare body, making note of every ridge of muscle, every taut line of sinew, every jutting inch of his penis pressed at her opening.

She wanted him now. Later they could dawdle over those pleasure points she'd not known she possessed. Later she'd love him as he'd loved her the first time.

The heat of him probing her most sensitive flesh wrenched a moan from her. She tossed her head back and straddled him, taking him in slowly when this time she sensed he ached to go fast.

His hands gripped her waist to help her set the pace. Slow, torturous glides that drew out the sensations until her body quivered and twanged.

On and on, the speed going minutely faster. Her body slicked with sweat, straining and alive like never before.

Here and now faded into a void in time as they came together faster, their bodies meshing perfectly, the sensations building into a white-hot burst of need.

"Now," she said, her voice strained with need.

"Whatever the lady desires."

His mouth captured hers, his fingers playing over where they joined. A slide of his thumb and her back bowed, sensations rippling through her like a skipping stone, going on and on.

He joined her, his body going taut on a grunt, then the spurt of his hot seed filled her, completing her.

She closed her eyes and held him close, branding every nuance on her mind, the texture of his skin, the tang of salt on her tongue, the feeling of rightness that settled over her like a warm blanket on a cold night.

His arms came around her as if to stop her from leaving. Not that Ellie had any intentions of deserting his bed this soon. She sighed, thinking she'd be content to stay like this forever. If only that were possible.

"I'll never get enough of you," he said.

She glided her palms up his corded arms. "I feel the same."

He dropped another kiss on her shoulder, his hands roaming her breasts, down her belly and slipping between her legs. She arched against him, desire flaring red-hot.

Words were unnecessary, though she wondered if he could sense the desperation coursing through her. The realization that when dawn broke, this ideal night they'd shared would be a memory. One she'd cherish forever.

His body shifted over hers again, fluid and taut with power. She wrapped her arms around his lean waist and arched to meet his thrust, pushing worries about families and heartache to the back of her mind.

There would be far too much time later to face reality.

This was perfect. And it hammered home the fact that the memory of what she'd shared with Reid would never be enough.

Chapter 23

The back door slammed and slammed hard. Reid rolled to his feet, unease hammering through at the same frantic pace as his heart.

"What was that?" Ellie asked, her voice drowsy.

"Company."

This time of night it couldn't be good. None of his men would come inside at this hour unless there was trouble.

That thought slammed into his head just as someone pounded up the back stairs. He grabbed his Peacemaker and moved to the door.

"Barclay! Where are you?" Moss—no, Ezra Kincaid asked.

Dammit, how had the outlaw gotten out of jail? Tavish sure as hell wouldn't have set him free.

He flicked a glance at the bed and Ellie sitting up wide-eyed, with the bed sheet clutched to her bare bosom. *Shit!*

"Get dressed and stay back," he ordered, but didn't waste time putting on jeans.

He stormed to the door and opened it. Hubert tottered at the end of the hall in his nightclothes while Ezra Kincaid ambled down the hall toward Reid, reeking of black powder and fear.

"Who the hell let you out of jail?" he asked.

Kincaid swore. "Some fool blew up the jail. Damn wonder it didn't kill us all."

He should've guessed. "One of your gang set on busting you out?"

"Hell, no! I ain't had a gang in nigh over three years."

Was the old man telling the truth? "Somebody sure went to some trouble to break you out."

"I ain't so sure. The explosion tore off the front of the jail," Kincaid said. "If that iron key ring hadn't been thrown back in my cell by the blast, I'd still be there."

That had him thinking someone had a bone to pick with Tavish. "The marshal okay?"

"He was knocked out cold, so I dragged him onto the boardwalk. But I didn't stick around to tend him with half the townsfolk heading that way to see what all the ruckus was about." The old man gave him a quick once over and scowled. "A mite cold to be standing round in the altogether."

"I was in bed."

Kincaid glanced back at Hubert, then squinted at Reid's bedroom door. "Where's Ellie Jo?"

"Reckon she's in bed, too." Never mind she was as naked as he.

Though Kincaid lived on the wrong side of the law, Reid knew he wouldn't cotton to him dallying with Ellie. It sure as hell wasn't something he wanted brought out now. As long as she stayed quiet and in his room, all would be fine.

The old man tipped his head back and eyed him like a hawk would a hare. "She ain't in her bed, 'cause I just checked. What's going on here?"

"Nothing that concerns you," he said, and sucked in a breath when he felt her small hand on his back.

Kincaid's eyes bugged. "Ellie Jo?"

She slipped in front of Reid as if trying to shield him from the old man, clutching the bedclothes around her. "Pa, what are you doing here?"

"I'd ask you the same, except it's mighty clear what's going on." Kincaid skewered him with a look that promised all hell would break loose if he didn't like the answer. "Well?"

So this is what it felt like to look down the barking end of a shotgun wedding. Oddly enough, he hadn't the inclination to fight it right now. Maybe ever?

"I suggest we all seek our beds," Ellie said. "Clearer heads will prevail in the morning."

Kincaid was clearly like a dog with a bone—he wanted to chew on this some more. "You're going to make this right."

Like hell he was! Erston used blackmail to force his hand with Cheryl. He wasn't about to let this old outlaw browbeat or threaten him to marry Ellie.

Nothing had changed. Until he had more to offer than dreams and promises, he wouldn't marry Ellie. Yet the thought of letting her go—

A deafening boom shattered the tension and shook the house. Ellie stumbled into Kincaid's arms. Hubert fell back against the wall.

Reid ran to the window to take stock of the ranch. A fireball roiled into the sky, illuminating the ranch as if it was day.

His ranch hands rushed from the bunkhouse and set to work dousing the flames. One errant spark near the hay barn and he'd lose his winter's supply of feed for the stock.

"What happened?" Ellie asked as she pressed to his side.

"The cook shack exploded." He whirled from the window to confront the old man, but Ezra Kincaid was gone.

"How could that have happened?" she asked. "Pa's been in jail, so the stove wouldn't have overheated."

"This wasn't an accident, Ellie."

He threw on his clothes, his gut twisting with the suspicion that this explosion was somehow connected to the one at the jail. Kincaid claimed that his cronies had no part in breaking him out. If that was true, then why make it look like it? Why come here and blow up the one place where Ezra Kincaid had held sway on the Crown Seven?

Reid jammed his feet into his boots then strapped his gun belt around his hips, welcoming the reassuring weight of his Peacemaker in its holster. He'd never killed a man or woman. Never thought to. Could he pull the trigger?

His gaze met Ellie's, and the fear he read in them stilled his heart a measure. Yep, he wouldn't hesitate to kill anyone who harmed her.

"Stay in the house with Hubert," he said.

"Be careful." She reached up and kissed him, a soft peck that hummed through his blood and teased him with the hope for something better in life. Something good and warm and true.

Gunshots peppered the air, a collage of volume that he recognized all too well. Sidearm and shotgun. It was the latter that forced him to end the kiss too soon.

He stared into her troubled eyes one last time then ran the length of the hall and pounded down the stairs, pushing soft thoughts of the woman he loved from his mind.

Loved? Hell, yes, he did love her. But he couldn't afford to go soft now. .

Hubert stood like a sentry at the rear door with an Adams percussion revolver clutched in his boney hands. "Godspeed, sir."

He dipped his chin in thanks. "Kincaid gone?"

"He's en route to the stables," Hubert said. "He said a varmint was after the horses."

A varmint of the two-legged variety, he'd wager.

Reid burst out the back door and broke into a dead run across the slush and mud. The stench of smoke clouded the air, and the horses' whinnies and stamping echoed with tension.

He drew his Peacemaker and headed to the bunkhouse, blinking as the smoke stung his eyes and made them tear. A tall man stepped from the gloom into his path, his face soot-covered, yet familiar.

"What the hell happened?" he asked Shane.

The cowboy's grim eyes met his. "Don't know, Slim. One minute I was picking my guitar, and the next an explosion damned near shifted the bunkhouse off its foundation."

"Anyone hurt?"

Shane shrugged. "Don't know."

"Where's Howard?"

"He headed to the stable right after supper."

A shotgun blast sounded ahead of them, followed by a horse's loud bugle. Rage pounded through Reid.

Dammit all, there was trouble with the thoroughbreds. He was off at a run toward the stables.

Shane kept pace with him. "Likely Kincaid is back."

That much was true, but was the old man in the thick of it trying to stop a rustler, or was he seeing that his plan came together as he made off with the herd?

Nervous whickers echoed up ahead. Hooves pounded the ground, coming their way.

Another shot split the air, this one more a bang. Likely a sidearm.

"They're about on us," Reid said, feeling the frozen ground rumble beneath his boots as the horses headed his way.

Neal burst from the smoky fog and nearly bowled him and Shane over. The three of them scrambled behind the shed just as nigh on twelve thousand pounds of terrified horseflesh thundered around them. A man's crazed whoop egged them on.

There was no way Reid could stop them. Nothing he could do but listen to his prize horses disappear into the night and hope one of Arlen's shots didn't plow into them, one of his men, or him.

"Saddle up and head after them," Reid said when the shooting stopped, for the trail would get colder the longer they waited.

Shane was already running to the pasture. But no amount of whistling or calling by either cowboy convinced their horses to come that close to the stench of black powder. Even Kaw refused to obey.

"We'll round 'em up." Shane and Neal took off across the pasture and were soon swallowed up in the haze that drifted from the remains of the cook shack.

Reid kicked a rock from his path and headed to the stables, pissed to high heaven that he'd failed. He stood in the empty paddock that had held his prize thoroughbreds and his dreams to raise horses and live out his life right here.

His ace in the hole—gone in a blink.

Despite having his men watch the horses day and night, it'd been disgustingly easy for Frank Arlen to steal them. Now he feared the bastard would run them into the ground getting away.

The rustler would push the herd hard and risk that a mare threw a foal. He wouldn't care if one of them broke the elegant legs that were unsuited to riding wild over this rough terrain.

He tipped his head back and stared at the moon, madder than hell and sick at heart. It was likely after midnight now. Who now owned the majority of the Crown Seven?

A faint moan came from the stable. He ran that way, frantically searching the dimly lighted interior for the source.

"Howard? Where the hell are you?" he asked.

Another moan answered him, this one slightly stronger. He ran down the aisle and searched each stall. Near the last one he spied his foreman, sprawled facedown.

Reid hustled over to him and knelt at his side, his insides twisting over the sight of blood soaking the foreman's trousers. Howard had caught a bullet in the leg.

"Hang on."

Reid scrambled to find toweling. He pressed it to Howard's thigh to staunch the blood.

"Arlen," Howard said, and winced.

"I know. It's been him all along."

A shrill whinny sounded outside. He looked up just as Kincaid hobbled into the stable leading a ganglylegged colt.

"How'd you manage to catch him?" Reid asked.

"Experience, boy." Kincaid half dragged the colt into a stall and closed the door. "When them horses took off out of here, I lassoed this little feller as they rounded the barn."

Reid shook his head. One colt saved out of a herd that was worth a fortune.

Kincaid ambled over to him. "Hell, Howard. How bad is it?"

"Burns like hell, Moss." Howard frowned. "Or should I call you Kincaid?"

"Makes no never mind." Kincaid knelt to examine the wound. "That bullet's got to come out."

Howard grimaced. "Then do it."

"That's beyond what I can do. Best get you back to the bunkhouse and fetch the doctor." Kincaid got to his feet with effort as Shane and Neal came running into the stable.

"What's going on here?" Shane asked, his hand hovering by his sidearm and his narrowed gaze locked on Kincaid.

"Howard was shot." Reid nodded at the old man. "He caught the colt as Arlen was making off with the herd."

Shane took it all in with narrowed eyes. "Reckon it's fitting that a rustler lassoed the colt. How'd you get out of jail?"

"You can haggle over that later," Reid said. "Help me carry Howard to the bunkhouse. Neal, snag a horse and ride for thunder into Maverick. Get Doc Neely out here as fast as you can, and tell the marshal that Frank Arlen rustled the herd. But don't tell a soul you saw Kincaid here."

"Yes, sir." Neal kicked up dust running from the stable.

Shane hesitated a moment then hurried to help move Howard. They went slow so they wouldn't jar him too badly, but every second gave Arlen time to secrete the herd.

As soon as Howard was settled in bed, Reid headed for the pastures. He whistled for Kaw. This time the gelding tossed his head and moved toward him, though he was still leery and skittish.

"That paint wouldn't let me near him," Shane said, topping the rise behind Kaw with four horses in tow.

Exactly why Reid had favored this horse. Kaw was loyal, but a stubborn cuss at times. Like now when time was short.

"You going after Arlen?" Shane asked.

"Soon as I can saddle up."

"I'm going with you," Kincaid said.

"Not a good idea," he said. "Tavish is likely to join us, and he might just shoot you this time instead of hauling your ass into jail."

Reid slipped the loop over Kaw's hard head and headed back to the barn a few steps behind Shane. Kaw pranced with nervous energy, his coat rippling like velvet caught in the wind. No doubt the smell of smoke still had him spooked. Low clouds of it hung around the outbuildings and house.

Shane turned the three horses into the paddock and tethered his mount to the fence. Reid did the same and then followed him into the tack room for their gear.

"You're going to need help rounding up them horses," Kincaid said and hefted a saddle off its tree. "The only thing I'm damn good at is rustling."

"We'll have to find the herd first," Reid said, and knew that wouldn't be easy in the dark.

"That colt will help us." Kincaid grinned. "That mare is going to be mighty restless when it's time to nurse and that colt ain't around. You mark my words."

Reid mulled that over. "It'll work."

Kincaid bobbed his white head. "I got a feeling he's been holed up close by all along. Easier for him to hide in plain sight with those horses."

Could he be right? If Arlen had a hiding place nearby,

he could easily double back after they'd ridden out. Ellie would be here with only Hubert to defend her.

"Shane, stay here and watch over Ellie," he said. "Once Arlen hides the herd, he might slip back here to raise more hell."

"I don't like this," Shane said.

Neither did he, but Ellie would be safer with Shane watching over things. "With Howard down, I need a man I can trust here while the old man and I go after the horses."

Shane slid Kincaid a dubious look, then dipped his chin. "You're the boss. But if you aren't back by sunup, I'll put men on guard duty and come looking for you."

"Fair enough."

Reid and the old outlaw stayed to the road that wound southwest, following a faint trail and Kincaid's gut feeling that Arlen had headed this way. He wasn't sure anymore.

A biting wind at his back proved the Chinook wind had come and gone, and clouds had shrouded the full moon. But the snow that had started falling right after they left the ranch now covered the tracks with a blanket of white.

Arlen could have veered off the road and be heading east or west. The sonofabitch could be out of the county.

If Arlen had a buyer lined up, those horses could be loaded onto a railcar and out of the state. Worry tied Reid's gut in knots. There was a good chance he'd never find Arlen or the herd.

Kincaid reined up sharp and tipped his head back. "I smell smoke."

He sniffed, catching the unmistakable scent of wood-smoke as well. That shouldn't be, at least not here. Even with the strong wind, smoke wouldn't carry that far and be that strong.

Nope, this fire was close.

He turned Kaw in a slow circle to get his bearings. They'd reached the northern edge of Rocky Point Ranch.

The road hugged the creek here. To the east, the ground stretched in a flat plain, but to the west it climbed a rocky hill to a shelf of land that was ten acres or more at best.

The remains of an early homestead was there, abandoned because pit vipers claimed it from the spring till frost. But the rattlers hibernated in the winter.

"Up ahead there's a trail that leads to an abandoned ranch," he said. "Arlen could be holed up there."

"How much cover?"

He wasn't sure. "As I recall, once you climb out of the arroyo, you're in the open."

Kincaid swore. "We'd best hope the snowfall shields us then."

They road in silence to the trail cut by wildlife. Midway down, the ground looked churned from hooves.

"This has to be it," Reid said, gaining a nod of agreement from Kincaid.

The old rustler reined his mount down the incline first. Kaw balked, not wanting to risk the hill that was made more treacherous by the near frozen mud.

He waited until Kincaid had crossed the creek and started up the other bank before urging Kaw to pick his path. The big gelding blew hard, but started down the slope. His hind legs slid under him once and nearly unseated Reid, but he leaned back as far as he dare and let Kaw get his legs under him again.

The old outlaw had already made it up the opposite

bank by the time he reached the creek. The gelding forded it and climbed the bank in a few powerful lunges.

Kincaid stood by a stand of trees, his back and his horse covered with snow. "Up ahead," he said.

He squinted but saw nothing but a wall of white before him. The only saving grace was if he couldn't see the cabin, Arlen couldn't see them. Or so he hoped.

They set off at a walk, the time crawling by until the dark outline of a cabin loomed before them. A soft whicker echoed up ahead, soon joined by another. Had to be his thoroughbreds.

"The weather is getting too dangerous to drive the horses out," he said.

"Didn't intend to," Kincaid said. "Horses will be fine where they are. It's that no-account inside we need to round up for the marshal."

"Can't just barge in." That'd likely gain them a gut full of lead. "You got an idea how to flush him out?"

"Sure do."

Kincaid cupped his hands around his mouth and let out a howl that raised the hair on Reid's nape and set the horses whickering and stamping. Hell, if he hadn't been watching the old outlaw, he'd swear a lone wolf was near.

"Come on." Kincaid reined his horse and set off around the far end of the cabin.

When they drew near to what remained of a barn, he let loose another howl. The horses snorted and began milling in the corral.

Kincaid dismounted and tied his horse to an old hitching rail on the far side of the barn. His hat, shoulders and back were now white with snow.

"I'm going to draw him out," Kincaid said. "Get the jump on him then. We likely won't get a second try."

The old outlaw ambled down the narrow finger of

land between the corral and the rocky cliff. Reid swung from the saddle and secured his gelding near the outlaw's mount, then angled back toward the cabin.

Muted light seeped from around the shutters on the window. Arlen was in there. Was he alone?

The plaintive howl of a wolf echoed from the murky darkness, throwing the horses into a nervous frenzy. He whispered his Peacemaker from the holster and eased toward the cabin door.

Tense moments passed before it opened and Arlen stepped out, a shotgun resting against his shoulder. Light poured out the door to pool around him.

"Drop it," Reid said, thumbing the hammer back on his sidearm.

Arlen didn't move. "I can pull the trigger and pepper the corral with buckshot long before you get a shot off to kill me."

It was a galling fact Reid didn't like acknowledging. Even if Arlen missed hitting the horses, they'd bolt. In this weather that'd likely result in them going down.

But he couldn't let Arlen get away either. He just hoped Kincaid didn't take it into his head to shoot Arlen because then they'd never get the truth out of him.

Reid damn sure wanted the whole truth.

"What did you do with the stallion you stole off me?" he asked.

"In a stall in the barn. Feller said I'd make more money off the stallion and the mares."

"You'll never see the money," he said, trying to divert Arlen's attention so he could get the jump on him.

That's all he needed. Once he lowered that shotgun, he'd plug him.

Arlen laughed. "Neither will you if I pull this trigger."

Damn him! "Why shoot the horses that can make you money when it's me you want dead?"

Just when he thought Arlen would aim that shotgun at him, a muffled sound came from beyond the corral. He hoped it was Kincaid getting the horses tethered together for the ride back to the Crown Seven.

"It was you who blew up the jail and the cook shack," he said. "Why?"

"Plain to see that with Kincaid busted out of jail, he and his gang would set off another explosion at the ranch so they could make off with the horses."

Reid had to hand it to him, for most people would believe that, including him. How wrong he'd been about Ezra Kincaid all these years.

"Why'd you kill that woman in Laramie?" he asked, when Arlen stepped back in the doorway.

Again Arlen let out a crazed laugh that stabbed Reid with chills. "She aimed to tell her beau what we'd been doing in the livery. Couldn't let her do that."

Disgust boiled in his gut. "You raped her."

"She asked for it, coming in the livery and insisting I hitch up a buggy for her." Arlen laughed. "I hitched her up, all right. Tossed her skirts and showed her who was boss. The little bitch fought like a wildcat."

Men like Arlen didn't deserve to draw air. "Drop the shotgun," he said again.

"Go to hell, Barclay."

"I'd rather send you there." His finger curled on the trigger, ready to squeeze.

"You gunned her down so she wouldn't identify you." Tavish's voice cracked like a whip just to the side of the cabin. "You lied to the law so they'd go after Kincaid."

Dammit, where was the old man? Had Tavish spotted

him? Or had Kincaid spied the lawman and taken off on foot?

Arlen sneered and steadied the shotgun as if planning to squeeze off a round. "What if I did? You can't prove a damned thing."

"I don't have to. I heard you bragging on how you got away with murder," Tavish said. "But not this time."

The crack of a rifle tore through the gloom, followed by a second one. Glass shattered inside the cabin and a flare of bright light arced out the door. Arlen staggered backward into the cabin with a guttural grunt and let go a shotgun blast at the same time.

The horses whickered, whinnied and charged in the corral, slamming into the rails so hard they groaned and cracked. Damn the man! It wouldn't take much for the horses to bolt.

He kept his back to the wall and eased to the door, half hoping he'd find a dead man instead of a trap. He heard the roar of flames before he peeked around the doorway.

The shattered remains of a kerosene lamp lay on the floor. So did Arlen. He stared at the ceiling, a black hole smack dab in the middle of his forehead.

Reid debated about rushing in to pull him out, but a timber gave way overhead. In a blink the roof collapsed on the old cabin.

Reid headed for the corral and the restive horses. Halfway there, Kincaid hobbled out of the darkness with Tavish right behind him. He was sure the lawman had a gun to the old man's back.

"Let him go," Reid said to Tavish.

"Can't do that. He's a wanted man."

"For rustling horses years back," he said. "He never killed that woman. You heard Arlen."

"I heard, but I can't absolve Kincaid on hearsay. I'd have to bring Arlen before the judge." Tavish glared at the cabin fully ablaze now. "Too late for that."

Reid hunched his stiff shoulders and refused to give up yet. This was Ellie's pa. He'd worked for Reid for a whole damned year without causing one stir. He'd still be working there if he hadn't gone into Maverick to buy Ellie that doll he'd neglected to get for her when she was a child.

"Let Ezra Kincaid die tonight," Reid said.

"You sonofabitch," the old man said. "After what you did to Ellie Jo—"

"I'm sticking my neck out for her," Reid said as he squared off against Tavish, the loud crackle and sizzle of wet logs in the background. "Who's to know if Kincaid died in the explosion at the Crown Seven, or in this fire?"

"That'd break my vow to uphold the law."

"No, that's righting a wrong," Reid said. "Kincaid is the man who witnessed a murder. If he hadn't gone after Arlen tonight, the no-account might have gotten away with murder."

"Kincaid is still a rustler."

"Let it go, Tavish. You got the man who killed Lisa True."

The marshal shoved Kincaid forward and stepped back, his gaze flicking from Reid to Kincaid, his Colt .45 gripped in one hand. "You want Ezra Kincaid dead? Fine. I'll end his miserable life right now."

Chapter 24

This had been the most troubled Christmas of her life. One week ago she'd come here for the sole purpose of spending the holiday with her pa, and talking him out of hunting down the real killer.

She'd struggled to put a meal on the table.

She'd made love with Reid and shamelessly enjoyed every kiss, every heated stroke, every breath they shared.

One week ago she'd viewed her time here as a brief visit before she assumed her new teaching job in California. Now her heart just wasn't into it.

No, her heart belonged to Reid Barclay.

She laid her palm on her chest and smiled, feeling the ring he'd given her press against her bosom. How could he possibly think he couldn't give her anything when he'd already given her torrid memories that would last her a lifetime?

The back door opened on a gust of icy air that chilled her to the bone. She knew who'd come home before Reid stalked into the kitchen. He looked ready to drop with exhaustion.

His glaze flicked from her to Hubert. "Ezra Kincaid is dead."

Ellie grabbed the back of the chair and swayed, feeling the stab of grief shoot right through her.

Even Hubert seemed dumbfounded by that cold announcement.

"What happened?" she managed to get out.

"Marshal Tavish shot him, but a fire started in the cabin he was holed up in and he was trapped." Reid shook his head, his mouth a grim line.

She dropped on the chair this time, sick at heart. Why was he telling her this so coldly?

"The horses, sir?" Hubert asked.

"Moss helped me bring them back," he said.

Her head snapped up and her gaze shot to his. Had she heard him right? "Moss?"

"Yep. He was there with me and Tavish when Kincaid died."

She read the truth in his eyes and realized something very wonderful had happened this Christmas. Somehow two men had decided to give her pa redemption.

The outlaw was dead.

Her pa had been reborn.

"Any chance Dade or Trey are here?" Reid asked, his dark eyes bright with hope.

"Unfortunately not, sir," Hubert said.

Reid ran a hand down his face and swore, but it was the bleak resignation in his midnight-blue eyes that broke her heart. "Reckon we can expect a visit from Erston soon."

She had nothing to say to that, for Reid would likely lose the ranch now. She just wished this proud, arrogant cowboy would realize that his own worth wasn't tied to the land.

* * *

Reid stood at the window admiring the thoroughbreds prancing in their corral. They'd been Kirby's dream that had passed on to him, and he'd done well with the breeding program.

He'd had such plans. But a drunken spree in Laramie two years ago changed his life, and not for the better.

It didn't matter now that Burl Erston had duped Kirby and him. The deal had had been made, and now the consequences had to be met.

He'd failed Kirby, his foster brothers, and himself.

He'd lost the ranch because he'd been so damned sure Dade and Trey would return to stake their claims. He'd believed he could beat Burl Erston at his own devious game.

A lone rider reined up in front of the house, the collar of his greatcoat turned up and a bowler planted squarely on his head. Speak of the devil—

Burl Erston dismounted and tied the horse's line to the iron hitching post. His swagger said it all.

Reid pushed away from the window and strode to his desk for what might be the last time. He held no hope that Erston had had a change of heart.

Nope, the man was heartless.

He cared about one thing. Money.

The office door swung open and Erston entered. His mockery of a smile proved he'd come to gloat.

"I wanted to be the first to inform you that I sold my shares of the Crown Seven," Erston said.

It was all Reid could do to hide his surprise. But damn, he sure hadn't expected that. While he was glad to have Erston out of his hair, he dreaded to learn who'd own controlling interest in the ranch.

"Who bought them?"

"A gentleman I happened to meet in Laramie." Erston poured himself a generous glass of bourbon. "I was at the depot when Mr. and Mrs. Charlton arrived. Once I realized why they were here, I invited them to share Christmas dinner with me at the boardinghouse. It seems Mrs. Charlton is looking for her long lost son who was taken from her at birth."

A pang of empathy eddied in him, for he knew the pain of growing up without a mother's love. "How old is the boy?"

"He's a grown man now." Erston let out a laugh that roused a real bad suspicion in Reid. "All she knew was the boy was placed in the Guardian Angel's Orphan Asylum. Can you believe that she and her husband are attempting to track down those boys who lived there?"

"There were a helluva lot of them," Reid said. "But I'm guessing you told her about me, Dade and Trey."

"Actually I didn't mention your foster brothers," he said. "It seemed more circumspect to keep the information at a minimum and hint that you may be this long lost son."

"You lying sonofabitch!" Reid's mother had died shortly after birthing him, and the midwife had taken him to the Guardian Angel's Orphan Asylum soon afterward.

"This is business. I was merely doing what I could to gain the price I was asking." Erston shrugged. "It should be interesting to see what happens when they learn the truth."

Reid grabbed the Englishman by the collar and slammed him up against the door. The man clawed at his hand, his eyes bulging and his face purpling.

"Get the hell off this ranch and don't ever come back." He shoved the man into the hall and came after him, fists bunched at his sides.

Erston stumbled backward to the door, cradling his throat and coughing violently. "My only regret," he said, wheezing deeply, "is that I won't be on hand to see you finally ruined."

The slamming of the door closed that troubled chapter on his life. But what did the next segment promise? Did this signal an end to his life here at the Crown as well?

"This is business, and the Charltons assumed they were doing their lost son a favor by buying shares in his failing ranch." Erston shrugged. "Who knows? Perhaps one of your foster brothers is this missing son."

"You know the chances of that being true are damn slim."

"Indeed so, but the economy is deplorable and I wish to get what I can out of the ranch and return to England. They offered a price I couldn't refuse," Erston said, his smile as stingy as his kindness. "It should be interesting to see what happens when they learn the truth."

"Don't give up, Reid," Ellie said.

He looked in the parlor to find her standing on a chair by the tree with the cornhusk angel in her hands. Sun streamed through the window and painted fiery streaks in her auburn hair, but it was the passion within her that lighted the fire in her eyes.

He strode into the room and stood before her, his hands coming up to cup her bottom. "I'm down to nothing, Ellie."

"That's not true," she said, threading her fingers through his hair so lightly he groaned with need. "You still have your horses. And you have me."

"But I've lost the ranch."

She shook her head, her smile sad. "Then you'll find a way to buy another one. This land doesn't define you. What's in your heart does."

Could it be that simple?

He was a heartbeat from grabbing her off the chair and showing her what was in his heart when the clearing of a throat shattered the mood. He gave Ellie a hand getting off the chair, then reluctantly let go of her and turned to find Hubert in the doorway.

An older couple stood behind him. Where the hell had they come from?

The gentleman wore a no-nonsense expression that didn't bode well, while the woman studied him with wide, hope-filled eyes. Ah, hell, were they the new owners?

"Mr. and Mrs. Charlton are here," Hubert said.

"Welcome to the Crown Seven." Reid strode forward and offered the man his hand. "Erston was by earlier to tell me he'd sold out to you. May I ask how long you'd been negotiating on this?"

The gentleman gave a firm shake. "It was a spur-of-the-moment decision we arrived at after talking at length with Mr. Erston. He led us to believe you were the young man my wife has been looking for."

He sent her a commiserating smile. "Erston mentioned it to me as well. Sorry he lied to you. Now if we can come to terms regarding the ranch—"

"May I see your nape?" Mrs. Charlton asked, the entreaty in her voice touching something deep inside him. "I was told that my son had a strawberry birthmark."

He knelt before the short woman who seemed desperate to find her son and let her part the hair at his nape. Her heavy exhalation told him what he already knew.

"You're not him," Mrs. Charlton said.

Reid got to his feet. "No, ma'am. My mother was from Ireland. She died giving me life."

"But you ended up in the Guardian Angel's Orphan Asylum," she said.

"Yep, along with forty other boys of differing ages." All urchins with no kin and no hope.

"Didn't you have any family?"

Distant relatives and a father who denounced him. "None that wanted me."

She laid her hand on his arm. "How many boys were near your age?"

Reid frowned, thinking. "Maybe a dozen."

"That's what we were led to believe," Mr. Charlton said. "We've tracked down over six men, and learned two have gone on to their reward."

"Any chance you've found Trey March or Dade Logan yet?" he asked.

The Charltons shook their heads, and he faced the possibility that one or both of his foster brothers were dead. That would explain why they'd never defied the bogus rustling charge and come to claim their shares.

So many questions that still needed answers. Would he ever find his foster brothers again?

"I understand you have thoroughbreds," Charlton said, and Reid welcomed the change of subject.

"Yes, sir, though I've got them up for sale right now."

"You giving up on raising horses?" Charlton asked.

"For now. I need the revenue to start over."

Charlton eyed him curiously. "Why would you want to do that when you own a share of this ranch?"

Reid spread his arms wide. "One sixth isn't much to hang a man's hat on."

"You want sole ownership," Charlton said.

He shook his head. "This ranch is the only home me, and my foster brothers, know. I wanted to keep it that way."

"If you agree to manage the ranch for me," Charlton

said, "I'll let you purchase your foster brothers' shares, providing one of them isn't our son."

Reid smiled, liking this man already. "You've got a deal, sir," he said and sealed the agreement with a firm handshake.

Moss poked his head in the parlor, eyes twinkling and pug nose red from the cold, as he scanned the room for Ellie. "I cooked enough for all of us tonight."

"Thank you," she said, and came to stand beside Reid as she greeted the couple. "I trust you're staying the night."

"If we won't be putting you out, dear," Mrs. Charlton said, as the jingle of sleigh bells drew close.

"I'm sure there's enough," she said, which Moss confirmed with a relaxed nod.

Reid peered out the window at the newcomer. Damn, he'd forgotten all about the man.

Moments later, Hubert had divested the visitor of his heavy frock coat and led him into the parlor. "Afternoon, reverend."

"Good day to you all too," the preacher said, glancing at the gathering. "I came as soon as I could, Mr. Barclay. Am I too late?"

Reid looked down at Ellie and smiled, certain he'd never had such a wild idea come over him. But it felt right.

"You're just in time," he said.

He took the cornhusk angel from Ellie and put it back atop the tree that she'd carefully decorated for his wedding. "You got to know I love you, Ellie."

She bobbed her head and smiled up at him with tear-filled eyes. "It's still good to hear it. You know I love you, too."

He nodded, his throat getting tight with emotion.

For a heartbeat, the enormity of what he was about to do hammered at his old fears again. This time, that suffocating punch to his gut was gone.

"Miss Eleanor Jo Cade," he began, and dropped on a knee and had the satisfaction of seeing her eyes go wide and her soft kissable lips part. "Will you do me the honor of becoming my wife?"

She laughed and cried and threw herself into his arms. "Yes," she said against his lips. "Yes."

He allowed one quick kiss that had him craving more and stood with her tucked against his side. Yep, he'd never felt this need for another woman before. Never experienced this fear that he'd open his eyes and she'd be gone.

"You still have that ring?" he asked her.

She tugged on the ribbon around her neck and handed him the gold band set with a trio of diamonds, warm from nestling between her breasts.

And so under the watchful eye of the cornhusk angel her mama had made, the misty eyes of an old outlaw who'd mended his ways, and the couple who were giving him a second chance to follow his dream, Reid Barclay married the woman who captured his heart and made him believe Christmas wishes do come true.

Romantic Suspense from
Lisa Jackson

See How She Dies	0-8217-7605-3	$6.99US/$9.99CAN
Final Scream	0-8217-7712-2	$7.99US/$10.99CAN
Wishes	0-8217-6309-1	$5.99US/$7.99CAN
Whispers	0-8217-7603-7	$6.99US/$9.99CAN
Twice Kissed	0-8217-6038-6	$5.99US/$7.99CAN
Unspoken	0-8217-6402-0	$6.50US/$8.50CAN
If She Only Knew	0-8217-6708-9	$6.50US/$8.50CAN
Hot Blooded	0-8217-6841-7	$6.99US/$9.99CAN
Cold Blooded	0-8217-6934-0	$6.99US/$9.99CAN
The Night Before	0-8217-6936-7	$6.99US/$9.99CAN
The Morning After	0-8217-7295-3	$6.99US/$9.99CAN
Deep Freeze	0-8217-7296-1	$7.99US/$10.99CAN
Fatal Burn	0-8217-7577-4	$7.99US/$10.99CAN
Shiver	0-8217-7578-2	$7.99US/$10.99CAN
Most Likely to Die	0-8217-7576-6	$7.99US/$10.99CAN
Absolute Fear	0-8217-7936-2	$7.99US/$9.49CAN
Almost Dead	0-8217-7579-0	$7.99US/$10.99CAN
Lost Souls	0-8217-7938-9	$7.99US/$10.99CAN
Left to Die	1-4201-0276-1	$7.99US/$10.99CAN
Wicked Game	1-4201-0338-5	$7.99US/$9.99CAN
Malice	0-8217-7940-0	$7.99US/$9.49CAN

Available Wherever Books Are Sold!
Visit our website at **www.kensingtonbooks.com**

All of us in the Christian higher-education enterprise are asking the same question: Can we use technology to educate students without foregoing the virtues inherent in our universities? These virtues define us: Christlike formation, faculty mentoring, character development, thoughtful and biblical integration, and the nurturing of a servant leader. Without these, we go limp. For anyone asking those questions, you need to read *Character Formation in Online Education*. Dr. Joanne Jung, a contemplative and historically grounded professor, guides thoughtful leaders through the complex and growing place of digital learning in Christian higher education today.

Barry H. Corey, President, Biola University

The future reality of online education has generated a good deal of anxiety among educators, particularly Christian educators who care about the personal and spiritual development of students. Joanne Jung has provided a vision for how online education may in fact open whole new opportunities for relationally and spiritually connecting with students in all kinds of fields where the traditional classroom sometimes fails. Online education in some cases provides the professor an opportunity to relate to more students and hear what is actually going on in their lives than they might in a physical classroom setting where there are more limitations on relational space. For some students this might be a very important and welcome change in their educational experience. There is much to think about and build upon in these pages.

John Coe, Director, Institute for Spiritual Formation; Professor of Spiritual Theology and Philosophy, Talbot School of Theology and Rosemead School of Psychology

The famous advertising man David Ogilvy believes a big idea is one he wishes he thought of himself. Joanne has written a book that I wish I wrote! My prediction is that the majority of learning in the lives of my children and grandchildren will be done on mobile devices in the future. Online education will dominate. Dr. Jung has given us the first real pathway to spiritual formation in cyberspace. Congratulations!

Michael K. Clifford, Education Entrepreneur, Philanthropist

The timing was perfect. I, the online education newbie, was eager to learn what to do. Joanne Jung was the master with a fresh new manual written just for people like me. I ate it up. What a fascinating collage of insights! Puritan history, positive psychology, spiritual mystery, and contemporary pedagogy, all woven together into a single guide to online education for those of us who are concerned not only with the accumulation of information but also in the development of Christian character. I put Joanne's suggestions into practice with passion: instructor presence and collaborative participation, lecture videos, teaming with a course designer, and more. Much to my surprise, both my students and I are really enjoying the online educational experience. And what is more, we are growing in our faith through the experience.

Evan B. Howard, Affiliate Associate Professor of Christian Spirituality, Fuller Theological Seminary; Founder and Director of Spirituality Shoppe: An Evangelical Center for the Study of Christian Spirituality

Character formation in online education? If that sounds like an oxymoron, get ready for a paradigm shift. And no one is better equipped to change the way we think about spiritual formation in the digital age than Joanne Jung. This book is the product of years of classroom experience from an educator who is both a leader in spiritual formation in the classroom and a pioneer in the application of distance-learning technology. And she's passionate. She cares about her students, she cares about her teaching, and she cares about making an impact for Christ's kingdom. Whether you are just preparing your first online class or have been working in the digital classroom for a decade, this book will bring fresh ideas and new inspiration. Read it. Your students will thank you!

Moyer Hubbard, Associate Professor, Talbot School
of Theology, Chair, New Testament Department

Can *character formation* and *online education* really coexist? In this brief, hands-on introductory guide, Joanne Jung demonstrates the realistic opportunities for bringing head and heart together in student learning. Employing a conversational style and laden with the details one wants to know, Jung encourages and empowers college teachers, in turn, to encourage and empower their students within this distinctive educational delivery system. Part Two, focusing on character formation, offers great ideas for going deeper, beyond the important but usual knowledge and competency learning outcomes. Furthermore, bonus features include guidance for first-time online instructors and insights about a robust conception of teaching and the integration of faith and learning that can stimulate veteran professors.

Klaus Issler, Professor of Christian Education and Theology,
Biola University; author, *Living into the Life of Jesus*

As we become more aware of the need for creating environments that are conducive to fostering and promoting spiritual formation in Christian distance education, this book helps everyone from the novice to the well-informed navigate the waters of online course development. Jung has developed a valuable instrument for guiding the practitioner toward an understanding of the integration between formative experiences through the relationships in community and learning content. Her book bridges the divide between online and hybrid education in a way that helps one apply basic principles of formation in technologically mediated learning environments.

Mary E. Lowe, Associate Dean and Professor, School of Divinity, Liberty University;
Executive Director, The Association of Christian Distance Education, Senior
Co-Chair, Council of Distance Learning Directors in Theological Education

The development of character during the formative years of higher education is a critical function of the college experience. Dr. Jung presents compelling arguments and practical approaches to online education and current technology tools that can enhance the learning and social experience.

David Metcalf, Director, METIL, Institute for Simulation
and Training University of Central Florida

CHARACTER FORMATION IN

ONLINE EDUCATION

Also by Joanne J. Jung

Knowing Grace:
Cultivating a Lifestyle of Godliness

Godly Conversation:
Rediscovering the Puritan
Practice of Conference

CHARACTER FORMATION IN

ONLINE EDUCATION

A Guide for Instructors, Administrators,
and Accrediting Agencies

JOANNE J. JUNG

ZONDERVAN

Character Formation in Online Education
Copyright © 2015 by Joanne J. Jung

This title is also available as a Zondervan ebook.
Visit www.zondervan.com/ebooks.

Requests for information should be addressed to:
Zondervan, 3900 *Sparks Dr. SE, Grand Rapids, Michigan* 49546

Library of Congress Cataloging-in-Publication Data

Jung, Joanne J.
    Character formation in online education : a guide for instructors, administrators,
and accrediting agencies / Joanne J. Jung.
        pages   cm
    ISBN 978-0-310-52030-6 (softcover)
    1. Web-based instruction. 2. Distance education. 3. Personality development.
I. Title.
LB1044.87.J845   2015
371.33'44678 – dc23   2015005046

All Scripture quotations, unless otherwise indicated, are taken from The Holy Bible, *New International Version®, NIV®.* Copyright © 1973, 1978, 1984, 2011 by Biblica, Inc.® Used by permission. All rights reserved worldwide.

Scripture quotations marked HCSB are from the Holman Christian Standard Bible®, Copyright © 1999, 2000, 2002, 2003, 2009 by Holman Bible Publishers. Used by permission. Holman Christian Standard Bible®, Holman CSN®, and HCSB® are federally registered trademarks of Holman Bible Publishers.

Scripture quotations marked NASB are from the *New American Standard Bible.* Copyright © 1960, 1962, 1963, 1968, 1971, 1972, 1973, 1975, 1977, 1995 by The Lockman Foundation. Used by permission.

Scripture quotations marked NRSV are from the *New Revised Standard Version of the Bible,* copyright © 1989 by the Division of Christian Education of the National Council of Churches of Christ in the United States of America, and are used by permission. All rights reserved.

Any Internet addresses (websites, blogs, etc.) and telephone numbers in this book are offered as a resource. They are not intended in any way to be or imply an endorsement by Zondervan, nor does Zondervan vouch for the content of these sites and numbers for the life of this book.

Cover Design: LUCAS Art and Design
Cover images: Masterfile
Interior design: Kait Lamphere

Printed in the United States of America

15 16 17 18 19 20 21 22 23 24 25 /DCI/ 20 19 18 17 16 15 14 13 12 11 10 9 8 7 6 5 4 3 2 1

CONTENTS

130708

TO THE READER

Character formation is grounded in Christian values, borne by belief in a triune God. He has ordained us as educators. We have been esteemed with the opportunity, responsibility, and honor to deeply impact our students' lives. *Character Formation in Online Education* provides practical ideas for customizing your online courses and improving your pedagogical methodology, irrespective of your discipline. As the reach of online education expands, so do the opportunities to effect real character formation. It is my hope that your students will not be the only ones to experience transformation.

FOREWORD

You are about to enjoy the great privilege of drinking deep from the well of a master. Dr. Joanne Jung is among the most skilled instructors I know. With seeming effortlessness she combines academic rigor, passionate teaching, effective course design, and heart for her students. I know of no better model from whom to learn the art and the craft of teaching.

Many of us regard online teaching as a barren land, devoid of the possibilities of true learning or the creation of a learning community. At Biola Dr. Jung has shown these stereotypes false. Although she enjoys sterling evaluations for her classroom teaching, Dr. Jung ventured into the world of digital delivery. She discovered there the possibilities for rich interaction and deep learning for her students, in some ways surpassing that which is possible in the traditional classroom. A passionate advocate for digital instruction, Dr. Jung here freely shares with the rest of us what she has learned.

Brimming with insights and practical advice, Dr. Jung's text breathes the commitment and concern of a skilled disciple-maker. It abounds with arresting insights. With painful realization I discerned my own early efforts at online teaching in her section "How to Create a Loser Course."

The book is clear, compelling, and practical.

Dr. Jung somehow manages to blend broad overview with organized and helpful detail, and the text is studded with suggestions and delightful examples.

This book delivers more than advertised. It is an excellent primer on good teaching in the digital age, whether the form of delivery is in the classroom, online, or hybrid. You hold in your hand one of the essential tools for successful teaching in the digital age.

Good teaching is student centered and outcome driven. Here you will find a trustworthy and sapient guide to both. Recognizing that today's students are digital natives, Dr. Jung embraces this reality and has discovered how to connect with them in ways that can surpass your expectations.

David Nystrom, author, *NIV Application Commentary: James*;
former Provost and Sr. Vice President, Biola University

RISING TO THE CHALLENGE

Advertising for online courses is ubiquitous: TV, radio, billboards, newspapers, magazines, the Internet. But are all online courses created equal? The general consensus among students is that online classes are easy. That descriptor, however, does not generally refer to the ease of access to these courses, though they are accessible. Nor does it describe the students' poolside relaxation while taking the course, though I'm sure that has been done. In this case, *easy* means completing some reading, adding to a discussion board, and submitting a final paper. The course is essentially taken in isolation with no requirement to interact or converse with anyone — the professor or other students. It is easy to simply go through the motions of learning in order to earn course credit.

On the instructional side, similar impressions exist. Imagine the appeal of teaching a class where the professor appears only in videos, students periodically respond to discussion questions, and a teaching assistant grades the assignments and final paper. Meanwhile, the professor sits on a sandy beach, sipping a tall iced mocha Frappuccino. These professors claim they teach an online course, but they are not really teaching and their students are not really learning. These courses are merely put on autopilot and thus are viewed as easy.

Compare this to a good, in-class learning experience where students are presented with engaging material and the rigors of the class are personally demanding. And of course, nothing beats the personal conversations before or after classes or during office hours where a student's interaction with her professor could change her life. Face-to-face classroom settings with the personal, unmediated presence of the professor and students can be very effective, but even these do not guarantee relational connections that foster learning. In physical classrooms, just as in online ones, teachers can seem detached and impersonal.

Cultivating effective pedagogy in an online class is possible. Learning outcomes and expectations need not be compromised. Students can engage in transformational learning that impacts their lives. This type of online class is not only possible but may even offer experiences superior to those found in on-campus classes.

Here's one example. In a typical on-campus class, there are times when a professor presents a question for large-group discussion. The percentage of students who respond is relatively low, perhaps 10–15 percent. Students who require time to process information and form their own thoughts are conscious of the time constraints. Before their viewpoints are defined enough to articulate and the risk is low enough to communicate those thoughts out loud, the opportunity to respond has already been seized by more prepared, spontaneous, or unreserved students. As a result, the usual handful of regulars contribute to discussions, but the majority of students prefer or feel forced to remain silent and less involved in the learning process. Meanwhile, the professor feels the need to continue presenting more information or responding to other questions or comments. One of my students, Zach P., once commented, "I am a person who might have input on a topic, but in a classroom setting, by the time I have gathered my thoughts, the conversation has moved on to the next topic."

The kind of well-organized and carefully designed online class described and promoted in the following pages uses a variety of visual, audio, and written media. Assignments are designed to foster interaction with fellow students and the professor. The depth of students' interaction is developed as they process thoughts, ideas, perspectives, and even feelings. The online format, an education without borders, provides a plethora of opportunities to engage with students in their learning and character formation.

Technology now allows the professor to take advantage of a number of features where students are able to see the personality behind the course—the Oz behind the curtain—as they are learning and become known and impacted by the professor. A part of the professor's life makes an imprint on students' lives. Online education, if it is going to effect character formation, deserves pedagogy that inspires.

Character formation is more than an outward, behavioral, or moral change. It deals with who one is now and who one is becoming over the long haul in his or her life. Whether in ordinary, everyday life or in the challenges and trials that force the true self to emerge, whether in the presence of eyewitnesses or in the solitude of seeming obscurity, character formation is an ongoing work. Godly character formation is aligned with spiritual formation, as its goal is growth in an honest relationship with self as a whole person, with others, and with God. It deals with the default self, the real self. It is developed by what one allows to enter most deeply into one's heart and soul and is the lifelong response to the grace of God by the power of his Spirit in growing likeness of the Son. God's Word informs this process, as evidence of this lifestyle of godliness has both inward and outward consequences: inward, a growing dependence and trust in God, who proves himself worthy of that trust; and outward, reconciled relationships with others, who matter a great deal to God. Our world needs more pervasively influential, Christ-centered, others-focused people.

There is skepticism among educators about character formation in online education. Many cannot imagine that real transformation can be achieved in any format other than in the traditional model of residential education with in-class face time. Profound spiritual formation, however, can and has happened through quality and effective learning in online education.

If you have settled for the "easy," uninvolved approach to online education, be warned. The following content will only serve to stir a discontent with that status quo. If, however, a desire is stirred in you to know more about the kind of professor, the kind of course, and the kind of character formation possible in your online classes, read on.

PART 1

RISING TO THE CHALLENGE

Chapter 1

LOG ON TO LEARN

Inspiring Students through an Online Course

The mediocre teacher tells.
The good teacher explains.
The superior teacher demonstrates.
The great teacher inspires.
William Arthur Ward (1921–1994)

I doubt William Ward ever imagined his words would apply to professors teaching online classes. Could he have envisioned that great teachers would seek to inspire through the effective use of learning management systems, email exchanges, embedded lecture videos, discussion boards, collaborative documents, and video conferences? Imagine his initial surprise and uneasiness. It might have foreshadowed our own. This book, however, is designed to help professors move beyond the anxiety of using technology to connect with students and to help professors experience the deep satisfaction of seeing the formative impact that online instruction can have on students' lives. Is telling part of online learning? Yes. Is explaining part of online learning? Clearly. Is demonstrating part of online learning? Definitely. Is inspiring part of online learning? It can and should be.

At the heart of a great teacher is the desire to invest in students, to make an impact toward observable differences in their lives. Time spent with a great teacher instills in the souls of students a deep, inborn fascination with learning and the satisfaction of having learned, which fosters growth and maturity. Times such as these cannot help but transform. Ralph Lynn reminds us, "Everything you learn influences who you are and what you can do."[1] Even when a new or different learning delivery system is introduced, the heart of a great teacher remains resolute, convinced that what is taught and learned transforms our students.

Here are three questions that demand the attention of a professor preparing to teach any course:

- What are the students to learn?
- How will they learn it?
- How will that learning and its impact on students' lives be assessed?

These questions are not foreign to teachers, even those who teach online classes. A different learning delivery system has no effect on the need for these questions to be fully addressed. You may think that, so far, there appears to be little difference between teaching an on-campus class and an online class, and you would basically be correct. In fact, starting with the elements common to both on-campus and online classes helps diffuse some of the anxiety that can accompany the creation and maintenance of an effective online course.

What Are Students to Learn?

The answer to this question is simply course content. Students are impressed when professors know their material (and you probably know your material better than you think you do), are passionate about it, and are enthusiastic about conveying it to others. Learners grow in confidence when professors know the material so well that they respond with empathy, skill, humility, and wisdom to students who need clarification, express doubts, or ask questions. These educators know that more than content is being learned; they know they are modeling the wisdom of living as a transformed human being. Great teachers are inclined to do this.

How Will They Learn It?

This is simply the way you go about conveying information — your methodology. How your students engage with you and the course material contributes to their fund of knowledge. Students have different learning preferences and styles, so employing a variety of teaching methods ensures the likelihood that a broader spectrum of students will engage and learn. Keeping in mind your particular learners, — i.e., age, background, motivations, familiarity with social media — you determine the appropriate form of teaching toward the best learning outcome.

Lectures are commonly used in higher education, and these remain a helpful means for communicating information, but they are certainly not the only way. For online courses, video-recorded lectures are often a given. These edited pieces of a professor in action are saved and embedded into a learning management system (LMS). They are fashioned to capture the essence of lecture content in order to attract and retain the viewer's attention. To broaden the scope of communicating information, however, there are ways the learner can engage with the professor and other learners through written, verbal, and video formats. Well-framed prompts and assignments foster not only critical thinking but also creative dialogue and effective learning communities.

A skillful educator knows these attitudes and tools. This knowledge, together with the desire and work of God's Spirit, makes for the greatest impact on students, regardless of the scholarly discipline. The Spirit's inspiration knows no bounds.

How Will That Learning and Its Impact on Students' Lives Be Assessed?

The most helpful course evaluations focus more on assessing student learning than on the professor's performance (or popularity). Learner-based assessments demonstrate what students have learned and how they are impacted toward change. This evidence links back to the learning outcomes that the professor determined at the outset of the course. The relationship between the initial learning goals and the evaluation is more cyclical than linear, in that the evaluations bring the professor's focus back to the first and second questions: Are your students learning what you promised they would? Are you delivering?

If their learning impacts their lives to the extent that they are changed, then you have taught. And if that learning has fostered character formation, then it can be assessed.

Keeping these three questions in mind helps one to think about the perks and challenges of teaching an online course. The perks for students are many. Easy navigation allows students to explore the entire course, gaining a clear sense of the rigors and expectations of the class. Similarly, clear guidelines and requirements for the course are always available in the LMS, while calendars automatically alert students to due dates for reading, projects, presentations, and written assignments. Expectations of students, in addition to what the students can expect from the professor, can be easily communicated through a short introductory video.

Additionally, videos are flexible: lecture videos embedded in an LMS allow students both to receive the benefit of direct class instruction and to accommodate their own schedule accordingly. The video format also allows students to replay something they may not have caught the first (or even the second) time through. And video segments are typically shorter because they need to be easy to download and view. An effective lecture segment must be specifically crafted and edited for a ten-minute delivery.

Finally, online courses afford a spectrum of learning activities that foster greater understanding of a given subject. In addition, evidence of student learning achievements, which may also demonstrate character formation, can be archived in a student's own electronic portfolio (e-portfolio).

For professors and their colleagues the perks are also wide ranging. For instance, after the initial setting up of a course, there is less preparation time for subsequent runs of a course. Thus the time typically spent on the traditional delivery of content is now invested in creating and maintaining a learning community, engaging in dialogue with students as they absorb the material, and experiencing the translation of that information into their lives. Partnering two or more online classes builds community among professors, and the students enjoy seeing the interaction between the professors.

Once recorded, video lectures are convenient and can be used for other purposes. They are available to the professor in the event of an illness or scheduling conflict and can be embedded into an LMS to be used even for on-campus classes. Other colleagues can view the material, for promotion purposes or in-service training, to ensure intentional sequencing with other courses within a program or for professional growth and learning.

Online courses also allow for simple evaluation. Plagiarism-detection programs are often built into an LMS. These give an immediate evaluation of the percentage of a work that appears elsewhere, the identity of that work, and the duplicated text verbatim of that outsourced work, whether within an institution or outside of it. On the positive side, learning outcomes are linked to an assessment tool, streamlining the process, and evidence of student spiritual growth can be archived, reviewed, appraised, and shared between colleagues.

Challenges also exist in online education. The desire for students to have effective and engaging learning experiences in an online course needs to outweigh the initial investment of time and mental energy required to create such a course. The professor will not only need to think through the overall flow of the course but also the sequential details, which can be time consuming. For many, there is a steep learning curve for adjusting to all that an LMS can offer, and coordinating and ensuring a user-friendly course that is intuitive for students to navigate as seamlessly as possible can be daunting. Training offered through an institution's digital learning office is recommended. Finally, professors must be intentional about structuring and building a strong learning community, as these communities afford effective opportunities for learning and character formation.

Great teachers are familiar with challenges. Such challenges, though, prompt them to achieve the kind of learning environments where they and their students thrive. These professors understand that an online course is far more than putting teaching videos online, having little or no communication with students, and then giving a final exam or receiving a final paper as the sum total of their classes. Refusing to settle for suboptimal courses, great teachers believe the most effective type of teaching—whether a statistics, language, biology, or theology course—affects the whole person.

The chapters in this book will help guide, equip, and encourage professors toward greater yields from their online course preparation. Resist the temptation to read only the chapters that appeal to your immediate interests or needs. Each chapter will address various aspects of the online course that together provide a more comprehensive perspective. The result will be a well-designed course that will prove mutually satisfying for both you and your students.

Note: Before we get too far ahead of ourselves, you may need to familiarize yourself with some terms. A glossary of terms, "Coming to Terms with Terms," is located in Appendix A. If you are already familiar with online classes, you may want to "gloss" over the glossary. Otherwise, spend a little time familiarizing yourself with these terms. You won't need to memorize them, but as these words or phrases pop up in this book or in a conversation, you will know where to go for a quick check.

Chapter 2

CHARTING A COURSE

Basics to Developing an Online Course

He who works with his hands is a laborer.
He who works with his hands and his head is a craftsman.
He who works with his hands and his
head and his heart is an artist.

St. Francis of Assisi

Techies, those who are skilled at using computers and other electronic devices, do not necessarily make good online professors. The misconception is that one needs to be beyond technologically literate and skilled in order to create, maintain, and succeed with an online course endeavor. Successful online courses, however, are the products of professors who allow their commitment to whom they teach, what they teach, and how they communicate to override their own fears in using technology. These professors are determined to explore the available technology that would benefit student learning. There is both an art and a science to successful online classes.

The Art of an Online Course

There are five basic qualifications that describe a successful online professor.

1. You communicate effectively and winsomely, manifesting care and dedication to students and their learning

All accredited academic institutions have avenues for learning outcome evaluations. Acquaint yourself with what these assessments mean. Do not assume the numbers tell everything. Ask a knowledgeable person from the office responsible for administering and collecting the data from these evaluations for a tutorial about interpreting the data. Consider also the honest critique of a colleague who has periodically sat in on a few of your class sessions. Establishing this kind of relationship lends itself to well-received peer reviews of pedagogy, which encourage positive change.

Ratemyprofessors.com is a popular website for undergraduate students to leave a comment or two about a professor. It is also a place to vent. Disregard the best and the worst of the comments. Take it all with a grain of salt or ignore the site altogether. Rarely are the comments specific enough to identify a particular trait or issue, but if a pattern persists, then you may want to revisit student comments from your course assessments and ask for input from a trusted colleague.

Professors who find it difficult to communicate a passion for their subject and their students will find even greater difficulty communicating that passion to students through an online course format. Students know bad teaching when they see it, and we all know bad teaching when we do it. Good teaching is good teaching and bad teaching is bad teaching, whether applied online or face-to-face. Commit yourself to improving your pedagogy; even the best online professors do this.

2. You know and communicate your course content well

You are an expert in your discipline, and you are committed to the learning your students must achieve. You have observed, however, that in this instant-information culture, the intake of information does not equate to knowledge or understanding. Perhaps you resonate with Michael Wesch's statement about students: "They'll be good at looking at Wikipedia, but most likely they've never edited Wikipedia."[2]

Together with others of your department, perhaps there have been discussions about what students at your institution must learn and master. In your courses, you understand there are myriad types of learners, and therefore you incorporate various styles of teaching and engagement with your students. You are flexible enough to pull a different approach from your bag of tools when you notice disengagement with your students or those contagious apathetic doldrums that can threaten any professor or classroom at any time. You've demonstrated this in the traditional classroom, and it works. Translating this for an online course requires thought, but you are willing to be surprised at the ease, creativity, effectiveness, and reward of these learning engagement techniques.

You do not suffer from what Chip and Dan Heath identify as the "curse of knowledge." The Heath brothers assert that learning involves someone, whether professor or peer, who understands what it means to *not* understand a particular concept or fact.[3] A professor may be so proficient in his own domain of expertise, with a propensity to be overly complex and abstract, that he is cursed by his own knowledge — cursed with the lack of ability to comprehend the learner's state of mind. Frustration and a lack of patience often result. You understand this concept, however, and are committed to connecting with students as they gain understanding and skills, even as you model what it is to be a thinker, a Christian, and a scholar.

The use of instructional and pedagogical techniques for the online medium focuses on acquiring skills to foster interaction and communication with and among students throughout the online learning endeavor. In the online course, your pedagogy and the knowledge of your discipline converge and are communicated through the means of technological instructional practices.

3. You understand what makes a good online learner

Not all students make good online learners. Some students learn that the hard way, discovering that online classes are not watered-down versions of traditional courses. Successful online learners expect a rigorous course that stimulates their learning. They are serious about meaningful learning and know that it requires self-discipline. Thus, they do not plan vacations or heavy work schedules while taking an online course. Even with these precautions, good online learners are willing to improve their time-management skills.

To aid online learners, you present an intuitive and well-organized course by creating a sequence of learning engagement activities that are easy to navigate. This applies to all elements of your course. You are acutely aware that student attention spans can be short. As John Medina explains, you have seconds to grab someone's attention and ten minutes to keep it.[4] You engage your students not for the sake of engagement but toward an end: learning. In seeking to sustain student engagement in a topic, you design particular elements in your course that challenge your students, while at the same time coming alongside them to offer your support and encouragement. They know you care.

4. You articulate instructions and expectations clearly

Clear instructions stem first from mapping out the learning requirements and activities a student will need to engage with and complete to most seamlessly progress through your course. The mental energy required in this process occupies most of your time in new course preparation. Evidence of this time investment appears in a well-constructed syllabus and synchronized course calendar. Your syllabus is the first, most helpful document required for developing an online course. From it and its synchronized calendar, you and anyone assisting with building the course can move forward in creating a course on the LMS. As with traditional classes, the syllabus should state your name, your contact information, the course description, the learning objectives, an overview of written and reading assignments, a grading rubric, and other course- and institution-specific information.

Being implicit or vague about course expectations yields frustration for both the students and you. Students need to know explicitly what will be expected of them to successfully complete your course, and it is imperative that you oblige. The extra time spent to ensure students understand the ownership and responsibility for their own learning is a wise investment.

However much technology you are comfortable using, you must make intelligent choices about using it well. You want to deliver your content in a way that maximizes its reception, but you also know that teaching is more than delivering content. José Bowen observes two things: the bad news about the Internet is that it makes the content you have to tell students less valuable because there are other people who can do that. The good news about the Internet is that it makes the "thinking" you are teaching students even more valuable.[5] The critical thinking you inspire, encourage, and expect from your students helps them to understand, analyze, and synthesize content toward personal transformation.

5. You recognize the importance of relationships in learning

You foster professor-student and student-student interaction; have experienced the satisfaction of communicating, encouraging, giving meaningful feedback, and engaging in a thriving learning community; and are convinced people learn more and learn more deeply in community than in isolation. You create an environment of trust, respect, support, and transparency. As students present challenges or risk expressing thoughts, you learn what motivates, interests, and worries them. You understand what it takes to be present and available to students in our highly distracted and distant culture.

When social presence is lacking, students experience high levels of frustration and disengagement, critical attitudes toward instruction, and lower levels of learning. When social presence is high, students experience greater satisfaction with the class, effectiveness of instruction, and a greater sense of community. Their achievement, in turn, is improved.[6] The success of an online course is directly related to the level of accessibility of the professor and effective, active engagement in the learning experience. It is not just mastery of skills or transfer of facts and information; it is about fostering students' desires to understand and grasp meaning and synthesize it for their own lives.

This takes attentiveness. It takes alertness to God's Spirit as he leads in the construction and sustaining of a course. The Spirit draws the professor's attention toward students, their stories, their needs, and the best ways to stimulate timely and meaningful dialogue and connection with them. How will you acknowledge a student's competence and transparency—especially when expressing matters of the soul? How will you support a student's sense of ownership of a course or foster a healthy connectivity among students? Your responses, whether through discussion posts, on graded papers, by email, in recorded media comments, or via video conferences, can reveal a dependency on God's Spirit and a commitment to the health of the learning community.

In all honesty, though you are instrumental and ultimately responsible for the successful creation, maintenance, and completion of an online course, such responsibility may lead to a control problem, one that is difficult to admit. Most of us encounter this as we wrestle with variations of "I know everything and you know nothing, so you must learn from me." This top-down approach inadvertently directs students to "figure out what the prof wants me to read or hear" versus engaging in their own learning and internalizing content toward transformation. Though more than the "guide on the side," online professors must also move away from the absolute, spotlighted "sage on the stage." Online education is not about you; it is about us. Professors become the "sage on the side," where "sage" means "service."

As an online course professor, you must take on additional roles, including facilitator of group discussions, implementer of strategic interactions, observer and evaluator of progress, in-house mentor, on-call tutor, ready encourager, and available guide. These external roles are best fulfilled by internal growth and maturity, which include your own alertness to and dependence on the work of God's Spirit, commitment to the authority of God's Word, and dedication to pursuing Christlikeness, as well as growth in prayerfulness and humility. The ability to be relational, transparent, encouraging, and attentive to the souls of others is a natural outgrowth of inward development.

Your roles and attributes contribute to building a learning community. You accept the responsibility of impacting the learning process, encouraging learners to pursue challenging goals, and promoting a presence that connects students together. It is energizing to witness students develop the skills to learn and to see how their learning influences transformation in their lives.

The structure that combines learning and community in an online class is the LMS. What follows are some features that LMSs provide to support the structure of any given course.

The Science of an Online Course: Features of a Good Learning Management System

A good LMS is like a Swiss Army knife. Known for its usefulness, adaptability, and multipurpose function, this knife generally has a sharp blade, a screwdriver, a can opener, and other various tools, each one functionally different. Some even include a flash drive, an MP3 player, a digital clock, and a laser pointer. Attached by a pivot-point mechanism, each tool is readily accessible. Different needs determine which implement will be used. The tools cannot all be used at once, but as a particular need arises, the appropriate tool is available.

Similarly, an LMS is equipped with many tools and features and usually includes a page where you can introduce yourself and your course with accompanying expectations, an announcement page for quick updates, a syllabus page for course information, and a calendar that lists upcoming due dates for students. Added to the basic gradebook are features that store and calculate student grades and weighted totals, inform participants of late assignments, offer formulas for dropping the lowest score, and embed typed, audio, or video comments into a student document. Also included are features such as a bulletin board, a conference room for individual or group meetings, email services, screen sharing, and collaborative documents. The LMS is the internal framework onto which the course materials are added. All information associated with the course becomes part of the LMS and is archived or stored. There is a current move toward storing all this data in the cloud. Privacy and security issues continue to be of concern and are subject to improvements in these areas.

The LMS is the one-stop location for the course. Although there are a number of LMSs available, effective ones share most of the same features. This book is LMS-neutral so that regardless of the LMS used, the information found on these pages can be readily applied.

The choice of which LMS is typically made by the academic institution, and technological improvements or the cost effectiveness of a new or updated system may persuade an institution to switch to a new LMS. Some systems are more intuitive than others, and some have higher learning curves than others. All of them offer assistance to users as they seek to build an effective learning environment and community with ease and minimal challenges.

To keep from becoming too overwhelmed with any LMS, start with the features you need to use, the must-haves for your course. Here are nine basic components of any online course; the first seven are essential, and you will find that the last two will quickly become must-haves. (See *Image 1: Menu Tabs*.)

Home page. This page simply welcomes the viewer and includes basic information like the school's name, the title of the course, and a brief welcome message from the professor. (See *Image 2: Home Page*.)

HIST 360

Home

Announcements

Syllabus

Modules

Discussions

Assignments

Grades

Conferences

Collaborations

Image 1: Menu Tabs

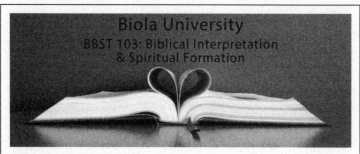

Welcome!

This course will address sound hermeneutics (the skill of reading and interpreting Scripture) as it applies to our growth in godliness. We'll be learning more about Christian spiritual transformation, the life-long process of becoming more like Christ for the glory of God. I am really looking forward to embarking on this journey of discovery together.

After reading the information on this home page, read the information found in the **Syllabus** folder on the left. You can see the weekly schedule and assignments in the **Modules** folder. Read the information in the "Getting Started" module and then complete the assignments for Week One. Refer to the "Course Calendar" for a quick overview of the semester. If you have any questions, please feel free to email me.

Blessings,

Dr. Jung

Image 2: Home Page

Announcements. Brief announcements from the professor are great ways to quickly inform students of updates or to provide FYIs. Students are apprised of new announcements as they are posted on the LMS. This page can save all of the announcements posted on the LMS over the entire length of the course. This feature is separate from the email services provided with all LMSs. In addition to the title and text of an announcement, there are options to post or to attach files. (See *Image 3: Announcements*.)

Library password
Hey, all. Just a reminder that the Library password for this class is "bbst103" and can be...   Jan 8

Turabian Footnotes
Here is a document that will help you with Turabian footnoting. Note especially th...   Jan 7

Welcome!
I am excited for this Interterm BBST 103 course. If you have taken a class previously...   Dec 4

Image 3: Announcements

Syllabus. The course syllabus should first include the professor's contact information (i.e., virtual office hours, email address, and possibly a cell phone number). A short course description is usually copied directly from the school catalog. All information pertaining to the course that students need to know must be included and readily available as a folder of its own. Within the folder, a link can be provided to view, print, or download the syllabus, or the complete syllabus can be displayed. As noted previously, this one document forms the basis for what will become the online course. A syllabus should also include a list of required textbooks and resources; course objectives and student learning outcomes; a list of assignments and assessments with point/percentage values and a brief description; a grading schema; policies on things like late assignments, academic honesty (plagiarism), and nondiscrimination; information on learning aids like disability services, support services, and library websites; and a course calendar.

Modules. Some LMSs call these content folders. The most effective modules are presented as weekly entities (for an intensive course, modules will be adapted as daily entities). Each module should be named by a week number and include key dates. (See *Image 4: Modules.*) A title reflecting the topic for that week could also be added. Within each module, it is essential to provide a schedule of the requirements due for that given week:

- *Required readings.* These readings can be assigned from a textbook or from PDF copies of works that are embedded directly into the module. Of course, these copies must be in compliance with federal copyright laws and your institution's copyright guidelines.

- *Videos and PowerPoint slides or presentations to view.* Capturing a professor's class lectures on video is a mainstay for many online courses. With proper planning and foresight, a professor's on-campus class lectures can be filmed over the duration of a course and then inserted into the online class. (Note: Time for editing and encoding the recorded lectures may require as much as six to twelve months, depending on the workload of the video team. Checking your school's policy and turnaround time is strongly recommended.) Keep in mind that video lectures should be fairly short in length. These shorter segments, which capture the essence of a teaching session, help facilitate student learning. Lengthy videos require more time to load and buffer when students have a slow Internet connection. These videos should be reviewed regularly and updated as needed.

• *Assignments that are due.* The due dates that are entered into an LMS will also appear in an electronic calendar that reminds students of upcoming assignment deadlines.

• *Whatever else may be helpful or encouraging,* such as links to additional resources.

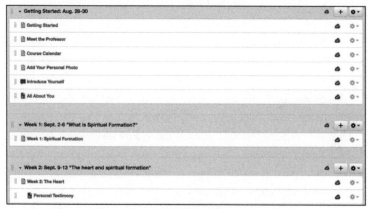

Image 4: Modules

Discussions. Sometimes called a discussion board, forum, or thread, this feature is one of the most effective ways for students to process the content of assignments and then to interact with each other as well as the professor. Discussions in a traditional classroom setting are synchronous (unmediated and in real time), and students see each other and the professor face-to-face. In online classes, however, discussions and student engagement must be strategically planned and implemented. These discussions should be scheduled frequently enough to ensure students stay engaged with course materials but with enough time between to allow for thoughtful responses from students' peers, the teaching assistant

(TA), and the professor. Intensive courses may require an increase in the frequency of interactive discussions. (See *Image 5: Discussions*.)

Discussions, group assignments or projects, and video conferences are important components in an online course that encourage student participation and help create a dynamic learning community. Well-framed discussion prompts or questions stimulate dialogue among students in a given small group and with the professor and can also include TAs. Students are typically required to respond to the initial prompts and then to respond to at least one to three other students' responses.

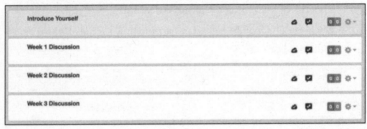

Image 5: Discussions

Assignments. Every assignment is to be submitted electronically to the LMS. The assignments folder will house the categories of assignments required as well as each individual assignment by name. Assignments might include discussion threads in small groups, written assignments (e.g., research papers or short essays), quizzes, the final exam, and a final paper or project.

The requirements for each submission are described in more detail, providing the student with guidelines for successful completion. Brevity and clarity are essential. Verbal instructions typically given in the classroom can be translated into written form. Adding a grading rubric to an assignment reinforces its requirements and lets students see both how their grades were calculated and the areas in which they need to improve. The grade assigned to each submitted document is directly linked to the grade book so that once scores or grades are entered for a required assignment, they are immediately calculated toward the student's overall grade or weighted total, ready for the student to view.

The grading of assignments provides unique opportunities for professors to connect with students. Many LMSs feature ways to leave comments on student assignments. Embedding comments directly into a submitted document reduces grading time, as does the option of adding either audio or video comments, which allows the professor to connect with students in a more profound way. Hearing the professor's voice clarify a point, expand on an idea, or pray over a concern mentioned in an assignment makes students aware of the professor's genuine care and concern more effectively than remarks penned on a page do. Video comments can be received with even more appreciation and impact, as seeing the face of the one speaking makes the message even more personal.

Grades/Grade Book. The professor and other authorized participants have access to view the grades, assignments submitted, and weighted total, in percentages, for each student. Some LMSs highlight assignments that have been submitted late. In addition, if a calculation involves dropping the lowest score of a set of assignments, some LMSs will highlight the lowest score that was not figured into the student's weighted total. The ease in accessing and viewing information pertinent to a course's grades saves time, energy, and sanity.

Two additional features in some LMSs are ones you will want to take advantage of to further engage students with their learning.

Conferences. Video conferences can seem a bit intimidating for professors as well as for students, but as the professor overcomes the fear or anxiety associated with their use, students find it easier to engage in community building. Professors may think their discipline does not warrant the use of video conferences; however, students will likely disagree. Even the simplest of connections conveys value and interest to a student whether the course is theology, mathematics, or statistics.

Collaborative Documents. Typically used by groups or pairs of students to collaborate on a given assignment, collaborative documents are easy to set up. Whether in Google Docs or a similar program, students can use these shared documents to work together on an assignment or respond to a prompt presented to the entire class. A collaborative document has advantages ranging from simple to significant. It can be used to collect information to help with something like coordinating volunteer drivers and riders for a class field trip (i.e., a hybrid class activity), or it can be as impactful as garnering reflections from a class-wide experience. These can be purposed as a learning activity or a reflections document, depending on the intent of the professor.

If you are feeling overwhelmed by the prospect of creating an online course, inadequate in your knowledge of technology and the LMS structure, and ready to close this book and give up, wait! When online classes first appeared, the professors who tended to join in were those who were somewhat tech savvy. They understood the language, concepts, and functions of the basic elements needed to create an online course. At this point, however, most online professors are *not* tech savvy, and the thought of learning to create an online course while fulfilling the usual research and writing responsibilities is intimidating.

This is where a course designer comes in. The next chapter explains how the professor and a skilled course designer, one who sees the course through the lenses of both the students and the professor, can work together to create an exceptional course. In circumstances where the services of a course designer are not available, the following chapter, with its design insights and guides, will be of even greater value and importance.

Chapter 3

PARTNERSHIPS THAT DELIVER

Tag-Teaming with a Course Designer[7]

Remember teamwork begins by building trust. And the only way to do that is to overcome our need for invulnerability.
Patrick Lencioni, *The Five Dysfunctions of a Team: A Leadership Fable*

Originally the term *tag team* referred to pro wrestling matches, where a pair of wrestlers would fight as a team and alternate being in the ring. Today a tag team signifies two or more people who work together, making it a good analogy for the relationship between a professor and a course designer. Of course, the ultimate goal in this case is not to pummel others (or each other) but rather to work collaboratively to create a well-designed course that facilitates students' learning and accomplishes the desired learning outcomes. Getting to that point, however, requires a mutual understanding of the roles professors and course designers have in this process.

Some professors prefer to give a brief overview of their course, provide their class materials, and then let the course designer put the course together, reviewing it afterward and specifying what needs to be changed, clarified, or corrected. Other faculty, however, want to sit down and build their own course with the course designer present to offer direction and assistance, especially with the LMS.

Still other professors feel uncomfortable relinquishing any aspect of their course to a course designer—perhaps because they fear they will demonstrate a lack of pedagogical or technical skills or because they are convinced that no one else is capable of organizing their course materials in a suitable manner. Sometimes techies fall into this category and try to design their own class, ending up with a course that is not only pedagogically less effective but also confusing and exasperating for students.

It is certainly possible for a professor to design his or her own course without the assistance of a course designer, but that may not be the most productive use of the professor's time. Course preparation, meeting with students, research, writing, department meetings, committee assignments, and speaking engagements, not to mention family responsibilities, afford precious little time to become an expert in the institution's LMS and to learn how to convert a traditional class into an online format.

When the professor and course designer combine their expertise and work as a tag team, each is allowed to do what he or she does best. The professor is the subject-matter expert, while the course designer is an educational professional and a specialist in the LMS who can provide valuable assistance with pedagogical issues, technical features of the LMS, and content structure of the course (including organization, formatting, and graphic layout). A well-designed course allows students to engage more quickly with the content of a course, rather than wasting time figuring out how to navigate the course elements. Students should never have to think, "I know it's in here somewhere, but where?"

The process of creating an online class together requires trust, humility, and mutual respect. Professors need to trust the course designer's judgment and view that person as a colleague who wants the class to be the best it can be for both the professor and students. Course designers need to demonstrate their qualifications by exercising their training in teaching methodology, educational psychology, differentiated learning, or human development. The result is a well-delivered online course.

Whether completely designing the online class or aiding the professor in the process, the course designer must first invest time reviewing the course syllabus and materials and dialoging with the professor to get a basic understanding of the course and to discern the professor's teaching style. Working together should be a constructive, comfortable experience as information is mutually exchanged. In the process, not only does the course designer learn more about the subject matter and form a relationship with the faculty member, the professor may acquire some new teaching ideas and technology skills.

Qualifications of a Skilled Course Designer

A course designer should:

- Understand that the course is being designed for students.
- Have educational training and preferably teaching experience in order to understand pedagogical issues—learning styles, rubrics, differentiated learning, multiple intelligences, Bloom's taxonomy, etc.
- Understand curriculum design.
- Be comfortable using technology and have technical expertise with a variety of tools such as Microsoft Office (Word and PowerPoint in particular), learning management systems, and basic HTML. Familiarity with programs such as Photoshop, Dreamweaver, Creative Commons, Adobe Reader/Acrobat, Jing, and Pixlr can be useful as well.
- Be detail oriented with exceptional organizational skills.
- Possess excellent writing, editing, and proofreading skills and be a grammar wizard.
- Be a lifelong learner, continuously learning and trying to keep current with new technology and educational best practices.
- Be a communicator and able to work collaboratively with others while maintaining a positive attitude.
- Know how to do research and be able to find answers to questions (and be honest enough to admit that there are some things he or she does not know).
- Be responsive to the professor's input and feedback.

Topics: Sanctification in the Christian Life

Readings:

- Packer, *Quest*, 16
- Bunyan, *Pilgrim's Progress*

Videos: Please watch the videos located below

Discussion 10: Please go to Class Discussion tab.
Initial posts should be made by 12 noon PT. Interaction with your colleague's post should be completed by 5:00 PM PT of the same day. Read and interact with responses posted by at least two other classmates on the discussion board each day.

Image 6: Before

THE
Pilgrim's Progress
FROM
THIS WORLD,
TO
That which is to come:
Delivered under the Similitude of a
DREAM

Topic: Puritan Theology -- Sanctification in the Christian Life

Readings:

- Packer, *Quest for Godliness*, 16
- Bunyan, *Pilgrim's Progress*

Assignments Due:

- Response paper on *Pilgrim's Progress*
- Week 10 Online Discussion

Lecture Videos: (embedded below)

- Sanctification in the Christian Life -- Part 1 and Part 2
- John Bunyan

Image 7: After

- Not be afraid to offer suggestions that could improve the class but also not be easily offended if those ideas are rejected, understanding that it is the professor's class and that the professor is ultimately responsible for the content—to students, administrators, the department chair, etc.

- Have some basic understanding of layout and design (See *Images 6 and 7: Before and After*). As in real estate, course design is all about "location, location, location." Where and how content is placed in an LMS can make for a more effective and enhanced learning experience.

An Eye for Design

Course design typically consists of five steps: analysis, design, development, implementation, and evaluation (aka the ADDIE model; see *Image 8*). Analysis involves making initial decisions about the course. Design entails writing course objectives and building content. Development includes adding or creating materials and assessments to make the course ready to be taught online. Implementation is delivering the online course to the learner. Evaluation focuses on the effectiveness of each of the prior phases.

Image 8: ADDIE Model of Instructional Design

From the professor's perspective, the first question that should be asked is, "What are students to learn in this course?" The answer to that question determines the course objectives, desired learning outcomes, and the selection of textbooks and other resources. The course designer then works with the professor to decide the best methods for communicating the course material and helps create or adjust assignments and activities that will make the learning achievable, relevant, and meaningful.

A skilled course designer does not merely copy and paste the syllabus, work sheets, and assignment information into the LMS. This professional organizes the course content, suggests appropriate instructional strategies to implement (e.g., interactive discussions, collaborative projects, case studies, embedded videos, and simulations), and helps identify and develop potential assessments for teaching effectiveness and student learning. The course designer provides support to the professor, but the main focus is on student learning.

A course designer must involve the professor as much as possible in the design process. One approach is to demonstrate options and ask for input. For example, a professor may want to embed a website URL in her online class. The course designer can show her several ways to embed it and then have the professor test them and send her feedback. Involving the professor communicates that her opinion is valued, thus strengthening the tag-team bond.

By utilizing sound instructional design principles, online classes are just as effective, interactive, and relevant as on-campus courses, maybe even more so. The key is to focus on teaching and learning—*not* on the technology. Computers and other electronic devices (e.g., tablets and smartphones) are simply the means of presenting the course. As more courses and programs are being taught online, learning has become more collaborative and interactive, requiring a change in pedagogy. For online learning to be truly effective, faculty must be willing to allow students to participate more fully in their learning. By asking insightful discussion questions that require critical thinking and processing of the course material, students can integrate their reading with personal experiences and prior knowledge and then learn from classmates as they interact with and respond to one another's posts. This level of engagement fosters significant learning.

Faculty Development

Even if a course designer creates the online course, it is helpful if professors receive in-service training on using the learning management system. We do not need to be experts, but we will want to be comfortable navigating within the course and assisting students with simple functions. The course designer is often a phone call or email away to help with more challenging questions and issues.

In-service training for an institution's LMS is frequently offered at different levels — from a couple of hours on how to use the most essential features to hour-long sessions split over a period of several weeks that provide more in-depth training on more complicated functions. Even if professors do not remember everything they learned in the training sessions, if they have seen it once, it will be easier to recall as they begin teaching courses. Almost every LMS also has a Help button built into the program where information can be readily accessed by professors and students alike.

A Checklist for Course Content

The presentation of the course material is important. Adding appropriate visuals can make the content more appealing and thus more likely to be read and remembered. The following checklist offers a concise guide to ensuring a well-developed course. Consider that your course content should:

- Be substantive and academically challenging rather than busywork.
- Be organized clearly and simply so that students can easily navigate the course.
- Offer a variety of learning activities, taking into consideration different learning styles, while providing opportunities for

students to share with and learn from each other. Examples of learning activities include individual or group projects, interactive online discussions, peer review, video or PowerPoint presentations, questions and answers, book reviews, critiques, interviews, research papers and projects, blogs, journals, quizzes, summaries, and portfolios.

- Spell out clear instructions for assignments, including detailed descriptions with specific guidelines, any length and style requirements, due date and time, how and where to submit the assignment, and the policy for late assignments.
- Be accurate; check for conflicting due dates, times, or information.
- Not have spelling or grammatical errors.
- Engage students; help them integrate what they are learning and encourage meaningful personal application.
- Foster dialogue, interaction, and communication, creating a learning community within the class.
- Include rubrics that inform students how assignments will be graded and that help the professor in aligning learning outcomes with assessments.
- Offer links to online library and research services.
- Include simple, effective graphics. Graphics not only make text more visually appealing but also help students recall data. Do not use antiquated graphics unless it intentionally illustrates a particular point or historic period.
- Ensure 24-7 technical support availability.

Team Support

The course designer does not work alone. Support may include a videographer to film class lectures or a postproduction coordinator who edits, encodes, and embeds videos; edits PowerPoint presentations and designs course banners and other visuals for the class (although the course designer may also be responsible for and skilled at editing

PowerPoint presentations and creating visuals). The expertise of this team helps a course look polished and professional. Professors ought to be able to say, "You make us look good," which is exactly what the support team is trying to do!

How to Create a Loser Course

Unfortunately some professors end up with poorly designed courses, usually due to lack of preparation beforehand. Here are the top ten foolproof ways to create a poorly designed course.

1. Use the same repetitive assignments every week, such as this one:
   - Watch the videos.
   - Read the assigned pages.
   - Answer the assigned questions.
   - Turn in the assignment by the required day and time.
   - Complete the discussion thread.

2. Ask the same discussion question week after week. The monotony is captivating. For example:
   - What did you think about this week's reading?
   - From the chapter(s) you read, share with your group what impact this reading had on you.

3. Assign busywork. Students thrive on assignments that ask them to outline every chapter to the paragraph level or that require them to write a two-hundred-word response to the discussion question and fifty-word responses to the posts of all of their thirty classmates.

4. Do not include rubrics for assignments. Let students be surprised by their grades and wonder what they did right or wrong.

5. Once the course is set up and started, go fishing and let the class run without you. Have the TA do the grading. No one will notice that you have checked out and are not present in the class.

6. Use pedagogically unsound assessments like, "Did you do the reading? Yes or no?" and "What percentage of the reading did you do?" (Of course, you might want to define the term *reading*. Does skimming count?)

7. Put all the assignments on one seemingly never-ending page in the LMS, including lots of links. Students enjoy treasure hunts. Whenever possible, link to documents instead of providing the actual text. Students will become more tech savvy and will develop their fine-motor skills as they practice clicking on the links and waiting patiently for them to open.

8. Make the online course text focused, especially with PowerPoint presentations, and do not include visuals. The more information you can get on a page, the better.

9. Do not use a spell checker or check grammar when creating the course content. Students will understand you are only human, or maybe they will not notice.

10. If you lecture in the physical classroom for an hour, make sure that your online video lecture captures every aspect of the on-site class, including student interactions that may not be applicable. Online students will not mind having to wait for long videos to download so they can get the "full experience" of the on-site classroom.

All kidding aside, these examples demonstrate poor pedagogy and hinder learning. If you find yourself doing any of these, look for a new approach that will improve your online course. The following chapters will help.

Focus on Students

On occasion, working with a course designer can seem less like a tag team and more like a wrestling match. I encourage professors not to take offense at course designers' feedback and to be open to their suggestions. The partnership can be a win-win situation for both the professor and students. After all, as this Image 9 depicts, the focus is the students.

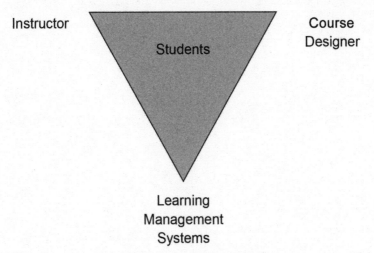

Instructor

Course
Designer

Learning
Management
Systems

Image 9: Students Are the Focus

Sometimes, a sense of camaraderie can develop between a professor and a course designer that results in the two becoming genuine friends. For instance, one morning I logged on to the home page of my online Puritan theology course to discover a photo of me attired in Puritan garb (complete with an apron, a bonnet, and a basket in hand), thanks to image-editing software. Over the course of working together, the course designer and I had become friends and had come to enjoy each other's senses of humor. In addition, the designer had attended an on-campus class meeting, met students, and personally observed the kind of relationships I had with my students, so she knew that both the students and I would appreciate a little levity in an otherwise serious course. And the students certainly did!

Whether or not you become friends with the course designers you work with, you and they can become an effective team. A course designer works with you to create your online class in a learning management system, where technology is simply the vehicle for delivering effective dialogical learning, as it was designed to be. At the center of attention are the students. And students should always remain the focus.

PART 2

ELEMENTS OF ONLINE CHARACTER FORMATION

Chapter 4

TAKING ONLINE CLASSROOM TECHNOLOGY TO GREATER DEPTHS

The Heart and Community

One never meets a mere human being.
C. S. Lewis

The heart is often misrepresented in American culture. Whether it is Céline Dion's "My Heart Will Go On" or Taylor Swift's "I Heart ?" or Tony Bennett's "I Left My Heart in San Francisco," the contemporary use of the word *heart* has popularized the idea that heart is exclusively linked to the human emotion of love or passion. We tend to valorize heart-based judgments as more true and authentic. But the heart has much more to do with how we live, as we mean when we speak of doing something wholeheartedly.

Effective teaching moves beyond a truncated understanding of the heart to incorporating the entire heart. In Proverbs 4:23 (HCSB), believers are warned: "Guard your heart above all else, for it is the source of life." Mentioned nearly one thousand times in God's Word, the heart is clearly important to him. Discovering more about the heart helps us understand its importance to him.

John Coe describes the heart as "the core of human personality and is the nexus of human will, affect, and intellect."[8] The intellect, which is the mind or thinking function of the heart, is where our thoughts are received, processed, and formed. Affect, or emotion, is tied to thoughts, because we have feelings about all thoughts; some elicit deep and profound feelings, while we could not care less about others. The will is an expression of what we actually do (or do not do) with our thoughts. These components of the heart—mind, emotion, and will—are often examined separately but were created to function together. They make up who we are. Our lives are our hearts in motion.

An approach to online teaching that focuses only on acquiring information focuses on the mind while marginalizing the emotions and will. The ability to form students' character depends on whether thoughts reach the level of emotion in the heart. Formational learning requires emotions to be involved, bringing greater value to what we understand, which prompts change.

John Kotter and Dan Cohen write, "People change what they do less because they are given analysis that shifts their *thinking* than because they are shown a truth that influences their *feelings*."[9] Though they are writing about the business world, their findings apply to academic settings. Successful organizations, and successful professors, recognize that both thinking and feeling are essential but that "the heart of change is in the emotions."[10] The key to change lies in making people feel differently. Kotter and Cohen's core pattern of "See-Feel-Change" has been shown to impact not only individuals but those around these individuals as well.[11] Joseph LeDoux, professor of neuroscience and psychology at New York University, adds, "Once emotions occur they become powerful motivators of future behaviors."[12]

Theologian Robert Saucy, in addressing the biblical understanding of the heart, describes human emotions as "sensors that are always evaluating the situations of our life with feelings of pleasure or displeasure, with resonance or dissonance."[13] Thinking or analysis that does not touch the emotions will produce little or no change. Human beings are more motivated to change when emotions are involved than when humans engage knowledge or analysis alone. How we feel about what we think has great potential for what we do.

The soul, too, is often misrepresented. There's Aretha Franklin, the Queen of Soul; the Kia Soul, a car; and, of course, soul food. Such broad use of the word diminishes the reality and importance of the human soul. In order to reclaim its importance, we need to understand that the soul's primary identity is "equated with the totality of the person created in the image of God."[14] The heart functions as the control center of the soul; therefore, what is known in the heart is known in the soul.

Even when Christians are asked about the soul, they tend to refer to it as the nonmaterial essence of who we are. Unfortunately, that is only partially correct. Scripture does not support the bifurcation of soul and body.[15] The two words in the Bible that are translated *soul*, *nephesh* in the Old Testament and *psuche* in the New Testament, describe living beings or human beings, not just the immaterial aspect of a person. Early in Genesis (2:7) we are told that the union of our body (the material substance) with our spirit (the immaterial substance) forms a living soul (*nephesh*). The soul, which includes the body, comes to mean "the whole person," all of what makes up the "self." All human beings are souls.

Considering the soul as only its immaterial aspect marginalizes the impact the body and its actions have on character formation in online education. When the body is excluded from an understanding of the soul, we ignore an important part of the soul: we unintentionally disregard the impact that physical actions and behaviors have on our soul. In an organic and dynamic way, matters that impact our souls, and thus our hearts, are manifested in how we live; the actions and behaviors of our lives impact our souls and thus our hearts. This holistic understanding of the soul allows us to address it with greater discernment.

Over the centuries, Christians have contemplated and written about the significance of the soul for our lives. Even when only the immaterial might be implied, one can still grasp the seriousness of matters of the soul. In the mid-1600s, Brian Duppa, Bishop of Winchester, wrote of the distance one can have with one's soul: "Why should the soul and I become such strangers? Are we like my two eyes, which have but an inch between them, yet never see one another? Or is it that we can so much more easily look on the souls of others with patience than on our own Wounded Souls?"[16] He then adds, "Whatever may become of my other friends, I hope that in my afflictions, I may at least have my soul to talk to—that neither sin nor the Devil could ever separate us."[17] Souls need attentive consideration.

Similarly, John Bunyan observes the soul as that which "God counts worthy to be the vessels to hold his grace—the graces of the Spirit in."[18] Intended to thrive on God's graces, we are inadequate people without them. We are poor souls when we are barren of the graces that are meant to fill the vessels of our lives. Growing one's consciousness of God's presence prepares us for the flood of grace intended to flow to the soul, the whole person.

This happens in character formation. It happens as we learn to think and learn to live our lives as Christians with a conspicuous faith, allowing ourselves to be vessels and conduits for the grace of the Holy Spirit's presence and power. This kind of reflection in online classes is possible through well-framed questions that keep the whole person in mind and through a strong learning community that recognizes that people learn best in positive relationships.

The Well-Framed Question

A prudent question is one-half of wisdom.
Francis Bacon

Questions are at the heart of learning. A good question affects intelligence, interest, attention, memory, and conduct. The quality of questions is more critical than the quantity to generate transformative learning and an integrative learning community. Well-framed questions promote the students' understanding of concepts and course material and encourage insightful engagement with peers and the professor. They help advance the line of discussion, inquiry, and reflection toward greater understanding of an idea or intellectual task. Vague or simplistic yes or no questions and mundane, repetitive questions fail to do this. Seize the opportunity to fashion investigative questions that help students discover truth for themselves.

Well-framed questions reveal something about the questioner; the answers reveal something about the respondent. Jesus asked questions, but not merely for the sake of asking questions. His questions were clear, brief, and practical, yet stimulating, personal, and adapted to the individual. They were intended to reach the heart of the matter, to cause people to think and feel, and to elicit a response that stemmed from careful consideration. Reflection is the brain's way of making connections toward grasping a concept or truth. Puritan pastor Richard Baxter understood the power of consideration and meditation "for the moving of the affections, and for the powerful imprinting of things in the heart."[19] Intentional reflection connects thoughts with emotions and leads to transformation. As Robert Saucy reminds us: "The deeper something is in our heart, the more it influences our life."[20]

Questions that impact character formation are those whose answers make a close connection between the subject matter and human emotion. These purposeful prompts further the engagement of the heart and have the greatest potential impact on the soul because they apply information, facts, and truths to students' lives. Well-framed questions force students to wrestle with or meditate on the information presented. The inclusion of the word *soul* in some questions and conversations is vital. Christian conversations are mostly devoid of the use of this word, yet every human being is a soul who requires attentive care, which ultimately means the heart receives attending as well. Here are two sample questions designed to elicit meaningful meditation:

- Paul writes in Colossians 3:23 (NASB), "Whatever you do, do your work heartily [with the soul], as for the Lord." In light of the biblical understanding of the soul, what challenges do you face in being obedient to God?
- Consider Psalm 119:11, 13. Is it more difficult for you to get the Word into your heart and soul or to speak when the Word impacts your life? Explain.

Meditating on a response to an effective prompt touches the emotions and affects the will, which results in living out what has been learned and embedded in the heart.

Brain Growth and Mindfulness Meditation

In an effective learning community, thought-provoking questions that aim at matters of the soul incline students to reflect or meditate on deep issues. Many people ask how to shorten the distance between head and heart. Richard Baxter would submit,

> Consideration opens the door between the head and the heart.... Now this is the great work of Consideration. O what rare men would they be, who have strong heads, and much learning and knowledge, if the obstructions between the Head and the Heart were but opened! and their Affections did but correspond to their Understandings.... He is the best Scholar who hath the readiest passage from the Ear to the Brain, but he is the best Christian, who hath the readiest passage from the Brain to the Heart; now Consideration is that on our parts that must open the passage though the Spirit open as the principal cause; inconsiderate men are stupid and senseless.[21]

Though meditation is a stranger to many, it is one of the most effective processes with which human beings effect life change. Meditation is not a stagnant exercise but one that forces a person to engage in thinking, to ask questions of the self, and to determine if a thought truly aligns with a belief. The seventeenth-century minister Jonathan Mitchel understood this: "One truth felt in Meditation, is worth a World, and it will make way for more."[22]

Massachusetts General Hospital researchers have observed the brain to explore the effects of mindfulness meditation. Meaningful self-awareness affects structural changes in two important parts of the brain: the left hippocampus and the amygdala. This kind of meditation helped increase the gray matter concentration of the hippocampus, an area important for learning, memory, and compassion.[23] On the other hand, stress-related disorders have been associated with smaller hippocampi.[24] (As a hopeful aside for the reader and this author, the hippocampus is well known for its ability to generate new neurons, and it has been shown that volume loss is reversible.[25]) The effects of mindfulness meditation on an individual's psychological well-being reach beyond the time spent in meditation and should inspire both students and professors to invest time in meditation.

To incorporate the self-awareness of mindfulness meditation with the God-awareness of biblical meditation is to create opportunities for students to engage in meditation that will embed truth more deeply in the heart. Meditation on the character and attributes of God—his sacrificial love, mercy, and kindness, to name a few—and on his movement throughout redemptive history provides abundant material not only for healthier gray matter but for transformative heart matter as well. Professors should allow students to think deeply in a way that incorporates biblical truth into their relevant fields of study, calling, relationships, and life purpose. Fortunately, Christians are not alone in this work. The Holy Spirit is a believer's Advocate and Counselor. He teaches, guides, and reminds Christians of why and how to think biblically about everything.

But the transformation doesn't end there. Not only are we impacted as individual souls directed by our hearts but also as souls created to thrive in community.

Connecting Thoughts with Emotions: The Community

Our culture perpetuates individualistic isolationism with its emphasis on the self. The iPhone, iPad, iTunes, and iPod reinforce the belief that it really is about me, or "i." Such radical autonomy is a constant temptation in contemporary society. Cultural anthropologist Michael Wesch observes that students are fluent in entertaining themselves but not in educating themselves. They may be digitally adept, but they have not developed the skills to use technology to educate themselves.[26] The ability to access information is not equivalent to acquiring knowledge. As educators, we are uniquely positioned to impact what students learn and how they mature in their learning and to foster critical thinking and discernment with the information they retrieve. The training in our various disciplines taught us to ask defining questions, to think broadly for resources, to pursue answers, to wrestle with apparent contradictions, to press through when we have hit the wall, to discover deep within ourselves the conviction that what we learn will indeed make a difference in our world. We then bring this posture to our students, and they are taking notice of what education looks like.

Christian education has always been more than delivering content or transferring information. It is committed to both academic excellence and spiritual transformation. Educators care about their academic discipline and Christian fidelity as they equip their students through an academic subject. They understand that knowledge without character formation limits true impact on students, their community, and the world. Students learn more when they believe that their professors care about their learning, and students are more engaged in their own spiritual transformation when they believe that their professors value transformation. The goal is character formation, and educators can provide opportunities for students to change something about themselves and grow as persons. This is best accomplished in a community that values knowing and being known. Learning together influences a deeper level of engagement.

Impactful learning in any season of life takes place in the context of affirming relationships. As human beings we have a fundamentally insatiable need for relationship. Being relational is in our nature because we are made in the image of God, who is communal. So no matter what the technology, people will use it to connect with others. The communal aspect of online learning conveys the value and role of each member in spiritually formative relationships, which include both professors and peers. Community makes possible a powerful structure for shaping and bringing about individual and corporate change. In community, emotional engagement is added to the shared experience and leads to changed behavior.

Creating an effective communal environment for learning can be challenging. Professors must consider schedules as well as the willingness and ability of both professor and students to engage in conversation and dialogue. Technology used well, however, has proven instrumental in addressing and accomplishing these tasks. Cultivating a presence in an online course community is critical. The professor who cultivates interaction with and between students breeds a "classroom away from the classroom" that is healthy enough to minimize the disadvantages of being geographically distant while maximizing the advantages of engaged learning to cultivate profound experiences of authentic Christian community. We will identify effective practices in the following chapter, but first let's consider the need to foster face-to-face community.

We would be remiss to ignore the need for students to take an intentional break from technology. Students must learn how to power off, to distance themselves from technology, and to engage in authentic face-to-face encounters in order to be present with others and avoid faking a self-image. One of my students, Riley, realized this in a very scientific and technological way:

> The other day I was sitting in the cafeteria eating dinner with a friend. He is a Chemical Engineering major and told me that he creates computer programs to solve his math and chemistry problems. I was blown away and I kept thinking, *How could anybody make a computer program that does his or her math homework?* I asked him to show me. He pulled out his computer, opened up the program, and walked me through it. I was amazed at what he was showing me. The program honestly looked like a different language, but I eventually started to see the basic structure of how it all worked. What he did next will stick with me for the rest of my life.
>
> My friend said, "Do you know what an image is?" I couldn't answer, so he pulled up an image and, using the computer programming software, showed me how an image is made and seen on a computer. As he put the image, which was written in a short code, into the program, a long grid of numbers popped up on the screen. And I mean long. It must have taken twenty seconds to load. He told me these numbers were all on a grid and make up what an image is. He then manipulated the image by changing some of the numbers. I was blown away by the fact that all digital images are merely grids and numbers. He then explained that anything digital, from an email to a text message, a viral YouTube video to an Instagram picture, is merely a series of numbers set in a grid. Simple

math problems and numbers run every digital device we have. The math problems, he said, are basic addition, subtraction, multiplication, and division, and the numbers are all zeros and ones. This is what runs apps, computer software, and digital devices.

I was blown away. After pausing, I asked him, "So the phone that I spend a vast majority of my day on, the Instagram picture I so badly want to upload, the computer I am so fixated with, is all just silicon and a series of numbers? That is what runs everything?" He simply said, "Yes."

I lean on my phone and my computer, my Twitter and my Instagram, and my email and my Internet for comfort, satisfaction. The weight of being fixated with technology while being inattentive to people really fell on me right then and there. There is nothing wrong with a computer or a phone. But I would sometimes rather be on my computer looking at grids and numbers that build an image rather than with [real] people. I am letting grids and numbers rob me of the joy that is found when I am in community with other people.[27]

We must encourage students to engage both in online communities mediated by technology and in students' own unmediated communities. Both provide the arenas for successful, character-forming interaction and conversations.

There is a difference between conversation and mere connection. The following chapter offers practical formats and prompts to move from connection to meaningful conversations that bring about learning in community.

Chapter 5

CONVERSATION FRIENDLY

Collaborative Learning Tools

Tell me and I forget. Teach me and I remember.
Involve me and I learn.

Benjamin Franklin

We should spend less time at universities filling our students'
minds with content by lecturing at them, and more time
igniting their creativity . . . by actually talking with them.

Daphne Koller

Cognitive anthropologists Jean Lave and Etienne Wenger observe, "Learning involves the whole person; it implies not only a relation to specific activities, but a relation to social communities—it implies becoming a full participant, a member, a kind of person."[28] A good online professor reinvests the time typically spent in the classroom or preparing lectures, both of which are now provided for students through the embedded lecture videos. The focus is now directed toward developing and implementing a collaborative learning strategy that involves students.

Small Matter, Big Impact

Whenever possible, use small groups in online classes. This is an important step toward developing a learning community. Prayerfully consider if these groups should be gender specific, discipline specific, or intentionally mixed, because forming appropriate groups carries great freedom and a need for strategy. Collaboration in small groups facilitates communication between members and with the professor. In a small group, students generally feel comfortable getting to know a few others, asking questions, and finding answers, while interacting with a whole classroom of students can be intimidating and cause isolation and separation.

Groups can be formed by geographic location, since scheduling chat times or video conferences should take time zones into consideration. The size of groups should be from five to eight people. This allows participants to cultivate greater transparency and trust, more meaningful dialogue, higher-order thinking, and effective problem solving. Groups smaller than five and larger than eight may find it difficult to accommodate the level of mutual dialogue that enhances learning. Well-planned group engagement helps students move from faceless anonymity to valued membership in a trusted learning community where they can experience character formation.

Collaborative Learning Tools and Ways to Use Them

Collaborative learning focuses on both the content and the process of learning. Participation, dialogue, and reciprocity are necessary for students to sense and know they are included in something greater than themselves. Meaningful dialogue, in a variety of formats, inspires critical thinking and reflection, combats mental inertia, and fosters transformation.

To simply "make conversation" means to speak in an artificial way, but there should be nothing artificial about fostering conversations that involve students in their learning processes. Three specific features in an LMS provide easy access to increased learning through conversation: discussion sessions, collaborative documents, and video conferences.

Give Your Students Something to Talk About

Discussion sessions have become a mainstay for online courses. As described earlier, this is where students engage with course materials in combination with well-framed discussion prompts or questions that stimulate dialogue among students in a small group and with the professor and teaching assistant. Students are typically required to respond first to professor-generated prompts and then to at least one other group member's response. The discussion thread created reveals the depth of engagement and understanding of course assignments. In a traditional classroom setting, time often limits good discussion. With this online feature, however, not only do students participate more, but the professor can also observe, contribute to, and guide these discussions in meaningful ways.

Use an initial "Introduce Yourself" discussion session, either with all students in the class or within the small groups you have created. A personal introduction is an excellent first step in creating an online environment in which students can get to know others and learn together. Some professors have students introduce themselves by creating videos, which all class participants can view. Others prefer to make these introductions in writing. Either way, this initial connection, prior to seeing and conversing with each other through later video conferences, has definite advantages.

There are many interesting people we have not had the pleasure of knowing because our first visual impression of them hinders our openness to initiate a conversation. By making personal introductions with written dialogue and conversations, even before a precourse video conference, students become acquainted with one another. As the course progresses, these relationships are solidified.

Tootsie is a 1982 comedy film that tells the story of a talented but volatile actor whose reputation for being difficult forced him to adopt a new identity as a woman in order to land a job. In a later interview, Dustin Hoffman recounts researching his starring role. He asked the movie studio to do makeup tests to make him look like a real woman. After their best efforts, Hoffman was shocked that he was not more attractive. "Now, make me a beautiful woman," he implored.

Disappointed when they told him that they had done the best they could, Hoffman went home to his wife and cried, insisting on the need to make this film. "I think I'm an interesting woman when I look at myself on the screen. And I know that if I met myself at a party, I would never talk to that character because she doesn't fulfill, physically, the demands that we are brought up to think—that women have to have in order for us to ask them out." With his voice cracking, he said to his wife, "There's too many interesting women I have—I have—I have not had the experience to know in this life because I have been brainwashed, and that was never a comedy for me."[29]

It is now common for people to know something about each other before they meet in person. Students find that this process minimizes the assumptions made about other class participants or members of a cohort. Whichever approach you choose, video or written, the LMS facilitates the introductory knowledge that establishes and grows a learning community.

LMS Examples

The following are examples of text that can be included in an online class to help promote community. Notice that a tone of community is set even *before* the course work begins. You or your course designer may want to modify the details in the following instructions to fit your class.

Example 1: Meet Your Classmates

In an online course, it is important to form the community of learners. This community usually results from the face-to-face contact and interpersonal communication of a traditional class. For this online course, we will be introducing ourselves through this forum. Please post a brief introductory paragraph or short video about yourself (city in which you currently live, year in college, major/minor), a photograph of and something interesting about yourself, and what you hope to gain from this course. Please do not include phone numbers or addresses.

Please do this before the first day of class as it helps build a purposeful learning community. We want to develop a strong learning community in this online class, which can only be accomplished as we get to know one another.

Example 2: Discussion Sessions/Threads

Here is an example of instructions for using the discussion sessions. Edit this for your own use as you build your course.

Discussion prompts are found on Canvas. After viewing the video lectures and completing the assigned reading, you will be expected to participate in discussions by 1) sharing your own response to the required reading by 6 PM and 2) based on the reading, responding to at least one post within your small group before 11:59 PM the same day.

Begin your response to other members of your group by addressing the person by name in order to lessen confusion. To add a personal picture to your Discussions, go to the Getting Started module and click on Add a Picture to Discussions. Adding a picture personalizes the discussion and helps everyone with voice and face recognition.

Characteristics of discussion sessions that are marked by intentional character formation are found in the following sections.

Regularity or Frequency of Discussion Sessions

The professor sets the regularity of discussion sessions. For a semester-long course, weekly sessions are reasonable. For intensive courses that last from five to eight weeks, a schedule of one or two sessions per week is suggested. This schedule helps establish a rhythm for students and assures them of the professor's desire for purposeful connection with them. Regular discussion sessions and similar formatting of the prompts allow the students to become accustomed to this learning feature.

Discussion Prompts

Each discussion session has prompts or questions to which students are required to respond. The professor's objectives ultimately determine the number of discussion prompts, but a good rule to follow is "You'll get more out of less." Prompts high in quality, not quantity, will reveal more student learning, application, and transformation. Two thought-provoking prompts can elicit deeper learning engagement than five lower-quality prompts that fail to scratch the surface of character formation.

Quality of Discussion Prompts

Well-framed, thoughtful questions that ask students to apply their knowledge to real-life situations are instrumental. Begin discussion threads with prompts that require evidence of students' understanding of and engagement with assigned material and avoid questions that require the student to simply reproduce facts or that can be answered by a quick Google search or by Siri.

Mindfully move toward prompts that foster formation. There are three categories of discussion prompts: low-quality, mediocre, and transformational.

Low-quality discussion prompts do little for character formation. These questions result in responses that require no depth and give little or no evidence of deep thinking or meaningful reflection. Simple, one-word responses or "search-highlight-copy" answers contribute little to learning. For example:

- Did you read Psalm 139?
- What did you think about the reading assignment?
- Did you enjoy what you read?
- Summarize the chapter from the assigned reading.

Mediocre discussion questions begin to address character formation but at a surface level. For example:

- What evidence of both good theology and human emotion is found in Psalm 139? How might this resonate with you?

- Share with your group some ways you've been thinking about extending friendship to a stranger and any anxiety or excitement that accompanies this exercise.

Transformational discussion prompts foster character formation. For example:

- How might a truth found in Psalm 139 impact how you relate to God? To yourself? To others in your community? God describes how he sees you. How does knowing that God views others the same way affect a difficult relationship you have with another? Be specific.
- How might sharing the good news of the gospel of Christ be "extending friendship to a stranger"? How might God be leading you in this to someone in your sphere of influence?
- What new aspect of your identity in Christ resonated with your soul? How does your identity in Christ inform a challenging situation God is using to prove the reality of your identity in him? Be specific.

The following prompts show a progression from content-oriented to formational questions for a biblical studies, an ethics, and an integration of faith and learning course.

Biblical Studies

- I trust you enjoyed Dr. Wilkie's presentation as she helped frame the film *Amazing Grace*. Take note of her discussion of Wedgewood's medallion imprint, "Am I not a man and a brother?" As you've studied and completed your paper on a passage from the genre of the Prophets, what connections/ thoughts do you have on social injustice, especially seen from God's perspective?
- Social injustice, a break in the horizontal relationship one has with others, is as much a sin as idolatry, a break in the vertical relationship one has with God. Social injustice begins with one

person, a soul. Christians are called to act justly, be merciful, and walk humbly with God. How has God brought to light an area where you are called to act justly, be merciful, and to walk humbly before him? Explain.

Ethics

- How would you summarize a Christian theology of death and dying?
- What challenges could you anticipate in discussing end-of-life matters with your parents?
- Create a mock advanced directive for yourself. What difficulties did you face in composing this?

Money, Sex, and Power

- Debt, ouch! What do you think about incurring debt and living with it?
- What did you find most interesting in Brooks's discussion (Chapter 5, "Does Money Buy Happiness?" in *Gross National Happiness*, 2008) on the relationship between money and happiness?
- How does your Christian faith influence the tendency to always want 40 percent more (Brooks, 118–119)? In other words, should this be different for a disciple of Christ? Why or why not?
- How much money is enough, and how do you know when you have enough? What habits can you cultivate now that will help you be content when you have more or less money?

Discussion prompts should be presented incrementally with an easy-to-more-difficult ordering. Consider the concept of the soul as the whole person when creating your discussion prompts and where the inclusion of the word *soul* would be appropriate. Note the last prompt in the first series. The use of the word *soul* in a discussion prompt, or any other question for that matter, forces one to stop and think. It is difficult to respond to questions about the soul without thoughtful consideration and reflection.

Through the careful and prayerful use of discussion prompts, students can discover the graces of God and have their spirits nourished. Students do not live in a vacuum, so take the opportunity to step into their lives. How is the truth of what they are learning getting expressed in their lives? This can be approached by asking questions such as, "What does this truth look like in your life?" or "What God-given opportunities might be clothed in this challenge?" or by commenting on how you have observed God working in an individual's life. Press students to be specific and to avoid superficial, cliché, or cosmetic answers. Take the opportunities to leave either a written or media comment for students. These validate their efforts and the encouragement can be deeply received.

Professor's Engagement in Discussion Threads

Give students enough time to begin to process the material that the prompts address. It is okay if their thoughts on a subject are not "correct." That is part of the process. Often another student will address that. Reading through the responses, though, allows the professor to interject Socratic-style questions or clarifying thoughts. Challenge members of a group to integrate their ideas.

Through discussion responses, professors can contribute to individuals or to the group as a whole. Exercise discernment when electing to send a comment to a group versus an individual. A personalized comment can be sent to a student, a more general one to a group. Meaningful comments made on these and other assignments give evidence of the professor's involvement with student learning and validate students' contributions and thought processes.

These comments can serve as an encouragement, include an additional thought-provoking question, be a platform for a personal anecdote, or provide an opportunity for a prayer. Prayer, offered on behalf of another, makes space for students to sense the commitment a professor has to their own journey with God and to others' journeys. This makes for an important point of contact. It is one thing to ask well-framed questions, even those that involve matters of the soul. It is another to respond to students when they articulate what God is revealing about himself and their hearts and souls. It is not uncommon for students to reveal past or present challenges or a particularly difficult issue they are facing.

Leaving a media comment particularly impacts students. Easy-to-use features in some learning management systems allow you to record sentiments, encouragements, or prayers. When you feel confident enough to do this, a deep connection is made. Be assured that the ability to delete and rerecord a media comment is always available.

Rubric for Discussion Responses

A timely response respects other discussion participants, affording them adequate time for multiple interactive entries. Responses should reflect the student's knowledge of the content read and viewed, though substantive posts need not be lengthy. Thoughtful reflection, signaling deep engagement with self and others, can be evaluated. A grading rubric is an efficient and informative assessment tool. (See *Image 10: Discussion Rubric.*)

CRITERIA	Excellent 4	Good 3	Average 2	Needs Improvement 1
Timeliness	All posts submitted on time	Majority of posts submitted on time	Several posts submitted on time	Frequently did not post on time
Quality	Well-written; no grammatical or spelling errors; appropriate length	Few grammatical or spelling errors; appropriate length	Some grammatical or spelling errors; questionable length	Numerous spelling and grammar errors; did not meet length requirement
Content	Relevant; responds to all discussion prompts; demonstrates an understanding of the course content	Posts closely related to discussion questions and course content	Posts occasionally off topic with little insight into the topic	Irrelevant posts that did not relate to the readings or course content
Application	Clearly adds perspective by including specific, personal, and real-life applications	Posts often include specific, personal, and real-life applications	Posts include somewhat specific, personal, and real-life applications	Posts rarely include specific, personal, and real-life applications
Interaction	Contributes to learning community through relevant, insightful, substantive responses	Frequently contributes to learning community	Occasionally contributes to learning community	Rarely contributes to learning community
				TOTAL

Image 10: Discussion Rubric

Grading student engagement on discussion threads can be challenging. Rubrics, which can be incorporated into the grading system of an LMS, ease the tension and provide the students with feedback based on objective parameters. Certain identifiable characteristics distinguish excellent contributions to the discussion threads from those of lesser quality. The criteria found in the rubric nearby can be used to assess the quality of the initial postings and response postings. The rubric offers a simple yet detailed means to assist the professor with grading while specifically informing the student of the assessment. In some learning management systems, after you click in the designated boxes, points are automatically totaled and inserted into the grade book.

Profit[able] Sharing: Collaborative Learning through Shared Documents

Collaborations. Just as the word implies, collaborations is a feature where more than one person contributes to the creation or building of a document. The LMS typically offers a collaborative document such as a Google Doc, Etherpad, wiki, or Padlet. The professor can create this document so students can coordinate carpools to an event, keep a cumulative prayer log, or cooperate on a group project. Students respond as individuals or as a group to the professor's prompts. The professor can choose to keep the collected responses anonymous or to identify students and can project them onto a screen during an on-campus session or simply let students view them online.

Web-based documents unite students over a common project, paper, or assignment. Such a document can be edited and viewed by multiple students simultaneously, or students can revisit it later to add their research, input, or opinions, since these electronic documents are available 24-7. The completed document can then be submitted to the professor on its due date.

A collaborative document can be used to present a text with which students are required to engage by adding comments, highlighting strong points, and offering constructive criticism. Here are a few suggestions:

1. Present a text laden with false information. Students must then identify and make corrections to that text.

2. Present a text that requires translation from a foreign language.

3. Ask students to peer edit one another's documents using the Add a Comment function.

4. Invite students to upload their own presentations for review.

5. Post an open letter from the Opinions section of the newspaper and have groups of students respond by gathering facts and contributing them to one document.

To increase the assignment's character-forming component as you consider the soul (body and spirit), you might ask students to reflect on a matter of personal interest stemming from the subject and to add those reflections to the document or to a separate collaborative document. Here are some reflection questions that correspond to the previous assignments:

1. How important is it to you to know and communicate truth?

2. What does your speaking a foreign language well communicate to a native speaker?

3. How can being corrected impact your pride/humility quotient?

4. What was the greatest challenge in presenting your project? How did you overcome it?

5. Do you work better as an individual or as a member of a team? Explain.

Additionally, the professor can effectively use a collaborative document to collect student comments, reflections, or contributions in either an asynchronous online format or synchronous hybrid course setting. The following example shows how a collaborative document can be used to further the learning process as students apply knowledge from their reading assignments to practical wisdom for living.

In a collaborative document, this explanation and prompt were used to elicit responses from a time spent in prayer:

You may be familiar with using the acronym ACTS for prayer. A for Adoration, adoring God for who he is. C for Confession. As we recognize who God is, it places us in a position of how we "miss the mark" and we respond in a time of confession. T is for Thanksgiving, where we often jump to thanking God for his blessings in our lives. Perhaps the first matter to be thankful for is the forgiveness received having confessed our sin before God. S is for Supplication, where we ask for things. Christians commonly spend most of their time in prayer in supplication, asking God for what we want or need in our lives. So, here is the brief exercise:

- Spend ten to fifteen minutes praying ACT, without the S.
- Afterward, collect your thoughts on this experience.
- In this collaborative document, anonymously add your brief reflections/takeaways from this exercise.

Here are a few of the online responses to the above prompt as they appeared in a collaborative document all students were able to view:

I thought about it as going to a friend or my dad and spending a second saying hello and then spending the rest of my visit just listing everything I needed them to do for me. They wouldn't really feel loved by me or feel like I even want to spend time with them. *Jessica V.*

In praying using ACT, I was able to realize how often I think of myself over God. I found that many times my mind would break away from God and I would start talking about my problems and myself. Without supplication, I thought about myself a lot, and I need to change to give glory to God. I understood how much God appears in my life even when I don't notice him. *Hunter G.*

Praying without supplication caused me to realize how little I give praise to God. Not only this but how difficult it can be to praise God. It is very hard for me to sit and adore him. At first I can rattle off a few attributes and then I draw a blank. God has revealed to me that I need to make it a better practice to just sit and praise him and give him glory in my day. The hardest part is just being there. *Kristin P.*

A meaningful prompt, using a collaborative document in an online course, brings together powerful individual experiences that can impact the entire class. The professor, now able to observe character formation in process, can follow up with further conversations through video conferences and posts on discussion threads. Even in a hybrid course, you will find that in less time than it takes to hear a few representative student voices face-to-face, you can provide a document where most if not all expressions, even the usually inhibited ones, are given a "voice."

When employed early in the course, the initial document serves as a baseline that can then be revisited near the close of the course for students to note changes in their thinking or perspectives on the same topic or matter. These reflections can be collected in a document to reference later or to use to assess learning outcomes for the course.

Students are encouraged when professors incorporate technology into their learning activities. Use these features judiciously and you will find the quantity and quality of responses mutually rewarding and transformative.

Lights. Camera. (Inter)Action: Collaborative Learning through Video Conferencing

A growing number of professors are using video conferences in their online courses and finding this feature less intimidating than they previously feared. As part of every good LMS, video conferences reveal the professor's desire to build and support a healthy learning community. These opportunities are valuable times to connect with students in an informal, user-friendly way. At the same time, video conferences help keep the professor alert, aware, and humble. Perhaps your reservations about using video conferences in your online course will dissipate in the time it will take to read the next few paragraphs.

LMSs continue to make video conference sessions easier to use, and they aim for clear and strong connections conducive to conversations without video or audio delays. Many LMSs have a video conference feature built into them, thus eliminating the need to resort to a program, outside of the learning platform, that professors and students would have to download and install separately on their computers.

Video conferences are best used not for teaching purposes but rather for following up or offering personal perspectives on previously viewed video lectures or completed assignments. When used between individuals or with small groups, dialogue is encouraged and community is furthered. Participants' names appear along with their real-time images, so professors do not have to memorize students' names ahead of time or be anxious about addressing a student by an incorrect name.

The professor sets the lengths and times of sessions. A good length for video conference sessions with groups is thirty minutes. This length of time seems doable, even for the quiet, more reserved student. The professor also determines the number of these scheduled blocks of time. Scheduled video conferences can accommodate the schedules of both students and professors and should take into account time zone differences and students' work and family obligations. Scheduling weekly conferences sometime in the earlier part of the week may be more helpful for the students, as would some sessions in the later part of a day. Students need to be advised before the start of the course that a webcam and microphone are essential tools for participating in the class. These tools are relatively inexpensive or sometimes can be borrowed from friends or checked out from the school's media lab.

The venue to hold video conferences may range from the comfort of your own home or office to any place where a strong Internet connection is available, preferably with little or no background noise or music or other people. Using different rooms in a home can give a personal touch and make it feel as though you are inviting students into your personal space. Students sometimes feel uneasy at the start of the video conferences even when they are in their own comfortable environment, yet within some sessions you can serendipitously meet parents, siblings, roommates, and even pets as they appear in the background of a student's screen (although pets are never as impressed as the other viewers).

It is also helpful for your teaching assistant to periodically join video conferences with you and your students. This gives your students the opportunity to become familiar with those who will likely give input on some of their assignments. The teaching assistant can also offer help in answering questions the students might have. During a video conference, you can also leave the screen and mute the sound, leaving the teaching assistant alone with the students for a few minutes. This gives students an opportunity to ask candid questions they find difficult to ask with you present. Upon returning, you can address anything that remains unanswered.

In many learning managements systems, students can initiate video conferences without the professor's involvement. These sessions allow students to work collaboratively, similar to unmediated, face-to-face settings. A professor can encourage the use of these sessions by mentioning it in a video conference discussion or by assigning weight to them.

Using Video Conferences Effectively

Inform the students or groups of students of the scheduled times designated for video conferences. Remind them to join the video conference at the scheduled times only and to be punctual. When initiating a video conference, consider inviting all the students and informing them to join at a specific, assigned time. This allows for one group of students to join after another group without your having to end one conference abruptly and start another with the next group. If some students show up early for their conference, it reminds those students that they are a part of a larger whole with other students in the course. Seize the opportunity and allow them to introduce themselves, fostering now an even larger community.

Leading a Video Conference

As the students join in, give them an opportunity to introduce themselves or to greet each other. An icebreaker may help: "What are you enjoying thus far in the course?" "What are some challenges?" Time management, workload, jobs, and other classes are common topics that you might bring up as a point of understanding or empathy. Introductory video conferences establish a welcoming and friendly tone for subsequent sessions. Informing students that they are being prayed for allows them to begin seeing a depth of care and trust found in an interactive learning community. As you grow more familiar with the students and they with you, it becomes easier to converse over course-related challenges, reflections, and assignments. When you embrace vulnerability, you can direct conversations toward heart and soul matters by sharing your own stories and brief observations on life matters or by asking how students' learning intersects with their life situations. When students present challenges as they think through and live out truth in their lives, respond with empathy, concern, openness, and prayer.

As you progress with the video conference, address any issues students may encounter and answer any questions they might have about the course, written or reading assignments, discussion threads, or LMS matters. One student commented that video conferences take discussion threads to a different level. If you as the professor have made observations about a group's participation in that week's discussion threads, for example, take the opportunity to offer your verbal comments. Students appreciate your suggestions, which help them foster their learning community, approach a particular assignment, or better understand a difficult reading assignment. This makes them feel like they have an inside track from the professor and provides additional points of contact and relationship building.

Keeping character formation in mind, consider the following ways to involve students in dialogue as participants in a video conference:

- Springboard from a comment made during the video conference. Be alert to what is being said. If students' answers resonate with you, say so. You might make a quick reference to your own life experience and to God's faithfulness in responding to you. If a student's answer needs more unpacking, ask, "What do you mean?" or "Can you give an example?" Consider what other members of the group might think, add, or contribute. Students appreciate efforts in getting to know them.

- Listen for the challenges that your students have. Challenges in our lives are God-ordained opportunities to give evidence of God's Spirit working in us. What challenges are your students experiencing in or while taking this course? How can they be found leaning on God even more?

- What differences can your students see in themselves since starting this course? How are they puzzled by what they are learning about God? What truth has them pondering a few minutes longer than usual? How has their love for God grown? How has their love for people grown?

As you approach the close of your live video session, consider giving your students a heads up. If the coming week is going to be challenging, tell them so. Or if there is something you want them to pay even closer attention to, let them know. You are offering lifelines to them as the rigors of your course mount. An easy way to remember what should be addressed in a video conference is "past, present, future." It is that simple.

Lastly, take the opportunity to pray for the students. Having listened intently to their concerns and knowing the tasks they have at hand, close the video conference with a short prayer. You impact your students when you model bringing others and their concerns before God.

Here are some student comments about video conferences used in an online course:

I am really thankful that the professor took the time to video conference with all of us and gave us the opportunity to see each other in "real life." These check-ins helped keep me motivated and informed, and I felt like I wasn't alone and overwhelmed with the readings and work by myself. *Rachel A.*

The video conferencing! I have to admit the start of it was a little nerve-racking since we hadn't all met yet, but we've definitely warmed up since the first one! This was probably one of the coolest things I had ever done with a class. It gave the class such a personal touch, and I really enjoyed that. *Dylan S.*

The video conferences brought my appreciation of community to a deeper level. As I waded through the readings and the papers, the video conferences allowed me to process everything *in community*. Through the video conferences, I was challenged, convicted, and encouraged in ways that no essay could ever replace. *Amanda H.*

Assessing the effective use of these features in an online course is not difficult. Feature-specific statements can be added to the Student Ratings of Instruction system used by your institution. These additional statements can be generated by the professor or may be standardized for online course offerings across the institution. Use the prompts below as a start.

1. The course assignments, materials, and engagement activities (e.g., online discussions) were well planned and properly sequenced.

2. The course assignments, materials, and engagement activities (e.g., online discussions) were structured to help establish an online learning community.

3. The video-conferencing sessions with the professor and other class members helped foster a learning community.

4. The in-person sessions (where applicable) contributed to assimilation of the course content.

5. The professor responded to questions and concerns according to the time frames articulated in the course syllabus.

6. The professor established a presence through his or her online interactivity throughout the course.

Chapter 6

PREMIUM BLEND

The Hybrid Course

If teaching is largely about faculty-student interaction, then we have to recognize that human interaction is changing.
José Antonio Bowen, *Teaching Naked: How Moving Technology Out of Your College Classroom Will Improve Student Learning*

Whether you are considering entering the world of teaching online by starting with a hybrid course or whether you've landed on conducting hybrid courses, you have discovered a highly successful format for learning in online education. Those teaching a completely online course may choose to skip to chapter seven, but then you might miss being surprised by the suggestions that can be used—with simple modifications—to further student learning in wholly online courses as well.

Hybrid or *blended* are terms used synonymously to describe courses where traditional face-to-face time complements online learning activities or experiences. Hybrid courses take advantage of the best features of both face-to-face and online learning. José Bowen states, "The best education of the future will be hybrid. There is value in physical contact with teachers, but there is also potential learning and real convenience in online coursework.... [For] most institutions, the primary question will be one of balance between face-to-face interaction and online resources."[30]

The professor, with the help of the course designer, determines what elements of a course translate best from a traditional to an online format. Hybrid courses do not treat the online component as an add-on to a traditional class or use the classroom time to repeat what is learned online. Much of the course content is provided online, and students interact and submit related assignments online as well. In a typical online hybrid course, students are first exposed to the course content through reading assignments and video lectures. They respond to this content in discussion threads and written assignments. The learning sequence continues with abbreviated on-campus sessions. These sessions further build the learning community and allow students to interact over the content learned. Because hybrid classes reduce seat time or classroom time in a brick-and-mortar facility, they can alleviate an institution's classroom shortage problems.

There are a number of effective ways to schedule the face-to-face classroom component of a hybrid. You may require weekly sessions, periodic sessions, or sessions at the beginning or end of an intensive course. If you schedule an in-class session at the beginning or end of the course, you should augment it with regular video conferences with students.

When a class meets in person, these are prime opportunities as a larger group to address student questions and facilitate interactive discussions. In addition, the professor can maximize student interaction and learning by incorporating activities designed to engage students and reinforce their learning, emphasize application of the course content, and build the learning community. (Some suggested activities are found shortly, in the "Bright Ideas" section.) The interaction establishes and generates excitement for learning and for learning within a given community.

To these on-campus sessions, the professor inherently brings his or her emotion and style of interaction.[31] As explained in chapter four, our emotions connect with our thought (mind) and behavior (will). This takes place in the heart. If our lives are our hearts in motion, then these classroom times can serve as opportunities for the professor to communicate passion, dedication, and love for a subject to the students. The virtual atmosphere created by the professor and course designer and the in-class atmosphere created by the professor are both indispensable contributions to the learning environment.

Flipped Classes

Whereas the traditional model introduces new content to students during class and assigns homework for outside class time, the flipped class introduces new content online and asks students to complete homework or collaborate on group projects under the guidance of the professor when they meet together as a class on campus. Described as a type of hybrid course, a flipped class is nuanced in two ways: the amount of online engagement and the purposeful design of the on-campus sessions. Hybrid courses range in the amount of online involvement they require, but flipped courses include significantly more online learning, thus shortening the on-campus time. The preclassroom, online sessions serve as a series of first-exposure segments that then focus the unmediated, face-to-face time on creative learning and application experiences. These activities and experiences are especially formative in the communal format that hybrid courses offer.

Bright Ideas: Learning Experiences for Hybrid or Flipped Classes

The following learning activities, typically done in student small groups, further establish and sustain hybrid learning communities. Some also have spiritual formation components that involve learners more deeply in their growth in godliness. Depending on the subject of a class lesson, a learning activity will usually precede a spiritual formation activity, which has its own distinct purpose. The following learning activities can be used for the face-to-face class sessions of hybrid or flipped classes, reframed to address specific course topics, and modified for courses that are completely online. The course designer can assist with these changes.

1. On a collaborative document, collect group responses to a well-framed prompt. Here are some examples of prompts that can be modified for a specific topic.
   a. Present a scenario where students are challenged to apply the information gleaned from their reading, writing,

or discussion thread assignments. Then ask students to change that scenario to reflect a real-life change in a situation; have them record the options, reactions, and responses that accompany this change; and have them evaluate the various group contributions.

   b. Ask students to identify themes from the film *The King's Speech*. Present them with the following questions: What does the film reveal about the natural human heart? How have you seen this truth of human brokenness demonstrated in the world? In your community? What evidence of God's redeeming purposes can be found in this film? In which roles, responsibilities, and accomplishments is your identity found? How does this align with your identity in Christ?

2. Take advantage of the use of smartphones. Ask each group of students to work together on a short script that is then captured on video using one phone's camera feature. The short clips, one minute in length, can be projected in class for all to see or posted on the LMS. Be sure you have the necessary cables to connect their devices to your computer. You might encourage students to create a commercial or news spot, clues from *Jeopardy!*, a "man on the street" interview, or a poem, mime, or rap.

   Another way to incorporate smartphones is to have students or groups of students text others. You might ask individual students to text a friend outside of class with a survey question and to bring the results to the class discussion. Or have groups of students text their response to a discussion question to another group, which can then agree, disagree, or expand on the received text. Continue this pattern with any other questions presented to the class.

3. Challenge the students to write a haiku on a given subject. On the screen, project the definition of a haiku and the topic on which the groups will focus. Have a member from each group then read their work aloud to the class.

4. For a survey of historical events, prepare some strips of paper, each with a brief description of an historical event. Mix the strips and place in a sealed envelope. Distribute one envelope to each small group of students, asking them to place the events in chronological order and to contribute their events to a single timeline in a collaborative document. The events may not be in the correct order, so you can review and further explain each event while one student edits the document. Students can revisit the document later for further study.

5. Show a TED Talk and discuss competing perspectives of a subject. For example, Brené Brown's "The Power of Vulnerability" can foster broad conversation.

   a. What are the truths, weaknesses, and implications of the assertions in this TED Talk?

   b. How do these assertions align with God's Word?

   c. What observations from your own life resonate with themes or arguments from this TED Talk?

   d. What are viable responses to these observations?

6. Using PowerPoint, create a *Jeopardy!* game board with answers and clues. Your course designer should be able to help create this or you can search for examples online. Appoint a "host" and divide the class into teams to answer the clues. Identify the group with the first correct verbal or written answer and reward them (be creative with this), which adds to the fun. For the exam, use the *Jeopardy!* clues and answers as part of a study guide.

7. Select four students to act as pastors, advertising agency representatives, or teachers. Meet in groups and have them deliver a five-minute sermon or presentation incorporating elements from readings, videos, discussion posts, and dialogue. These can be captured on video for a later posting on the LMS.

8. People enjoy stories. Allow opportunities throughout the course for students to share their own life stories. Students

appreciate when you begin with your own story and are more apt to share their own personal journeys. Students are also impacted by guest colleagues who share their story, even as an integration piece.

9. When students arrive with their intended group presentations, surprise them with a "sudden change in plans," such as a change in the time allowed for the presentation, an audience whose spoken language is not English, or an equipment breakdown so that the group must work together in responding to the "emergency." They (and you) will discover how they respond to or cope with unexpected change.

10. If you are using social media in your hybrid course, mention the students with the best tweets, Instagram posts, or Tumblr blogs of the week. Be sure to distribute these accolades among a number of students, not highlighting the same students every week. Create a discussion around the circumstances behind these student contributions.

11. Project a shared collaborative document onto a screen for all to see. Students receive immediate feedback as they observe the document develop and expand as rapidly as they type. The sound of keyboard typing and seeing other students add their reflections or responses encourages more students to contribute as well. Depending on how the prompts are set up, the document may become an outline for the lecture. The following is an example of a prompt and the subsequent student responses, which have become the lecture outline:

In groups of two to three, add to the collaborative document on the seven deadly sins. Include the blind side of the sin, a contemporary example, and a way God's Spirit desires to move through you in that situation.

Pride

1. The blind side of the sin
   - Insensitivity
   - Not valuing others/disrespecting the values of other people
   - Cycle of trying to satisfy your need of appreciation through pride (tearing others down to lift yourself up)

2. Contemporary example
   - Avoiding a responsibility or a task because you believe that it is beneath your talents and skills
   - Not cleaning up the mess after a classroom party, because it's the janitor's job, not yours
   - Being frustrated/annoyed with those of a different personality
   - Responding with "Good" or some kind of superficial, put-together answer when people ask how you're doing even though the reality is that you are probably struggling with things and could use the care and help of others

3. A way God's Spirit desires to move through you in that situation
   - A reminder that you are fully dependent on him and all "good" acts are for his glory and not your own. Learning ways to love and care for others with a humble heart and loving them for who they are, not for gains they can bring you

Serendipitous Acts of the Professoriate

Hybrid courses allow students to observe the community dynamics of their faculty. In a live, unrehearsed environment, a colleague can just happen to show up or can be scheduled as a guest speaker. Whether playful or serious, these acts of the professoriate only add to the advantages of hybrid courses.

Of course, these moments can be enjoyed in an online format too. By simply adding a professor to the LMS, he or she can be introduced to your class, can make a "special announcement" or appearance, and can even persuade students to respond to a dialogue created between professors. Students sense and enjoy the camaraderie among faculty.

Chapter 7

BUT I TEACH MATH!

Integrating Faith and Learning[32]

*Divine knowledge, and Human Learning, are the
right and left eye of the World; as the Sun and
Moon are to the Universe, the eclipsing of either
of them leaves the World in darkness.*

Richard Mayo[33]

*Vocation is the place where our deep gladness
meets the world's deep need.*

Frederick Buechner

There are some who feel that the Christian faith and scholastic learning are diametrically opposed and antithetical to each other. Not so! Rather, the two are harmonious companions. Faith in God is deepened as we learn and understand more about ourselves and our world, regardless of the subject matter—whether mathematics, science, business, or the humanities. Likewise, learning is expanded when we comprehend the majesty of God's handiwork in creation and the world around us. The writer of Proverbs asserts, "Blessed are those who find wisdom, those who gain understanding" (3:13), and "Get wisdom. Though it cost all you have, get understanding" (4:7). Conversely, only the unwise do not wish to learn: "Fools despise wisdom and instruction" (1:7). It is God who gives knowledge and understanding (Dan. 1:17).

At the core of the integration of faith and learning is the mandate for Christians to participate with God in seeking creation's greatest good and bringing about its flourishing in ways that honor its Creator (Gen. 1:26, 28). This involves applying a biblical or Christian worldview to all of life. The goal is to use acquired knowledge—how we think, act, and live within culture—to participate in God's plan to redeem culture to its fullest potential, its realized good, and his revealed glory.

This chapter addresses the practical side of the integration of faith and academic disciplines in an online format. It is important to note, however, that a model of integration where faith is merely a quick supplement or insertion into a discipline creates a compartmentalized life, devoid of an authentic biblical worldview and lifestyle. Therefore, let us first identify what the integration of faith and learning is not.

To meet a quota or an institutional requirement, some professors erroneously implement the integration of faith and learning by tacking a Scripture verse onto a principle where it may—or may not—fit or by starting class with a short devotional that has little or no relevance to the subject matter or to students' lives. In some cases, an attempt to integrate faith and learning may unfortunately be inserted on the last day of class.

Integrating faith and learning is not limited to any particular subject or discipline; it is applicable to all. It is fallacious to think that professors who teach courses in theology or biblical studies do not need to be intentional about integrating faith and learning or that courses in the arts and sciences, for example, do not need such integration. Professors must communicate their subject matter with biblical integration and application. Incorporating faith and learning into all disciplines is crucial to living lives of integrity and purpose.

Broadly, the integration of faith and learning is a conversation between Christian beliefs and the best of academic learning in all disciplines. The goal is to guide learners so they are able to formulate essential questions that emerge from study in the academic discipline, to discover insights that arise from the questions that connect the discipline with relevant biblical concepts, and to respond to the insights with a plan to act and engage with culture. Once a question has been framed, the conversation continues for the purpose of discovering insights that connect the best of the discipline with the relevant theological concepts. The identification of points of congruence, complementarity, conflict, or continued questioning furthers the discussion.

Because the integration of faith and learning is not just a cognitive process, one must respond to the insights with a plan to act, to engage creation or culture. Richard Baxter notes, "Reason is at the strongest when it is most in action."[34] David Williams echoes this thought, saying, "Reality is not what our knowledge mirrors; rather, reality is that with which our knowledge participates."[35] True and deepening knowledge requires action. It is easy to see a linear sequence from thought to emotion to expressed actions of the will, but in fact, actions have a double-back impact on the emotion (feeling) and thought (thinking). Actions flow from the emotion of the heart but also have an effect on the heart's emotion.[36] C.S. Lewis observes, "The rule for all of us is perfectly simple. Do not waste time bothering whether you 'love' your neighbor; act as if you did. As soon as we do this we find one of the great secrets. When you are behaving as if you loved someone, you will presently come to love him."[37] In this, one can begin to see the mutual effect the mind, emotion, and will have on one another in the heart and in character formation.

It is a small step outside the box of online learning to imagine the ways a student can engage in his or her own milieu and community. Geographical distances may separate the professor from the student, but the student is present in his or her own corner of the world. The online professor may not engage with students in an unmediated way, but that does not preclude the students from interacting with their own present reality.

Adding experiential components or actions—aspects of the will—to the learning process affords opportunities to practice a principle or truth, strengthening what is thought (mind) and felt (emotion), thus allowing that truth to be more deeply known. Interestingly, the absence of such opportunities, the lack of an expression for the will, can impede knowing and feeling.

The most effective level of learning and knowing will involve knowledge that is lived out in actions. As meditation on God's Word embeds that truth in one's heart, so too do actions affect the heart and soul as noted in chapter four. The following are sample discussion prompts for thoughtful reflection and experiential components that assist students in engaging with integrative theologies and character formation. Note that examples for science, technology, engineering, and mathematics are included because though these classes are often taught online, the integration may not seem as obvious for the professors who teach these courses. So instead of throwing their hands up in surrender, professors can use the following prompts and experiential components and tailor them for their courses in order to increase character formation and the integration of faith and learning. These should serve as a catalyst to help professors think integratively. You need only start with modifying one or two prompts. Consider how your own experiences of living out your faith within your discipline might be translated into a thoughtfully engaging prompt, hypothetical scenario, or real-life experiment.

You may be tempted to read only the sections on integrating theology into your own discipline, but I suggest reading through all the following sections. Perhaps an even broader integration can be found in asking questions of this kind: What does psychology have to do with biology?—art with business?—bioethics with sociology or math? Posing such questions to students who represent various disciplines would be mutually beneficial for critical thinking. The more explicit we can become with the integration of faith and learning, including cross-disciplinary integration, the more our students will grasp the scope and intricacies of a purposeful Creator and his orderly, integrated creation.

Sociology

Is America guilty of some of the same sins against the poor that led Old Testament prophets to condemn Israel and ultimately contributed to God's sending Israel into exile?

- How is poverty associated with racial tensions in the United States? What is the role of the church and what is the role of the government in fighting poverty?
- *Experiential component:* Form a small group and plan a daytime walking tour of an area known for its poverty and human suffering.

- *Experiential component:* Visit two local churches of different socioeconomic levels for Sunday services and then describe your observations, questions, and the impact this experience had on your view of the worship or experience of God. How has your opinion changed from your experience?

Psychology

How does a scriptural understanding of forgiveness differ from the descriptions of forgiveness found in humanistic psychology literature? How are they similar? How do they compare or contrast with one another?

- Is forgiveness different for Christians than for non-Christians? If so, how? How would you describe the forgiveness you have extended to another?

- What might one be overlooking when emphasis is placed on "forgiving yourself" rather than on receiving the breadth and depth of God's forgiveness?

- *Experiential component:* Interview two individuals regarding their experiences of being injured by another in some way and needing to extend forgiveness. As you focus on the forgiveness, collect their reflections on when they decided to forgive, what that entailed, and what that process was like for them. Write your reflections from this assignment. What impacted your view of forgiveness in a specific situation you have experienced?

- *Experiential component:* Forgiven people find it easier to forgive. The apostle Paul states, "Just as the Lord has forgiven you, so you also must forgive" (Col. 3:13 NRSV). Spend time with God in prayer over that for which you have been completely forgiven. What does your forgiveness of another look like? As God's Spirit leads, extend forgiveness to someone whom you have harbored unforgiveness toward. If needed, seek counsel from another to help you with this process.

General Science

How do the choices we make have an impact on nature and those we come in contact with?

- Read Genesis 1. In which day of creation were bacteria made? In Genesis 1 plants and animals are said to have been created "according to their kind." What is a kind? A species? A genus?

- How do the immensity of the universe and the vastness of time affect your understanding of God? Does God seem more impossible? More great? More worthy of your worship or gratitude? What is your soul's response into a glimpse of God's majesty? How does this impact your relationship to him? To others? Be specific.

- *Experiential component:* Amaze Me Project — Take a long hard look at a twelve-inch square of creation from different perspectives. Use the naked eye, a camera, a magnifying glass, binoculars, or a microscope. Present your findings in a way that will astound and cause a person to praise the God of creation. This may be in the form of a photographic slideshow, a series of electron micrographs taken of things you found in that square foot of creation, an original poem, or another original work of art.

Biblical Studies and Spiritual Formation

Describe hospitality as you understand it.

- How does the following quote from Parker Palmer differ from your initial idea of hospitality? He describes hospitality as "inviting the stranger into our private space, whether that be the space of our home or the space of our personal awareness and concern. And when we do so, some important transformations occur. Our private space is suddenly enlarged; no longer tight and cramped and restricted, but open and expansive and free. And our space may also be illumined.... Hospitality to the stranger gives us a chance to see our own lives afresh, through different eyes."[38]

- Explore these Bible passages on biblical hospitality: 1 Timothy 3:2; Job 31:32; Hebrews 13:2; and Leviticus 19:33–34 or Luke 14:12–14. Place each verse into one of these categories: indicates true discipleship, is the responsibility of leaders, crosses social barriers (race or class and status), or is commanded by God.

- *Experiential component:* Biblical hospitality involves extending friendship to a stranger. God has done this to us in that we are no longer strangers but are now family. As you grow more sensitive to God's Spirit, follow his lead where he challenges you to extend friendship to a stranger. Comment on your experience in the discussion thread.

Bioethics and Human Reproduction

Related to matters of human life, which ethical issues are private matters and which should be subject to governmental control and policy?

- How does a holistic Christian ethic of the sanctity of life affect the realm of reproductive technologies?

- If embryos can be formed through means other than egg fusing with sperm (somatic cell nuclear transfer, twinning, iPS cells), when does life begin? Do you have to know where life begins to take a reasoned ethical position?

- What does it mean to be made in the image of God? What difference does this truth make in how you view yourself? In how you view and treat others?

- *Experiential component:* Imagine yourself as a baby growing in your mother's womb. What are your desires, fears, and curiosities? What questions might you have for God? Share these ponderings with a family member or close friend.

Diet, Drugs, and Disease

On the topic of food production and consumption, which ethical issues are private matters and which should be subject to governmental control and policy?

- What do you understand the term *organic* to mean?
- What is a GMO food?
- What advantages and disadvantages are there in GMO foods?
- *Experiential component:* Visit a local organic farm or fruit/vegetable stand. Ask the farmers or sellers what unique approaches to farming they promote. Why? Ask about their faith: Does spirituality play a role in their farming practices or their view of food?

English

Read two to four stories from other cultures (e.g., Native American, Asian, African) about the creation of the world and then compare and contrast those with the biblical account. How do the different stories relate to your own cultures and beliefs?

- Until the twentieth century the Bible and *The Pilgrim's Progress* were standard books in English-speaking households, and both have been translated into hundreds of languages around the world. Why were these books so important? What impact have they had on people's lives?
- C. S. Lewis's prolific writings include fantasy, science fiction, theology, poetry, essays, radio addresses, and apologetics. Read *The Lion, the Witch, and the Wardrobe.* Why do children and adults alike enjoy this book? Give specific examples of how Lewis integrated his Christian faith in his storytelling. Describe in detail his use of symbolism, imagery, and allegory in the book.
- Watch a movie version of *The Lion, the Witch, and the Wardrobe* and use a Venn diagram or other chart to compare and contrast the book and the movie.

- *Experiential component:* C. S. Lewis said, "I believe in Christianity as I believe that the Sun has risen, not only because I see it, but because by it I see everything else."[39] Create a short video expressing how your beliefs affect the way you think, act, and live.

Foreign Language

Memorize the Lord's Prayer in another language.

- Identify your favorite Bible verse and explain why it is meaningful to you in the target language.
- Write a psalm on an attribute of God or personalize an existing one.
- *Experiential component:* Use the target language to write your testimony of how you came to know Jesus Christ as your personal Lord and Savior. Share your testimony with someone from the target culture.

Business

What function does business serve from a biblical perspective? Are there purposes beyond that of providing a context to share your faith and love others?

- When you stand before Christ, what aspects of your business will he ask you about and why? What will he have observed as his Spirit led you in decisions you made?
- God provides ordinary and material goods as part of common grace. How should Christians view and value these? What are the pitfalls and blessings of valuing material goods? Identify a potential pitfall or blessing in your life. How might this pitfall damage or this blessing heal those around you?
- How does your use of technology reflect the person you want to be?
- *Experiential component:* Is there such a thing as a Christian company? What are the criteria for a business to be regarded as

being Christian? Companies such as Hobby Lobby and Chick-fil-A are touted as companies that practice Christian values. Do some online research on a company that you consider to be Christian. How does the company fit your description of a Christian company? Visit this company in person and determine if and how their Christian values are reflected. If you were the business owner, what would you change or retain to reflect Christian values?

Mathematics

One million earths would fit into a space the size of our sun. What aspects of your being and purpose are challenged or encouraged by this truth?

- Chaos theory shows us that some equations and physical systems are practically impossible to predict more than just a little bit into the future. Since God knows the future, how does this help you think about God's power and wisdom?

- *Experiential component:* Find some images and videos online of the Mandelbrot set and read about how it is calculated. The visual images are created from a really simple equation. What does this tell you about a God who knows and controls the whole world?

- In what way does the realization that God is omniscient and in control affect how you live your life today?

Statistics

In what ways have you observed or experienced the orderliness of God and his creation?

- *Experiential component:* The law of large numbers and the central limit theorem display the orderliness of the universe, which points to the very nature of God. Explore these with the following exercise:

a. Predict the shape of the distribution of twelve dice rolls. Next, predict the distribution of all of the dice rolls of the class combined. Then predict the distribution of the means of each student's twelve rolls. Share your predictions with your group members.

b. Roll twelve dice (or one die twelve times) and record the values and the mean. Submit these figures to your professor.

c. After your professor has compiled the figures, view the histograms of the submitted values and means. How does your prediction compare with your twelve dice rolls?

d. Discuss the fact that this *always* happens. From the light years between stars and the earth to the nanometers between electrons, the means of *all* variables tend to the one bell curve, which reveals a profound order in the universe that reflects its one Designer.

e. Read Romans 1:20. What impact does knowing God as the God of order have on your soul and in a present situation?

The aforementioned suggestions are intended to help professors envision how to integrate faith and learning in practical ways for different subjects. Some colleges and universities offer assistance and direction with this. For example, the Office of Faith and Learning at Biola University has short but detailed how-to videos to help professors integrate biblical truths into many academic disciplines. An introductory video to iFLIPs, Internet Faith Learning Integration Presentations, can be found at *http://open.biola.edu/resources/technology-in-the-classroom-video-iflips* and a catalog of iFLIP videos is located in Appendix B.

The Most Influential Integration Component

Theories and narratives are one of the principal ways to begin and continue the integration discussion. One narrative, however, remains key to influencing and inspiring students as they grapple with their own integration of faith and learning—yours! As effective as the content and structure of the online course is, they cannot substitute for an authentic, transparent, caring educator.

Professors are responsible not only for teaching course content but also for *how* it is taught. Even in an online course, they must be mentors and must be present for students both effectively and personally. The word *integration* comes from the word *integritās*, from which we get the word *integrity*. Students search for and desire access to someone who is honest about manifesting a life of faithfulness and authenticity.[40] How these integrators think, discern, make choices, and live out a consistent commitment to God and others is crucial — essentially modeling integration in a way that allows student access to that process. Students desire to observe and interact with those whose Spirit-led, heart-directed souls are characterized by a solid biblical worldview and a lack of hypocrisy. The fact that students want to see a professor's personal relationship with God means that the integration of faith and learning is something profoundly meaningful to them.[41]

Researchers continue to affirm Randall Sorenson's findings that what contributes most to a student's integration of faith and learning is how well students can determine the convergence of a professor's authentic, dynamic, and growing relationship with God and the professor's nondefensive, emotionally unguarded, and even vulnerable relationship with students. Sorenson summarized this point as follows:

> Too often we think that teaching students our integrative models is what they need in order to learn integration. Often what they want, however, is not our models but ourselves — or perhaps more accurately, they want us to model our own integration, and to give them access to our own relationship before God in an open and nondefensive manner. It is as though when they have access to us as not just professors but persons, and to our ongoing life before God — doubts and all, our joys and our terrors — students are well served in finding their own integrative pilgrimage.[42]

The relational attachment that students, both graduate and undergraduate, have with their mentors is the most effective way they learn integration. Professors are often the mentors who personally model that integration for students. Elizabeth Hall and her colleagues identified five traits that are significant to the process of integration: self-revealing, caring, welcoming, dedicated, and open-minded.[43] *Self-revealing* refers to the transparent and humble nature with which professors describe their personal, professional, and spiritual knowledge and experiences. *Caring* reflects the personal involvement of a professor in students' lives outside the classroom. *Welcoming* involves opportunities for discussion and ongoing conversations about topics of interest, which form a large part of the integration of faith and learning. *Dedicated* refers to the faculty member's passion, heartfelt desire for, and belief in what he or she is doing and communicating through the integration of faith and learning. *Open-minded* means fostering a climate in which students can mutually share thoughts and opinions, recognize differences, and wrestle with integrative issues.[44] These relational processes reflect the value of Spirit-filled, Christ-like lives and the significant influence such professors can have on their students.

Discussions about integrating faith and learning are often unscripted and spring from a lifestyle that models a biblical worldview, a life of godly character and integrity. As such, integration exercises may not be a part of every class session, since it takes time to build an infrastructure of discernment, understanding, and transparency. To exhibit your passion for and dedication to integrating faith and learning in the classroom, you can bring new ideas, engaging questions, and challenging scenarios to a conversation and can demonstrate how various concepts fit together. Start with a concept with which the students are familiar and then introduce them to a fact they have yet to learn. Encourage students to think outside the box, which fosters critical thinking, and explain why you chose that approach.

The importance of being present and conversant with students cannot be overemphasized, even in a course that at the outset may not seem to be inclined toward the integration of faith and learning. Even a statistics course can be shown as a function of God's creation, but the professor is the key to integration. One student in an online statistics course reflected on her experience of unreturned emails and unanswered phone calls to the professor. The student avowed that she would have felt less like a faceless, nameless number if the professor had made even a minimal effort to respond to her inquiries. With the communication features of most LMSs—discussion threads, collaborations, video conferences, written or media comments on graded assignments, and of course, announcements, emails, and audiovisual comments—professors have no excuse for not being present in online courses.

Professors have a tremendous opportunity to awaken and inspire faith in their students. They have been given the noble responsibility of equipping students with knowledge, and that knowledge is not merely intellectual but is also knowledge of how to live. It is imperative that professors recognize and stalwartly accept the remarkable task of integrating faith and learning.

Chapter 8

SOCIAL MEDIA

Forming Character with 140 Characters

The Digital Revolution is about orthopraxis —
right practice — not orthotechnology.
Elizabeth Drescher, *Tweet If You Heart Jesus*

The previous chapters have established that character formation happens in relationships, and relationships are effectively fostered in online classes by combining course content with purposeful assignments, meaningful feedback, discussions prompts, personal interaction, video conferences, and collaborative documents to establish a viable, sustainable learning community. But juxtapose character formation with social media, and it can be puzzling.

We live in a highly mobile society, connecting with one another in ways unimaginable to the ordinary person merely a decade or so ago. Social media, the means of connecting with others in a virtual community, depends on mobile and web-based technologies like applications (apps) and text messaging (texting) for individuals and groups of people to create, share, collaborate, and discuss user-generated content. Emerging in the early 2000s, these technologies include social networking sites, video-sharing sites, and blogging and microblogging platforms.[45]

This chapter describes popular social media sites, demonstrates how they might be used in an online class format to foster connections between professors and students, and addresses a few concerns that come with using social media in your class. The aim of this chapter is to help you become more informed about social media in case you decide to incorporate it into your online class. After all, about 70 percent of online students spend ten or more hours online weekly, in addition to their online studies. They visit social networking sites most often, followed by news and shopping sites.[46] Participation in one or more social networking sites is normal for our students and usually assumed. Only about 10 percent do not have a profile on any social networking site.[47]

There's a good chance you already use social media. The University of Massachusetts Dartmouth found that 70 percent of faculty used Facebook, though not typically for their classes. If you are not among them, do not feel pressured to use social media in a class. Pressure is not the best kind of motivation. If, however, you have an interest in incorporating the dynamics of social media into your class, the following information may serve to further that decision. In addition to Facebook, you've probably encountered a few other social networking sites (e.g., Twitter, Instagram, Pinterest). These sites may or may not be familiar to you, but it is helpful to recognize them and know basic facts about each.

- **Facebook:** At the time of this writing, Facebook is the most popular online social networking service. Founded in 2004, it has grown to over one billion active users. Professors can create common-interest groups using private Facebook groups to connect with students in a course. Although Facebook may be the best option for connecting with family and friends, a growing drawback for students is that Mom and Dad are probably their "friends" on Facebook.

- **Flickr:** This popular photo- and video-management website, acquired by Yahoo! Inc. in 2005, is used widely by photo researchers and bloggers, and hosts images that can be embedded in blogs and social media.

- **Google+:** Once a single social networking service, Google+ appears to be reorganizing and splitting into separate services: Photos and Streams. Streams may be the collecting of Google+ posts. Google Hangouts will remain the messaging and video-conferencing service.

- **Instagram:** Launched in 2010 as a social networking service, Instagram enables its users to share square-shaped photos and short videos (up to fifteen seconds long) and to apply digital filters to them before posting them on a variety of sites like Facebook, Twitter, Tumblr, and Flickr. Images are usually accompanied by five words or fewer.

- **LinkedIn:** Launched in 2003, LinkedIn is a professional networking service geared toward business rather than social connections. This site is available in over 20 languages, making it an effective global service for professionals and prospective college graduates.

- **Pinterest:** A visual discovery tool that people use to collect ideas, projects, and interests. Pinterest users bookmark images called "pins" to create a collection on a "board," which they can share with other users. Pinterest is a strong favorite among women, but the number of male users is growing. Pinterest has become an effective tool for businesses.

- **Snapchat:** A favorite among college-aged students and younger, this site allows "snaps," photos or videos with accompanying text and drawings, to be sent to a specified list of recipients. Users can set the time limit for which a snap can be viewed before being hidden from the recipient's device. As of April 2014, the average time for viewing was from one to ten seconds. Users beware: although snaps seem to disappear, they are all still traceable.

- **SoundCloud:** This online audio-distribution platform, the audio version of YouTube, enables creators to upload, record, promote, and share their originally created sounds. This audio-sharing renaissance platform is particularly fast growing.

- **Tumblr:** Owned by Yahoo! Inc., Tumblr is a social networking website that allows its users, primarily sixteen- to twenty-five-year-olds, to post multimedia and other content to a short blog. Blogs can be made private and users can follow other users' blogs. Many use it for "fandom"—fan art, commentaries on popular media, artistic GIFs, television show jokes, and philosophic humor. At times it becomes a space for collaborative art, which creates a sense of community as people feed off of each other, building on the previous commentary or adding to the creative piece.

- **Twitter:** Created and launched in 2006, this site allows users to post a short 140-character text message called a tweet. *Tweet* was named 2009 Word of the Year. Users keep up-to-date with others by "following" them. As an online social networking service, Twitter is useful for finding the latest chatter or for monitoring current events. Twitter was the first platform that supported hashtag usage. *Hashtag*—a word or unspaced phrase prefixed by the # symbol and used to mark key words or topics in a tweet—was recognized as the Word of the Year in 2012 by the American Dialect Society and in June 2014 was added to the Oxford English Dictionary.

- **Vimeo:** Founded in 2004, Vimeo is a video-sharing website where users can upload, share, and view videos. Vimeo users often embed their videos into social networking sites such as Facebook. Videos are of high quality, but the site is less interactive.

- **Vine:** Twitter's video-sharing service allows its users to record and share six-second looping videos, or "video loops," on social media sites such as Facebook and Twitter.

- **YouTube:** Owned by Google, this video-sharing website allows people to create and share videos and to surf the site in an effort to build more community.

Look Both Ways

Before considering using a social networking site, check for a social media platform that may already be provided in your LMS. It should function similarly to sites outside of the LMS. Determine ahead of time the way you will use it, its purpose, its boundaries, the rules for engagement, and the appropriateness for the learner. Whatever technology is available, it should be used to connect with people. Danah Boyd asserts that it is not so much that students are addicted to social media as much as they are addicted to each other[48] and to an accompanying "fomo" (fear of missing out).

Because community remains important to college students, educators must consider social media's complications and address them in order to use it wisely. One way that social media affects relationships is through a sense of isonection. *Isonection* describes people who are well connected on social media yet are very lonely and isolated. The term originated from Tony Beliz who combined the words *isolation* and *connection*.[49] Sherry Turkle, who studies how devices and online personas are redefining human connection and communication, maintains that people need to engage in conversation and self-reflection and need to know that someone listens because we feel alone.[50]

Professors must also be aware of students' media literacy, the ability of users to apply critical skills to understand biases in advertising and to determine the credibility of works found on the Internet. Because students use social media as a news source and truth finder, they need the input of educated faculty to assist them in discerning the value of published works and readily available information.

Be purposeful and strategic with the use of social media in your online courses. Coordinate the social media prompts with your assignments. And as your students post, be sure to reply, "like," or follow in ways appropriate for the platform. Highlight some of your responses, perhaps through a class announcement on the LMS. This validates not only students' efforts but also their personhood.

The growing number of professors who use social media as part of the designed engagement for their courses is providing students with an upper hand for their future. Employers assume graduating students use social media, and they expect them to understand how to use it for more than just personal enjoyment. Incorporating social media into one's teaching can help students learn how to use social media professionally by observing how teachers and staff use it well.

Best and Worst Practices for Using Social Media

The platforms previously described are not foolproof. If you decide to try one, choose the one that best fits you and your course. As with any practice, consider the parameters of social media usage. It may benefit your students and save you time, embarrassment, and potential regrets. The following are the top five things to do and top five things to not do when using social media.

Top Five Dos

1. **Do Encourage:** Your words influence souls, even if not expressed directly to your students.

2. **Do Champion:** Give evidence that you support your students. Be a strong voice in their lives.

3. **Do Reflect Values:** Consider how your values are reflected in everything you share.

4. **Do Engage:** Plan on interacting, not spying. Students want to know you see them.

5. **Do Humanize:** Do not be afraid to be personable. Your warmth, friendliness, and humor contribute to the one-to-one feel of social media.

Top Five Don'ts

1. **Don't Complain:** Don't complain or be critical, especially about students. This can feel like backstabbing or betrayal of trust.

2. **Don't Overshare:** Students want to be seen and known, but they value the distinctive relationship they have with you as the professor. They want to see that you are human, but they do not want to be your best friend.

3. **Don't Underestimate Your Influence:** Young people treasure friendships and mentors, and you have an incredible opportunity to be influential.

4. **Don't Be Creepy:** It is awkward to jump into a conversation uninvited, and it is the same thing on social media. You are not their primary audience; their peers are.

5. **Don't Discount Value:** Consider the dynamics of social media and use it well.[51]

Decide how you want to employ social media in your class, set up the parameters of what you want shared, and aim for quality content that is published frequently. You can require a specific number or frequency (perhaps weekly) of posts on a social media site during a course. You can then collate, evaluate, and assess these posts for quality and quantity of participation. They might include connections the students have made between content learned and observations in their world (a news item, art project, or serendipitous conversation), thoughts stemming from a reading or written assignment that was particularly meaningful, or questions and ideas that impact their understanding of the course's subject matter, who God is, and what he is doing.

Social media is one means of interacting; it is a tool. When used well, it can be an asset for learning that allows students and information to be more easily accessed and interconnected. Social media also extends the sense of the professor's presence and becomes an aid in the integration of faith and learning. Whether it's through 140-character tweets on Twitter or microblogs on Tumblr, students are looking for ways to be social, so be a healthy model for them. The reward for your efforts will emerge over time and tweets as you witness changes in students' thinking processes, a greater attentiveness to their own integration of faith and learning, changes in their biblical worldview, and reflections on applied knowledge that transforms their own character—all shared experiences within the course's community.

PART 3

BUILDING
BETTER
OUTCOMES

Chapter 9

ASSESSMENT

It's about Stewardship

*Faculty need support from each other and from
administrators to become engaged in assessment.*
Trudy W. Banta and Catherine A. Palomba,
*Assessment Essentials: Planning, Implementing, and
Improving Assessment in Higher Education*

For educators, the assessment of course learning outcomes is a subject
often dreaded, a sentiment that is echoed for online education. Many
ask, "Why can't I just teach?" or "What do I have to do to look good?"
Although professors recognize the need for assessment, sometimes they
feel as though an outside accreditation or governing body is trying to
intrude in their teaching, classroom, or online course. Assessment can
also touch a sensitive spot and make one ponder: *Am I really teaching
what I say I am? Am I doing it effectively? Are students learning? What
if the evaluations say I am not doing a good job?* There is a fear of being
erroneously judged, which may also play a part in the apathy toward
assessment. Couple this with knowing that it requires a lot of time and
effort to be an effective teacher, and one has a recipe for prolonged
indifference and resentment.

Of course, the teaching/learning center in your academic institution (often called the Office of Academic Effectiveness or Instructional
Effectiveness) faces the pressures and realities of graduation rates,
retention, and job placement, along with growing student debt. These
colleagues shoulder the responsibility of supporting the academic
institution's response to these critical issues. Assessment places them
between these accountabilities and accurate evaluation of the learning taking place. Although the teaching/learning center is the hub for

collecting, collating, and interpreting this necessary information, it is more than a storehouse for such data. This office provides academic departments with access to accurate data for critical decision-making.

As professors, we instinctively recognize the need for assessment and appreciate the benefit of thinking about the goals of our courses and the learning outcomes for our students. This may be even more important for online education. With the constant threat of low-quality education available in online formats, valuable and life-changing student learning can become a low priority. Assessment done well, however, helps ensure that professors continue to inspire and that students continue to receive the valuable learning they need to navigate their lives, careers, and future in years to come. It is not about doing whatever it takes to look good but rather about doing what it takes to teach well. This motivates great teachers. If you have ever found yourself tweaking a syllabus because of a new book you have read or changing an assignment to better reflect what you want your students to experience, then you are doing assessment; you are improving your teaching. Protocols implemented by academic institutions are just the avenues that prove this; they are a means for educational improvement.

And in a real sense, assessment is about stewardship. It is a response to what you have been given. As a professor, you have been given a responsibility to oversee the learning that takes place under your watchful care, and assessment helps ensure that learning occurs and occurs effectively.

Not only is assessment a matter of good stewardship, it is something scholars do. When you read a journal article or review a book, you look at the source. You determine its validity. You assess whether the information presented is true and verifiable. In the same way, when you claim to teach, instruct, and educate, assessments give evidence of those claims. Here are some pertinent questions to ask in order to do an informal self-assessment of your online teaching. Great online teachers care enough to candidly answer these questions, assess their own efforts, and make changes.

- How well do your students write and discuss what they are learning?
- In what ways do you encourage faculty-student contact?
- How well do your students work with one another on substantive tasks?
- Do you give prompt and frequent feedback to students about their progress?
- In what ways do you communicate high expectations?
- In what ways do you explicitly communicate standards and grading criteria?
- What are some ways you help students achieve those expectations and meet the criteria?
- How do you respect diverse talents and learning styles?
- In what ways do you use problems, questions, or issues as points of entry into the subject matter and as sources of motivation for sustained inquiry?
- How do you make courses assignment-centered rather than merely text-and lecture-centered and then focus on helping students successfully complete the assignments?[52]

Assessment requires taking action. If it did not, perhaps professors would not drag their feet as often or for so long. That action comes in different forms. It may mean reviewing your course syllabi to weed out assignments that are simply busywork, both for students and for you. An indication of this can be the little time and attention you spend grading these kinds of assignments.

It may mean asking your students. It is easy to think that all you need to look at are students' grades as evidence of whether they "got it" or not. There is, however, more to the learning process than the grade earned at the end of a course. Offer a prompt on a collaborative document asking them to give advice, encouragement, or challenges to students taking the same course in the future. If you've developed a good relationship with students, you may receive helpful feedback when you ask students for ways the course aided their learning and could be improved.

You might also take action by allowing yourself to be inspired. Meet with a colleague to brainstorm ideas that have proven successful and then evaluate the ideas and tweak them for your own students. Or spend some time in reflection to determine the life events that have robbed you of the joy and purpose that teaching brought you in former years. Then share these with a trusted friend and colleague to get back on track. Finally, try reading a book designed to refresh your calling as a professor and then reboot with fresh ideas for communicating with your students. They may seem to speak a different language, but the joy of your commitment to their learning transcends many generational and cultural gaps. Here are a few recommended readings:

- Susan A. Ambrose, et al., *How Learning Works: 7 Research-based Principles for Smart Teaching* (San Francisco: Jossey-Bass, 2010). Geared toward faculty in higher education, this book links research findings and experiments with practical suggestions for classroom use.

- Ken Bain, *What the Best College Teachers Do* (Cambridge: Harvard University Press, 2004). You won't be disappointed that there is no list of dos and don'ts in this book. Instead, Bain offers research-based teaching strategies of knowing, engaging, and challenging students by focusing on the character, attitudes, and practices that effective teachers do well.

- José Bowen, *Teaching Naked: How Moving Technology Out of Your College Classroom Will Improve Student Learning* (San Francisco: Jossey-Bass, 2012). Bowen stresses creating an environment conducive to student learning and highlights the use of technology in fostering student-faculty interaction. This allows "naked"—i.e., face-to-face—interaction between faculty and students to increase the value and effectiveness of education.

- Chip Heath and Dan Heath, *Made to Stick: Why Some Ideas Survive and Others Die* (New York: Random House, 2008). This well-researched, collaborative work identifies barriers to learning while fostering ways people connect with ideas. Teachers are not the only ones who desire their ideas to be communicated and to stick.

- Wilbert McKeachie and Marilla Svinicki, *McKeachie's Teaching Tips: Strategies, Research, and Theory for College and University Teachers* (Boston: Houghton Mifflin, 2006). Aiming at those who teach college-level classes, McKeachie and Svinicki offer strong introductions and overviews of key concepts and theories critical for novice and continuing instructors. This comprehensive collection of advice and ideas stimulates thinking about effective instruction.

- Parker J. Palmer, *The Courage to Teach: Exploring the Inner Landscape of a Teacher's Life* (San Francisco: Jossey-Bass, 1998). "Good teaching comes from the identity and integrity of the teacher," writes Palmer. He addresses the character formation of a teacher, looking at the inward matters of the teaching soul and connecting it, or reconnecting it, with its vocation and students.

- James E. Zull, *The Art of Changing the Brain* (Sterling, VA: Stylus, 2002). Zull uses nontechnical language to provide knowledge about the brain. This knowledge of learning processes informs teaching strategies.

Each of the aforementioned actions takes time and requires a healthy measure of humility. How willing are you to engage in these actions or conversations for the sake of impacting students with what you know and how you teach what you know? Is your humility quotient higher than any accompanying fear factor? If your answer is yes to either of these questions, you have just accomplished the most challenging part of moving toward effective assessment. Read on, the rest is quite simple.

Walvoord and Banta define assessment as "the systematic collection of information about student learning, using the time, knowledge, expertise, and resources available, in order to inform decisions that affect student learning."[53] Assessment builds on what you are already doing, so keep it simple. Accrediting agencies exist to provide a means of accountability for educational institutions to ensure high standards of academic quality and effectiveness whether in a brick-and-mortar or online format. The systems they use are designed to help enhance student learning, to draw on the best aspects of academic culture, and to be sustainable in terms of time and resources.[54] Currently, accrediting bodies and state and federal governments are focused on learning outcomes and a holistic community rather than on individual professors. They want to determine the quality and integrity of an earned degree. The questions they ask revolve around three areas of concentration:

1. **Goals:** What will students be able to do once they have successfully completed the course of study? How will they have learned and been transformed because of what and how well they have learned?

2. **Evidence:** What evidence do you have that students have achieved the goals you have set for them? What influences their learning the most?

3. **Action:** How can the results of an assessment shed light on areas inside or outside the classroom that need attention? What support is needed to improve or sustain student learning?

Beware of Assessment Pitfalls

Watch out for these pitfalls while you are assessing your teaching. First, if your compliance is driven by external demands, assessment becomes legalistic and one simply asks, "What is the least we can do to pass?" Assessment can also turn into "adult busywork" if it is simply gathering data no one will use and dumping that information into an assessment file. That is not assessment. Finally, a too-complicated process adds to the unnecessary burden of "too much work."

To avoid these, focus on streamlining the process by looking for "quality" data versus the "quantity" of data. And as data are collected and interpreted, acknowledge when substantial improvements or efforts to maintain a high-quality education are discovered. The aim of this evaluation process is to improve performance and maintain a high level of learning.

Changed from Nouns to Verbs

Bloom's taxonomy is a teaching tool used to help evaluate levels of instruction and student learning. Developed and originally published in the 1950s by a committee of educators chaired by educational psychologist Benjamin Bloom, the taxonomy was designed to assist educators in designing curriculum and exams. In the mid-1990s, Lorin Anderson, a former student of Bloom, revisited Bloom's taxonomy. Most notable were Anderson's changes from nouns to verbs and a slight rearranging of the categories. (See *Image 11: Revised Bloom's Taxonomy*.) These shifts reflect more outcome-oriented language and a more active form of thinking, which are perhaps helpful in providing educators with terminology useful for assessment. Compare the old steps and the revised steps in the chart nearby.[55] Notice that "Knowledge" has been converted to "Remember" and that the highest level of development is now "Create" rather than "Evaluation."

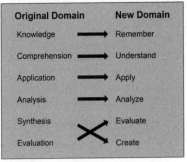

Image 11: Revised Bloom's Taxonomy

"Remember" and "Understand" reflect lower levels of learning and typically appear in 100- or 200-level courses, which tend to be foundational for mastering the skills assessed in higher-level courses.

Based on this revised taxonomy, an expanded version of Bloom's work follows.[56] (See *Image 12: Expanded Bloom's Taxonomy*.) Moving from the inner circle outward are descriptive words and suggestions for connecting an outcome with an activity. These are helpful when you coordinate your learning outcomes with assignments.

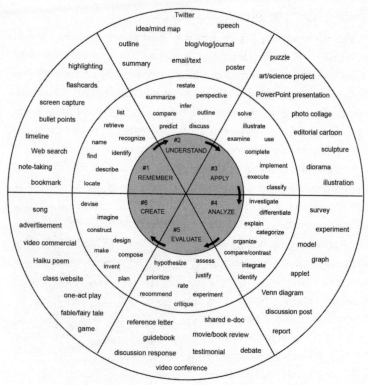

Image 12: Expanded Bloom's Taxonomy

Assignments must be clearly described and their outcomes clearly understood by students. These parameters help link student learning with learning outcomes and hopefully make the steps toward assessment seem less daunting. The first steps for assessment are as follows:

1. Each department's learning outcomes are those mutually agreed on by that department's faculty as necessary for successful completion by students who major or minor in that discipline. These and the learning outcomes for every course offered in a specific discipline need to be clearly stated in the course syllabus.

2. Be sure students have a clear understanding of the learning goals, the things they should be able to do that demonstrate that they have learned. These should be stated using specific

verbs (*apply, analyze, evaluate,* or *create,* rather than *know* or *understand*) and should be readily available to students and articulated periodically throughout the course. Mention what they will learn to do and ask often how well they are learning. Students should be able to see a strong connection between the assignments required for the course and what they are learning. If your course is taught by a number of other faculty members, there is great benefit in consistency in learning goals—for students, faculty, and administrators. Although learning outcomes and objectives should be the same for every section of the course, there remains great latitude for individual teaching styles and approaches within each individual class.

3. Gather information about what students are learning from conversations, collaborative documents, class or small-group discussions, assignments, exams, and extracurricular activities. This information indicates progress and can serve to improve student learning in your classes. Sometimes this starts by asking a few simple questions: How is this idea beginning to make sense? How are you tracking with me? What has been the most beneficial in your learning in this class? The least helpful?

4. Keep records and share this feedback and your responses to it with other colleagues who teach additional sections of the same course and/or with your department chair. Once collated and interpreted, this information provides valuable information to a department.

Learning outcomes for any course, online or otherwise, are specific abilities your students will be able to do upon the conclusion of your course. Align these outcomes with certain aspects of the assignments you require. Your assignments should build on each other and lead toward the achievement of the outcomes stated clearly in your course syllabus.

Notice this sequence in the following example of outcomes spelled out in the course syllabus for the course Biblical Interpretation and Spiritual Formation:

Sample Syllabus: Biblical Interpretation and Spiritual Formation

Bible Department's Program Learning Outcome:

- Identify the basic contents [and theology] of all books of the Old and New Testaments and apply the biblical teaching for Christian faith and practice through reliable and faithful methods of interpretation.

Student Learning Outcomes for the Course:

- Interpret select representative biblical texts toward an accurate meaning by using principles of interpretation for genre-based hermeneutics.
- Write personal contemporary applications and observable differences that are relevant to expressing truths found in Bible passages.

IDEA Objectives:

- Learning fundamental principles, generalizations, or theories. (This is an essential emphasis for this course.)
- Learning to apply course material (to improve thinking, problem solving, and decisions). (This is an essential emphasis.)
- Developing a clearer understanding of, and commitment to, personal values. (This is an essential emphasis.)

The objectives of the IDEA (Individual Development and Educational Assessment) survey or other student ratings of instruction systems are pieces that contribute to the learning outcomes. A sample assignment that addresses the above objectives is provided in the next section.

Competency-based education or learning looks at the process of learning, not just its outcome. It is learner-focused. As the learner moves through a series of competency successes, they progress toward mastery.

Rubrics Rule

When students wonder about or ask for explanations of grades for assignments, they are curious about what criteria you used to assign those scores. Rubrics are guides that list specific criteria for grading papers, projects, tests, or other course assignments. They serve as the bridge between the abstract and the assessable, the subjective and the objective. As professors, we naturally use a rubric when grading assignments; however, often it is just in our heads instead of on paper. Since rubrics help explain to students our expectations and how and why specific scores were earned, it is essential to provide a written rubric for assignments that they can view. Students are able to more quickly evaluate the strengths and weaknesses of their submitted work in order to improve it and subsequent assignments.

Rubrics, in fact, are the foundational construct for assessment. Using them consistently and efficiently helps students to see more clearly the intentional sequencing in their own process of learning. At the same time, clear and concise rubrics assist each faculty member and department, ensuring that content is successfully learned and supporting the success of student learning in that discipline.

Sample Assignment: Scripture and Interpretation Meditation

For each of the genres of Scripture explored, interpret passages according to the following format. Each paper is to be approximately two pages, typed, and double spaced.

1. Approach each passage with prayer and dependence on God's Spirit for understanding and obedience. Read and reread the meditation passage.

2. Identify the genre of the biblical passage. Give a brief description of the genre before identifying its particular interpretive principles. Briefly describe or explain each principle.

3. Using headings (if these are helpful to you), identify the author with a brief bio, date, and audience of the book. Make

observations regarding historical, cultural, or literary background of the passage. How does this passage fit into the rest of the chapter? The theme of the book?

4. State the "big idea" of the selected passage in one sentence by reading and rereading the surrounding passages.

5. With the help of a good commentary (or commentaries), apply the appropriate interpretive principles to determine the meaning of the passage.

6. Spend thirty minutes meditating on the meaning, importance, and significance of the passage on your soul.

7. Having established the boundaries of the original application by the original author, make a contemporary application that does not violate the author's original intent. What impact or relevance does this passage have on your own present spiritual formation? What might God's Spirit be leading and empowering you to do in a present relationship or situation? What observable difference is there in this relationship or situation as you know and act on God's truth? Be specific.

Assessment: These assignments will be scored according to a rubric, assessing the level of completion of the required elements.

Here is the rubric for this assignment. (See *Image 13: Assignment Rubric*.)

Scripture Interpretation and Meditation Rubric				
Criteria	**Ratings**			**Points**
Timeliness *Submitted on time*	On time 2 pts		Late 0 pts	2 pts
Content organization/development *Relevant, well-developed ideas with evidence of understanding*	Excellent 3 pts	Adequate 2 pts	Needs improvement 1 pts	3 pts
Grammar/punctuation *Uses correct grammar, punctuation, & spelling*	1-2 errors 2 pts	3-4 errors 1 pts	Many errors 0 pts	2 pts
Integration of theology & praxis *Demonstrates integration of content with personal application*	Excellent 3 pts	Adequate 2 pts	Needs improvement 1 pts	3 pts
			Total points: 10	

Image 13: Assignment Rubric

The "Integration" component in this rubric addresses the character formation aspect of the assignment. See questions 6 and 7 in the sample assignment instructions. An expanded description of this component could include, "After spending time reflecting on the meaning of the passage, address significance and application. What impact does this truth from God's Word have on your life right now? What observable difference is there as you rely on God's Spirit for understanding and then his power to live out that conviction? Be specific."

Your assignment instructions must be as specific as possible in order to direct your students toward greater transparency with God, their community, and themselves. Do not settle for trite or cliché answers. Press students to wrestle with what it means to know, trust, and obey God as it relates to the material in each particular course. Most students have been trained to write in the third person, and now they'll need to write in first person. It is challenging. In this learning process, though, they learn to grow more candid and truthful with God and others. These documented texts become evidence of students' character formation, available and ready for assessment.

The LMS is a most useful tool for streamlining assessment. Students' work and a rubric can be linked directly to an assessment tool, making it easy to compile data and evaluate progress toward achieving the desired outcomes. The information helps substantiate effective learning, identify students at risk, and support the institution's accreditation process.

Assessment Is a Good Thing

Good, healthy communication and vigorous exchanges among the faculty of a department are key to assessment and can be a challenging aspect for academic institutions that find themselves functioning in silos. Movement in this direction indicates scholarly humility and an institution-wide focus on integrity, on delivering what the institution promises to do. It is the academic department, which is made up of specialists, that defines what mastery looks like. Assessment purposes must be specific and have agreement, thus turning inward and communal.

Rather than succumbing to the external demands of an accrediting agency's compliance model, a department asks, "What do we believe our students should be able to know and demonstrate?" Prove that your students are progressing toward mastery, not just to accrediting agencies, the academic institution, your department chair, or colleagues, but also to yourself. Demonstrate that the approach you take in your distinct style of online pedagogy works, or discover that it needs improving and humbly address that for the sake of your students and their futures. As you do, you will make your course, department, and institution stand out. Assessment is a good thing. It pushes us to make our courses and our teaching the best they can be. Great professors do this, and as they do, students can experience authentic character formation, even in online education.

Conclusion

Great professors inspire students. They've always done so in traditional classrooms; now they get to do it in online classes as well. The added dimension of inspiring students toward character formation has been the focus of this work. As students are inspired, their souls are impacted, their hearts are transformed, their lives are changed, and their impact on others becomes boundless. Students in online classes should experience a real sense of community and never feel that they are alone with the computer screen. Community is important and all the more so in online classes. Character formation is important and all the more so as our world needs knowledgeable men and women of integrity and virtue. To a roomful of college presidents from a wide range of private institutions, New York Times columnist David Brooks stated, "The Christian schools are the ones most serious about teaching character. Others don't. [L]eaders [from a well-known Ivy League university] decided recently they wanted to teach students about character, but they gave up because they didn't know how."[57]

The growing numbers of online courses provide strategic intersections between learning and character formation. This book has not offered lofty ideas, imagined for the ideal online class, but rather practical guidance borne out of real-life online teaching experiences. Seeking to bring about character formation in students can be a challenge but is well worth the investment. There is nothing quite like witnessing lives being transformed before your very eyes (even if it is on a computer screen).

May your experience teaching online classes be rich and your efforts to foster character formation be rewarded. And may the words of a former student of mine encourage you in this endeavor: "Take your tools. Take your ideas. And create something that will inspire the world."[58] Great professors do this.

APPENDIX A

Coming to Terms with Terms

Apps: Applications.

Asynchronous learning: Any form of communication or learning in which participants do not have to be available at the same time. This can include discussion threads and collaboration documents.

Bandwidth: Measured in hertz (Hz). The amount of data, usually measured in bits per second, that can be sent through a given communications channel.

Blog: A contraction of the words *web* and *log*, a blog is a site for discussion or informational posts. Posts are discrete entries typically displayed most recent first. Used as a verb, one can blog; used as a noun, one can create a blog.

Browser or Web browser: A software application for connecting to websites and browsing the Internet. Some more popular browsers include Chrome, developed by Google; Firefox, developed by Mozilla; Internet Explorer, developed by Microsoft; Netscape Navigator, developed by Netscape; and Safari, developed by Apple.

Chat: A chat room is an Internet-based "place" where two or more individuals or groups of individuals connect to have real-time (synchronous) typed conversations. Chats can be used for virtual "office hours" or as a place where groups of students can interact with each other to discuss projects, assignments, etc.

Cloud: Web storage space outside of a computer where information can be saved while remaining accessible. Cloud storage providers include Dropbox, iCloud, and Google Drive.

Collaborative learning: A variety of educational approaches that use features of an LMS so that students can work together to search for understanding, meaning, or solutions or to create a product of their learning.

Course designer: Also known as an instructional designer, curriculum developer, or curriculum design specialist, this person works alongside an educator to build classes in an LMS, ensuring that creative, purposeful, and engaging instruction is based on learning objectives and learner needs.

Course Management System: See *Learning Management System (LMS)*.

Database: An information file that is organized to easily access, manage, and update data.

Digital immigrant: Any individual born before the existence of digital technology and who learned to use some form of it later in life (often much later in life). Their numbers are declining. Both this term and *digital native* were coined and popularized by Marc Prensky.

Digital learning: Also known as distance education or distributed learning, a model in which learners and instructors are separated by time and place. Educational practices include a combination of media and technologies.

Digital native: Anyone who grows up with the digital world as the norm. They are native speakers of the language of computers, video games, and the Internet. Their numbers are growing.

Discussion board: An LMS feature that consists of posts or threads and allows individuals of a group to contribute to an online conversation, creating a series of asynchronous messages on a particular topic. The interaction potential of this feature between peers and professors is great.

Discussion prompt: A well-framed question or comment that fosters learning, critical thinking, and the building of a learning community as students respond to and engage with each other.

Download: To copy onto one's own machine a file or program from another device or computer system.

Emoticon: A symbol that conveys an emotion, which can be difficult to do in text-based communication (e.g., a smiley face ☺). Since there is no guarantee that the meaning of an emoticon will be accurately translated, invest the time to first communicate well with written words and then perhaps add an emoticon.

Engagement: Meaningful interaction between students, course materials, and the professor that enables learning.

E-portfolio: Short for electronic portfolio; a user-managed collection of electronic evidence that can be organized, archived, displayed, and shared for personal, educational, or marketplace purposes.

Face-to-face course: A class where participants are physically present in one place at the same time; also called a traditional course. In such a course a web-based LMS might be used only to post the syllabus and assignments.

Flipped class: A type of hybrid course where students engage with instruction online through an LMS and then meet regularly (e.g., weekly) with the professor on site for homework exercises and discussion. Students generally work through a significant amount of the coursework online through recorded lecture videos, readings, quizzes, and other resources. Classroom time allows students to interact with the instructor; augments online coursework through problem-solving, practical exercises, lab work, learning activities, and presentation of current research; and builds a learning community.

Hybrid course: Also known as a blended course; an online, distance-learning course that also incorporates face-to-face class meetings. A substantial proportion of the content (30–79 percent) is delivered online and thus reduces the number of on-campus meetings. This format takes advantage of the best of both traditional and online learning.

Import/Export: These terms refer to data sent from one program to another, similar to the movement of products between countries for trade or sale.

Instructional design: A systematic approach to course development that ensures that specific learning objectives are accomplished through various pedagogical approaches. It is the process by which learning and instructional principles, resources, activities, and assessments are formatted into online, technology-assisted courses.

Learning community: A group of individuals who collaboratively engage in critical discourse and reflection, using both synchronous and asynchronous activities to cultivate learning and critical thinking together.

Learning Management System (LMS): Software that delivers full courses online and may also handle registration, grading, and related functions. Among the over 150 LMSs, the more widely used ones include Blackboard, Canvas, Desire2Learn (D2L), Moodle, OpenClass, and Sakai. Some institutions design their own LMS.

Link: Short for *hyperlink*, a connection within a website or document that, when clicked, opens another location or element within the same or another website.

Logging on: The process of connecting to a computer network. It involves more than turning on the computer and typically requires a password.

Lurking: The activity of reading posts in a discussion thread but only occasionally posting or responding to a post.

Module: Some LMSs refer to these as *folders*. Modules are self-contained segments of learning that introduce key ideas and provide links to videos, reading, written assignments, and discussion boards or forums. These are the building blocks of a course.

Netiquette: Socially acceptable behavior in an online context. The dos and don'ts of online communication.

Online course: A course where all the content is delivered online. There are typically no requirements for face-to-face meetings between students and instructor, though they may meet through video conferencing.

PDF: Short for portable document format. A file type that allows documents to be viewed in their original format and appearance with the layout, spacing, and margins intact.

Post: A message put into an LMS such as on a discussion thread or in response to a submitted assignment.

Professional development: The opportunities for faculty to learn or improve their technological skills through in-service training, workshops, conferences, or private or group tutorials.

Real time: Describes an environment in which information or interaction is received and responded to with no time delay. See *Synchronous*.

Rubric: A grid-like tool that communicates the consistent criteria for evaluating a particular task or assignment. Rubrics aim at accurate, fair assessment and mutual understanding between instructor and student.

Scroll: Moving up, down, left, or right on the computer screen.

Search engine: An Internet application that enables a user to search for specific content, as defined by the user, on the web. The top three search engines are Google, Yahoo!, and Bing; Google is the most popular.

Server: A networked computer that allows those connected to it to jointly access information, help, or services.

Social contagion: The mutual influence people have on each other, which usually tapers off after about three degrees of separation (a friend of a friend of a friend).

Social network: A website or application whose users communicate and influence each other using posts, comments, messages, pictures, or videos to share news, ideas, updates, knowledge, values, or beliefs.

Synchronous: Generally used to describe online, real-time communication between individuals who are not in the same place; the opposite of asynchronous.

TED Talks: A global set of conferences owned by the Sapling Foundation that operates under the slogan "Ideas Worth Spreading" and brings together people from three worlds: technology, entertainment, and design. Typically using the form of storytelling, speakers present their ideas in innovative and engaging ways in a maximum of eighteen minutes.

Teleconferencing: Two-way communication between two or more people in different locations. This can be via phone or computer, audio-only or audio and video.

Threaded discussion: See *Discussion board* and *Discussion prompt*.

Traditional course: Course where content is delivered in person but may be technologically enhanced with minimal use of a learning management system. See also *Web-facilitated*.

Twitter: An online social networking service that allows users to send and read short messages called tweets.

Upload: Send data to a device or computer system.

Video conference: A communication between two or more people or groups of people in different locations that includes both video and audio.

Web 2.0 tools: Blogs, wikis, social media, and mobile devices such as smartphones and tablets.

Web-facilitated: A course that uses web-based technology to facilitate what is essentially a face-to-face course. May use an LMS or web pages to post the syllabus and assignments.

Wiki: Stemming from the Hawaiian word for *quick*, a collaborative document that allows users to edit its content.

APPENDIX B

iFLIP Catalog

Link:

http://open.biola.edu/groups/iflips

List of topics:

The Conversational Model of Integration: Overview

Introduces a model for integrating faith and learning that is based on conversations—in this case, a conversation between the historic Christian faith and the best of human learning.

The Conversational Model of Integration:
The How-To's of Integration

Gives a simple acronym (TRACE) for the integration of faith and learning. It can be particularly helpful for structuring student projects or presentations.

The Conversational Model of Integration: Topics

What if your academic discipline is far removed from theology? This iFLIP gives some ways to build integrative bridges in disciplines where integration may not seem easy or natural.

The Concept of Revelation

We talk about God's revelation and often simply mean the Bible. However, for the integration of faith and learning, it is important to understand precisely what we mean by revelation and how this connects to both Scripture and science.

General and Special Revelation

How are general and special revelation like one another, and how do they differ?

General Revelation and Modern Science

Is modern science a form of general revelation? If so, in what sense? If not, why not, and how should we understand it from a biblical perspective?

A Conversation: Mathematics and Limits of Knowledge

This conversation between a theologian and a mathematician models some of the points of shared interest that can be used to integrate faith and learning.

Mathematics and Limits of Knowledge

Puzzles in mathematics about the limits of knowledge open intriguing connections to the limits of knowledge in theology.

Spiritual Life in the Classroom

What can we model about the Christian life within the normal activities of the classroom?

Kingdom and Culture

How should Christians understand human culture? Is it an act of rebellion against God? A necessary evil? Or a way that God has ordained for human beings to live?

Minding the Gap

Sometimes our desire to integrate the findings of the modern academy with the teachings of Scripture presses us to blur important distinctions. It is important to "mind the gap" when integrating faith and learning.

GRATITUDES

Only God could weave three seemingly unrelated threads of my life together—spiritual formation, online education, and the English Puritan practice of conference—to produce this book. I continue to be grateful for and humbled by his calling in my life and for the way God has used focuses that are important to me to equip those who inspire others.

Along this journey, he has placed those who have provided timely encouragement and needed support.

Dennis Dirks, Michael Wilkins, Clint Arnold, Scott Rae, and Doug Huffman—Talbot deans past and present—provided the sabbatical in which much of the research and writing of this book was completed. Matt Williams helped me say no so that I could remain more focused and rested. Dave Bourgeois, Ron Hannaford, Rebecca Hong, Carolyn Kim, Elizabeth Kobayashi, Rick Langer, Rhonda McEwen, Bob Saucy†, Laura Springer, Behzad Varamini, Matthew Weathers, Maria Wilbar, and Jason Wilson gave of their time and expertise. Biola students, beyond those whose quotes are found in this book, have added to the reward of teaching online classes. Mike and Carolyn Parkinson of Trinity Ranch let me use their Montana log cabin. Nancy Hoffman, whose multidisciplinary background and understanding of online teaching from both the student and instructor viewpoints provided valuable input. She is more than an excellent instructional designer; she has become my friend. Madison Trammel could not have been a more supportive and skillful editor. I have been blessed beyond measure through my treasured family—Norm, Adriane and Sean, Mason, Ashley, Cami, and Tyler—whose humor, love, and encouragement will always find a place in my heart and soul.

NOTES

1. Ralph Lynn, quoted by Ken Bain, *What the Best College Teachers Do* (Harvard University Press, 2011), 84.
2. Michael Wesch, "Digital Ethnography" (lecture, Biola University, La Mirada, CA, 2013).
3. Chip Heath and Dan Heath, *Made to Stick: Why Some Ideas Survive and Others Die* (New York: Random House, 2008), 20.
4. John Medina, *Brain Rules (Updated and Expanded): 12 Principles for Surviving and Thriving at Work, Home, and School*, 2nd ed. (Seattle: Pear Press, 2014), 2.
5. Jose Bowen, "Using Technology to Power Integrative Thinking" (Imagination Summit, Biola University, La Mirada, CA, March 21, 2014).
6. Paul Gorsky and Ina Blau, "Online Teaching Effectiveness: A Tale of Two Instructors," *International Review of Research in Open and Distance Learning* 10, no. 3 (May 28, 2009).
7. Nancy Hoffman authored this chapter and allowed me to adapt it for this book.
8. John Coe, "Heart," in *Dictionary of Christian Spirituality*, ed. Glen G. Scorgie (Grand Rapids: Zondervan, 2011), 495.
9. John P. Kotter and Dan S. Cohen, *The Heart of Change: Real Life Stories of How People Change Their Organizations* (Boston: Harvard Business Review Press, 2012), 1.
10. Kotter, *The Heart of Change*, 2.
11. Kotter, *The Heart of Change*, 10–11.
12. Joseph LeDoux, *The Emotional Brain: The Mysterious Underpinnings of Emotional Life* (New York: Simon & Schuster, 1998), 19.
13. Robert Saucy, *Minding the Heart: The Way of Spiritual Transformation* (Grand Rapids: Kregel, 2013), 84.
14. Wil Hernandez, "Soul," in *Dictionary of Christian Spirituality*, ed. Glen G. Scorgie (Grand Rapids: Zondervan, 2011), 764–765.

15. Jesus spoke of a separation of soul and body in Matthew 10:28, but he was addressing what happens at death when the soul or person is separated from the body, resulting in a disembodied soul. In Revelation 6:9, the apostle John identified the disembodied souls of those who were martyred. These disembodied souls would be incomplete souls because though the soul remains the real person with or without being embodied, it is designed for embodiment. For Christians, this will happen at Christ's second coming, when believers receive new, resurrected bodies.

16. Brian Duppa, *The Soules Soliloquie* (London, 1648), 5. Updated in modern language.

17. Duppa, *The Soules Soliloquie*, 5.

18. John Bunyan, *The Greatness of the Soul* (London, 1683), 50.

19. Richard Baxter, *The Saints' Everlasting Rest* (London, 1650), 720.

20. Saucy, *Minding the Heart*, 82.

21. Baxter, *Saints' Everlasting Rest*, 720.

22. Jonathan Mitchel, *A Discourse of the Glory* (Boston, 1721), 282.

23. Britta K. Hölzel, et al., "Mindfulness Practice Leads to Increases in Regional Brain Gray Matter Density," *Psychiatry Research: Neuroimaging* 191, no. 1 (2011): 36, 41.

24. Hölzel, "Mindfulness," 40.

25. Hölzel, "Mindfulness," 41.

26. Michael Wesch, "Digital Ethnography" (Lecture, Biola University, La Mirada, CA, 2013).

27. I thank Riley Mailman for "A Write-Up on Technology," April 2013.

28. Jean Lave and Etienne Wenger, *Situated Learning: Legitimate Peripheral Participation* (Cambridge: Cambridge University Press, 1991), 53.

29. "Dustin Hoffman on TOOTSIE and his character Dorothy Michaels," American Film Institute, accessed March 18, 2015, https://youtu.be/xPAat-T1uhE.

30. José Bowen, *Teaching Naked: How Moving Technology Out of Your College Classroom Will Improve Student Learning* (San Francisco: Jossey-Bass, 2012), 237.

31. Rosemary M. Lehman and Simone C. O. Conceição, *Creating a Sense of Presence in Online Teaching: How to "Be There" for Distance Learners* (San Francisco: Jossey-Bass, 2010), 9.

32. I am indebted to Rick Langer, director of the Office for Integration of Faith and Learning at Biola University, for his expertise, which contributed to the writing of this chapter.

33. Richard Mayo, *The Life and Death of Edmund Staunton*, (London: Printed for Ths. Parkhurst, 1673). As a nonconformist minister, Mayo pens his reflections on his predecessor, Edmund Staunton, an ejected minister, college head, and Puritan divine.

34. Baxter, *Saints' Everlasting Rest*, 723.

35. David Alan Williams, "Knowing as Participation: Toward an Intersection between Psychology and Postcritical Epistemology," in *Care for the Soul: Exploring the Intersection of Psychology and Theology*, ed. Mark R. McMinn and Timothy R. Phillips (Downers Grove, IL: InterVarsity Press, 2001), 343.

36. Saucy, *Minding the Heart*, 192.

37. C. S. Lewis, *Mere Christianity*, rev. ed. (New York: Macmillan, 1960), 101.

38. Parker Palmer, *The Company of Strangers: Christians and the Renewal of America's Public Life* (New York: Crossroad, 1981), 69.

39. C. S. Lewis, "Is Theology Poetry?" in *The Weight of Glory: And Other Addresses* (San Francisco: HarperSanFrancisco, 2001), 140.

40. Randall L. Sorenson, et al., "National Collaborative Research on How Students Learn Integration: Final Report," in *Psychology and Christianity Integration: Seminal Works That Shaped the Movement*, eds. Daryl H. Stevenson, Brian E. Eck, and Peter C. Hill (Batavia, IL: Christian Association for Psychological Studies, Inc., 2007), 350.

41. Sorenson, "Collaborative Research," 350.

42. R. Staton, Randall L. Sorenson, and H. Vande Kemp, "How Students Learn Integration: Replication of the Sorenson (1997a) Model," *Journal of Psychology and Theology* 26 (Winter 1998): 348.

43. M. Elizabeth Hall, et al., "The Other Side of the Podium: Student Perspectives on Learning Integration," *Journal of Psychology and Theology* 37, no. 1 (2009): 17.

44. Hall, "Other Side of the Podium," 19.

45. Danah Boyd, *It's Complicated: The Social Lives of Networked Teens* (New Haven: Yale University Press, 2014), 6.

46. C. B. Aslanian and D. L. Clinefelter, *Online College Students 2012: Comprehensive Data on Demands and Preferences* (Louisville: The Learning House, 2012), 26.

47. Aslanian, *Online College Students*, 24.

48. Boyd, *It's Complicated*, 80.

49. Tony Beliz is deputy director of the L.A. County Department of Mental Health Emergency Outreach Bureau and is quoted in "Fighting the Stigma," February 2011, accessed August 24, 2014, www.socalphysician. net.

50. Sherry Turkle, "Connected, but Alone?" TED Talk, accessed February 22, 2015, http://www.youtube.com/watch?v=t7Xr3AsBEK4.

51. I thank my colleague Carolyn Mae Kim for her knowledge, skill, practice, and shared wisdom in using social media inside and outside the classroom.

52. Modified from B. E. Walvoord, "Making the Grading Process Fair, Time-Efficient, and Useful for Student Learning and Using the Grading Process for Departmental Decision." Used with permission.

53. Barbara E. Walvoord and Trudy W. Banta, *Assessment Clear and Simple: A Practical Guide for Institutions, Departments, and General Education* (San Francisco: Jossey-Bass, 2010), 2.

54. Walvoord, *Assessment*, 3.

55. Lorin W. Anderson, David R. Krathwohl, and Peter W. Airasian, *A Taxonomy of Learning, Teaching, and Assessing: A Revision of Bloom's Taxonomy of Educational Objectives* (New York: Longman, 2001), 31.

56. Created by Nancy Hoffman.

57. David Brooks, lecture.

58. Zach King, "The Storyteller in All of Us," TED Talk, accessed February 21, 2015, https://www.youtube.com/watch?v=VMIpxqeoI1c.